The Girl
in the
Painting

BOOKS BY RENITA D'SILVA

Monsoon Memories
The Forgotten Daughter
The Stolen Girl
A Sister's Promise
A Mother's Secret
A Daughter's Courage
Beneath an Indian Sky

The Girl
in the
Painting

RENITA D'SILVA

Bookouture

Published by Bookouture in 2019

An imprint of StoryFire Ltd.

Carmelite House
50 Victoria Embankment
London EC4Y 0DZ

www.bookouture.com

ISBN: 978-1-78681-650-4
eBook ISBN: 978-1-78681-649-8

For my niece and godchild, Bhavna Rachel. A beauty inside and out. An all-round superstar: brilliant writer, singer, musician, while also being very wise. May your star always shine, my lovely.

And for my sister, Irita Sheryl. Gentle, graceful, loving, forgiving. I'm so lucky to have you.

In memory of my father, Cyril D'Silva, 1947–2018. Beloved. Sorely missed.

Prologue

England 2000

Margaret

Twilight

Margaret sits in the arbour in the grounds of what was once her childhood home and is now a hospice, waiting for her granddaughter to arrive. She has a feeling Emma will visit today, and over the years she has learned to trust her feelings.

She is sitting in the same spot – although a different bench, this one hardy metal, not glossy walnut lovingly polished by Albert – where her mother had once perched almost a century ago, looking at the angel that has borne witness to and survived so much. It is faded now, its white marble dingy yellow, and yet still bearing testament to her brother's brief life. It centres her.

She has touched the base of the angel, felt the markings there like she used to as a young child – how naive she was then, so happily innocent of all that was to come – lovingly tracing her brother's name etched into the smooth stone.

As always when she's here, the icy caress of snow-sprinkled air on her wizened cheeks, the angel constant, she marvels at the serendipitous miracle that has enabled her to spend the twilight of her life at the place that is caretaker of her happiest memories.

She has come full circle.

There's exquisite comfort in coming to terms with her life in the place where it started.

She feels so close to them here, her loved ones, knowing they are waiting, separated only by the ethereal curtain that cloisters this world from the next. Now she understands that during her long life, despite at times having felt bereft, solitary, she never *was* alone – they had been watching over her, looking out for her. The thought of reuniting with them, including, in particular, the love of her life, brings in equal parts joy and longing.

'Not long now,' she whispers.

But before she goes, there's something she must do.

She fingers the envelope in the pocket of her dress, put there when she woke this morning, knowing with absolute conviction that Emma would come. The official wording on the deeds, yellow with age, crackling with importance; the letter scented with nostalgia, memories of a land once loved, never forgotten.

She closes her eyes and pictures the house: wide and sprawling, tinted copper as if sprouted from dust.

She pictures her granddaughter's slender hands pushing open the ornate wooden door, stepping where she had once…

She thinks of the painting that was created beside the stream, swollen water glimmering starburst silver, the opposite bank dotted with saris singing in kaleidoscopic colour as they dried on rocks, the spiced grit taste of humid heat, cinnamon tea and companionship.

The painting of a girl, stark sadness in her eyes.

Margaret will give the envelope to her beautiful granddaughter and say, 'These are the deeds to my house in India.'

She will navigate Emma's surprise, field her granddaughter's questions with the imperiousness that is the prerogative of great age.

She will hand Emma the painting, conceived beside a babbling brook pregnant with rain, and she will ask her granddaughter for one last wish – the final request of a dying woman.

'Please,' she will say. 'Go to India. There's a woman I'd like you to find. Archana. She and I... It's a long story.' Margaret will close her eyes, everything that happened flashing briefly before tightly shut lids, spawning moisture tangy with regret and ache.

'When you do find Archana,' she will continue when she is able to speak, 'give her this painting. Tell her... tell her that I understand why she did what she did, that I forgave her for it a long time ago. Ask her, please, to forgive me.'

PART 1

SISTERS

Chapter One

England 1913

Margaret

Seeker

'…twenty-eight, twenty-nine, thirty. Here I come!' Margaret opens her eyes and looks about the grounds. The world is a bright, joyful green, scented with summer: grass and nectar.

Robins sing, pigeons peck at worms, squirrels nibble at acorns and magpies admire their shimmering reflection in the water of the fountain. Her sisters, however, are nowhere to be seen.

Albert is hacking away at the rose bushes with his pruning shears, a riot of colourful petals festooning his feet. He is mumbling to himself as he works.

He does that a lot. Margaret, perpetually curious, had once tasked him about it.

'Oh, never you worry your pretty little head, Miss. Tis between me and the plants, it is.'

'Does talking to them help?' she'd queried, wide-eyed.

He'd laughed, a throaty chuckle that morphed into a phlegmy cough, so she moved backwards ever so slightly just in case her new dress, lavender silk tulle with white lace flowers, got spattered.

'Go on, Miss, off with you.' Waving Margaret away and turning to his beloved plants, his hands quite brown, encrusted with mud that had settled in the grooves of his skin.

*

The air tastes golden, a hint of smoke overlaid with lavender. A giggle wafts from the house on a burst of honeyed breeze – maids gossiping as they go about their chores. Sheets billow, puffed-up ghost selves of their owners – it's wash day; Peggy will be wearing a scowl, her face a thundering storm, her hands chafed pink and peeling from all the scrubbing.

'Does it hurt?' Margaret had made the mistake of asking, staring at Peggy's palms, like the fat slabs of ham that Father likes in his sandwiches, in horrified wonder.

'What do you think?' Peggy had growled.

'You're too curious for your own good, Meg,' her sisters admonish her. 'It'll get you into trouble, if you're not careful.'

'But how else do I find out things?' she asked.

'Do you *have* to know about everything?' Her oldest sister, Evie, smiling fondly.

'Of course! How can you *not* want to know?'

Perhaps when Peggy's not looking they can play the tent game with the washing, Margaret thinks; if she can find her sisters, that is. This hide and seek is getting tedious – she always ends up seeker. It's not fair.

Margaret scrunches up her eyes in concentration, her gaze flitting this way and that like the yellow and black striped furry bees alighting on the flowers, spoilt for choice. Try as she might, she cannot spot her sisters. But she *will* find them.

She lifts up the skirt of her dress and runs past the fountain spewing greenish-white diamond-speckled water. Past the folly, a quick look inside: no, they're not in there.

Into the copse of fruit trees, plum and cherry, apple and pear. The vinegar green scent of ripening fruit. Chirping birds.

Of her sisters, no sign. She plucks a cherry. Spits it out. Red but not ripe. Deceptive. She wants rid of the bitter taste in her mouth.

And then, her eyes adjusting. Behind the apple trees. A flash of silver. Evie's wheelchair sticking out of the copse.

'Ha! Found you.'

It's always a wonder to Margaret how her sister manages to hide herself so neatly despite the wheelchair. It's a cumbersome contraption and yet Evie never complains, despite not being able to join in with Margaret and Winnie in most of their games, content to sit and watch. It is also why they end up playing hide and seek so often, for it is one of the games Evie *can* play, Albert helping her to her hiding place.

'Why are you always in that chair? Why can't you walk and run, like us?' Margaret had asked when she was just beginning to make sense of the world around her.

'Meggie, you can't—' Winnie had admonished but Evie had interrupted her with, 'I had a disease called polio when I was younger than you. It made my legs weak, look...'

Evie had pulled off the blanket that always covered her legs and lifted her skirt, and Margaret had burst into tears at the sight of the twisted twigs that passed for her sister's legs.

Now, Evie grins. 'Took you long enough. Where's Winnie, then?' And, seeing Margaret's face, 'I'll help you?'

Despite the wheelchair Evie has a knack for divining hiding places, no matter how intricate, which is why she is rarely seeker.

'I'll find her myself.'

'Do you have to be so stubborn, Meg?'

Margaret bites her lower lip, determined. She might be the youngest but that does not mean she needs help.

She runs past the vegetable garden, cabbages and cauliflower, carrots and potatoes dug up by Albert and waiting to be collected, and into the walled section that her sisters call 'the secret garden'.

A butterfly, brilliant yellow, flits among the roses; a burst of sunshine in the foliage.

Something catches the corner of Margaret's eye. A gleam of inky violet clashing with the rainbow-hued flowers.

'You shouldn't have worn your favourite dress, Winnie,' she says, laughing, as she hauls her sister out from behind the waterfall of blooms.

'Oh, Meg—' Winnie begins but then stops, cocking her ear.

Nurse's voice, faint but distinct, carrying across the garden so Albert stretches and squints towards the house, one palm shielding his eyes. 'Miss Evie, Miss Winnie, Miss Meg, you're to come in for tea.'

'Not already, surely? I wanted to play the tent game among the sheets,' Margaret complains.

'Come along now.' Winnie good-naturedly tucks her arm through Margaret's.

'You smell like a rose bush.' Margaret scrunches up her nose and Winnie giggles. It's the sweetest sound – tinkling water and pealing bells – and Margaret can't help but join in.

She falls in step beside Winnie, pushing Evie's wheelchair between them, a rhythm perfected through practice.

Evie, Margaret's gentle eldest sister, is patient and knowing, answering all of her questions, holding the skipping rope, uncomplaining – both about Margaret's demands and about the fact that she can't take part herself – while Margaret perfects her leapfrogging antics.

Winnie, Margaret's middle sister, is sweet and soft-hearted, quick to tears. She has adopted all the rats in the scullery, so traps for them have to be laid in secret, and carcasses hidden from Miss Winnie – for everyone loves her and they would go to any lengths to protect her.

Winnie has also named the rabbits that devour Albert's plants, and keeps some as pets, much to his disgust.

'Nuisances,' he harrumphs, shooing them off but not daring to do much else, for fear of making Winnie cry.

Winnie begs scraps off Cook – who refuses, of course. Cook is a termagant, her pies as wonderful, her desserts as sweet as she is sour. When no scraps are forthcoming from Cook or the kitchen staff (who are all more afraid of incurring Cook's wrath than about upsetting Winnie), she saves food off her own plate for her pets.

'Look at the state of you!' Nurse tuts when she sees them. 'I've a job to make you presentable. Your father expects you in the orangery at four o'clock sharp.'

'Father is here?' Margaret asks. Father very rarely joins them for tea, unless it's one of their birthdays.

'Yes.' Nurse smiles, secrets glinting in her eyes. 'I think he and your mother have something to tell you.'

'What is—' Margaret, always impatient, begins.

'You'll find out soon enough, Miss Meg. Upstairs with you and Miss Winnie. Miss Evie, I'll help you up.'

Mother and Father are seated at the long table in the orangery when Margaret skips downstairs after Winnie, Evie carried down to her wheelchair by Nurse, all of them scrubbed clean and shiny.

Tea is laid out, formally, something they don't do when Father is not around. They sit at the kitchen table instead, with the warm scent of baking, Cook bustling around them while simultaneously bossing her staff.

Mother beams indulgently as they sit opposite her and Father. She is glowing, Margaret notices.

The table is laden with cucumber and egg sandwiches, vanilla sponge and custard tarts.

'Good afternoon, girls,' their father says and Margaret's attention focuses on him. He is smiling widely, his moustache gleaming with well-being.

'Mother, Father, what is it you want to tell us?' Margaret asks, not having, unlike her sisters, the reticence to keep her mouth shut when she wants to know something.

'There's a time and place for everything, Meg,' Mother likes to say when Margaret speaks out of turn. 'Sometimes, no matter how pressing the need to know something, you have to wait for the right time to ask, or not ask at all, as the situation demands.'

'But how do I know when to ask and when not to? How do I know when is the right time and when isn't?'

'You'll learn.' Her mother always smiles fondly at her. 'My firecracker of a daughter.'

This time though, Margaret's out-of-turn question is met with a grin from Father.

'We have good news,' he says, eyes twinkling, his hand resting on Mother's. 'You are to have a sibling.'

Margaret claps her hands in delight, setting Father's teacup rattling in its saucer. 'We'll have a brother this time, I'm certain!' Her sisters' awed faces reflect her joy. 'When are we to meet him, Father?'

'In the new year. In the meantime, you are to take good care of your mother, and not to trouble her too much.'

'Yes, Father,' Margaret chimes in unison with her sisters, her heart overflowing at the thought of a little brother to cosset and boss, she no longer the youngest but a responsible older sister, looked up to and admired.

Chapter Two

India 1918

Archana

Good Girls

'What're you doing?' Archana asks of her big sister, although she knows perfectly well that Radha, in cahoots with their good-for-nothing neighbours, Sinthu and Dinesh, is planning a raid on old Bhim's orchard. Archana has been eavesdropping on their frenzied discussion from behind the banyan tree, the scent of sap and intrigue, her heart thrumming with the fear her sister obviously lacks, at the idea of sneaking out at night with *boys* to *steal* fruit.

'Why are you here?' Radha makes a face at Archana.

'You know you shouldn't be talking to boys,' Archana says. 'Especially now Ma and Da are actively looking for a husband for you.' Archana and Radha's parents have decreed that at fourteen, Radha is of marriageable age – she will soon be leaving the missionary school they both attend.

'Respectable girls don't talk to boys, they don't even look at them, and they surely don't shoot pebbles at them with a catapult from the top of a banyan tree! What were you thinking, Radha? You're blessed with good looks, which will guarantee a good match. Don't render them useless by getting a bad reputation,' their mother had yelled when the village bully's mother had complained to her about her tomboy daughter. 'And you' – her mother had turned on Archana. 'God knows you need everything going for you with your sooty complexion and that limp – I worry if we can get you married *at all*, but if you're caught mixing with boys and worse, being mean to them…'

'But, Ma, I—' Archana had begun.

'She didn't do anything,' Radha had cut in, eyes flashing. 'Why're you scolding her?'

Her sister drove Archana crazy. She could be mean to her, but she was also her staunchest defender, her best friend.

'Why're you here?' Radha repeats. 'I'm busy.'

Sinthu and Dinesh nod along, looking brightly, avidly, at Radha, in her thrall like everyone who comes in contact with her.

'I came looking for you. Ma said to come home as soon as we could. In fact, she didn't want you to attend school at all today, remember? That suitor is coming to see you.'

Radha huffs. 'I better go or I'll never hear the end of it,' she says to her companions, who sport identical disappointed expressions.

Radha stands, dusting her skirt, her veil slipping from her face in the process. All the boys in the field that serves as a school playground turn to look at her, starry-eyed, mouths wide and gaping.

Sinthu and Dinesh stand too, the other boys shooting envious glances, wishing they were in their hallowed position: friends and confidants of the prettiest girl in the village. Radha is different from every other girl: she not only talks to boys, unlike the other girls, who only afford them coy glances from beneath their veils, she also plays with them – but *only* these two boys, which makes her even more irresistible to the others.

Archana has overheard Aiman, the village bully, ask his gang, 'What does she *see* in them?', his voice a combination of disdain, anger and jealousy. Radha, laying siege from between the branches of a banyan tree, had just unerringly hit him with a pebble from a catapult.

'Sinthu and Dinesh appreciate me for who I am,' Radha likes to say.

Which means, Archana knows, that they allow her to lead them, willingly, into scrapes. Archana reluctantly tags along too, afraid of getting caught but not wanting to be left behind and, most of all, wanting to keep an eye on her sister, to try to stop her from going too far, save her from herself.

As they walk home, the sun a hard ball, Archana dragging her left leg, significantly shorter than the right, she asks, 'Are you worried?'

Despite the sheen of sweat, her hair coming loose from her plait and crowding her forehead, falling in her eyes – she has not bothered with her veil as there is nobody else around – Radha glows.

She throws her lovely face to the wide, cloudless sky and laughs. 'Worried? Why?'

It is hot. The sun beating down, harsh, relentless. The air perfumed with baked earth and roasted cinnamon, pungent with fermenting fruit, gritty with dust.

Archana is tired, her right leg aching from doing the work on behalf of both of her legs. 'About marrying someone you don't know.'

'Oh, I'll make sure I know him,' her sister says, with that supreme, effortless confidence that Archana both envies and loves. Radha knowing that she can charm anybody, that they will love her, twirling in the middle of the dirt road, the skirt of her salwar ballooning in a graceful arc, bright with reflected sunlight, tinted orange with dust, sequinned with pebbles from squatting on mud. Spinning effortlessly in a way Archana can never do. A goddess with the whole world at her – equally aligned – feet.

'What if he dies and you have to do sati?' This has been playing on Archana's mind since their mother explained that a dutiful wife, if her husband died before her, burned on his funeral pyre. It was the greatest sacrifice a wife could make; she would then be hallowed, venerated alongside goddesses!

'Would you do it, Ma, if Da died?' Archana had asked, lower lip trembling with dread, imagining her father dying and her mother sacrificing herself as well.

'Of course. It would be an honour,' her mother had replied, massaging her hair with coconut oil.

'Who would look after us, then?' Archana had queried, head aching with upset.

'The villagers would, happily, for my sati would rain good fortune upon the entire village.'

Archana prayed her father wouldn't die anytime soon. And although she hoped she'd get married, if only to ease her mother's worry, she also wished her husband would live a long while – she didn't want to be burned alive, no matter how much she was venerated afterward. And it went without saying that she wished the same for the man her sister would marry – Archana didn't want her sister dying before her time either!

'Oh, Archana!' Radha's laughter jolts Archana into the present. 'You're such a worrier!' There is affection in her voice. 'Let me get married first!'

'Are you really planning to raid Bhim's orchard?' Archana asks, changing the topic to more immediate concerns.

Radha looks archly at her. 'Why not? Don't tell me I can't. Scaredy-cat!' Her tone teasing, musical with mirth.

Archana had been about to do just that, but… 'Can I come?' she asks instead.

Her sister tucks her hand in hers, sweaty and slick, a rare show of affection. She pinches Archana's cheek. 'When has saying no ever stopped you, eh? You may not be as openly bold as me, but in your quiet manner, you always get your way.'

'Wait for me,' Archana calls, dragging her unwieldy, unaccommodating leg along as fast as she can in an effort to catch up with Radha.

'Hurry up, then. Did you *have* to tag along?' her sister huffs, stopping to catch a breath. 'At this rate, the others will get the best fruit and we'll be left with the dregs. Bruised cashews, stunted mangoes. A bit like you,' Radha says, and sniffs as Archana reaches her, panting from the effort.

Together, they make their way between the fields. It is dark but their path is lit by golden pinpricks of light – glow-worms. The air tastes of fruit and secrets, of companionship and daring.

They sit among the trees of Bhim's orchard and eat the stolen fruit. Honey sweet and syrupy golden.

It will be worth it, Archana thinks, even if they are caught, for this moment. Squatting among the branches, Archana perched on the lowest one, so her uneven feet touch the ground. Her sister and neighbours in the branches above. Her stomach properly full for the first time in what feels like for ever – at home there is never enough food to go round, the best morsels reserved for their father after his hard work in the fields; the three of them make do with what is left.

'Hey!' A call among the fields. 'Thief! Stop!'

A light bobbing towards them. The smell of Bhim's sweat. Tart. Sour.

'Run,' the boys call, jumping off the trees.

'Come, Archana,' Radha hisses, her sister's fruity breath on Archana's face tasting of fear.

Archana tries, Radha pulling her along. But she can't run fast enough.

Chapter Three

1913–14

Margaret

Farewell

Mother is shut in her room, has been for *days*.

'She's ill.' Father curt. His radiance of the past few months, the happiness emanating from him at the anticipation of having a son, no longer in evidence.

'Is our brother making her unwell…?' Margaret has so many questions that they trip over her tongue in their rush to drop out. She knows that their sibling – who they're all convinced will be a boy, their much-longed-for brother – is growing in her mother's stomach, that he will come out when it is time. But how? Is it time now? Is that what's making her mother ill?

Father's face taut, sharp, like it never is with her, his moustache drooping, gives Margaret pause, causing the curl of worry that had bloomed in her chest since Mother was confined to her room to become a flood, threatening to drown her.

Despite being lit with inner joy, Mother had appeared wan the last few months. She walked strangely, and fell asleep in the middle of the day sometimes, even when Margaret was talking to her.

And now Mother has disappeared into her room and hasn't been out for ages. The doctor has been with his big black bag, looking grim. Nurse and the rest of the staff venture in and out, but Margaret and her sisters are not allowed in. How is that fair?

'Is this what happened when we were born? Did we make Mother ill too…?' she's tried.

'That's quite enough, Miss.' Margaret is whisked away by Nurse and, unceremoniously, put to bed.

It's so frustrating, nobody telling her or her sisters *anything*, only walking about with long faces.

It leaves Margaret with no recourse but to take matters into her own hands.

That evening, when Nurse has retired to her room, Margaret slips down the corridor to Mother's room, looming shadows, huge and unfamiliar, making the short walk seem endless and strange, sinister, distorted.

The door to Mother's room is shut, as expected, and despite her bravado in coming here, Margaret finds herself afraid to open it, worried about what she might find. She presses her ear to the door and when she hears the moans, low and pitiful, her mother's voice but in a cadence, thick with pain, that Margaret has never encountered, she rushes back down the corridor, her small feet swallowed by the shadows, and into bed, burying her face in her pillow, trying to smother the sounds she has heard, willing the mother she knows back.

The next few days drag, full of worries, gargantuan, insurmountable. Everyone, from Father to Peggy and Jane, the housemaid, even Albert, sporting grave, sombre visages. Margaret, for the first time, does not have any questions – she is afraid to ask, afraid in case someone replies, confirming her worst fears. She spends her nights with the pillow pulled down over her head, and yet she fancies she hears moans. She wonders what is going on behind that closed door to Mother's room, where the doctor goes daily with his ominous black bag, but she dares not ask.

Then, when Margaret has convinced herself she will never see Mother again, the door to her room opens and she emerges, spent, smaller somehow. Dark circles under her eyes accentuating her paleness. So delicate that Margaret worries that if she touches her, she will disappear. A wraith. An angel.

Once again they are summoned to the orangery for tea.

Mother – the diminished, fragile version that has emerged from her room – smiles as her daughters sit opposite her and Father, but it is a smile that smacks of devastation, that is more sad than when she is crying.

Father is morose, his face not lighting up when he sees them as usual, his moustache sallow, not shiny like always.

'Mother, are you quite alright now? Why were you in your room? Why have you asked us here?' Margaret is unable to stop the questions that have found release now that her mother is returned to her, even when Winnie bumps her knee with hers, a gentle remonstrance. 'When is our brother…?'

At the mention of 'brother', her mother shuts her eyes. Her father sighs, rubbing his face with his hand, causing his moustache to droop even more.

Margaret's sisters have given up all pretence of eating, their sandwiches halfway to their mouths. Margaret fidgets in her chair.

The silence is loud, oppressive.

Once again, Margaret is compelled by an urge to break it.

'Something's the matter, isn't it?' she says. 'Mother, why're you sad? Father, why're you looking so grim?'

Mother opens her eyes, emitting a fake little tinkle of a laugh. It has no joy in it. 'Oh, Meg, must you…'

'Alice,' Father says, laying a palm on Mother's hand so her words dry up.

Father takes a deep breath and looks at each of them in turn. 'Girls, your brother... He... We named him George, after me.'

'He's *arrived*?' If so, then where is he? And why are her parents sad when they've been looking forward to his arrival so very much?

Mother lifts a hand to her lips. She looks ashen.

'He...' Once again, her father rubs a hand across his face. His voice when it comes is thick. 'He was not breathing when he... He's with the angels now.'

Angels? Margaret doesn't understand. She opens her mouth to ask what it means but Evie lays a warning hand on hers. Her sisters' faces mirror their mother's, drained of all colour.

'It is your mother's wish that we install an angel statue in the walled garden to remember your brother by,' her father is saying, but it is as if his voice is coming from far away as his earlier words reverberate in Margaret's mind, their implication finally dawning.

Not breathing.

The sandwich is heavy and sodden, unpalatable, in Margaret's mouth.

Outside, birds twitter, celebrating the buttery gold, early spring sunshine. Albert grumbles to himself as he works the soil. Daffodils nod in the sugary breeze. Jane hums hymns, her voice high and sweet, as she dusts the mounted portraits in the hall. From the kitchen waft the faint sounds of Cook giving one of her girls a piece of her mind.

But here in the orangery, with the doughy taste of bread, the sweet vanilla fragrance of cake, the silence is pungent with questions, stilted with shock and a terrible understanding as Margaret and her sisters come to terms with this, their first brush with death.

*

It is a time when Father is preoccupied, with no time for his daughters, his shoulders hunched, face pinched, moustache limp, and Mother is always sad, her grey eyes stormy with grief. She sits in the walled garden, with its profusion of cascading roses in all colours, the rich, syrupy amber fragrance of blooms and the newly installed angel statue a memorial to a lost son: George's name is inscribed on the white marble base.

Margaret worries about her wisp of a mother, sitting outdoors, shivering under the blanket, when she has not been well, wondering why nobody, not Father nor Nurse, will reason with her instead of indulging her by wrapping yet another blanket round her thin, barely-there shoulders.

It is a time when the house is mired in silences, heavy and mournful, stifling, even Margaret succumbing to their sombre spell, all her myriad questions completely choked out of her.

Some months later, one afternoon, Father comes upon them in the orangery. Mother and Evie are sewing, Winnie and Margaret daydreaming.

Father's face, until recently weighted with care, is now bright with determination, eyes shining, moustache twitching with purpose.

'Alice,' he says, taking their mother's hand. 'I've signed up to do my bit for the war effort, like we discussed.'

War.

Up until now, although Margaret knows of Peggy's beau, Jane's fiancé, Cook's son and others from the village who have enlisted, excited to be fighting for their country, war has been a vaguely distant concept, something that is happening elsewhere, to other people.

But now it is here, in this room, insistent, demanding notice.

Margaret feels fierce pride rise up in her chest on her father's behalf, and it is reflected in her sisters' and mother's eyes.

'George, that's very brave of you,' their mother says.

Father gathers their mother in his arms and smiles over her shoulder at his daughters, beckoning for them to come and join in the embrace.

Margaret is gratified – this is the first time their father has really looked at them, involved them, since their brother died. It is as if, with his death, their brother stole a vital, thriving part of their parents' personality. But now, it appears Father has come back to them, only to be leaving to fight very soon.

He bends down and lifts Evie effortlessly from her wheelchair into his embrace, one arm round their mother, Winnie and Margaret leaning into him.

'I'm doing this for my country and for us, Alice. You've needed me but I...' their father murmurs as he bends down to kiss their mother, 'I've been floundering. If I do this, I believe I...'

'I'm proud of you for it,' their mother whispers, as they all hold each other, a family again, fractured by loss but, for the moment, together, bound by love, courage and war.

They bid farewell to Father on a Saturday.

The station is crowded with families taking leave of their loved ones. Margaret, her sisters and parents jostle among the crush of people and the trunks being loaded onto the train, which is belching huge clouds of steam that stain the sky an angry, scowling black.

The smell of sweat and perfume, adrenaline and excitement. Passionate kisses, earnest promises, fervent declarations. A party atmosphere, an energy in the air, hope, enthusiasm, ardent patriotism undeterred by the reek of burning coal and smoke.

Margaret shivers in her new dress, although it is quite mild. A dip in her stomach, as if she is going to be sick: heady pride mingling with nerves at saying goodbye to Father, only recently theirs again after having lost him to grief when George was stillborn. Winnie clinging to Father's legs, Evie in her wheelchair beside him.

Mother's beautiful grey eyes soft and shimmering, mirroring the autumn sky, her gaze full of love and pride, focused on Father.

Around them, mothers are pressing packets of sandwiches into sons' hands, boys hardly older than Evie. The boys look excited but their mothers and betrotheds wear the same expression as Mother, their smiles bright, their eyes raw and hungry as they commit their loved ones' every feature to memory.

'Be sure to write,' they remonstrate. 'Eat those sandwiches before they get soggy, mind.'

'This war'll be over soon. We'll be home by Christmas,' their sons and fiancés, husbands and brothers reassure them.

The train hisses, emitting a long, low hoot in a burst of steam, sounding impatient.

Mother buries her face in Father's chest, and all around them, women hold on to their husbands, their fiancés, their sons; children angle into their fathers' embrace, like Margaret and her sisters are doing, loath to let go.

Father kisses Mother and then gently disentangles himself from her arms. He pastes kisses on Evie's cheek, Winnie's, Margaret's. He smells of lime and tobacco, as familiar as comfort. As love.

'Look after your mother for me, girls.' His voice determinedly cheerful.

He climbs onto the train and stands at the doorway of his first class compartment, alongside the other men crowding there, doffing his hat to Mother as the train groans and squeals and starts to move with a great big shrug as if it is a real living thing, a monster eating men and belching smoke and puffs of hot air.

Margaret feels her heart heave in her chest. She is shivery all over.

She is aware of Evie's hand circling her waist, her sister pulling Margaret into her lap on her wheelchair. 'There, there, Meg,' Evie whispers but her voice is squeaky. She passes Margaret her handkerchief.

Margaret wants to say, 'I don't need it,' but her voice is salty; her throat feels all choked up.

She is angling for a glimpse of her father, who is smiling at them, hard, although she can see that beneath the stiff moustache his lips are aquiver.

All around them wives, mothers, children wave with all their might, handkerchiefs flying in unison.

Margaret stares until Father's face wavers and is indistinguishable from all the others and then with a groan and a whistle, the train rounds the corner, the station a mass of women and children tucking their handkerchiefs away and pulling themselves up stiff and straight, although a vital part of them feels loose, astray.

Gone.

'He'll be back before we know it,' Mother says, brightly, but her mouth droops even as she tries for a smile.

In the months that follow, the war insinuates itself into their lives, making itself comfortable, an ever-present guest. The sense of excitement with which men and boys signed up for the war is replaced by a resigned acceptance, the knowledge that the war is much bigger and nastier than anyone expected, lasting far longer than they thought, claiming sons and fathers, friends and relatives, limbs and hearts, indiscriminately.

Staff leave one by one, some to do their bit for the war effort, others because help is needed at home, until there are only Cook, Jane, Peggy and Albert left.

Peggy is constantly worrying about her beau, and Jane about her fiancé. They wait for letters, pining when they don't arrive and grumbling and fretful when they do, and most words are crossed out.

Letters from Father are a great event. Every day Mother keeps watch for the postmistress and when she doesn't arrive, she is morose.

On those days when she sees the postmistress cycle up the hill from her vantage position at the window, Mother rushes downstairs to greet her, opening the door herself, too impatient to wait for Peggy to pause in her chores and attend to it.

Mother caresses her letter with the same gentleness with which she strokes Margaret's cheek when saying goodnight. She brings it to her nose, breathing in deeply as if it holds some scent of her father, when Margaret knows all it smells of is the damp sliminess of having lain in the postmistress's bag and the pungent tartness of then having been handled by her snuff-stained fingers.

Margaret watches Mother take the letter into the orangery and, seated in her favourite armchair, open it reverently, running her fingers softly over her husband's handwriting. Only then does she read it carefully, once, then again, Margaret observing her eyes move down the page. Once she has digested the contents she looks up, smiling, her eyes bright and glassy, taking a moment to focus.

'Meg, there you are. Fetch your sisters, my dear.'

Once they're all in the orangery, Mother reads out the bits of the letter where Father has written a few sentences to each of them, her voice high and girlish, giddy with happiness.

*

In the years to come, this is what Margaret will remember. The sound of her mother's voice as she read her husband's letter out to her daughters. The expression on her face, love and yearning as she smoothed out her husband's missive from the warfront, as she caressed his words, her eyes soft, mouth slightly open, as if she was touching him.

Chapter Four

England 2000

Emma

Nightmare

No, it can't be. It just cannot.

Emma stares at the computer, her heart beating out a nightmare.

There must be some mistake.

But even as she checks and cross-checks, as she rereads David's paper and compares it to the damning evidence on her computer, archived material unearthed during her own research, she knows there is none.

She rubs her stunned eyes. The world blurs, the scent of old documents and unearthed secrets, betrayal, heartache and disappointment.

Outside her window city lights blink wearily, buses trundle by, tourists head back to their hotels, garishly dressed good-timers in clothes too skimpy for the chilly damp line up at clubs, high-pitched skeins of conversation drifting into her office.

When Emma announced this project, taking up where David had left off with his paper, the one that made him famous, the one for which she has just found out he fabricated the evidence – cleverly, of course, which is why it hasn't been discovered until now – David had tried his hardest to put her off.

'I've finally decided on a project,' she'd said, turning to him, eyes sparkling, as she explained just what it was.

She'd anticipated a witty comeback before he expressed delight, as was his way.

But he was wan, colour draining from his face. 'I don't think it's a good idea. You're underestimating the scope of the research you need to do. Believe me, you don't have that kind of time, not with your teaching commitments and Chloe…'

Her upset at his reaction, his lack of support, made her sharp. 'I'll make the time.'

'It'll take too long. I'll see even less of you than I do already.'

She wondered if he might be jealous as he turned away from her, pulling the pillow over his head, shutting her out. She was continuing where he'd left off, after all – it was something, he'd once confided, he'd always meant to do.

But she was too piqued at him putting a dampener on her joy, doubting whether she could take on the project, to make an effort to assuage him.

She had fumed and seethed all night. It was not as if she was stepping on his toes; he had retired, for God's sake! The project was wide open for anyone to pursue and instead of being glad that she had taken the opportunity to do so, he was sore.

She woke up more determined than ever to see the project through, his reaction only serving to spur her on.

It never occurred to her that he might be afraid of being found out. Especially given her nature, how dogged she was when something didn't quite add up, which was how she had discovered David's hoax: the smallest sliver of discrepancy.

Emma didn't like discrepancies, minuscule or not. And so she'd pursued it, never imagining for a moment that David's greatest legacy was backed by fabricated evidence; without it, the paper that made his name had no legs.

*

David had come round eventually, reluctantly, when he realised Emma was not giving up on the project just because he thought she should.

Every night he waited up for her.

'How's it going?' he asked, handing her the cup of green tea he knew she liked before bed. ('You're so low-maintenance, my love,' he liked to joke. 'Not wine or beer or spirits, just green tea!')

They snuggled on the sofa, David sipping his wine, Emma her tea, his hand massaging the cricks out of her neck.

'You don't have to wait up for me,' she'd say, leaning into him, the half-light of the TV screen casting shadows on his face, BBC presenter grim as she recounted more horrors wrought by humans on one another.

'I know I don't have to. I *want* to.' He'd smile. 'Tell me how it's going,' he'd prompt.

She'd yawn, setting down her teacup. 'Do you really want to talk about it? I'd much rather go to bed.'

'It makes me feel alive. I've missed it since retirement and this way I can vicariously join in.'

Now, tasting betrayal, roiling blue at the back of her throat, she understands that what she took to be his supportiveness, evidence of his love, was really a fact-finding mission. He was trying to glean just how much she knew with regards to his hoax.

Were his hints and helpful suggestions – 'I wouldn't do that if I were you. I'd focus on the Sherpa rather than the Maori, they have more to offer.' – all ways of pushing her off the track, deflecting her from discovering his deception?

Emma pushes her hair back from her face, devastated as she second-guesses every one of David's actions, realising that what she took to be love, caring, was anything but.

It wasn't just David trying to protect himself, this was also him lying to her, deliberately sabotaging her research. David no longer worked; Emma was the main breadwinner, and yet... He'd been willing to damage her own work in order to cover up for what he'd done, even knowing that it would be their daughter who would suffer from the fallout.

David had broken Emma's heart before, when he abandoned her while she was pregnant with Chloe. It had hurt then, but now... This...

She had taken David back, despite his failings. Chloe loved her father.

But, seeing his every action in a new light, Emma wonders: Has David really cared for her and Chloe, for anyone at all apart from himself?

Reluctantly, Emma gathers her things, knowing she can't put off going home for ever.

The corridor is brightly lit but deserted, offices bearing an abandoned look, desolate in the harsh light. She is the last to leave, as is always the case when she is reaching the crux of the paper, where, with critical, focused research, it all comes together. Before David moved in with them, she used to do this at home, after Chloe was in bed, staying up most of the night.

Her eight-year-old would find her: 'Mum, you've fallen asleep on the sofa again!' Hands on her hips. Her sweet, high-pitched little-girl voice.

Now, thanks to David, Emma can stay later in the office, doing her research work after her teaching duties and not having to worry about rushing to pick Chloe up and ferry her to after-school clubs – but sometimes, she misses when it used to be just the two of them, her and Chloe against the world, before David – Emma's lover, Chloe's dad – came to live with them.

David.

The thought of facing him after finding out what he has done makes her sick.

She sighs tiredly and, bundling her coat round her, her scarf looping her neck, braves the outdoors.

The cold slaps her with freezing fingers, invading every part of her not covered, the top of her wrist where her glove doesn't quite reach. She walks briskly, head down, braced against the frost-tipped wind, ice and exhaust, snatches of phone conversations, a man drunkenly weaving past, singing off-key, screeching tyres, a long-drawn-out horn, a string of expletives.

A scuffle outside a bar. Wild eyes, faces tight with anger, raised, fisted hands.

We all have something to deal with, she thinks.

He'll have a good explanation, she thinks.

I must have got it wrong, she tells herself, even though she knows in the depths of her heart that she hasn't.

David, fiercely intelligent, intensely charming, always getting what he wants. David of the wonderful, all-seeing eyes.

David, unscrupulous?

Yes, the deepest part of her answers.

She loves him, admires and idolises him, but, if she is honest with herself, doesn't completely trust him since he left her in the lurch when she found out she was pregnant with his daughter and needed him most, only coming back to Emma when *he* needed *her*.

Perhaps this is why she is shocked at what she found out, upset, but not surprised, not really.

Her bus comes, a grinding of brakes, doors opening with sing-song beeps. She climbs to the upper deck and, resting her head against the pane, cool and soothing, and closing her eyes, tries not to think of what is to come.

Chapter Five

1915

Margaret

Vigilant

'Beg pardon, Marm, Jane can't come in today. She sent word.'
Peggy stands deferentially beside Mother's armchair.

The doors to the garden are open and an autumn-flavoured breeze, tart with woodsmoke and ripe apples, drifts in. Evie's daydreaming in her wheelchair, while beside her on the settee, Winnie writes in her diary, a small smile playing on her face.

Margaret is sprawled on the chaise longue reading, willing Peggy to go away so she can get on with her book.

'It's her fiancé, Marm. She got the telegram this morning.'

'Oh!'

'Marm? Oh dear!'

Margaret, galvanised into action by the alarm in Peggy's voice, shuts her book and turns to Mother, Evie and Winnie doing the same.

Their mother has pricked herself. Mother, who can sew with her eyes closed! She sits there, face pale as winter mist, while blood, vulgar scarlet, dots the blanched skin of her finger.

Peggy uses her apron to stem the flow while Winnie holds Mother's other hand. 'Are you alright, Mother?'

But Mother is not listening to her. Her eyes are fixed on Peggy's bent head. 'Jane… how is she taking it?'

'She's awful cut up, Marm, as is to be expected.' Peggy's trying hard to be nonchalant, Margaret can tell, but her voice is pinched all the same.

'You've heard from your Freddie?'

'Yes, Marm, last week I did.'

Mother nods, her eyes far away, looking across the garden to something beyond. She must be counting the days from when she last received a letter from Father, Margaret surmises.

Margaret is quick at maths. 'Father's letter arrived ten days ago,' she says.

Mother startles and looks at her, her lips, the bruised pink of a blustery dawn, rising in a small smile. 'You're a gem, Meggie. You always know just what I'm thinking.' Then, closing her eyes as if the effort of smiling has cost her, 'I'll rest now.'

That afternoon, Mother says, 'Girls, let's wander down to the village. We'll drop this hamper off to Jane on the way. Although,' she adds, her voice low, almost a mumble, as if she is speaking to herself, 'I daresay it won't be much help.'

Margaret and her sisters exchange a look, equal parts worry and caring. Mother suggests a walk down to the village whenever it has been too long between Father's letters, on the pretext of needing to stretch her legs. She makes sure to suggest it in the afternoon, after the postmistress has finished her rounds and is sure to be back at the post office.

Gerry the groom having signed up and none of them knowing how to ride – their mother didn't think it fair for Margaret and Winnie to learn when Evie couldn't – they have to walk everywhere, Margaret and Winnie taking turns to push Evie. Gerry's wife comes up from the village every day to look after the horses, but there are no more carriage rides for them.

The war that everyone thought would end by Christmas of last year is dragging on, the party atmosphere that had accompanied the initial fluster of goodbyes to loved ones no longer in evidence.

The big house feels vast and cavernous without the chattering, busy industry of the staff – there's only Cook and Peggy left, now. Even Albert has given his notice, and it looks like Jane won't be coming back now either.

Leaves have started to turn, a riot of deep yellow, golden russet, blood orange. Blackberries ripen in bushes beside the road, bees and flies drunk on them. The air is perfumed with hawthorn, honeysuckle and wild garlic. Crab apples ferment in the sunshine.

In the village, after having delivered the hamper to Jane's red-eyed but grateful and obsequious mother – Jane was in bed, indisposed – they walk towards the post office.

Before the war, a trip into the village would involve ice cream at Mrs Armstrong's. Margaret and her sisters would consider the ice cream on offer: strawberry, luscious pink; blackberry, deepest purple and, of course, chocolate: rich velvety brown. Mrs Armstrong would look on indulgently. They would debate whether to choose something else this time, before settling on chocolate, as always.

But now the dairy is boarded up, Mrs Armstrong having left to stay with relatives up north.

'Sensible thing to do,' Cook had grunted when she relayed this news to Mother, 'what with us being at risk from air raids. I'm considering moving somewhere safe too, Marm. As you should, if you don't mind me saying.'

Winnie had blanched at Cook's warning but Margaret wondered how they would look and sound, these giant machines wielding destruction from the air, another recent, menacing threat of this beastly war.

Mother, noting Winnie's pale face, had said lightly, 'We'll be fine. Belgian refugees are being evacuated to Kent. Surely if there was a danger of air attacks they wouldn't come *here*?'

'But they said on the wireless, Marm…'

'Scaremongering.' Mother laughed, although her voice shook a little. 'I'm thinking of opening up the house to wounded soldiers. I've heard there's a need for hospitals and Lord knows, we've enough empty rooms. I'll write to your father, girls, asking what he thinks of the idea…' Her voice rising in that blend of hope and wistfulness she got whenever she spoke of letters to or from Father.

'That's a good idea, Mother,' Margaret declared, picturing herself nursing brave soldiers felled by war. 'We've been doing our bit at school, too, knitting socks and mittens for the front line.'

'And digging up the playing fields to create vegetable patches,' Winnie pitched in, colour returning to her cheeks.

'You must write and tell your father. He'll be so proud of his girls.' Mother smiled fondly at them.

Now, as they approach the post office, Mother's steps quicken. She appears to be holding her lips together with effort, every so often touching her face as if to make sure it is still there.

'Any post for me, Mrs Norris?' The raw hope in Mother's voice makes Margaret embarrassed and tearful all at once. She wants to shut her ears to the sound like she used to shut her eyes when Father would kiss Mother.

'Not today, Marm,' the postmistress says softly, her voice kind. 'If there was, I'd have brought it up to you.'

'It hasn't fallen down the sides of your bag, by any chance?'

And again, Margaret resists the urge to make herself small and disappear. Her sisters fidget and avoid each other's eyes – Margaret knows they're feeling the same way.

'I'll look again, if you like.' Margaret notes the pity in the postmistress's gaze. Perhaps her mother sees it too, for she shuts her own eyes. Or perhaps that's just the hope that this time there *will* be a letter, elusive, that has slipped into the folds of Mrs Norris's bag.

'Thank you.' Mother's voice is cloyingly grateful.

Sometimes, late at night, when Margaret startles awake to the owls cooing and wind howling outside and goes in search of Mother, she finds her not asleep in bed, but sitting by the window in the corridor outside her room, from which she can see into the walled garden and the angel within it.

Mother is always silhouetted against silken blackness, ghoulish shadows dancing upon her starkly white, vulnerable face. The window is slightly open, inky sky, silvery sliver of moon, curtains flapping eagerly as the night breeze imparts, through its hushed rustling, breathless stories of escapades.

Margaret does not go to Mother, somehow sensing she wants to be alone in her contemplation of the angel in the arbour through the window, the dancing curtains. Her shoulders are hunched, sharp-angled, her face raw, her palms joined.

So pale, wraithlike in her nightgown.

Margaret hides behind a pillar and keeps watch upon her mother in secret, the cool solidity of the pillar, the iron and marble, clandestine taste of pressing night, rendering time fluid, elastic.

In the months since Father went to war, Mother has become brittle, fragile, her smiles papery, cracking at the edges, her eyes perpetually holding the shine of hope and torment.

In those undulating, secret hours, Margaret wonders what would become of Mother if Father did not come back, like so many men. As soon as she thinks it, her mind shies away from the thought.

No.

It won't happen. It *can't*.

One night when Mother is conducting her nightly vigil by the corridor window, Margaret creeps into her room and, ensconced in sheets smelling of her mother – lavender and longing – she studies Father's letters, much thumbed and arrayed beside Mother's pillow. Margaret knows they are private – except for the parts Mother reads out to her and her sisters – but she misses Father, worries about him, and his letters make her feel closer to him; which is why, she realises, her mother waits for them so eagerly. Margaret also wants to understand the woman her mother has become since their father went away and she hopes the letters – which her mother reads and rereads, a secret smile playing on her face – will hold clues.

For Margaret worries that Mother will revert to the way she was after George was stillborn – a shadow of her usual self. Mother had come back to them after that terrible time, albeit with less happiness behind her smile. If something were to happen to Father, would they lose Mother too?

But Father's letters, far from reassuring Margaret, upset her, for Margaret discovers that Father, much as he loves his daughters, struggled more than she had realised to recover from George's death. Father had written: 'I signed up to do my duty to my country, and also to get over my continued sorrow at the loss of George – I think you know how much I have tried and failed to put it behind me, Alice.'

Margaret sets down the letters carefully beside Mother's pillow and leaves the room, her chest tight with hurt, eyes prickling with the peppery sting of tears, resolving not to read correspondence meant for Mother's eyes only again.

'No letter today, Marm, but I'll be sure to come up to the house as soon as there is one.' The postmistress tries for upbeat, but Margaret feels something in Mother's body crumple, like a cake taken too soon out of the oven. Margaret stands upright and leans against Mother, as though it is she who is holding Mother up.

'Marm, have you heard about the air raids up in London? Kent is at risk too, I've heard it said. We'd do well to be careful, Marm. Vigilant.'

'Yes, thank you very much, Mrs Norris,' Mother says, graciously.

Then she walks away, expecting her daughters to follow, straight-backed, stiff, as if, should she let herself loosen even a little, she would break.

Chapter Six

1918

Archana

A Visitor

Archana and Radha in the orchard in the middle of the night, sated on stolen fruit, trying to run from the scene of the crime, Archana's cursed limp holding them back.

Bobbing light, Bhim's pungent breath, rushing closer.

'Hurry, Archana. Please.' Radha begging.

'You go,' Archana cries, sweet fruit gone sour with fear in her mouth. 'I'll…'

'I'm not going without you,' Radha whispers.

The boys are far ahead, darting shadows in the distance.

Bhim is gaining on the girls.

'We'll be in so much trouble.' Radha's breath hitching on a sob.

'Come,' Archana says, taking command, upset by her sister's distress, her frantic mind working to find a solution.

Bhim's footsteps almost upon them.

Think, Archana, think.

She grabs her sister's hand and pulls her into the ditch, a lizard scurrying away, just as Bhim reaches them. Something brushes against their crouching legs. Archana's weaker foot throbs in agony. The smell of mulch and earth and organic matter. The rustling of nocturnal animals in the undergrowth.

Her heart is beating so loud she's afraid Bhim will hear. Panic-flavoured darkness, thick and pressing. Gasping, adrenaline-suffused breaths, damped down, held in. Her sister's sweat; her panic, vinegary, anxious.

The weak light from Bhim's candle sweeps towards them. It flickers and, just as it is about to reveal them, dies in a gust of breeze.

'I'll get you,' Bhim spits, his voice hoarse with panting, acidic and phlegmy, ending in a cough.

Archana feels a hysterical giggle bubble in her throat. With all her willpower, she stifles it.

Bhim stands there, just beside them, shaking his hand furiously at the darkness.

They wait, holding their breath, Archana's leg aching, a horrified thrill in her wildly beating chest, her sister's perspiring hand in hers.

Another gust of wind. The rumble of thunder.

No, please, gods. She does not want there to be lightning, for surely it will reveal them.

Go, Bhim.

And as if her desperate prayer has been heard, Bhim turns and hobbles away just as an arc of lightning splits the sky. They stay there, in the ditch, the smell of fear and mud and clandestine adventure as Bhim's footsteps recede into the distance, as the heavens open and they are soaked.

Afterward, her sister's arms round her, her voice sweet and light, her breath smelling of raindrops, flavoured with heady relief. 'That was *so* exciting.'

'A bit too exciting, if you ask me,' Archana says drily, and Radha laughs, cascading honey, shimmering gold.

They walk back in the rain, slipping discreetly into their hut, the dog stirring under the tamarind tree, opening one eye, then both, and dancing around their legs in delight and welcome, heeding their soft entreaties for quiet. They create wet and muddy tracks on the cow-dung-swept floor of the one room where they all sleep, quietly taking up their positions on the mat on either side of their mother, who is snoring gently with her mouth open. Their father is in his corner, fast asleep as well.

The next morning, Archana and Radha wake to their mother's sighs. 'The rain has caused the mud to come in again.'

When her mother collects fresh dung from their only cow to sweep the floor clean, guilt propels Archana to say, for it is herself and Radha who dragged in the mud after their midnight escapade, 'I'll do it.'

'You're a good girl.' Her mother smiles. 'If someone sees past your limp and dark skin, please gods, and marries you, he'll be lucky indeed.'

It is Sunday, a day off school.

Archana prefers school to being at home; she loves learning. She knows Radha likes school too, which is why she has begged to stay on until she is married, but for a different reason to Archana's.

'At home, it's one chore after another. At least at school I can sit down, instead of carrying water, sweeping the floor, washing clothes, cooking, milking the cow...' she grumbles to Archana.

The school is run by missionary nuns and so is closed on Sundays while they attend church.

'You are all welcome,' the nuns have declared more than once.

But even though Radha has pleaded with their mother, curious to know what goes on in church, in what way the nuns' God, who looks human (the nuns have shown them pictures and told them Bible stories) is different from their many gods, they have not been allowed to go.

'The main reason we're sending you to school is to pass the time until you're married. What's this nonsense about attending church when you complain about coming with me to the temple even once a month?' their mother cried.

Archana is scrubbing the breakfast dishes by the washing stone when the dog, who has been nipping at her legs, starts barking frenziedly. She looks up to see Bhim making his way through the fields towards their hut.

Archana's heart misses a beat. Pulling her sari *pallu* over her head to cover her face in the presence of a man, she sidles up to her sister, who is shelling knobbly brown tamarind.

Her sister squeezes her hand, imparting comfort, while draping her own *pallu* carelessly over her head, the movement graceful like everything Radha does.

Bhim's gaze sweeps over them, at once disdainful and knowing, lingering on Radha.

'Ma,' Radha calls, 'you have a visitor.'

Their mother appears in the doorway of their hut, wiping her hand on her sari, her face flustered and red from the heat of the hearth, her eyes wet from chopping onions. Archana experiences a jolt of fierce affection for her, even as she tries to swallow down her fear, tasting of saliva and iron.

'Come in,' Ma says, eyes worried, darting to her daughters.

She is mentally making note of if she has enough tea leaves, if there is any milk remaining, so she can offer Bhim tea, Archana knows.

'No, I…'

Archana sees her mother relax, a smile finally reaching her eyes and then flitting away as she puzzles over why he is here. 'Has something happened?'

'Yes, as a matter of fact.' Bhim clears his throat. 'Someone raided my orchard last night. I was wondering if your girls know anything about it.' His gaze again skipping over Archana, settling once more on Radha.

'Why would they?' Her mother is bemused. 'They were at home, sleeping beside me.'

'Oh.' Bhim's smile is mean and calculating, revealing urine-yellow stumps for teeth. 'Only that I found this shawl in the ditch this morning a few paces from where my fruit was stolen. I'm pretty sure it belongs to your girls.'

He holds up the distinctive saffron and maroon cloth cut from an old sari of their mother's that Radha had taken along to use as a pouch to carry surplus fruit. Archana can see Radha's eyes widen with worry and fear; the bravado that she has adopted for Bhim, the facade, dropping.

Their mother peers at the shawl, then, her face red as she recognises her sari, turns to Archana and Radha, her gaze enquiring, embarrassed, upset, all at once.

Radha looks set to cry.

But before her mother can open her mouth, Archana somehow, as she did the previous night, garners courage just as Radha loses hers and says, 'I lost it in school yesterday.'

'Why take it to school?' her mother asks, still looking suspicious and mortified.

'The nuns gave me some books. I took it to bring them home in.'

Her mother's face clears. She turns to Bhim, whose jaw is set, his mean gaze on Radha, whose eyes – all that is visible of her face through the *pallu* covering it – crinkle in a relieved smile.

'Thanks for bringing it round,' Ma says, taking the shawl. 'I hope you find the thief.'

With one last angry glance at Radha, Bhim leaves. He has the measure of them but he cannot prove it.

'I don't know how he could think you had anything to do with the theft,' Ma grumbles, shaking her head and returning indoors.

Archana's hands tremble and she cannot stop them shaking, a nervous reaction after the fact. Her sister takes Archana's quivering hands in hers, holding them until the jitteriness stops. 'Good thinking, little one. You are the best,' Radha whispers.

The dog dances around them, licking their feet, the fruity air tasting of relief and love as their mother shouts from the doorway: 'Get on with your chores. You've wasted enough time already!'

Chapter Seven

1915

Margaret

Fireworks

'Your Aunt Helen has written. She's worried for our safety, especially now the air raids have begun in earnest, and has invited us to stay with her until the threat passes,' Mother says to Margaret and her sisters, looking pensive.

Cook, who's come in with oat biscuits – she's brilliant at concocting dishes that are tasty despite the rationing, but is as grumpy as ever, if not more so – says, 'You should take up her offer, Marm, if you don't mind me saying. We're in the direct line of attack, we are. I won't be here much longer – I'm leaving in a couple of weeks to stay with my nephew. It's not safe for us here, Marm.'

'Oh.' Mother's eyebrows scrunch together in thought.

'Peggy's considering moving too,' Cook adds as she leaves the room.

'I'll write to your father asking what he thinks we should do. I'd like to stay put and do our bit by opening up the house to wounded soldiers rather than go to my sister...' Mother says.

'How will we get on without Cook or Peggy? They're the only ones left and we just about manage as it is!' Margaret exclaims.

Winnie scrunches up her nose. 'I'd rather stay here. I don't like the farm – it smells. And our cousins make fun of us, call us names.'

'It's safe,' Evie says, gently.

Margaret looks to Mother. 'I think we should leave immediately.'

Evie adds, 'We could do our bit for the war effort at the farm just as well as here.'

Mother blinks, her eyes taking a minute to lose the starry-eyed distance that clouds them when she thinks of Father and focus on her daughters. 'Ummm... I think we'll wait a couple of weeks, girls, until we hear back from your father.' She pushes her chin out in that way she has when she's decided something. 'I don't imagine we're as much at risk as everyone's making out. If a reply doesn't arrive within the fortnight, we'll go to my sister.'

'But Mother!' Margaret cries, exchanging worried glances with Evie. 'Air raids are *dangerous*. We were told about them at school.'

Mother smiles gently. 'Nothing will happen in a fortnight, surely. And there might even be a reply from your father asking us to stay put, that we're worrying for nothing.'

Three nights later, when Margaret hears the loud bang, the smell of smoke edging into her consciousness, persistently nudging her awake, she thinks at first that it is fireworks.

She loves fireworks. They remind her of sitting on Father's shoulders – her privilege, being the youngest, although she did (grudgingly) allow Winnie a turn – and watching the display on the occasion of the King's birthday. The scorching thrall of smoke and excitement, the breeze stroking their cheeks with a tingling, conspiratorial buzz, the village spread out below, the sky lit up in an explosion of colour, the taste of fire and embers.

Afterward, they had had hot soup, curtains open to the night, enigmatic ebony, swollen with intrigue, bats flitting, charged wind hissing among branches, the grass dark and secret with shadows, the sky lighting up once and again with a stray firecracker, the burnt caramel taste of contentment. Margaret's stomach warm with potato and leek soup, spiced with herbs, thick chunks of hearty bread dipped in it. Dozing off on the settee, she and her sisters wedged between their parents, comfort and love. The feeling of being rocked as she was carried to bed, hammocked in her father's arms, the thud, thud of his beating heart, his smell of tobacco and lime, his beard brushing her cheek as he leaned in to kiss her, tucking the quilt up around her chin: 'Goodnight, Margaret.'

Now she jolts awake and thinks: fireworks. Then the realisation that Father is away fighting a war. Dense choking waves of smoke. The hot taste of fire, strangling her, making it hard to breathe.

She coughs and, hand over her mouth, fights the ambush of smoke, pushing open the door to her room. The corridor spills with smoke, rushing navy clouds. It smarts her eyes, plugs her throat, hurting, stabbing, obstructing.

What's going on? she wants to cry but she cannot speak, gasping for breath.

Evie, she thinks.

Evie will be trapped.

Margaret trips through smoke, making her way to Evie's room, counting steps in her head, knowing how many it takes to get there, having played the game many times before.

'Evie.' She bangs on her sister's door.

'Meggie,' she hears. Evie's voice, weak, strangled.

'I'm coming for you.'

Margaret tries to push open the door, but it is swollen in the frame by heat and stuck hard.

'Help,' she cries through a hoarse, burning, ash-clogged throat. 'Someone, please help. Mother? Winnie? Peggy? Cook?'

But all she can see are billowing navy clouds. No people. Just heat pressing, smoke choking, a gasp in her chest.

With all her strength she pushes at Evie's door, but it is wedged fast and try as she might, tears stinging her scalded face, she cannot wrestle it open.

Fury and impotence, blistering black.

'Evie,' she calls, even as she batters furiously at her sister's door, willing it to open. 'I'm getting help. I'll be straight back.'

She stumbles to Winnie's room. It is wide open, taken hostage by smoke. Winnie's bed is empty – she has got out.

Mother.

Once again, she counts steps to take her mind off the scorching heat, the difficulty in taking a breath, her worry about Evie prisoner in her room. Mother's door is shut.

Margaret bangs on the boiling wood. 'Mother!'

No sound from inside. She tries to open the door but this one too is stuck fast. She pounds on it, calling for Mother, desperation coating her burning throat. 'Mother, Mother!' But there is only the hissing of the flames.

Perhaps Mother was in the corridor, looking at the angel in the arbour. Margaret nurses this lifeline of a thought, turning to rush along the corridor to the spot where her mother keeps watch, pushing despair away. She has things to do, a sister to rescue. Evie *needs* her.

She stumbles along the corridor only to be met by a column of orange flames blocking her path.

Blistering wretchedness sizzling her throat, stabbing her eyes. She pushes it away fiercely. No time to wallow.

Evie, she *must* save Evie.

She cannot climb upstairs to the servants' section. It is blocked by a towering wall of fire.

She turns to go back to Evie, try her door again, but she is obstructed by fire that, in the space of a few moments, seems to have spread and is *everywhere*.

Please, not near Evie's room. Please let Evie be safe.

She has no choice but to go down. Her heart wails at leaving her sister behind, but she knows she has no other option – she cannot reach Evie, she needs to get help.

At nineteen steps she is at the stairs, the banister blistering hot to the touch.

She stumbles down, eyes blinded by smoke that roils and churns, topped by flames, giddy apricot. She is trying to call for Winnie, her mother, Peggy, Cook, gagging on her words instead, the fiery fumes, smog and ash invading her lungs, making her tremble, want to collapse, give up, give in.

No. Evie's up there all alone, waiting for me to rescue her.

Instead, she counts, pushing herself to make it all the way down.

Panic and fear, wild in her chest, constricting it more than the smoke. What on earth is happening? Where is everyone?

She pushes aside, with immense effort, the terror squeezing what breath remains from her.

And then she is downstairs, a slap of scorching heat, scalding, branding.

'Winnie? Mother? Peggy? Cook?'

No response. Only fire hissing, advancing.

Twenty steps to the front door.

She can do this.

...nineteen, twenty.

She emerges from the front door in a wheezing, turbid singe of smoke onto the burning grass. She squints, the darkness pushed aside by the living, leaping flames, casting everything in a demonic orange glow.

There, in the distance, two figures on the grass. Mother and Winnie?

She runs across the grounds, naked feet searing, blistering, outrunning the smoke-topped flames. How could she have imagined this to be fireworks?

She finally reaches grass that hasn't been scorched, although it's hot to the slap of her bare feet, as if it carries the imprint of the fire.

'Meg!' Winnie's arms round her. She is sobbing. Huge, gagging tears. Despite her urgency and upset regarding Evie, Margaret experiences a fierce burst of affection and relief.

Winnie, in her nightgown, the pungent reek of fire and horror. Scalding hot to the touch. And yet shivering uncontrollably as if she cannot get warm. Her skin boiling and blackened. Peggy beside her, coughing. Not Mother.

Even as Margaret opens her mouth to ask for help, she scans the grounds for Mother. 'Evie's inside, we need to save her.'

'Miss…' Peggy's voice is as charred as Margaret's. 'We can't go indoors.'

Peggy gestures at the flames eating Margaret's home, the conflagration lighting up the surroundings bright as a summer's afternoon although it is night, rendering the darkness muggy although the trees are bare and dusted with frost.

'You don't understand.' Margaret turns on Peggy. 'Evie is *inside.*' Her voice an incensed, smouldering, raging whisper.

'Miss—'

'Please,' she begs. 'I couldn't open her door by myself. You *have* to come with me.' Tugging urgently at Peggy's scorched nightdress.

Peggy puts her arms round Margaret, and Margaret fights the urge to collapse into them. Her sister is waiting.

'No, Miss, you can't. It's sheer madness to attempt to go in. You won't come out.'

Peggy, instead of responding to Margaret's urgency, her pleas, is holding Margaret back!

'It's madness to stay here while my sister… my sister… She's *trapped*, don't you understand?' Her voice a screech even though her throat is singed. 'She can't get out! She's waiting for me to come for her… Please, please… And Mother…' Her voice flailing. 'Mother might be trapped too…'

Margaret thrashes against the surprisingly strong constraints of Peggy's arms, blisters bursting open and weeping the tears she is too horrified and panicked to shed as lights bob up the hill – wide-eyed villagers in their pyjamas and nightgowns arriving with buckets of water, pale and muttering.

'Air raid,' Margaret hears. 'Biggest house around here, obvious target, come to think of it.' The villagers' voices soft with shock and sympathy.

Peggy says, soothing, 'Help is here. Shhh… it's alright. They'll find Marm and your sister.' But she does not release Margaret.

'I promised I'd come for Evie,' Margaret sobs.

'It's not safe, Miss.' Peggy rubs a smoke-stained arm across her leaking nose, the other still gripping Margaret in a vice-like, impossible to escape, hold.

'She's inside, waiting for me. She's *trapped*.'

Help is coming, Evie, she says in her head, while out loud she pleads, her voice rasping, despairing, 'Please, Peggy, let me go,' kicking and fighting Peggy, whose face, lit up by the inferno, is bruised and suppurated with ash and burns.

Old Mr Seeton, who acts as fireman now that the firemen have been called up to war, ineffectually tries to put out the flames with the aid of the villagers, Margaret calling to them, 'My sister is inside and…'

Her eyes scanning the grounds. No sign of Mother.

'…and possibly Mother.'

It is then that Margaret collapses onto boiling earth, hot but not as scalding as the agony in her heart.

Chapter Eight

1920

Archana

Vulnerable

'Radha, what are you *doing*?' Archana asks, blinking as her eyes adjust to the gloominess of their hut after the bright sunshine outdoors.

She can just about make out her sister, lying on the mat with… a *boy*. No, a man! *Inside* their house, when their mother has always emphasised that even looking sideways at a boy or man is enough to ruin a girl, destroy her reputation.

Her sister pats her sari back into place, looking flustered, her hair awry.

'What are *you* doing back so soon?' Radha's voice shakes a little and this scares Archana even more than the man in their home. Her sister's voice *never* trembles, not even when she has great big fights with Ma and Da about refusing every proposal for her hand.

'I… The nun who teaches us took ill.' Archana's voice quivers too, but with shock. 'They allowed us to come home early. Where is Ma? Do she or Da know…?' She nods towards the man, his head bent and shoulders slouched. He is silhouetted in the doorway briefly as he slinks outdoors and away, and it is then that Archana recognises him.

'Radha.' Her voice a stunned whisper. 'He's the untouchable from—'

Radha grabs her arms. 'Please' – her grip hard, her breath sour – 'Don't tell Ma and Da.'

Her sister has been distant these past months, preoccupied, not wanting Archana anywhere near her, giving her the slip more than once – it's been easy for Radha to do so, as she left school the previous year.

'Is he the reason you've been avoiding me and saying no to all the proposals you get?'

'I don't want to marry the person *they* choose for me. I want to make my own destiny.'

'But Radha, you can't choose *him*. He's an untouchable! You'll be ostracised – if Ma and Da ever agree, that is.'

'I love him.' Radha is sporting the stubborn look she gets when their parents chastise her for letting yet another proposal go.

'You *can't*. He's an *untouchable*,' Archana repeats as if that might make her sister see sense. 'And you let him inside our house! What will Ma and Da—?'

'You're not to tell them.' Her sister fierce.

'Where *is* Ma?' Archana asks, knowing Da is tilling fields, willing her parents here, now. Her sister is scaring her, as is what she thought she saw as she entered the hut, before her eyes adjusted to the light... A nightmare, an illusion, surely? She wills it away.

'Promise me, Archana.'

Once, she would have loved conspiring with her sister, innocent times, like that raid on Bhim's orchard, only two years but feeling like a lifetime ago. She wants *that* sister back, not *this* Radha, who has been so remote and is now frightening her with her intensity, her insistence that she loves this entirely unsuitable man, wanting Archana to keep quiet about it.

But Archana doesn't want to keep this from her parents. It feels too huge.

The weight of her sister's secret presses down on her that afternoon when her mother comes back from visiting a sick relative in the next village, and is touchingly pleased when Radha sweetly offers her spiced tea, tells her to put her feet up, serves her rice and pickle. When their father comes home from the fields, worn out, Radha serves him dinner too, Archana heating water for his wash, the soothing scent of boiling water, burning twigs. Da smiling fondly. 'My good girls.'

Archana lies down that night beside her sister and her mother, her dreams punctuated by her father's snores from across the room, and fights dread, even as Radha sleeps beside her in the space where the man was before. Archana fancies she can smell him, the air inside their hut rank, tainted by his presence, and is not at all surprised when she startles awake crying, and her mother shushes her: 'Go to sleep. You had a nightmare, that's all.'

Radha's eyes meet hers, glinting bright with warning in the shadowy seething dark, conspiracy in them, the secret she is imploring Archana to keep, against Archana's will.

'What's the matter?' Archana asks her sister. 'Are you not feeling well?'

It is very early in the morning, a few weeks after Archana discovered the man with her sister in their hut, Archana having been woken by her sister surreptitiously getting up from the mat they share with their mother.

Their mother and father, tired out from a long day's work, will sleep through anything.

Radha is retching under the banyan trees behind the house. The dog is rubbing his body against Radha's legs, offering comfort. In the chilly pre-dawn light, the air stroking their cheeks smelling of night and secrets, her sister looks insubstantial, her thin body bent like a question mark, her fair skin glowing, eyes huge and stark.

Archana puts her arms round Radha, rubbing her sister's frail shoulders, goose-bumped and vulnerable.

'Is it the fish from last night?' she whispers, when Radha, finally spent, rests her forehead against Archana's.

At the word 'fish', her sister goes green again and, turning, retches some more. There is nothing left inside her stomach and yet she vomits, again and again.

Afterward, Archana holds her sister in the soft quiet peppered with unasked questions, sharp with misgiving, the dog licking their feet. Rustling in the bushes beside them, nocturnal animals returning to their lair.

This is the closest Archana has felt to Radha in a long time. And yet…

Her sister's fragile shoulders shaking. Her indomitable sister emotional, smelling of sick, upset.

The scent of jasmine and dew-speckled air and unease. The taste of dawn, chilly with a hint of freshness, black curling at the edges, pushed away by the pink-streaked smile of morning. The flavour of alarm, an anxious gasp in Archana's throat.

Standing there, holding her sister as she sobs, soundlessly, her silent crying more scary than anything Archana has experienced until now, even the time she encountered a cobra on the path, hissing and showing its forked tongue. She had turned and run as fast as she could (not fast at all, given her limp), anticipating, all the while, the snake's fangs sinking into her leg, venom flooding her body. Once she had cleared the fields, crossed the stream, she had looked back, panting. The snake was still where she had left it, its hood up. It lounged proudly on the path, daring anyone to come upon it. She had been spared. That was when she had cried, tears of sheer relief.

Now, reciprocal tears tremble on her cheeks at her sister's upset. Radha reeks of fear, yellow tinged with violet. Archana can feel it pulsing through her body, feeding into her own fear. Her sister is terrified. Of what?

A thrill of premonition shudders through Archana.

And somehow, even before Radha opens her mouth to speak, Archana knows that this is the moment their life will change, that nothing is going to be the same again.

PART 2

....

HOPE

Chapter Nine

1916

Margaret

All-Consuming

'Winnie?' Margaret whispers. 'Do you feel at home here?'

Margaret and Winnie are in the draughty room assigned to them in the attic of Aunt Helen's farmhouse, the very place Mother had postponed coming to by a fortnight, in the process losing, to an air raid, her life and that of her oldest daughter, along with the home she had wanted to open up to wounded soldiers.

The room is cold, wind howling against the windows like a banshee out for revenge, and Margaret shivers, unable to get warm, although when she closes her eyes she sees fire: all-consuming, all-encompassing coppery flames.

Winnie sniffs, turning to her side on the hard pallet that passes for a bed, so she faces Margaret.

Her features are in shadow but Margaret can just make out her sister's eyes, once bright, now anguished, in the moonlight angling into the room on a squalling wintry gust. 'Meggie, this *is* home now. There is no other.' Her voice tender but stoic.

Margaret closes her eyes, unable to look at her surviving sister. Flames dance in front of her tightly shut lids, and she hears Evie's voice, choked, small, calling, 'Meggie.' A plea from her trapped, immobile sister that she was unable to heed.

The pain is constant, as is the image of flames singeing her beloved sister, smoke strangling the breath out of her as she waited for Margaret to rescue her. Evie who was so patient and gentle to the end, who must have held out hope Margaret *would* come, even as she died. Evie, kind and motherly, always smiling despite being confined to her wheelchair. Evie, who had once confided in her sisters, eyes shining, as they fantasised about their futures, 'I want to have at least five children – three girls, like us, and two boys.'

Winnie is waiting, so Margaret coughs out the question that sticks in her throat, tormenting her. 'Why do I get to live when they— Evie…?' Her voice breaking, rendering her unable to continue.

'Oh, Meggie!' Winnie's hand snakes across the small gap between their beds, populated with the spectres of their missing family, and squeezes Margaret's.

Margaret looks up at the ceiling, which is broody with shadows, unable to meet her sister's earnest gaze. 'If we had left immediately Aunt Helen's letter arrived, inviting us to stay, if Mother had not decided otherwise, we would *all* be here…' She shuts her eyes tight, the image so perfect, exquisitely painful, entirely possible if only they could go back a few weeks and do it again, differently…

'Meggie.' Her sister's voice gentle, her hand warm in Margaret's, the only warmth in this room. 'There's no point thinking this way.'

'Oh, but I do,' Margaret whispers, so softly that Winnie doesn't hear, the ceiling undulating before her agonised eyes. 'I do.'

'You're smelly and a sissy!'

'I'm not!' Margaret shakes her fist at her taunting cousin Robbie.

'And useless with it. Taking ages to do your chores. Your mother taught you nothing but hoity-toity airs and graces—'

'Don't you dare!'

And Margaret is on him, pummelling him with her fists and her legs until she is dragged away by the ear, her breathing heavy, face red. Snot drips from her nose because it is freezing, always cold here. And she cannot wipe it away either for she is being hauled by Uncle Robert to the pigsty.

'Clean it,' her uncle bites out through clenched teeth. 'God knows, all the farmhands have left to join up. No help, the farm going to the pits and your aunt insisting on taking you in, two more mouths to feed.'

Their uncle's litany since Margaret and Winnie arrived.

'Your mother married above her station and now we're lumbered with you two, who will not pull your weight.'

'My mother might have married above her station, but Aunt Helen married below it, more's the pity,' Margaret wants to say, but she bites her lower lip to keep her words in. Too late to defend her mother against her uncle's vitriol. Too late to do anything at all for her mother and sister…

'Does Father know about the… the air raid?' Margaret had asked Aunt Helen when they first arrived.

It was her uncle who answered, from his customary position in the armchair beside the hearth. 'I've written to his regiment. Whether the letter reaches him is another matter. And until he makes arrangements for you, we are burdened with two additional mouths to feed, as if our own were not enough.'

'Robert…' Aunt Helen cautioned from the sink, where she was scrubbing potatoes for supper.

'Father has put money aside for us, for when we come of age.' Margaret willed her voice not to break, recalling her mother in the orangery, Margaret ensconced in her lap, her sisters on the settee.

'Mother,' Margaret had said, playing with her mother's pearl necklace, which reflected the weak spring sunshine in its ivory depths. 'This is beautiful.'

'You'll get it one day. You'll each get something of mine, and your father has made sure you'll all get a dowry when you come of age.'

'And until then,' her uncle had snapped, jolting Margaret from her reverie – happiness and agony where her family was safe and whole – 'what shall we feed you on?'

'Robert, that's quite enough.' Her aunt turned from the sink with such ferocity that water droplets dribbled onto the floor in a wide shimmering arc.

One day, a few weeks later, when Margaret heard her aunt refer to 'Alice's girls', she had loitered in the shadows behind the doorway, the scent of mildew, cobwebs and secrets, a spider edging away from her along its gossamer thread, and eavesdropped.

'They're a drain on us. You said we should take them in, they'd be a help on the farm now all the farmhands have left, but they're useless.' Her uncle grunted his disapproval vehemently.

'We'll be compensated.' Her aunt's tone placatory. 'The solicitor sent a note. He's waiting to hear from their father, but even if not, he'll be sending money regularly for the girls' upkeep – apparently their father made some arrangement when he signed up for just this eventuality.'

Her uncle had grunted again, but this time with approval.

Margaret had slipped away, feeling grateful to her father for his foresight and also devastated, picturing his face as they had said goodbye at the station, how he had looked at them as if committing them to memory, knowing, she is beginning to understand, even then, that there was a possibility he might not see his family again…

She'd gone to the room in the attic, thinking of Father, missing him, recalling how when he was around they'd all felt secure, contented, except during those dark, dismal times after George's stillbirth. She and Winnie needed Father now – their only remaining family – and yet there was no word from him. No letter, no intimation to let them know he knew of the air raid, that he felt the loss of Mother and Evie as keenly as they did. No words of comfort.

Nothing.

And again Margaret wondered, as she'd taken to doing lately, if perhaps things would be different if George hadn't died? Father had signed up for the war partly to get over losing George, she knew from surreptitiously reading his letters to Mother. Would he have signed up as eagerly as he had – the first among his friends – if George had lived? And would that have made a difference?

Father, why haven't you written? We miss you. Don't you miss us? Are you angry with us for not managing to save Mother and Evie?

If George was alive, here with us, would you write? Would you come home to him?

'If Mother or Evie were to see you now, they wouldn't recognise you, that's for sure,' Winnie says with a sigh when Margaret gets into a fight at school yet again, with their cousin Robbie as is most usual, her hair in a tizzy, her clothes a mess.

'Where's that sweet little Meggie gone, eh? The one who drove all of us crazy with her continual questions.' A wistful smile on Winnie's face as she checks Margaret's person for scrapes, wounds, marks of battle.

Margaret thinks, no, she *knows*, that that other Margaret died in the fire and the one who has taken her place is formed of guilt, loss, anger; a hard carapace, purple-shelled, impenetrable, carrying the cruelly snuffed out souls of Mother and Evie – living for them as much as for herself, hoping for redemption by looking out for Winnie, not letting her down as she did Evie when it mattered, when she needed her most.

Margaret sniffs as she cleans out the pigsty, the pigs grunting placidly around her. The stink makes her want to gag but she gets on with it, teeth gritted. As Winnie reminds her every so often, this is their life now.

Chapter Ten

2000

Emma

Less Than Perfect

Emma rests her head against the window of the bus, which bears the ghostly imprint of a thousand hands, her breath fogging the pane. The musty scent of steaming clothes, wet glass and hopelessness.

She closes her eyes and thinks of David. The only man she has ever loved. The father of her child.

He will be in the living room, the blue light from the television trailing shadows on his chiselled face. He will be drinking wine and waiting up for her.

Down the corridor and across the bedroom from theirs, their daughter will be fast asleep with Cuddles, her stuffed bear – not much stuffing left now, Emma having sneakily washed him a few times – and Blanky. All the other soft toys Chloe obsessively collects keeping watch.

Emma's home, her sanctuary. Her loves: Chloe and David. The roots that she has yearned for all her life, finally in place.

Is she willing to destroy all she has worked for, the life she has longed for, the life she finally has?

But if what I have found is true, then it is already destroyed. David has destroyed it.

Again.

Emma has looked up to him, idolised him, ever since she saw
him first on TV. She's put him on a pedestal, refusing to see his
flaws despite having ample cause. But now she has no choice but
to acknowledge that the man she loves is fallible. Human. Quali-
ties she hasn't allowed him as she persisted in her hero-worship
of him – even though he's proved less than perfect before.

But now…

What she has discovered undermines the very reason she fell
in love with him in the first place. His work. The paper that
made him famous.

The bus stops with a jerk and grinding of brakes, a noisy sigh.
A man, back hunched against the icy wind, gets off. A gaggle
of noisy teenagers, beer bottles in hand, climb to the top of the
bus. They sit at the back. Emma is right up at the front and yet
she can hear them, laughing, calling each other names. She is
glad of the distraction, although the only other person upstairs,
a middle-aged man, goes downstairs.

'You like the maths teacher, Mr Clarke, don't you?' A snarky
boy's voice carrying to where Emma is sitting, a smirk in it. 'Look,
she's blushing. She fancies that stuffed suit. He's married, you
know, with children.'

The others laughing.

'He's ancient,' another boy drawls. 'What's wrong with you?'

'Chicks dig that, mate.'

Slumped in her seat, Emma stares sightlessly out of the
window, her gaze blurred by tears.

She is crying for the girl she once was, newly arrived in
Cambridge, in awe of the formidable Dr David McEwan with
his Scottish accent, his rugged good looks, his formidable
intelligence, his groundbreaking research paper that made him

famous, spawning TV appearances and book deals, the way his blue eyes looked right at you, into you.

Dr David McEwan was the reason Emma chose to read history at Cambridge. He had been present at her selection interview and although he had not asked any questions, his assessing gaze had speared her as she answered questions the other academics in the panel put to her. When she had finished he had given a quick nod, smiling at her, and she felt singled out, special, a warm glow spreading through her. She knew then that she would get in.

And she had.

Then to arrive and find that he would be teaching her! And, by the end of her first year, to be picked to help him with his research – oh, the heady joy of that time!

A screech of high-pitched laughter from the back of the bus.

She startles, her head knocking against the glass.

She wipes her face, soggy with nostalgia, regret and upset for the choices she made that have led her here.

Now she is faced with another choice.

Should she confront David, or let it be?

If she confronts him, and he *is* culpable (and part of her still hopes he isn't, although she has conclusive proof showing otherwise), what will she do then?

Will she have the courage to out him, show him up for the fraud he is, knowing that it will cause a media circus, that she will be breaking up their family in a very public way?

It would be the right thing to do, but what about Chloe?

What would seeing her parents on opposite sides of a much-publicised scandal, witnessing her father's name reviled, finding out that her mother was responsible for it, do to her beloved, impressionable daughter?

Chloe has accepted David, welcomed him into their lives without question in that innocent, wholehearted way of children. She loves him unconditionally, completely, and despite everything, even given what she's just found out, Emma loves him too.

Can she do this? Will she?

Chapter Eleven

1917

Margaret

Touch

'Margaret, you did a good job feeding the horses.' Aunt Helen beams, patting Margaret's back.

Margaret pulls away, flinching from her aunt's touch.

Aunt Helen's face falls.

Winnie, who is chopping onions and sniffing vigorously, eyes running, notices and shakes her head at Margaret.

Later, Winnie corners Margaret in their attic room. 'Meggie, you shouldn't have pulled away from Aunt Helen. She tries very hard, you know, to make us feel at home here.'

'She's not Mother.'

Mother – evoking in Margaret complicated feelings of love and loss, sorrow and anger.

Winnie, exasperated: 'Meggie, Mother is no longer here. You have to accept that.'

Margaret turns away from her sister so Winnie won't see the press of tears stinging her eyes. Winnie rarely raises her voice, and she never has to Margaret before. It is a shock.

As if she has divined Margaret's upset, Winnie puts her arms round her.

Her sister's touch is the only one Margaret can bear, but she feels distant from Winnie too, something she hadn't thought possible.

Losing her mother and oldest sister, worrying about Father – they haven't had a letter or visit from him since the air raid – has made her hard and sharp, removed from everything and everyone, even Winnie.

'This is our life now and Aunt Helen our guardian. You have to accept it, Meggie. Please.'

Winnie is trying to adjust to her new life – she grieves for Mother and Evie every night (thinking Margaret asleep and unaware) and somehow this allows her to wake up and face another day. Margaret envies her sister – while Winnie is attempting to move on, Margaret cannot accept this life, for it was not meant to be theirs, not without Mother and Evie being here with them. She longs for the past, their times together as a complete, unfractured family in their childhood home, the repository and curator of happy memories, when war was just a rumour, something to be ignored, batted away like a persistent buzzing wasp...

'Will this war ever end?' Winnie asks that night, as they huddle on their cold, hard mattresses in the freezing room in the attic, hands linked across their cots for warmth and solace.

Margaret knows it is still going strong. She has heard it on the wireless that her uncle likes to listen to in the kitchen of an evening while cradling his mug of ale.

Should she lie, tell Winnie that the war will be over soon? As soon as the thought hovers, she is overcome by a fierce burst of anger directed at their mother, followed by a conflicted avalanche of emotions – sorrow, love and guilt – for raging at Mother when she is dead.

But… if Mother had not refused to see the reality of war, if she had accepted the possibility of air raids instead of airily assuming everything would be alright, Margaret wouldn't be lying awake every night. For when she closes her eyes she sees Evie, trapped in her room, waiting for Margaret to rescue her. When Margaret does drift off to sleep, she hears her sister's voice, weak, pleading help, rescue: 'Meggie…'

And so she tells Winnie the truth, knowing there is no point in sugar-coating it as it will only cause hurt and confusion later. She is aware that they cannot be complacent, that they must prepare instead for more hardship. 'It's not looking like this war will end anytime soon.'

'Oh.' Winnie's voice small. Then, at once hopeful and anxious, 'Father? Do you think he's alright?'

In her question, Margaret reading the worry they both don't want to voice. Why hasn't Father written? Why hasn't he visited when others have returned to be with their families, if only for a couple of days?

And again, copper-tinged flames blooming in front of Margaret's eyes, the villagers ineffectually trying to put out the fire while she fought Peggy to be allowed to go to her sister, staring at the glowing embers of what used to be their childhood home and hoping, wishing, that Mother and Evie had somehow escaped unscathed and would come to them at any moment.

'It's not fair, is it? Robbie and Hilda get to have their father with them, just because Uncle Robert's weak eyesight makes him exempt from signing up. Perhaps if Father hadn't gone away to war…' Winnie, usually so philosophical and accepting of their fate, showing a rare moment of pensiveness, upset.

Margaret has dwelled on this during those seemingly endless, lonely hours of night when exhaustion drags her eyes closed and Evie's immobile body, tormented by flames, haunts her.

Privately, she thinks their family started unravelling when George, the much-longed-for son and heir, was stillborn. Mother had come back to them afterward, albeit more fragile, grief lurking behind every smile, but Father... A vital part of him was lost and perhaps he had hoped, by signing up and doing his bit for his country, to reclaim it. Had he? Where is he now? Why hasn't he been in touch with or visited his remaining family, his grieving daughters, undone by loss? Would it be different if George was alive?

Out loud she says, gently, repeating what Winnie has said to her many a time over the preceding months, 'It's done now.'

Margaret is not the naive girl she once was. She understands now that life can change in an instant, that nothing is safe or to be taken for granted. That they cannot rely on anyone – that even adults are powerless in the face of war and tragedy.

Listening to her sister's sniffles, shivering in their draughty room, the blankets not enough to keep them warm, Margaret vows that she will make her own destiny as soon as she is able, that she will depend on no one.

Before, she and her sisters used to smell of lavender and bergamot, lemon and the outdoors. Now, no matter how much she scrubs herself with the bar of soap, her skin red-raw and sore, she cannot rid herself of the reek of the farm – hay and manure and animal. It sticks to her clothes, it gets under her skin.

She thinks of the angel in the garden, with the name of her brother, who never got to live, etched onto it. She had run her fingers along George's name, pearly indentations on marble, warm and soft to the touch like sun-kissed skin, secretly hoping that just by sheer force of will she could bring him to life. Now, she pictures the angel with more names added: Evie, Alice.

'Margaret, your painting is hard to look at,' Miss Pym says.

Behind Margaret, her cousin Robbie sniggers loud enough for her to hear.

The brief was to depict where you belong.

Margaret has painted two girls, representing herself and Winnie – tarred with smoke, touched by death – in a hollow purple shell, encasing nothingness; the shell touches images – their childhood home, their parents, their sister – yet is bare inside, to indicate that the girls carry all these other elements, they are formed of them but are now essentially empty, belonging nowhere.

She had painted it in a feverish rush and when she finished, she had felt a small part of her settle, the act of putting her emotions on the page providing a slight relief to the roiling mess her heart has been since the air raid.

The painting had felt intensely personal and she had not wanted to share it with anyone, resolving to paint something else for Miss Pym's assignment instead.

Winnie had come into their attic room just as Margaret was stowing it under her mattress.

'What are you hiding away?' she had asked, wrestling the painting from Margaret.

She was silent for a good while, and then, eyes brimming, she'd said only, 'Oh, Meg!' and enveloped Margaret in her arms.

The next day, when Margaret looked for the painting, it wasn't there.

'I handed it in to Miss Pym,' Winnie said when Margaret asked her where it was.

'I—' Margaret began but Winnie cut in, 'I think it's brilliant. Sad, but amazing and heartfelt. You have real talent, Meg, and it's time you were recognised for it.'

*

Winnie, what have you done? Margaret thinks now, her cheeks hot with mortification.

'It exudes emotion,' Miss Pym is saying. 'And pain. It made me cry. It does exactly what art should do – evoke a reaction in the viewer. You are really very good.' Miss Pym smiles at Margaret, approval and commiseration – she has lost her father and a brother to the war, Margaret knows.

Winnie glows with pride on Margaret's behalf, her smile bursting out of her face as she shoots Margaret a 'What did I tell you?' look, while their cousins scowl. They are all in the same class although there's three years between them – there are not enough teachers so they've been clumped together.

Later, as they walk to what passes for home, lagging behind their cousins, Winnie pats Margaret's arm. 'See, Meg? Miss Pym was so impressed. Well done!'

It is summer again, almost time for the holidays, hedges aglow with ripening blackberries, stinging nettles, honeysuckle and thistle. The aroma of maturing produce, the droning of happy bees.

Up ahead their cousin Robbie, hearing Winnie's remark, turns, his lips parting in a sneer. 'You've got to be good at *something* seeing as you're rubbish at farm work. We need an extra pair of hands just undoing your mistakes. And it's not like you're new any more. You've been here *ages*.'

Winnie ignores him, squeezing Margaret's hand, a warning not to take the bait.

Winnie has grown tall and willowy in the last year, her eyes long-lashed violet, face ethereal, causing boys to flock to her and Robbie to become even more mean.

In a way her cousin is right. School is Margaret's respite. She works hard at her lessons, seeing them as her out, convinced learning will give her the freedom she yearns for, escape from the farm, which does not and will never feel like home.

She has found that while she's waiting to leave the farm for good, two things provide temporary solace: books, lent to Margaret by Miss Pym, and art.

Margaret draws all the time, using whatever medium is to hand. Etchings created with charcoal from the fire, sketches of life on the farm: her sister asleep, the slender, perfect lines of her. Margaret's self-portrait: knee-deep in muck in the pigsty, at home with the pigs, who watch placidly, patiently. Brambles, alive with thorns, piercing the blackberries, juice dripping, tangy purple. Her cousins, with their perpetual sneers. The room she shares with Winnie in the attic. Her uncle, his beer belly, his face flushed puce with drink. Her aunt: pursed lips and anxious gaze.

When Margaret is without any material to draw with, she sketches in her head, while cleaning the pigsty and doing all the more difficult, dirtier jobs around the farm that their cousins make sure to leave for them and which Margaret takes on to spare Winnie, without her knowledge.

Sometimes as she shovels the mud and dirt she talks out loud, to alleviate the loneliness that seems to dog her, even when with Winnie, the otherness she feels, as if removed from everyone around her, the pigs looking on serenely. The slop, sick-coloured and sour, sloshes and overflows, splashing her shoes, which are squelchy with mud.

'Talking to yourself?' she hears. 'Or to the animals? You really are quite mad.' Robbie, sneering as always.

She sniffs, rubbing a hand across her face to remove any trace of wetness, and walks out of the sty, ignoring him, not deigning to reply.

Chapter Twelve

1920

Archana

Shame

'Radha, how could you?' their mother cries, hitting her own head against the wall of their hut, again and again, the mud cracking, tinting her forehead powdery red as if the skin is peeling off her face in bloody wisps.

Radha cowers in the corner, by the hearth. Tears rolling down her face. One hand wrapped protectively round her stomach. Archana has her arms round her sister, Radha's delicate shoulders rocking in Archana's grasp.

Their father is slumped on the floor by the front door. Both parents look defeated, their mother's forehead having really started bleeding now, a bruised, dust-stained bump where she has been repeatedly battering it.

'Ma, don't,' Archana manages when her mother goes to bash her head again, her voice small, her stomach roiling, her whole body protesting at this rupture in her family, all of them swallowed up by misery.

Her mother's devastated gaze lands on Archana.

'Eh, Radha, did you spare a thought for your sister when you did this? Did you stop to think about what you were doing, destroying your future, destroying us? Did you give a thought to anyone but yourself?' she bites out, her breath stumbling on a sob.

Her father's head sinks lower into the tomb of his lap.

'How will we show our faces in the village? How will your father go to work now, after this dishonour? How will we get Archana married? It was difficult enough with her limp and her dark skin but now, it's impossible. Did you think of that?' Her mother's voice a vanquished husk, a brooding lament.

Unbearable.

In her arms, her sister crumbles. Archana's mouth fills with salt and brine. Iron and blood. The taste of a family splintering, hearts breaking.

'An untouchable, of all people! You're carrying the child of an untouchable. Shame on you! Leave. You're dead to us!'

Her sister flinches sharply. Her shoulders heave. Her breath hitches.

'Ma, what are you saying?' Archana speaks up, her voice a squeak of shock and upset.

'Here.' Her mother scrambles behind the hearth and digs out a small bag clinking with gold bangles. She throws it to Radha. 'Take the dowry we were saving for you. Part of the dowry *I* brought when I married your father. The other part is for your sister, if she's ever able to get a proposal after this disgrace. This scandal. After what you've done…'

Her sister speaks. One word. A plea. 'Ma…'

'No.' Her mother turns away. Her voice shakes and yet she says, 'You lost the right to call me that when you did what you did with an untouchable. We may be poor but we're of good caste. How could you?'

She bangs her forehead against the wall again.

'Go and don't darken our doorstep again. As far as we're concerned you're dead to us.'

That word again! Archana shivers. 'Ma,' she wails as her sister, eyes swollen, face crumpled, gently frees herself from Archana's grasp. 'Don't do this.'

'Don't you see, child' – Archana's mother grabs her by the shoulders – 'she's ruined your chances. She's ruined *us*. We were proud of her beauty, her light skin. But to what end? Look what she's done!'

'Ma, she's your *child*! Da,' Archana pleads, 'do something.'

But her father's face is buried in his lap. He will not respond. Her mother has released her grip on Archana and turned away.

Urgently, Archana squeezes her sister's hand. 'Don't go. They'll come round.'

But her sister is tucking the bag containing her dowry into her sari skirt, her face ravaged, shiny with tears and yet as beautiful as ever. She strokes Archana's face, tenderly wiping away the tears. 'I'm so sorry. I did not think.' She gulps. 'I didn't mean for this to happen.' She rests her forehead against Archana's and they stand like that for a beat, their heads touching, the taste of sorrow and love.

Then Radha gathers her clothes, bundles them into a sari, knotting it into a parcel. She squats down, touching their mother's feet. Their mother turns away, but from the way her hunched shoulders move, Archana can see that she too is weeping.

Radha does the same to her father, who moves his legs, folding them under him, not looking at either of his daughters, or his wife.

Radha sniffs and pulls her veil over her head. She walks away, looking flimsy and insubstantial as she stops at the tamarind tree and turns to gaze one last time at her home, her parents who are turned away from her and Archana, the dog dancing at her feet and barking, a volley of worried staccato yaps. He too knows something is not right.

'Radha, don't. This is *not* the answer, don't you see, Ma, Da…' Archana, who has until now been rooted to the spot in shock, refusing to believe that her sister is actually leaving, makes to run after her, bring her back, force their parents to see sense.

But she is stopped by a low howl.

Her sister, who has resumed walking, stops as well, turns.

Their father is sprawled on the mud by the doorway where he was sitting just before, clutching at his heart. The howl, a weird sound, hollow with pain, is coming from him.

Their mother rushes to him, squatting beside him, her tear-swollen eyes stunned, veil falling from her face in chagrin. 'What's the matter? Tell me, please?' Her voice pleading and panicked all at once.

Archana cannot move and her sister is the same, stranded beneath the tamarind tree, knotted sari containing her belongings on her shoulder, face wet with tears, dog lapping the dust off her feet.

Their father jerks once, twice. Then he is still, the stillness even more shocking than the howling.

Their mother bends low, resting her head on his heart. It takes Archana a horrified moment that seems to stretch to a year to understand that she is listening for his heartbeat.

An endless minute of taut silence as her father lies on the dirt by the doorway, absolutely rigid.

Then her mother lifts up her head, her agonised, wild and yet strangely empty gaze connecting briefly with Archana's before her face crumples and she keens loud and long and then with a terrifying crash brings her hands to the mud.

Archana flinches, her eyes never leaving the still form of her father. She knows that her sister, beneath the tamarind tree, is doing the same. The dog leaves her sister's side, ambles up to her father, sniffs him and then sets up a mournful wail.

Her mother brings her hands down again and again. Her glass bangles splinter and litter the mud beside the unmoving form of her husband, shards glinting brightly in the orange dirt. Blood burgeons on her mother's bare wrists, the skin exposed without its habitual sheath of multi-hued bangles and speckled shiny red.

The dog cries, a plaintive whine of prolonged distress.

Her mother lifts her bleeding hands, naked without their adornment of bangles, up to her face and with her muddy palms wipes the vermilion circle that she paints on her forehead every morning, the mark of a married woman, off her bruised and battered, dust- and bloodstained face.

Archana stares, not wanting to comprehend what she is seeing.

There must be some mistake. Her mother must have got it wrong.

With legs that jerk and stumble, she goes to her father.

His hands clutching his heart. His eyes wide open and pained, looking at nothing.

She sits beside him, then very gently lays her head on his chest, between his hands. It is chillingly still. Not rising and falling like it should. His heart silent, no longer beating out the rhythm of life.

No, she screams. But nothing comes from her numb mouth.

Her dazed eyes connect with her sister. Radha's gaze, desperate, pleading with her at first and then, perhaps reading something in her eyes, defeated, bleeding grief.

Radha starts walking towards them.

'Stop,' their mother yells in a blood-curdling tone Archana has never heard before. 'You've made me a widow.' Her voice breaks on the word, then gains steam once more. Dripping sorrow, suffused with rage, cloudburst crimson. 'You've taken your father's life. Happy now?'

Archana lifts her head from her father's immobile body. Her sister's face, pale. Washed raw. Hurting.

'Ma, no…' she begins.

But her mother ignores her, violent fury overlaid with pain. 'I have only one daughter.'

'Ma…' Looking to her mother, wanting her to soothe like she used to when she was a child, tell her this is all a mistake. A nightmare she will wake up from soon. 'Please.'

She doesn't know what she is asking: for her father to live. For her sister to stay. For everything to go back to before.

Her sister's face devastated. Radha nods, once, tears falling unchecked as she stares at her father, perhaps willing him, like Archana herself is, to wake up, make everything alright.

'Radha,' Archana calls urgently as her sister turns away, her voice hoarse, throat dry and desperate.

Her sister's shoulders slump. She takes one step forward.

'Radha,' Archana's voice a plaintive reed. 'I cannot lose you too.'

'She brought this upon us,' her mother sobs. 'Let her go before she does more harm.'

'No.' Archana stands, makes to go after her sister.

'You *will* stay here.' Her mother's voice breaking.

'Ma, please,' Archana tries.

'Let me go, Archana,' Radha says, her voice soft but carrying in the mournful, grief-suffused breeze. 'It's for the best.'

'How so?' Archana cries. 'Radha, please…'

'Look after Ma. Don't be like me.' Radha's voice weighed down with pain.

'*Now* she speaks sense, when it's too late,' her mother spits, tears coursing down her face.

Once again, Archana makes to run to her sister.

'No, you stay here.' Her mother, eyes bloodshot, face and hands bloody and bare, holds her back.

Archana struggles in her mother's arms, her familiar scent of fried onions and chilli powder and sweat and now grief, the taste of heartbreak and loss as she watches, helpless, her sister walk away.

Chapter Thirteen

1918

Margaret

Selfish

Margaret is wiping her shoes on the carpet – she's just back from taking the dog for a walk and the fields were soggy – and has her hand on the kitchen door ready to push it open, when she hears her aunt's voice.

'I miss Alice, yet I'm cross with her. I wrote inviting her and her girls to come and stay with us until the threat of air raids passed.'

'Without asking me,' her uncle grumbles. 'How were you planning to feed them all?'

'We'd have managed. At least my sister would be alive.' Margaret's aunt sniffs. 'But Alice… she dallied, waiting for a letter from that husband of hers. If only she'd come, she'd be safe.'

Margaret rests her cheek against the cool, rain-speckled wood of the kitchen door, the dog looking at her with empathic brown eyes before standing on two paws and nuzzling into her side, offering comfort.

'And now I've finally received a response to the umpteenth letter I wrote enquiring after Alice's husband. The official line is that he's missing in action but it appears that the fool, on receiving news of her death, put himself in the line of enemy bullets and gladly received them, not giving a thought to his two surviving children. How selfish is…'

Margaret has heard enough. She charges into the kitchen, silencing her aunt, who pauses mid-flow, hand on her throat, and blinks rapidly, her eyes bright.

Margaret's uncle, lounging in the armchair by the fire, squints at his niece over the top of his mug of ale. He takes a gulp and wipes his beard with the back of his hand.

'Now, where did you come—' her aunt begins.

But Margaret, who has managed to gather herself, squeaks past the briny lump sitting square on her chest, 'He wouldn't do that. Father…?'

Despite herself, her voice rises in question.

Her uncle grunts, taking another big sip of his ale with a loud slurp, bubbly white froth freckling his orange moustache.

'Of course not, dear.' Her aunt flusters, voice kind as she opens her arms out to Margaret.

Margaret looks at this woman, a thin, reedy version of her beautiful mother, and she cannot bear it.

Aunt Helen waits but Margaret will not go to her, this woman who cannot give the comfort she needs.

Margaret turns away but not before she sees her aunt's face fall, her arms dropping to her side.

As Margaret walks away, up to her and Winnie's room, she hears her uncle scoff, 'What did I tell you? Ungrateful squirt, looking down her nose at us, thinking she's too good for us! Your sister marrying above her station, giving herself and her daughters ideas. The other one's not so bad, but this one… Nothing but trouble.'

That night in the draughty attic room, Margaret fights sleep while pretending to snooze. This is what she does every night, affecting sleep until her sister's hand goes slack in hers and her breathing eases into gentle snores. Sometimes Winnie cries out and Margaret knows she is dreaming of fire.

This is why Margaret is afraid to sleep. When slumber does take her captive against her will she hears the staccato burst of what she assumed was fireworks that fateful night, and then she is ablaze, burning, boiling, destroyed, the old, innocent Margaret gone, a new hard girl taking her place, crusted with the blue-black, prickly scab of guilt – for not being able to save Evie – and anger, directed at her mother for wanting to hear from Father and deciding to stay at home longer, thus choosing love for her husband over the safety of her daughters, and at herself for being angry at her mother.

She debates whether to tell Winnie what she overheard her aunt say regarding their father, unable to find the words, the terrible knowledge, the weight of it crushing her lungs, leaving her gasping.

Father, you wouldn't do that, surely? Would you not spare a thought for your younger two daughters? Or was living for us, living at all, quite unfathomable after you heard Mother had died?

What if George, your coveted son and heir, had lived? Would you have made sure you survived if there was a son to come home to?

'Father's not coming back, is he?' Winnie says, jolting Margaret out of her terrible musings.

Margaret looks sharply at her sister. Does she know about their father?

But Winnie is just ruminating, her eyes not knowing but bleak, looking gloomily out the window at the sliver of moon in a cloudless sky studded with stars.

It's a hot, muggy night. Every so often an owl toots and bats flit past their window. A fox cries, mournful, despondent, and the tops of trees whisper in the occasional honeysuckle- and primrose-scented breeze.

Winnie, usually determinedly upbeat no matter how bad things get, sometimes lapses into melancholy from which it takes a while to rouse her, as if the effort of trying to be happy has quite worn her out.

At these times it is Margaret – whose normal stance since the air raid that displaced them is a defensive prickliness, leaving for Winnie the sweetness and light – who tries to jolly her sister into optimism again, their roles reversing.

Margaret thinks again of the overheard burden of knowledge. Should she tell Winnie the whole truth, break her heart? She could just say, 'Father's missing in action.' This way she could protect her sister from the heartache she herself is suffering. But what if her sister finds out from someone else? Isn't it kinder that Winnie hears it from her rather than from their aunt, or worse, their uncle?

And in any case, if there's one thing Margaret has learned since the air raid, it is that hiding hard realities does not do any good. Truth has a way of making itself known, one way or another. Their mother had shied away from the reality of war, assuming nothing bad would happen, refusing to accept the possibility of an air raid, and it has led them here…

Margaret takes a deep, fortifying breath. Then she opens her mouth and shares with her sister the devastating rumour concerning their father – that most likely he offered himself as target to the enemy when he heard of his wife and eldest daughter's deaths, the thought of his surviving daughters not enough to sustain him.

'I… I thought, since God took Mother and Evie, Father at least would be spared,' Winnie sobs, 'But it turns out… it turns out…'

Holding her sister, Margaret has a sudden vision of that day at the train station, the pungent aroma of steam and goodbyes, the whisper of myriad assurances and promises, the seasoning of a thousand unshed tears, Winnie clinging to Father's legs.

'I was able to face everything because I knew, I *knew*, Meggie,' Winnie cries, 'that Father would be back and make everything alright. But now…'

She bunches the handkerchief Margaret has handed her, paying no heed to her running nose and eyes.

'How could he, Meggie? *Why* did he?'

Chapter Fourteen

1922

Archana

Voices

Voices. As she nears the house.

Archana's heart jumps. A thrill of hope holding her body hostage. Her sister! Welcomed back by her mother, the feud having gone on long enough.

Then, as the low rumble of sounds distinguish themselves into recognisable voices…

Her mother's voice, high-pitched, excited.

Excited.

This is the first time Archana has heard her mother sound anything other than bitter, weary, since her father died…

And then, wonder of wonders, her mother laughs!

Her laughter is fake, a glassy tinkle tinged with mania. But, fake or not, Archana cannot recall the last time her mother smiled properly, let alone laughed.

In the months following her father's death, her sister's leaving and, subsequently, their abrupt fall into ignominy, their ostracism from village society, her mother has become an aggrieved, exhausted husk of her former self.

Her mother did not do sati with her husband after all.

'There's no one to ask me to do it,' she said tearfully to Archana. 'I'm considered impure now, because of our untouchable association.'

It was, for Archana, the one good thing during that dark time. She couldn't have borne it if she had lost her mother too.

'I would gladly have sacrificed myself on your father's pyre even without the support of the villagers. But Archana, I couldn't abandon you to an uncertain fate. I couldn't leave you alone to suffer…'

It made Archana feel guilty, knowing that her mother would rather have died with her husband, that she suffered the indignity of exclusion, the hardships of their present life, for Archana's sake. She felt weighted down with the burden of this as her mother struggled to make ends meet, her face lined with worry, hair prematurely grey, eyebrows bunched with care, eyes hooded with hurt as people she had known for years turned away when they saw her coming.

Much as Archana tried not to, she resented her sister for reducing their mother to a shadow of her former self; she blamed her for their father's death. But she also missed Radha furiously. She felt her absence keenly. She wanted her back.

Her mother's laughter trills, creating pleasant flutters of joy in Archana's heart. It *is* her sister who has caused this welcome change, their mother having reconciled with her at long last—

A man's low murmuring.

Archana's heart falls.

Not her sister at all. The feud still ongoing. Her hope immature.

Over the last couple of years, Archana had tried countless times to persuade her mother to end the feud.

'She's your daughter.'

'She killed your father.'

'She is the mother of your grandchild.'

'That poor child. Casteless. Untouchable for father, fallen woman for mother.'

'But, Ma…'

'She's dead to me.'

Archana frustrated. Feeling the familiar sour-bitter tang of upset and helplessness. Anger at her mother for her stubbornness, her sister for her foolishness.

All their lives, Archana and Radha have understood their duty. What they must do as good daughters. It has been drilled into them by their mother, when they were young and she massaged coconut oil – which they could ill afford – into their hair and onto their limbs, trying to stretch and manipulate Archana's leg to its right size by sheer will, it seemed: 'Otherwise no one will marry you.'

Their mother reiterated her advice when she applied wet gram flour to Archana's face in a bid to lighten her complexion, the paste drying and cracking, a splintered yellow mask, only her eyes glinting through, bright black in a ravaged yellow, shattering landscape, Radha laughing: 'You look like a ghost.'

It would have been so easy for Radha: she had had myriad proposals, eligible bachelors falling over themselves to marry her, all of whom she rejected with that supreme confidence that added to her charm.

'I'm waiting for the right man,' she'd say serenely when their mother complained that she would never get married at this rate.

And after all that, she fell in love with, of all people, an untouchable.

Radha had written to Archana, care of the nuns at the missionary school, when her son, Kishan, was born, and Archana, grateful and emotional at finally hearing from her sister and knowing her whereabouts, and at having a nephew, had mentioned it to her mother that evening, the first of many times she'd tried to broach the subject of reuniting with Radha.

'Over my dead body!' her mother spat. 'Tear up the letter and throw it in the fire,' she commanded.

Over the last two years, unbeknownst to her mother, Archana has sneaked to Radha's village, two villages over, several times, walking all the way there and back, dragging her bad leg behind her, to see her sister, her nephew and newly arrived niece.

Archana has never once, in all those times, met Radha's husband.

When she asks Radha where he is, she sighs deeply, wearily. 'In the arrack shop.'

After the first few times, Archana asked, archly, 'Does he ever come home to his family?'

'Sometimes,' Radha mumbled.

Archana had looked at her, shocked. 'And others?'

'Some days I find him and bring him home. Others, I let him sleep it off.' Radha paused, her eyes far away and haunted. Then, 'It's soul-destroying, cleaning toilets, and being maligned for it, taking abuse because of your caste.'

Archana knew that the basest of jobs such as cleaning toilets were the only ones allowed untouchables.

'He thought…' Radha paused, overcome. 'He thought marrying me would set him apart, but instead we are even more tainted, our children casteless…'

Her sister's eyes shone with pain so Archana gathered her in her arms, stifling the question burning in her throat: 'He obviously married you for what he thought you could give him – respect, status. Why did *you* marry him?' and suppressing the anger consuming her: 'You fool! You could have had everything.

Instead, you make excuses for your drunkard, self-pitying louse of a husband…'

Radha lives on the very outskirts of the village, beside a ditch over-flowing with rubbish, the taint of faeces, the scent of desperation, in the section reserved for untouchables. Her beautiful face now haggard, permanently tired. Lines etched into it. Her glow fading. She looks older than her years, wiped down, reduced by life.

The first time Archana walked all that way to see her sister she found her living in a hovel smaller than the one-room hut they'd grown up in, rats feasting on the rubbish festering in the ditch just outside, the sweet, stale reek of filth, Radha's eyes dull and without their bright, happy, devil-may-care spark. It took all of Archana's effort not to cry. Rant.

She had smiled instead. Allowed herself to be enveloped in her sister's embrace. Her sister too thin, shoulders bony and protruding. Her smile not reaching her eyes, which were heavy and dark, full of things she would not say, of everything that had occurred since she left home, so many months' worth of distance. Her sister, to whom Archana had once been so close, to whom she could talk of anything.

Archana was conscious of a fierce, festering rage.

If only you had done your duty, listened to our parents, allowed them to choose.

That evening, her mother said, 'You're quiet. How was school?'

'Fine.' Hating herself for lying to her mother. Hating her sister for putting her in this position. Hating her mother for her intractability.

She told herself she wouldn't go back. She couldn't bear to see her sister like that.

But she had.

Bunking school every so often, making up excuses for the nuns.

And every time she thought: *You fell in love, married him. For this?*

And on the walk back, long and excruciating, her trailing leg throbbing, telling herself: *Radha is constrained by the decisions she's made. Ma is constrained by her longing for acceptance. I will try my hardest to make Ma proud. But I will* not *be constrained.*

When Archana visits, Radha's very first question is, 'How is Ma?'

'She's fine,' Archana lies, knowing that Radha knows she's lying. Both of them complicit, yet keeping up this charade, every single time.

'Does she ask after me and my children?'

Archana tries not to wince at the naked hope colouring Radha's soft voice bright white.

'She does.' Archana cannot meet her sister's eyes, flinching from the raw ache there, knowing she'll read in them the question Radha cannot ask: 'Why does she not visit or ask me to visit, then?'

There was once a time when they could speak about anything at all with each other. But now they hide behind obfuscations and lies, all the things they cannot say an unbridgeable chasm between them.

Radha sighs. 'I just wish my children had the chance to know their grandmother. I wish things could have been different.' The closest she will come to admitting her guilt. Her sadness. To showing the remorse she must feel.

And again, Archana is consumed by rage for what her sister did and sorrow for her life now. She wants to take Radha in her arms and soothe her like she did her nephew when he fell down and scraped his knees. And she wants to hit Radha, rage at her for destroying their family along with the sunny future they had envisioned for her.

Archana is forever battling these opposite emotions with regard to her sister: fury and sympathy, indignation and love; and it tires her, wrings her out emotionally and makes her feel guilty most of all.

A fly buzzes close to Archana's face. She swats it, annoyed, coming back into the present. She has been standing on the path, lost in musing. Water burbling beside her, the soundtrack to her thoughts.

The voices inside their hut, so very out of place…

Since Radha eloped they've become pariahs.

'People your father grew up with spit on the road when they see us; they don't want to set eyes on us in case we bring bad luck. This is what your sister has done to us.' Her mother sniffs, her voice bile-green with resentment, purple with hurt, when they sit outside the hut in the gathering dusk, laughter and chatter from their neighbours gathered in one of the adjoining huts drifting to them, knowing they are not welcome to join in as her mother would once have done. 'I'd rather have died than endured this humiliation.' She's taken to repeating this at least once a day, her words knives that stab Archana, bleeding hurt. 'Your father's is the perfect fate, ignorant of our sorry state of affairs, and in an ideal world, I would be sharing the afterlife with him, having done sati. But I couldn't take the risk that the villagers would look after you as they would have done if I was doing sati in normal circumstances. *Nothing* of our circumstance is normal, Archana, and I couldn't abandon you to an uncertain fate. I couldn't bear to think that you would have no recourse if I sacrificed myself on your father's pyre but to live with your disgraced sister, a destiny I wouldn't wish on my worst enemy, if the villagers did not step up to look after you. And after they shunned us, not one of them turning up to keep vigil beside your father's dead body, as soon as they got word of what Radha had done, how could I be certain?'

Her mother is living a cursed life, a life she doesn't want, for Archana's sake. It makes Archana even more determined to make her mother happy, proud of her.

And now, for the first time since that terrible day when Archana lost her father to a heart attack and her sister to her unsuitable lover, they have visitors!

Archana is on the path between the fields, directly underneath her hut, which is at the top of the hill. The stream gurgles merrily, tiny fishes' scales flashing as they dart past, slimy weeds fluttering lazily in the water.

A cow tethered to the post in the next field but one tugs at its rope, its liquid brown eyes regarding Archana mournfully. The air smells of ripe mango and heat, grit and earth.

Archana is on her way back from school.

When their father died, after their sister left to marry her untouchable, her mother had wanted Archana, then fourteen, to stop school, find work.

But there was no work to find. Everybody turned them away, the villagers not even deigning to talk to them.

'These were our friends, people we have known and helped turning away from us, abandoning us in our time of need!' her mother cried, her voice jaundiced yellow with hurt.

With no jobs forthcoming, Archana had begged her mother to continue at school. 'The nuns don't care about what has happened. Their religion doesn't have caste, they'll still treat me the same.'

Her mother's mouth a downward moue of upset, lines tugging at the corners of her eyes. 'It can't hurt, I suppose. I can't see you getting married, not after what Rad—' Her mother biting off her sister's name as if it choked her to utter it. 'It's not as if you're inundated with proposals.'

Her mother is tired, whipped to bitterness by the hand life has dealt her, working, always working. Her hands deftly stuffing tobacco mixture into betel leaves and shaping them into beedies – the man from town, a friend of a friend of Archana's father, who gives her mother this commission, not caring that she is a pariah as long as she meets the target number of beedies per day that he has set her.

When Archana's mother has a spare moment, which is almost never, she sews: booties and clothes for newborns, sequins onto saris, churidars from patterned cloth (the same man who gives her the beedie work also giving her the sewing commission when he happened to see one of the blouses she had sewed for Archana), her mother's eyes peering at the cloth, the evening air perfumed with candle wax and impossible dreams, sweet amber.

Archana loves school. It's a respite from her mother's perpetual weariness and upset, her sister's absence, her father's death. She doesn't care that the other children ignore and shun her. Reading gives her joy. It transports her to other worlds where she can forget the ache of missing her sister and kind, taciturn father, her mother's bitterness and resentment, her hurt and exhaustion.

Archana loves speaking in English, which she has picked up quickly. The pleasure on the nuns' faces: 'You're a bright spark, Archana, a joy to teach. Pupils like you make teaching worthwhile.'

At school, with the nuns, she is not defined by her limp, her dark complexion, her sister's actions, and there is exquisite freedom in that. The nuns only judge her by how she absorbs and applies the knowledge they impart, and it is something she can control as opposed to being out of her hands. To be judged for who she is and not by her disability, her looks or her sister's actions is a gift that she treasures immensely.

'You might be the brightest student I've ever taught,' Sister Mildred had declared just that morning, smiling fondly at her. 'You should go to college. I'm sure you'll win a scholarship. We'll help with your application. Speak to your mother – see what she says.'

Throughout the day Sister Mildred's words have fanned her hopes, given them wings. She sees herself going to college, taking her mother away from this village where she is hurt daily by the small snubs dealt them by people who were once friends. She will get a job in the city, and her mother will be proud, her lined face finally relaxing into smiles. Archana will somehow persuade her to forgive Radha and perhaps, one day, she might even bring her sister and her children to the city…

Radha's husband does not feature in these dreams. Whereas Archana's mother blames Radha, Archana chooses to direct all her ire at the man for whom Radha gave up everything. This way she can love Radha without also secretly hating her a tiny bit; she can be angry on her sister's behalf rather than angry *at* her. Hence Radha's husband is denied entry into her fantasy of college and working and giving her mother and sister a better life than the one they currently have, a vision so real and accessible she could reach out and touch it…

*

Her legs covered in dust, flies hovering, mosquitoes feasting on flesh, but she doesn't notice, experiencing a warm glow as she pictures telling her mother, 'Ma, the nuns think I'll get a scholarship to college. That means the college will *pay* me to do what I love!'

'Stop getting these ideas in your head. They're not for the likes of us,' her mother will grumble. 'You have to get married.'

'Ma, the villagers go out of their way to avoid us, why will anyone marry me? But if I study…'

And here, Archana will detail her fantasy and her mother will smile, pat her cheek and say, 'You're a good girl. Yes, okay, you can go to college.'

A small, sane voice in her head intervenes in her imaginings. *If she says no, what will you do then?*

She thinks of Radha. Her haggard, worn face. Her bruised eyes that have seen too much.

I will convince her that this is for the best.

But before she does, Archana thinks, briskly striding the last few steps towards home, she needs to find out who is visiting them, village pariahs, and why; to whom these curious, unaccustomed voices that have made Ma laugh belong…

Chapter Fifteen

1919

Margaret

Anticipation

For several weeks after learning that Father is not coming back, Winnie hardly moves from her bed in the attic, refusing to engage, to eat. It appears she is grieving for Mother and Evie all over again, as well as for Father.

Though she is alright for months at a time, every so often Winnie suffers bouts of sadness. Usually when she succumbs to upset Margaret is able to rouse her in a day or two. But this time, nothing Margaret tries works. Winnie remains as cheerless and desolate as ever.

Margaret is beside herself with anxiety, second-guessing her decision to tell Winnie the truth about Father instead of shielding her from it.

Aunt Helen makes several trips to the attic a day with plates of food, trying to persuade Winnie to eat, wringing her hands when she refuses. Even Uncle Robert is moved to enquire after Winnie. In her gentle way, Winnie has won their hearts.

It is the dance – the biggest in town and the first one this season – that finally brings Winnie out of her fug. Margaret hears about it at school – everyone is abuzz with the news, a low hum of excitement putting a spring in their step, a welcome change after the endless bad news and distress of the war. Margaret's classmates plan outfits, not paying attention to teachers, doodling dress patterns in notebooks instead. For the umpteenth time Margaret wishes Winnie was here with her instead of grieving in their attic room at the farm – but Winnie has finished school and has no desire to study further, while that is all Margaret wants to do. Study. Go away to university. Escape the farm.

'The annual spring ball is taking place next weekend,' Margaret says to Winnie when she gets home from school. 'It's rumoured Baron Cohen will be attending.'

The Baron has returned from the war a hero. He owns a huge estate on the outskirts of town, easily thrice the size of Winnie and Margaret's childhood home. The sisters had stumbled upon the mansion while blackberry-picking. It was mysterious and secretive with an air of desertion, appearing to be scowling down at them, as beautiful as it was forbidding. They had run all the way back to the farm, blackberries scattering from their skirts, their mouths stained violet with juice.

Winnie looks up at the mention of Baron Cohen, her face tear-spattered, hair messy. And yet as beautiful as ever.

'Really?' She sniffs, wiping her face with the back of her arm, succeeding only in spreading her tears all over her face so it glows with a bright, wet sheen. 'He's rumoured to be a recluse.'

Margaret bites her lip to keep the thrill from showing on her face – this is the first time since she heard about their father that Winnie has shown an interest in anything.

'Shall we attend?' Margaret asks.

But Winnie just shrugs, burying her head deeper into the pillow.

The thrill Margaret had experienced fizzles into nothing. If this can't rouse her sister from the dark mood that plagues her, it is cause for worry indeed. But when she goes upstairs after supper, she finds Winnie in their room, busily sketching dress patterns in one of Margaret's sketchbooks, and she breathes a sigh of joyful relief.

The dance hall is crowded with bodies, packed with sweat and rose water, excitement and anticipation, promises exchanged in a single, intent, loaded glance, the taste of the future, expectant and sweet, one with the war behind them. Happiness and hope now that the country is emerging slowly from the rubble and devastation of the war.

Margaret lounges in a corner, feeling as always apart, other, removed from the cheer, the buoyancy pervading the room, even as she watches her sister dance. Gay, her skirts swinging, her hair flying, face aglow, Winnie, the loveliest of the three of them – a stabbing pang at the thought of Evie, who was most like their mother, another pang.

Winnie, glorious, basking in the attention she is lavished with, the other girls in the room watching jealously even as Margaret looks on with fierce pride on Winnie's behalf and relief that finally her sister is herself again.

Lost in thought as she is, it takes Margaret some minutes to register the sudden silence that has descended upon the dance hall, the giggling and chatter, the flirting and the extravagant compliments having quieted, so there is only the music playing and the dancers swaying.

Margaret follows the arc of the crowd's gaze. A man in the doorway, scanning the hall, tall and broad, his bearing regal, haughty.

Margaret watches as his eyes zone in on her sister, easily the best and most beautiful dancer in the room, looking like a sprite, otherworldly, the yellow silk of her dress catching the light and glinting gold, matching Winnie's hair, a cascading waterfall, the skirt swirling elegantly around her shapely legs.

Margaret watches the man approach her sister, the dancers making way for his determined stride. She sees the exact moment Winnie notices him. Her sister's smile falters, although she does not stop dancing. A blush seeps colour into her face, already flushed rose from exertion, making her look even more beautiful, if possible. The man falls in step beside her, taking over from Winnie's dance partner, a mere, pimpled youth in comparison to this man's masculinity, as easily and carelessly as if it is his right. He whispers something in Winnie's ear. She smiles, her eyes bright beacons, her face a picture, a story unfolding, a gift.

And even before Margaret is party to the whispers that have started up furiously as if making up for the sudden hush, she understands who this man is and she knows that what will happen next is inevitable, that perhaps she was expecting it even as she coaxed her sister out of grief and urged her to come to this ball.

Did I engineer it? she will ask herself in the coming weeks.

Did I want this to happen? she will wonder as she tosses and turns, unable to sleep, in the cold attic room.

Did I subconsciously bring this about because I'm tired of looking out for Winnie? she will chastise herself when Winnie announces that the Baron has asked for her hand in marriage.

Margaret will ask, 'Are you sure you want to accept?'

And Winnie will reply, with conviction, 'Absolutely.'

'Isn't it too soon?'

'Meggie, he loves me.' Winnie's face beaming; Margaret's sister, who has ached for love since she lost Mother and Evie and Father.

Margaret will reiterate, 'He's much older than you,' even as her conscience chides, *too little, too late.*

Winnie will repeat, gently, 'But he loves me, Meggie, he'll look after me like you do, almost as well as you do.'

'*Almost* as well?' Margaret will ask.

'Better, but I don't want to upset you.' Winnie will laugh – oh, how Margaret loves the sound of her sister's unbridled, merry laughter!

And Margaret will feel relief spreading through her entire being, rendering her loose-limbed with joy on behalf of her sister.

But that night she will toss and turn once more, as she has so often been doing during the dragging, violet hours of darkness, her sister radiant beside her, her face alight with dreams of happy-ever-afters.

I want to study, to go to university and not have to worry about my sister, so I have fobbed her off to the Baron.

She is old enough to make up her mind, older and wiser than you. Do not presume to exaggerate your influence upon her life, her conscience will chime.

And yet, she will wonder and she will worry, questions going round and round, piercing daggers of blame in her head.

Chapter Sixteen

1922

Archana

Foreboding

'Ah, here she is,' Ma says, and there is pulsing anticipation in her voice, something Archana hasn't heard for a very long time.

Archana's mother is sitting under the tamarind tree in their small courtyard with a bald-headed man, another older man and a wrinkled woman, the air spiced cinnamon, pungent tamarind, the dog sat by the washing stone and eyeing the visitors beadily, butterflies alighting on hibiscus flowers, bright red as promises.

'Bring tea for the visitors, Archana.'

Archana pulls the veil down over her face and goes into the hut, the dog, having bounded up to her in joyous welcome, now squatting on the doorstep and looking longingly inside, golden eyes pleading, tongue out and panting.

Archana's heart feels leaden, her feet sluggish with foreboding.

She hears snippets as she boils the water with the tea leaves, using the last of the milk they were saving, the milk that had to last them the week. She crushes ginger, splits cardamom pods and adds the black seeds to the bubbling tea.

'Good girl,' she hears. 'Not like her sister.'

Her mother's voice sour as she says it – the first time she has voluntarily referred to Radha since she left. When Archana tries to bring the subject up she refuses to talk, shouting at Archana to stop.

'I didn't realise her limp was that pronounced. We were told it wasn't…' It is the wrinkled woman speaking, her voice harsh as the scrape of a fingernail on a scab.

'It doesn't hold her back,' her mother says brightly. 'And she's very healthy otherwise.'

'Dark,' the woman spits as if speaking of a vile act.

'Yes, but *good*,' her mother is emphasising. 'Dutiful. Hard-working.'

'Since she's not bringing any dowry, given your circumstances…'

Even hidden away in the hut, Archana can feel the heat of her mother's blush.

'… she'll need to work. We cannot afford…'

Archana's dreams of college, so real just a few hours ago, now fading fast.

The spiced tea threatening to overflow as her eyes blur.

'Yes, of course. She's happy to.'

I'm not, Ma. I want to study. The words dying on her tongue before they're allowed access.

As if picking up on her distress, the dog whining from the doorway.

She takes the tea out to the visitors, her palms trembling as she hands the tumblers out.

She peruses the bald man through her veil. This man who represents the end to her dreams.

He is almost as old as her father was when he died, she surmises. The even older couple with him must be his parents.

'She'll do,' the woman is saying.

Her mother lights up as if a fire has been lit inside her. Truly happy after a very long time.

Archana's heart heavy as her mother asks her to touch their feet.

After they leave, her mother, beaming, sobbing, holding Archana, her smell of onions and sweat and hard graft. 'It's happened, the miracle I was hoping for! You're getting married to a respectable man from a *good* family.'

She looks at her mother then and her mother reads the unasked question in her eyes.

'His previous two wives died in childbirth. The children too. Nobody will give their daughters to him. They're convinced he's cursed. Then somehow they found out about you and came to us…'

Her mother pauses to wipe her tears – happy for a change – with her *pallu* and Archana tries not to shudder.

If I marry him – and it appears from your joy that you've already decided so – will the fate of his previous two wives be mine too?

She opens her mouth to tell her mother about college, the nuns' conviction that she will get a scholarship, the alternate future awaiting her, the one *she* wants.

'I thought you'd never be married after what your sister did. How lucky we are, how blessed! Perhaps finally the bad luck that has plagued us since your sister did what she did will lift. Now people won't cross the road when we approach. We will no longer be known as the relatives of the untouchables; the mother and sister of the girl who married a *shudra* and killed her father…'

Her mother – who wanted to do sati, die with her husband, but has endured a hard slog of a half-life for Archana's sake – looking, in her happiness, like the young girl she must have once been. Looking like her sister did before she married, beautiful and luminous. The weary lines around her face gone.

'We'll go to the temple tomorrow, give thanks.'

Archana has seen what her sister's wilfulness did to her parents. She cannot shatter her mother, devastate her; she will not.

And so, the words she had prepared to convince her mother about college, the dreams that flared briefly, die, as Archana closes her mouth again.

Chapter Seventeen

1921

Margaret

Self-Portrait

'Aunt, Uncle, I've won a place to read art at King's College London. I'll be leaving next month. Thank you for taking Winnie and myself in and looking after us. We've appreciated it so very much.' Margaret relays the speech she has carefully prepared to her guardians.

Her uncle sets his glass down on the carpet by the hearth, beside which he is sitting in his armchair, his face flushed rose with drink and the heat of the fireplace. Her aunt looks up from her sewing, looking for an instant just like Mother, the golden light from the fire dancing upon her face and setting it aglow. It is after supper and her cousins have already retired to their rooms, but Margaret has hung back to tell her guardians of her plans, the acceptance letter from university burning a hole in her pocket.

Winnie is married, a baroness, glowing and gracious, mistress of her huge mansion, in her element. Her utter dejection on receiving the news of Father had jolted Margaret more than she could put into words; for a time, when Winnie was refusing to eat, Margaret had panicked that she would lose her only remaining family. But now, though she misses her sister dreadfully, her worry with regards to Winnie has eased for Winnie is absolutely, delightfully content.

'I am so *happy*, Meggie,' she says whenever Margaret visits, and Margaret can see the evidence of it shining out of her face, which is unfurrowed, carefree, like when they were children.

Although Margaret isn't quite sure about the Baron – a bit too haughty for her liking, a little too full of himself – she cannot dispute the fact that he loves Winnie, worships her. His eyes soften when he looks at her, his gaze following her around the room. In fact, his whole person appears to mellow when he is with Winnie, so he becomes a softer, more malleable version of himself.

It eases Margaret's guilt while at the same time creating more. She wants her sister to be happy but she is not sure if it is for Winnie's sake or her own. Perhaps both…

Nevertheless, once Margaret was absolutely convinced that Winnie was truly happy and not just putting on an act for her benefit – she had achieved this by turning up at her sister's home unannounced on several occasions at various times of day, irritating the Baron, who saw through her, but delighting Winnie, who didn't – she had pushed her doubts aside and approached her art teacher, Miss Pym, enlisting her help in applying to university.

She had created a portfolio of paintings and sketches: the farm, with all its attendant muck, the endless rolling fields, newborn kids on unsteady feet, chickens pecking at the dirt, placid horses with caramel eyes, ewes suckling newborn lambs, gorse bushes and bluebells, sunburst dandelions and velvet blackberries, a pig stuck in a stile. People: her uncle's frown, her aunt's perpetual weariness, captured in the slump of her shoulders, in the tired hair crowding beady, sunken eyes. Her cousins with their sneers. Her classmates. Her sister. The Baron (she cannot think of him as Andrew despite Winnie's insistence).

She also drew herself. A self-portrait. Fire consuming all that was precious to her. And Margaret standing in the midst of it, fire devouring her from within. Guilt. Anger. Ambition. Grief. Unbelonging.

She had sent off her application, portfolio attached, and waited.

And waited.

She went about her chores as always, but took care to intercept the post every morning, harking back in her memory to the days when her mother would keep watch for the postmistress, hoping for a missive from her husband.

When the letter finally arrived, with its official university crest, stiff white paper, the smell of importance, addressed to *her*, she could almost not believe it. She had held it for a long time, walking with it to the stile, the fields around her alive with bird-song, starry celandine and flowering lilac thistles, bright yellow buttercups and sunshine-hearted daisies like blessings. The mossy woodiness of the stile bolstering her. The scent of green grass wet with last night's rain. Magpies chattering, pigeons gossiping and cooing, a robin alighting, worm in its beak. The cows lowing as they grazed. A bushy-tailed squirrel disappearing up a tree.

This is where she often came to sketch when her chores were done, the world bursting with the aroma of ripening berries, nectar-rich flowers and fecund earth. The flavour of an English spring, mulchy with loss, seeded with sorrow, the memory of all the missing, felled by war. Their bodies buried in battlefields far from home, her father among them. Her mother and sister, killed in their house which should, by rights, have been a place of safety.

Trembling fingers as she opened the letter.

She read it once, then again.

Unbidden, at what should have been her happiest moment she thought of Evie. Her gentle, patient sister. Who had waited for Margaret to rescue her. Waited and hoped even as she burned…

Why did Margaret get to live when Evie didn't?

And yet here she was, holding in her hands the escape she had always wanted. The opportunity for a life more than this one on the farm, a respite from the perpetual loneliness that dogged her, the feeling of otherness…

The chance to *belong*, to feel part of something again. Perhaps at university, among students who enjoyed learning, like her, she would find that part of her that was lost, untethered when her childhood home burned down.

She wanted to be happy, as Winnie was.

She wanted to create.

Sketching, painting, afforded an outlet for everything she could not say, the feelings within her, secret and hurtful, the questions that plagued her: had her sister Evie lived, what would she have been? Would she have wanted to study, like Margaret, or be mistress of her own household, like Winnie? Evie loved the garden. She loved to sew. She wanted children, at least five…

At the ball, when Winnie met her beau, now her husband, Margaret had thought of Evie. Everything Margaret did, every new experience she had, she wondered what Evie would have made of it.

She was living for Evie as much as for herself.

We are going to university, Evie, she whispered, tasting the words, their surprising sweetness.

She brushed her eyes, which were streaming. Above her among the tree branches a bird cawed, plaintive.

She understood then – the stile hard and sun-warmed against her back, the honeyed spring air brushing her salty cheeks, flowers nodding, squirrels foraging – why her mother liked to contemplate the angel inscribed with the name of her stillborn son. She was fashioning a life for him, wondering, had he lived, how his life would have panned out. She was carrying him, living for him, alongside her daughters and herself.

The farm dog, Bowie, bounded up to Margaret, licked her face with his sloppy tongue. He knew uncannily when she was in need of comfort. She buried her face in his warm flank. 'I'll miss you when I'm gone.'

Now, in the kitchen of the farmhouse, the pungent scent of her uncle's ale mingling with the lingering aroma of the mutton pie they had had for supper, congealing gravy, embers, her aunt and uncle look at Margaret as if she is mad.

'What about marriage?' her aunt asks, finally.

'I want to study first.' She is firm.

'And money?'

'I've won a scholarship. It covers living expenses.'

'A scholarship?' her aunt repeats, seemingly unable to picture it.

'And there's my inheritance.'

'That's dowry for when you get married. *If* you do, what with your fancy ideas.' Her aunt sniffs.

'Let her go,' her uncle says, taking a long, loud slurp of his drink.

Her aunt stares at her a moment longer, then nods, her shoulders drooping in their customary slump, and picks up her sewing.

Margaret is dismissed. It is done.

Now all that remains is to tell Winnie.

'I'm so proud of you!' Winnie squeals, throwing her arms around Margaret. 'You set your heart on something and you do it. You're amazing, Meggie.'

'Will you be okay?'

'I'll be *fine*. I'll miss you though. Come and visit often.'

'I will.'

Winnie squeezes Margaret's hand, beaming. 'Isn't it wonderful that we've both got what we want? I wanted to marry, be mistress of my household, and here I am.' She waves her arm around her opulent house as if not quite believing it, even after all these months. She is luminous, looking even more beautiful than before, if possible. Marriage suits her. 'And you get to study like you wanted. My clever sister. Mother and Father and Evie would be so proud.'

And there it is, out in the open. The shadow looming over their every joy. But even that cannot douse Winnie's glow for more than a minute.

'Go live your life, Meg.'

Margaret holds her sister close. 'I'll see you soon.'

And then she readies herself to walk away into a new life.

A different unknown.

PART 3

....

COMFORTABLE

Chapter Eighteen

1922

Margaret

Nerves

Margaret stands unobtrusively in an alcove tucked into a corner of the gallery, nursing her glass, inhaling the fragrance of the lilies that adorn the room, set artfully around the great hall in giant vases. She is standing behind one such vase, her face obscured by the flowers, trying to quell her panic, nerves rampant as she watches people arrive: elegant, beautifully attired ladies, suave gentlemen, all of them confident in their own skin.

Here I am on the outskirts again, looking in.

That familiar, lonely angst of otherness, a constant since being displaced from her childhood home by the fire in the aftermath of the air raid.

After Winnie married, once Margaret won her scholarship here, she had dared to hope that she too would fit in like her sister, who has found her place, at home with being a baroness, effortlessly blending in with her elaborate surroundings as if she had been born to them – which in a way she had, they all had, before fate intervened.

But in Margaret's lodgings at the King's College Hostel for women, she is awkward, shy. She is the scholarship girl and she knows that the other girls, so sure of themselves, know it. She feels out of place in her hand-sewn dresses, her drabness while they are bursts of extravagant colour in their beautiful gowns. She listens to their heated discussion on all manner of topics, from the latest fashion trends to the vote for women, and she wants to join in but finds she cannot. Perhaps it is the years on the farm that mean she feels only at home with animals. At school too, the other children were so much in thrall to her bully of a cousin that they did not befriend Margaret or Winnie, although many of the boys would ogle Winnie from a distance.

And so Margaret paints. Her feelings of displacement, of not belonging, come out in her etchings, as does her guilt at not being able to rescue her sister, the ache of missing her living sister, the house she grew up in with her sisters and parents, and even the farm with its menagerie she has grown to love: the pigs with their wet snouts, the gentle horses, the cows with their placid eyes, the farm dog, Bowie, the stile against which she would lean and draw while looking out over the bluebell- and dandelion-festooned fields.

It is only when she is painting that she feels truly herself.

'These are so good that we have to exhibit them,' her life art teacher, Mrs Imelda Danbourne, declared when she saw Margaret's paintings.

Mrs Danbourne has taken Margaret under her wing. 'When I saw the portfolio you sent with your application, I knew we had to have you at any cost. This sort of talent only comes every so often.'

Each year she chose one student's work to display at an exhibition she hosted at the university, using the art studio with access to the road as the gallery so guests could alight from their cabs and come straight in. She set it up like a proper exhibition, sending invitations to all of her contacts in the art industry.

This year, she had picked Margaret.

'It's an honour to be chosen. Many artists have begun their career this way,' her classmates had said to Margaret, eyes flashing with envy.

'But my paintings… they're private. I don't really mean for them to be…'

'Why are you here then?' The envy congealing into something hard, angry, flashing red. 'If you didn't want your work to be seen, noticed, you shouldn't have applied to read art.'

After Winnie married, I was lonely. The feeling of otherness, always present, intensified, choking me. I thought education would provide escape and since I love painting, I applied to this course. She wanted to say all this, defend herself, but when she opened her mouth, the words would not come.

She wanted to tell Mrs Danbourne, 'I enjoy painting but I do it for myself. I love this course – I want to complete it, get my degree. But I don't want to be singled out.' But after her classmates' reactions, she couldn't do it. She wanted to belong, be accepted. If she refused this honour, which the others would have been grateful for, she would come across as churlish; in fact, she already was.

And so she allowed herself to be swept along on the wave of Mrs Danbourne's enthusiasm; and if she was honest, she was touched and more than a little thrilled at her teacher's genuine passion for her paintings. But it also made her all the more scared and she couldn't sleep at night for worry as the day of the exhibition drew inexorably closer. What if Mrs Danbourne's contacts and friends in the art world did not like her paintings? Had it happened before with any of her protégés? She was too afraid to ask.

When Margaret first stepped into the art studio masquerading as a gallery and looked at her paintings, her feelings, her inner turmoil, up there for everyone to see, hanging between giant vases of lilies positioned for maximum aesthetic impact, she wanted to turn and run. It was like being flayed alive, turned inside out for everyone's inspection, their commentary on her *self.*

Now she waits as the doors to the gallery open, as the crowd spills inside, the women self-assured, resplendent in their dresses, at home on the arms of their men, the scent of expensive perfume and anticipation, suits rustling, gowns shimmering, light reflecting off pearls and tiepins, twinkling in eyes.

They walk indoors and stop short, pausing mid-chatter, mouths open. The smiles on faces freezing.

Complete silence as everyone takes in Margaret's paintings.

What are they thinking?

She looks to the front of the room, where Mrs Danbourne is, trying to gauge her reaction to this reaction. But her teacher's face is turned away.

This was such a bad idea.

Margaret's head throbbing, her cheeks hot, mouth bitter and tangy with brine, an obstruction in her throat when she swallows.

They hate her paintings. Of course they do.

How dare I presume otherwise? What was I thinking? Why did I agree to this?

These people, judging her innermost thoughts, her pain. Set out in paint. It is like they are erasing her from inside out, so there will be nothing of her left.

She has never felt more other.

Then, a burst of sound. The room erupting all at once.

Applause.

Applause?

Cheers. Loud, frenzied discussion. Hullabaloo.

People dispersing to stand in front of individual paintings, dissecting them with partners, friends. Arguing about their meaning. Putting their own interpretations upon Margaret's thoughts.

Salt in her mouth. Heart beating in staccato, panicked frenzy.

Is this relief? It feels like fear. Of a different sort than before, but fear all the same.

The crowd seeking out Mrs Danbourne.

'Where is the artist?'

She wants to blend even further into the lilies. She feels exposed, raw, hollow, vulnerable, like she will burst into tears or burst open and spill out in a splattered mess.

'There's so much pain in these paintings, layer upon layer. Every brushstroke is so complex – it's the angst of a country at war, losing their sons and fathers to the greater cause,' a lady in pink satin declares, sniffing and wiping her eyes with an embroidered handkerchief.

Around the room other women are doing the same while men clear their throats and rub their jaws, contemplating the paintings, *her* paintings.

It is a revelation to Margaret.

She knows that once you've shared something you've created, you lose ownership, that everyone experiences it in their own unique way. This is the beauty, the power, the point of art. But what she didn't realise was how art also brings people together. By giving voice to her private pain through the medium of her paintings, she has touched a nerve with this audience. Her pain, although personal to her, is shared by a nation. Every single one of the people in this room has lost someone to the war and Margaret's hurt, on display in her paintings, speaks to them, the wounds they hide behind their dazzling clothes and bright smiles.

All this while she has felt separate, apart from everyone else, but standing here, beside these people whom she thought confident, assured, she realises that they have all suffered too and that her pain, while intensely private, is not isolated.

Perhaps, she thinks, *they feel different too, other, like me, they just hide it better...*

'Is the artist around? We'd like to meet her.'

Mrs Danbourne surreptitiously glances over at Margaret. She shakes her head, slipping even more into the shadows of the alcove behind the giant vase of lilies. Although she is beginning to understand that these people are not all that different from her, she is still not ready to meet them. She feels shy, out of her depth.

Mrs Danbourne, in her characteristic way, moves the conversation away, directing the woman who's asked to meet the artist to another of Margaret's paintings.

'This one is profound,' a woman says, her voice quivering with emotion.

It is a portrait of Margaret scrubbing herself raw, trying to scour herself of guilt at not being able to help her sister. The skin falls off her in long strips, as she brushes and scrapes, but the guilt is indelible. It is embedded too deep, spilling out of her eyes, haunted, desolate, weeping blood – not hers but that of those no longer here, pale shadows in the background.

Margaret had painted it on the anniversary of the air raid. The day they lost their childhood, their home, everything dear to them. It had been the first she had spent away from Winnie. She had written to her sister and then she had painted, putting all her sorrow into this painting.

Winnie's reply, when it came, said, 'I forgot it was the anniversary. I'm expecting a child. It's time to look forward and not back, Meg.'

Margaret had read those words: 'I'm expecting a child' and felt joy curling around the empty spaces in her heart.

Winnie is creating a future, forging ahead, putting the past to rest. Margaret wishes she could too.

Will she ever?

Her reverie is interrupted by Mrs Danbourne's voice, pleasure and warm affection. 'Vanessa, you came.'

An elegant couple ascending the steps to the makeshift gallery. The woman, thin, distinguished. Something about her familiar.

Mrs Danbourne beaming at her, arms outstretched.

'I had to see for myself. You haven't been this complimentary about a student since… well since myself.' The woman smiles coyly at Mrs Danbourne.

Mrs Danbourne chuckles even as it dawns on Margaret just who this is.

The woman enters the room. Stops. Standing very still. Her gaze on Margaret's paintings rapt. Sharp.

'And?' Mrs Danbourne asks.

The woman looks at each painting in turn. Margaret's heart pounding a litany. *Please.*

All of her earlier misgivings dispersed, scattering like dandelion seeds. If this woman is who she thinks she is – Vanessa Bell, her university's famous (and notorious, Margaret has heard it whispered about, because of her unconventional, scandalous lifestyle) alumnus and Mrs Danbourne's star pupil – then she wants her to like her paintings.

'This one…' she says at last.

Vanessa is standing in front of the painting that means the most to Margaret, the one that she absolutely didn't want to part with, not wanting even Mrs Danbourne to see it. It is of a girl split into pieces, each piece containing within it yearning, burning souls, separated, branded by fire. One piece represents the struggle Margaret experiences daily, trying to live not only for herself but also for Evie, how it feels as if Evie is part of her, yet always the guilt of letting her sister down when she needed her most eating away at her. The other pieces represent her struggle with herself regarding her continued and unresolved anger at her mother – for deciding to stay at home, making light of the threat of air raids at great cost to herself and her children, and Margaret's anger and upset at her father for not considering his surviving daughters worth living for.

'It is viscerally emotive. Very powerful,' Vanessa says.

Margaret finds that she is shaking – the most intimate of her paintings has won the approval of this famous artist!

'What do you think, Duncan?' Vanessa links her arm casually through that of the man with her.

'This is quite a collection. I like all of them, but I agree with you – there's something really special about this one,' he says.

Mrs Danbourne nods as if this is nothing more than she expected. 'You have as usual homed in on the best one, the painting *I* liked the most and the one the artist did not want to part with. In fact, it was a job convincing her to part with any of them at all!'

'I can see why. There's something intensely private and at the same time deeply compelling about these paintings, which is a big part of their appeal.' A pause. 'So, can I meet this artist then?'

And this time, instead of deflecting the question, Miss Danbourne leads Vanessa towards Margaret's alcove, saying, gaily, 'Come on out of hiding, Margaret. Mrs Bell wants to meet you.'

Margaret, nervous and self-conscious in her shabby gown, paint ingrained in her fingernails, comes out from behind the giant vase, briefly meeting Mrs Danbourne's gaze, which proclaims, quite clearly, 'I couldn't allow this opportunity to pass you by.'

'Pleased to make your acquaintance, Miss...' Mrs Bell's voice is smoky, deep and rich with a hint of gravel.

'Thornber.'

'Miss Thornber. You possess rare talent. Are you free next weekend?'

'Er...'

'If you are, come down to Charleston and spend it with us. You'll make the acquaintance of several artists and writers and I look forward to meeting with you in a more intimate setting and getting to know you better.'

There is a gasp from the people nearest Vanessa, apparently at this invitation so casually extended to Margaret.

But Vanessa pays no heed, her piercing gaze pinning Margaret.

'I like your paintings. They have soul, or perhaps they hold your soul.' Her keen eyes seeming to bore into the soul Margaret has tried to empty into her paintings. 'Your work emotes in the rawest way the vulnerability within us all.'

Margaret stares at her, speechless. This poised and accomplished woman *understands*.

'Of course they're not perfect. You need to work harder, delve further, explore those layers that you're only hinting at in these paintings. Which is why you should come to Charleston.' She smiles. 'You'll meet like-minded people, several artists among them. Plenty of inspiration so you can work at developing your style and perfecting your talent.'

Margaret watches them go, taking some of the life from the gathering in their wake.

The room erupts in excited gossip.

'What did I tell you?' Mrs Danbourne beams. 'You've the stamp of approval from two of the best artists in London. And I say... An invitation to join the Bloomsbury Group! Make sure you *are* free at the weekend…' She winks and moves aside to allow the crush of people descending on Margaret access.

Everyone's gaze trained upon her, wanting to talk to her.

And she, still registering what Vanessa Bell and Duncan Grant, established artists, said about her paintings, their amazing invitation, stammers through her answers to the questions that keep coming from all sides – 'What inspires you?' 'You seem to use dark colours, bold and unflinching. Is that a conscious choice?' 'Will you take up Mrs Bell's invitation?' – smiling so hard her cheeks ache, unaccustomed to using those particular muscles quite so much.

Chapter Nineteen

1922

Archana

Puppet

'We can't afford a big wedding,' Archana's mother-in-law-to-be declares. 'We spent all our savings on the previous two weddings. We spared no expense. But that is why your Archana will now have to work. And why we cannot afford a huge celebration.' She sniffs loudly. 'We are not like others leaving the wedding to the girl's parents – we'll share the cost. We're generous…'

'Of course.' Archana's mother nods eagerly, finally managing to interrupt the other woman's monologue, get a word in.

'And broad-minded.'

'*Very* broad-minded.'

Archana hates how her mother is reduced to a sycophantic puppet in her would-be in-laws' presence.

A flash of anger directed at Radha. Radha's mistakes have reduced them to this: her mother suffering, trying to make ends meet, her once lustrous hair straggly grey under her widow's veil, eyes permanently squinting from sewing in the half-dark, the multiplying lines on her face, old before her time; and Archana herself, swallowing her dreams to allow for her mother's on her behalf.

Radha chose love. To what end? She is not happy either.

Deep down Archana knows Radha is not to blame. Even if Radha had not done as she did, she doubts her parents would have allowed Archana to go to college: 'A woman's place is at home. Get those ideas out of your head! Your duty is to make a good marriage.' She never quite believed her fantasies of college would come true, but, for the brief while it took to walk home from school the fateful day of her proposal from this man with his overpowering mother, she had had hope.

Her father's dying is not her sister's fault either, but a small part of Archana cannot help blaming Radha for it. In any case, she believes that what Radha did was a catalyst, exacerbating the factors that led to her father's death.

'We're broad-minded,' her mother-in-law-to-be repeats in her trembling, old-woman voice. 'Nobody else would choose your daughter, with her limp and her mustard-seed complexion, not to mention her sister's antics, but we're welcoming her into our home with open arms. And we will chip in for the wedding although it is the girl's responsibility…'

Archana bites her tongue to stop from lashing out at this old woman who is repeating the same things over and over, making her mother feel more beholden and grateful than she is already.

'We will—' her mother begins.

'No. We insist. But as you know, given her sister, and our tragedies, we want a small wedding.'

'We don't want a big one either,' Archana's mother hurriedly adds before the woman interrupts again.

'And we'd prefer it if you didn't bring up the sister and the unfortunate untouchable association.'

'O-of course,' her mother blusters, her face filling with colour.

Chapter Twenty

1922

Margaret

Recollection

Margaret stands at the burnished brown door of the house –
Charleston, Vanessa Bell had called it, as if it was a person in its
own right – her overnight bag beside her, and sounds the knocker.
She is shaking all over, as much from nerves as from nostalgia.

This elegant house with ivy creeping up its walls, its russet gold,
timeworn bricks imprinted with the past, its solidity, its stature,
brings memories of her childhood home. If she closes her eyes, she
can almost hear the voices of her sisters, high and angelic, their
laughter as they played hide and seek with her, Albert the gardener
humming a tune off-rhythm as he trimmed the rose bushes, their
sweet scent mingling with the earthy aroma of rosemary, the tart
tang of parsley and peppermint from the herb garden.

She blinks, pushing the recollection, so very real, away.

Now is not the time, she tells herself sternly, startling as a heron
alights upon the pond, majestic sweep of wings, droplets of water
splashing in an arc, shimmering bluish white.

On the honeysuckle-flavoured breeze laughter – not that of
little girls but of women, high and lilting, accompanied by mas-
culine rumbles, spiced smoke carrying the scent of grilled meat.

What if she's forgotten she invited me at all?

*

It has been a roller coaster of a week. Word of Vanessa Bell's praise of Margaret's paintings had spread throughout the halls by the time she returned from the exhibition. All week, people she doesn't know have been coming up to speak with her. She is no longer the *scholarship girl*, but the *artist* lucky and talented enough to be invited to spend the weekend with the Bloomsbury Group.

'You're going up at the weekend, aren't you?' Mrs Danbourne had said, two days ago. 'It's an opportunity you cannot afford to miss.'

'I—'

'You *are* going, Margaret.' Mrs Danbourne stern, and Margaret had no recourse but to nod, unable to voice the doubts that had been assailing her as the weekend drew closer: *What if she didn't really mean it? What if she's forgotten? What will I wear?*

Mrs Danbourne reminded Margaret, in an oblique way, of her mother. They looked not at all alike, but it was their manner, the kindness interspersed with firmness, the strength in their core, the twinkle that sometimes danced in Mrs Danbourne's eyes, the way her face softened when she looked at her.

'It will do you a world of good to get away, meet like-minded people. It will inspire your work.' Mrs Danbourne smiled.

It is too late now to change her mind. Margaret tastes summer, sweat and trepidation on her lips as the door is swung open.

'Follow me, Madam,' the butler says in a formal, dirge-like voice, picking up her bag. She is led through various rooms, a glimpse of vast spaces populated with art, inviting and electrifying even in the briefest of peeks, making her want to ask the butler to stop, wait a minute, or an hour while she examines every one. Portraits and oils, pastels and watercolours, each one exquisite, she can see even from the barest glance. Glimpses of elaborate furnishings that provide a plush background for the main adornment: art.

Her heart thudding, raucous with nerves, as the faint strains of laughter and banter carrying through the windows get louder, sunshine-yellow sounds of happiness and companionship. The zesty saltiness of roasting meat, flavoured smoke and well-being. The glossy ruby taste of wine and wit.

Through the open doors and into the vast, wide gardens.

And again, she sees her childhood self counting, going in search of her sisters, flashes of colour among the flowers. Here too, an explosion of colour. Women in beautiful gowns. Men wearing jazzy neckties. Some sitting on chairs, others standing, yet others grouped on the lawn, under the fruit trees. Everyone seeming happy and at home. Comfortable.

She wants to be part of it all. An inclination as strong as the one to turn tail and run. Opposing forces, equally urgent, pulling her in opposite directions, so that she stops short. Her heart noisy, frantic, as much with excitement as with apprehension.

Then, a hand thrust out, a face lit up, the fragrance of lavender and turpentine.

'Margaret.' Vanessa Bell. 'Welcome to Charleston.' Her breath smoke and vinegar.

Margaret's heart settling. Then singing.

She did *mean it. She remembers me.*

'Let me introduce you to everyone.'

A whirlwind of names, smiles, bright flashes of teeth.

A woman who looks like Vanessa but whose eyes have a darkness, fathomless. 'My sister, Virginia.'

Her sister the writer.

'Ah, you're Mrs Danbourne's protégée. My sister was quite taken by your paintings and believe me, it takes a lot to impress her.' A brief flash of a smile lighting up her face, then, her gaze genuinely curious, 'So tell me, why do you paint?'

Margaret starts talking and is surprised by the ease of it. She is welcomed, easily, effortlessly into the group. Conversation flows fluidly and without pause, her shyness, her fear vanishing in the wake of this warmth, this casual acceptance of *her* as one of *them*.

She feels like she is on fire, but this time, a fire of zeal.

For the first time since the air raid that took her mother and sister and changed the course of her life, feeling confident in her own skin. Alive in a way she wasn't before.

Margaret is invited back the following weekend and a new routine is formed.

She travels down to Charleston every weekend, and during the week she is often invited to spend the evening at Vanessa's busy, colourful house in Gordon Square, bursting with art and sculpture, a homage to creativity.

The Bloomsbury Group's complete disregard for the rules of society is freeing, especially after living at the farm, her uncle with his chip on the shoulder about being from a lower stratum of society than Margaret and Winnie and punishing the girls for this, assuming their unhappiness was because they were judging their aunt and uncle's way of life rather than from losing their parents, their sister, their home.

The Bloomsbury Group take lovers as they wish, they switch husbands and partners, they do not care for what people think or say; all they care about is art. And although it was disconcerting at first, their blasé attitude to relationships, their many and change-able lovers across both genders, now Margaret is completely used to it. It is freeing that when she is with them, she is judged and celebrated for her work, not for how she looks, where she has come from, her past, her class, her place in society.

Above all, the realisation that they are like her: hurting, haunted by secret pains. Trying to get their angst out through their art, whether it be drawing or writing or sculpture. She is not alone in feeling as she did and the thought is freeing. Everyone has lost someone in the war and they all harbour their own private torment, anger and guilt, which is why her paintings resonate with them, hence that moment of stunned silence when Vanessa and Duncan first saw them displayed at Mrs Danbourne's exhibition of her work.

Being accepted as part of the Bloomsbury Group transforms Margaret. She perfects the art of appearing assured despite being nervous inside. The more she practises this the easier it gets, a woman comfortable in her own skin emerging in place of the lonely girl who talked to pigs while cleaning out the sty, trying to make sense of herself and her place in the world. Gradually, she shrugs off her mantle of scholarship girl. She smiles more than she ever did, despite her smiles being tinged with sorrow, weighted with the loss that she, along with a nation of war survivors, will always carry.

She is able to talk to her housemates (hiding her nerves behind a poised exterior rehearsed in front of the scratched mirror in her room), participate in discussions, form opinions, shoulder them, instead of hovering in corners eavesdropping, feeling unable to join in. She is slowly becoming one of the self-assured people she admired (and hoped to emulate but despaired she never could) when she first arrived at university, having discovered their secret – to *appear* confident so often that it becomes natural, almost instinctive.

Margaret has, finally, come into her own.

Chapter Twenty-One

2000

Emma

Apology

David is in the living room – the curtains aren't drawn, so Emma can see him from the street. He is slumped on the sofa, his head pushed back, mouth open, fast asleep.

Emma waits outside, smothered in shadows, reluctant to step inside her own home, spying on her love in the grey-blue cold, her breath visible in front of her, freezing puffs.

An empty glass in David's hand, his receding hairline, that head of black curls he was once so proud of now sparse silver.

He looks old.

She had thought he was old when she first saw him on TV, old but cool, dashing and enigmatic, with that wonderfully buoyant head of curls, those youthful eyes that crinkled pleasingly at the corners. But it was what he said and the way he said it, his words speaking directly to the rootless teenager who craved convention and belonging that Emma had been, fed up of travelling, lonely in a crowd, not fitting in with her mother's hippy friends.

'History both teaches and gives us warning. Through our history, we make sense of who we are.' David's mellifluous voice, his Highland accent out of place in the commune in Spain where Emma and her mum were at the time.

Somehow those words connected with Emma and she watched mesmerised while the other kids messed about and their parents –

her mum among them – lounged outside on sun-bleached grass, smoking, singing and dancing.

'I still make time to teach undergraduates at Cambridge. It was in fact a question asked by one of my students that kindled the idea for my paper…' David had stated, looking intensely and conspiratorially at the camera as if he was talking only to Emma.

In the caravan, someone said, 'What's that guy droning on about?' and went to switch off the television.

Emma had pounced on him, furious: 'Leave it be!'

'Someone has a crush,' the boy crooned but Emma ignored him, her concentration focused on the screen.

It was then that Emma made up her mind to read history – not just anywhere, but at Cambridge. She also decided she'd had enough of travelling – she wanted to stay put in one place and concentrate on her studies.

When she asked her mother – for the umpteenth time – if they could give up their nomadic lifestyle and return home, she had a fit as always. But this time, Emma didn't give up, give in like she usually did. She called her grandmother – the only one who could get round Emma's mother. And so it was at the end of that summer, Emma started at boarding school in England. She had never been happier. Thanks to David, the trajectory of her life changed.

Almost all her life, Emma has idolised David, looked up to him. She loved him from afar for years and when she realised her goal of getting into Cambridge and finally *did* meet him, her hero, and he reciprocated her interest, singled her out for his affections, it didn't matter that he was married, taken. It felt right. Inevitable. Validation of the love – augmented by hero-worship – that she had harboured for him for most of her life. Now, she looks at him, fallen asleep on the sofa while waiting up for her, the father of her child, and it is as if she is seeing him for the first time, seeing him as he truly is.

Despite having had her heart broken by him that first time, when he stayed with his wife and abandoned Emma, pregnant and alone, when he came to her years later, after his wife kicked him out, she had forgiven him and taken him back. For to her he would always be the great Dr David McEwan whose paper had spawned television appearances, one of which changed her life. Emma did not, or could not, see that by the time he came knocking on her door, she had moved on, become someone in her own right, while he had retired. She couldn't see past her desire to trust him – she believed he'd bring stability to her life because she didn't have that in her childhood, and she equated the stability she finally found at boarding school with him.

Why didn't she learn from her mistake? Why, instead of guarding her heart against his particular, torturous brand of hurt, had she opened it up to him again? Why had she compounded it by allowing her daughter – *their* daughter – to offer her heart to him as well, when Emma knows that he is not careful with hearts, that he runs slipshod over them?

Because he is the only man Emma has ever loved. It is a gasp in her throat, a salt-and-brine lump in her chest. It makes her tired.

She had always been a mature girl, far too grown-up for her age, but loving David is the most immature and irrational thing she has done. He had that effect on her.

He has let her down, disappointed her, upset her, outraged her, but through it all, she has loved him. When she was his student and lover, he'd led her to believe – and she had naively bought into the idea – that she was *the* one; that he was stuck in a marriage he didn't want because of the kids. It was only after his rejection of her that she found out about all the others, a long line of students including the one who had given him the idea for the research paper that made him famous.

When his wife finally kicked him out, he knew to come to Emma, not any of his other 'favoured' ex-students, ex-lovers. And, after he had apologised and grovelled, despite what he had done, everything he had done, she took him in, as he knew she would.

Fool.

He has fitted into her life and her child's. He has unleashed his charisma and charm on his daughter too and Emma has watched her fall for it, much as she herself had done.

Within a few weeks of David's re-entry into Emma's life, her daughter was calling him 'Daddy'. And there is no question that he adores her as much as she does him. He has taught her to play chess; he reads to her, patiently explains the mysteries of the world to her.

'I always wanted a little girl,' he said to Emma one night. 'Thanks for giving me the gift of Chloe.'

She had stood up then, wordlessly, clutching her pillow and going to the spare room. She did not speak to him for two days.

'I'm sorry,' he said over and over. 'When you told me you were pregnant I... I wasn't thinking straight. I was scared, which is why I asked you to get rid of... of the baby.'

'That's Chloe you wanted rid of.'

'Of course now that I... There's no excuse, I behaved abominably. But I thought I had too much to lose. My wife, my sons... I'm so sorry.'

When her anger gave way to weary acceptance she had, like countless other times, accepted his apology, forgiven him.

Stupid fool.

Her best years given to David, her daughter shared with him.

For years Chloe was hers alone; they were a tight, composed, happy unit of two. Then David entered their lives again, Emma proudly showing off their daughter – *Look, this is who we made together! Isn't she wonderful?*

David's eyes welling, amazement and yes, love.

But David's brand of love – not eternal.

She *knew* this. And yet.

And yet, she shared her life with him again, opened up her daughter to his fickle love…

Why?

Because I've been blinded by my hero-worship of him ever since I first saw him on television.

Now that that's fallen away, Emma is finally seeing David for who he really is. But if she acts on what she has found out, *she* will be the one to break their family unit, break her daughter's heart.

She sighs, takes a deep breath, pushes herself out of the shadows and up the small path, edged by the minuscule garden that she resolves every spring and summer to do something about, sighing with relief when autumn kicks in and she has a good excuse to ignore the weeds: *I'll make it look nice next year, too late now.*

The sound of her key in the lock must have registered, for when she comes into the living room, David is awake. He sets the empty wine glass down, rubs his eyes, smiles at her.

That smile she fell in love with, blue and crinkly, warmth and love.

'What's the time? I might have had a wee kip.'

She pulls the curtains closed.

He comes up behind her, drawing her to him.

His solidness. His smell of cloves and comfort. She breathes it in.

Then gently she pushes him away.

'What is it?' he asks.

'The paper I'm working on, David.'

'Yes?'

The weak yellow light of the lamp serves only to cast his face in shadow. Have his eyes widened slightly? Is that fear darkening his pupils, or is she imagining it?

'In the course of my research I…'

He takes a step backward. Crosses his chest with his arms, as if protecting himself.

Now she can see his face and she is not imagining the fear. She isn't.

Don't say it, he's pleading with his eyes.

She feels her heart sink, her body collapse in on itself.

Despite her findings, her doubts regarding David's integrity, she has been wishing that when confronted, he would laugh off her worries, get angry with her for suspecting him, come up with an explanation so simple yet perfect that she would laugh at herself, her pointless anxiety.

But David's reaction…

He is guilty. Reduced. Shattered. Small.

'Why, David? Why did you—?'

He holds up his hand to stop her. Then, so softly that she has to strain to hear, he once again, with only a few words, breaks her heart.

'I've been waiting for this all these years, but I never thought it would be you, of all people, who would expose me.'

She closes her eyes. If she shuts them tight enough perhaps this will go away, this knowledge, this truth.

'Yes, I've fabricated the evidence, but the ideas I put forward have changed society, the way we think. Good has come out of my paper, Emma. You have to see the bigger picture.'

Anger thrumming through her voice so it sounds fragmented. 'What I see is your colossal arrogance. So convinced what you were putting forward was right that, when you couldn't get the sources to back you up, you *made some up.*'

'What if I did?' His eyes flashing. 'That paper makes sense. The very fact that no one has twigged about the fake evidence until now is proof. It provides a simple, elegant way of solving problems society faces today based on examples from the past. It has changed our thinking for the *better*! Isn't that enough for you? Do you always have to do things by the book? Isn't it advisable to bend the rules sometimes when you know you're right?'

His voice, desperation and fiery, passionate anger. The same passion that once drew her to him. Not now.

Now all she feels is weariness. Immense fatigue.

Once again, her lover has proved that he is not the man she hoped he was. But this time something is different. This time, instead of making excuses for him, she believes it.

For now, her eyes are open and she is finally seeing David the man rather than David the hero.

Chapter Twenty-Two

1922

Margaret

Lifeline

'Hello there.' An accented voice behind Margaret, dark and rich like the thick chocolate Cook would make on winter evenings when frost-tipped wind howled in the denuded trees and Margaret and her sisters cosied up by the fireplace beside Mother and Father, watching flames dance on the crisping wood.

Margaret turns towards the speaker. Warm, twinkling eyes that match his voice, deep and fathomless. His skin the glorious, glossy ebony of polished wood.

Her first reaction is surprise. This man with his stunning looks, his sculpted, regal profile, looks like he belongs in a palace rising from fired earth, vivid, sun-spiced amber, not in an English country garden with its muted greens and golds here at Charleston.

But really, nothing to do with the Bloomsbury Group should surprise her.

Margaret is still a regular guest at Charleston. She arrives on the Friday evening, staying until Sunday. She is an acknowledged member of the Bloomsbury Group.

The discussions run late into the night in the grounds here at Charleston, the sky ink and pearls, conversations petering out into silences that are comfortable. Margaret savours every warm, companionable minute, never wanting these evenings to end.

What she loves best, admires most about the Bloomsbury Group, is that they live in utter defiance of society and its rules. It is freeing and wonderful to be included among these accepting, open-minded people. But although Margaret has come out of herself since her art exhibition, where she met Vanessa, she's still not brave enough to emulate the Bloomsbury Group in this, their complete disregard for the norms of society. She is content to stay on the sidelines, watching everything, avidly taking it in.

'Live a little,' her friends urge. 'You need experience, *life* experience, unshackled by societal decrees, to be a better painter.'

They like that she is thrilled, in awe of their antics, and ham them up for her benefit. They tease her affectionately, trying to set her up with men – and women too sometimes, the more to see her eyes widen with shock.

'I'm waiting for the right person to come along,' she says, eyes twinkling when they raise eyebrows at her use of the genderless 'person'.

'Is there something you're not telling us?'

'That's for me to know and you to find out.' She laughs.

They laugh along with her. 'You're not such an innocent after all. Try to bring some of that mischief into your paintings, they could do with lightening up.'

The man beside her raises an eyebrow. 'Are you surprised by me, Miss?'

She flushes, caught out. Heat rising up her neck, mottling her face. 'No, I… I…'

Words fail her, appraised as she is by his spiced marigold eyes.

'I'm reading law at Cambridge. I was invited here by Lytton Strachey. He went to my college and his father and mine are great friends. They met through work in India.'

'Yes, of course. I...' *Why is she behaving like this? Lost for words.*

It is his gaze, sun-warmed sandstone, bright and focused on her, that is rendering her mute, making her regress to the shy waif she was when she first came to university. But that girl has gone. The Margaret she is now is confident – or at least pretends to be.

She swallows, gets what she wants to say past her clogged throat, tasting of embarrassment, bright yellow. 'You don't have to explain yourself to me. I... I'm a guest here too.' And then, in a bright, defiant burst: 'I was thinking I'd like to paint you. You have such a princely bearing – any royal blood in your family?'

He smiles – a rainbow in a storm-chased sky. 'I can never gauge what reaction my presence is going to evoke here in England. Most often it is shock and distaste; people don't want me near them – so my default stance is defiance. I've never been asked this, however.' His eyes twinkling honey-gold. 'Sorry to disappoint, but my family has absolutely no royal connections.' And, his gaze softening, 'Apologies if I came across rude. Shall we start again?'

I really would like to paint you, Margaret thinks, surprised by the impulse.

Since she's come to university, other than her emotions she's mostly painted the dead – Evie, Mother, Father. Although Father is still 'missing in action', and neither his death nor the rumour that he placed himself in the line of enemy fire has been confirmed, Margaret feels deep in her heart – and she knows Winnie does too – that their father is no more.

Margaret sketches her missing family members over and over, trying to commit their features, their mannerisms, to paper before fickle memory wipes them away completely – a process that has already begun, for she struggles to recall the shape of her father's chin, the particular tilt of her mother's head when she was thinking, the radiance of Evie's smile...

At the farm painting was escape, a lifeline. She would lean against the stile, mossy velvet, breathe in the fragrance of honeysuckle and wild garlic, blackberries and ripe apples and dying summer, and she'd paint the meadow spread out around her, dotted with mushrooms and bluebells, woody earth, fecund green, blackbirds calling from the trees above.

Now she only paints what tugs at her emotions, makes her bleed, care, feel. She does not paint Winnie, although she misses her intensely. For her sister is happy, the letters Margaret receives from her religiously every week bursting with news and enthusiasm. Winnie is a mother now, completely besotted with her firstborn son, Toby.

Margaret had travelled up to see him and Winnie. She had held her nephew, a tiny, squirming bundle, and thought of her mother. How happy she would have been, how proud. She had looked at her sister's glowing face, tired but jubilant, and in her shining eyes she had seen her musings reflected.

'Mother would have been ecstatic, and so would Evie. Father would have clapped Andrew's shoulder and declared, "Jolly good, old chap, well done,"' Winnie had said.

Margaret and Winnie had held each other and wept, then, for their beloved dead, the past, all that was lost nestling alongside this baby, the future, between them.

'Miss?'

His eyes are pools of liquid caramel flecked with amber, bringing to mind mellow rays filtering through a forest canopy at sunset. To paint them, she would mix gold with yellow to get that rich toffee hue, temper it with a dab of violet, a touch of green to perfect the lemony indigo streaks…

He blinks and she comes to her senses with a jolt.

She's been staring *again*, she realises, hot colour flooding her face. She forces herself to smile, biting her lower lip in an attempt to conceal how flustered she feels.

'You're an artist?' he asks.

'We're all artists here, of one kind or another.' She aims for cool and collected but her reply falls short, pinned as she is in his gazelle-like gaze.

'I'm not.' He holds his hands up, palms outward. 'I'm a lawyer. I tagged along at Strachey's bidding.'

'Do you always do Strachey's bidding?' she asks, feeling completely off-kilter while he stands there unfazed, smiling warmly at her. She wants him to lose his cool.

But he laughs instead and it is a delightful, infectious sound, like festive bubbles popping. 'Not always, but this time I'm glad I did.'

'Why?' she asks archly, aware she's flirting – she, Margaret! – her heart conducting a symphony in her chest.

'Because I've made your acquaintance. You are quite simply the loveliest person I've met.'

And now she blushes, properly, and he laughs again, seemingly delighted by her discomfort.

Vanessa comes to where they are standing, beneath the apple trees, their feet grinding blossom, the scent of consternation and nectar, the flavour of cut grass.

'You've met Suraj, I see.'

'I…'

'Suraj, this is Margaret. A very talented—'

'Margaret. *The* artist. The one you're all talking about.'

'Yes!' she beams, winking at Margaret as her face is, once again, suffused with colour.

'Vanessa,' someone calls and Vanessa glides away, as casually and suddenly as she'd appeared.

'You truly are the most beautiful woman I've met,' he says, leaning close so he's whispering in her ear, Margaret's skin standing out in delicious goosebumps of anticipation.

She keeps her voice light. 'I'm sure you say that to every woman you meet.'

His gaze seems to pierce the innermost, secret part of her soul, the one that harbours her deepest desires. 'You're the only woman I've said it to.'

She manages a small laugh.

'And you're not only heart-stoppingly beautiful but incredibly talented as well, so I've heard.'

Her cheeks on fire. He's obviously trying his luck with her but nevertheless she can't help being flattered, warmed. His eyes soft, glowing orange as they look at her.

She could stand here and listen to his chocolatey, melodious voice for ever.

'What drives you? Why do you paint?'

'It's a compulsion, as necessary, as inevitable, as breathing.'

'Ah,' he says and again that look, deep and searching, that seems to penetrate all her defences. 'But I think there's more than that. Something you're not telling me.'

She's at once surprised by and accepting of his perception. Although he is obviously flirting with her, she understands somehow that he sees more than everyone else. There's something about him – a reserve – despite his twinkling, flattering gaze, that makes him sensitive to everything she herself is holding back.

'No matter, I will get it out of you. If not now, then very soon.' He smiles lazily, his tawny eyes devouring her.

She is aware of a connection with this man, instant and deep. Something she has never felt before with anyone. It makes her bold.

'What's your story?' she asks.

Despite his easy-going manner, she senses hidden flickers of pain reflected in the warm copper light from his eyes. He too is hiding something, he too holds back.

The day is ebbing, the setting sun transforming the sky into an artist's palette of pinks and ochre golds, casting navy streaks on the grass, dancing shadows on the faces of friends deep in conversation.

'I'm from India,' he says. 'Here to learn the law so I can take over my father's practice when I return home.'

India.

Why does she feel this kinship, sudden and unexplained, for this man from the other side of the world? Is it the haunted shadows she can sense, stealing the light from his eyes?

Why does she experience a pang when he talks about going back to India?

She has only spoken to him for a few minutes but it is like she's known him always.

'I miss India.' His eyes liquid, his tone: notes on a violin, burnished blue. 'Here, I... I feel displaced. Not quite belonging.'

She touches him then, unthinking, as he puts into words what she herself has felt since the air raid that destroyed her family.

A pat on his hand.

And again that connection, charged, binding. She wants to leave her hand on his for ever, even as she retrieves it.

He looks at her, his gaze molten honey, and she knows he feels it too.

'I understand,' she says, and he doesn't ask how, why.

He nods and there is an understanding between them, distinct, tangible.

Electric.

The next morning, as dawn streaks the sky creamy shades of velvet rose, Margaret, having tossed and turned all night, rendered restless by a pair of all-seeing dark eyes, dresses and slips out of the house with her sketchbook.

She walks along the ridge of the downs, the sea in the distance a sheet of silver, moist air perfumed with morning depositing soothing caresses upon her flushed cheeks. She squats on grass shimmering with dew, and watches the day begin over the water.

As the sun climbs over the horizon, she sketches warm brown eyes, inviting confidences from her, inciting her to impart more than she should.

'You're up early.'

She startles, dropping the sketchbook. It falls face down and she is glad. It would have been mortifying if he knew she was sketching him.

'You scared me,' she says.

But she's not surprised. Somehow, she knew he would come, she's been expecting him. She's willed him to and he's here. With her. Sharing her secret place.

'I'm sorry. I didn't mean to.' He squats down beside her, as heedless of the moisture seeping into his clothes as she is.

A butterfly flutters on a blade of grass beside them, butter-cream with sapphire dots.

'I like coming here in the mornings, watching the sun rise,' she says. 'This view has always comforted me. The sea, timeless, bigger than all of us, the living and all the dead. It will be here a hundred years from now raging against the rocks, spitting spray.' She is comfortable enough with him, she realises, to say whatever comes to mind without fear of him judging her – it is as if she has known him always, instead of having met him just the previous day.

'You're a poet as well as an artist!' His eyes aglow with admiration.

She laughs, delight and embarrassment at his compliment.

'You're right though. There's something infinitely calming about this place. It almost inspires me to pick up a brush myself.'

She turns to him. 'Why don't you?'

'Believe me, you'd regret saying that if you saw my efforts! I'm happy to just sit here with you and enjoy the view.'

Sit here with you. Bright fire burning in her stomach.

The tantalising scent of new day, the taste of new beginnings and wild excitement, the land below them glowing in the morning sunshine, dipping into the sea, which shimmers and undulates, a distant roar, the crash of waves on rocks, an arc of frothy spray, creamy blue.

'Do you believe in destiny?' he asks after a while.

She considers his question.

It would be so easy to write the air raid off as destiny, fate. If she believed that Evie and Mother were *meant* to die that day, she would be absolved of the guilt she feels at not being able to save her sister, for living while she died.

Evie, with her wide smile, her gentle manner, her disability that she managed quietly and uncomplainingly. Why was she not meant to live?

And what about that other reality, the one Margaret visits often despite it torturing her with its tantalising glimpses into an alternative outcome, where Mother does not dally and they go to the farm, *all* of them, and are safe, alive, together…

He must read the words she cannot say for his eyes soften, his gaze mellifluous gold. '*I* do,' he says. 'I think we were destined to meet, you and I. It is as if everything that has happened in my life has been so I can get to this point – the two of us meeting. For I have never felt as comfortable with another human being as I do with you.'

And again she is speechless, drowning in his earnest gaze. For that is *exactly* how she feels and she knows even as he opens his mouth what he is going to say next.

'It is as if I have known you for ever.'

Later, they walk back together, joining the others in the kitchen as they cobble together breakfast: thick hunks of crusty bread with lashings of strawberry jam and golden butter from the farm down the road, washed down with great mugs of strong tea sweetened with two cubes of sugar.

When the weekend draws to a close, Suraj, who has never left her side, asks, 'Will you be here next week?'

'Yes,' she says, overwhelmed by that charged thrill she feels in his company.

'Then I will be too.' He is smiling and yet there is pain in his eyes, sorrow at their parting, the torment she herself feels.

How, she wonders, is it possible to understand someone, know what they are thinking, what they are not saying, when you haven't been acquainted for more than two days?

How is it possible to miss them with every fibre of your being, the world rendered colourless without them, when they were strangers just a few days ago?

And yet, it is so.

They part as friends, or in truth, something more, their gazes lingering on each other until the last possible minute of parting, knowing that they will yearn, separately, for the following weekend when they *will* meet again.

Chapter Twenty-Three

1922

Archana

Inauspicious

'Ma,' Archana says when her would-be in-laws have left after setting out their terms for the wedding. 'Does this mean we cannot invite Radha?'

'Don't say her name in this house,' her mother hisses, her face hard. 'She's brought nothing but bad luck and finally, it is lifting. Didn't you hear what your in-laws said? We cannot invite her, and even if we did, do you want to start off your married life on an inauspicious note?'

'Ma, it's your daugh—'

'Archana.' Her mother cups her face in her palm and the way she says her name, the tenderness in her voice, stalls Archana's argument. 'You're a good girl. You've given me such solace these months without your father. Get married, give your husband and in-laws the child they want. Live your life.'

'But, Ma…'

Her mother sighs, her hand dropping tiredly. Archana feels bereft without her mother holding her. 'Nobody drinks from the same cup or eats from the same plate as an untouchable. Nobody will attend your wedding if she is here.'

'Ma, she is…'

'You must think me a monster. But I'm not heartless.' Her mother's eyes fill. 'I miss her, I do.'

Archana jumps at this admission, this softness displayed by her mother. 'Then come, we can visit her. She'll be—'

Her mother's face closes up, severe. 'No. I cannot. I will not.'

Archana leaves it. She has seen the chink in her mother's armour; she will exploit it, to her sister's advantage, later. But now, she has a more pressing matter to discuss.

'Ma, after I'm married, you'll be all alone. How will you…?'

'Don't you worry about me. You're only a few miles away, in the next village. I'll manage.'

'And your livelihood?'

'How much do I need, eh? I can get by with the beedies and the sewing.'

'Promise me you'll not sew at night.' Archana shudders as she pictures her mother's hair getting caught in the candle, burning, her face alight.

'I promise.' Her mother cups her chin again, gently. 'I know you love your studies. I'm sorry you have to give them up. The nuns talked to me, tried to convince me to get you to stay on.'

Now it is Archana's eyes that fill. The air tasting of mango and jackfruit and lost chances caressing her face. The dog dancing around their legs.

'It's my duty to get married,' she says when she can speak, convincing herself.

Her mother nods.

'Your in-laws have found work for you as a servant up at the landlord's mansion in their village.'

Hope there are books, she thinks. Then chides herself, *You'll be working! When will you have the time to read? And even if by some outrageous chance you do have a spare moment, you cannot read their books, mere servant that you are. You've given up your dream of studying to get married; be a dutiful wife, don't have ideas above your station…*

Chapter Twenty-Four

1922

Margaret

Connection

Margaret is unsettled all week, counting down to the weekend, molten caramel eyes populating her dreams, keeping her company during waking hours. She draws sketch after sketch of Suraj, but it isn't the same as seeing him, being with him. The thrill of their remembered conversations, the flavour of his company…

The weekend arrives too slowly, and when it finally does, she is ready and waiting, excited and nervous. Has she imagined the connection she feels? Is she making more of this than she should?

She arrives at Charleston in a frenzy of anticipation and nerves.

Suraj is not there.

Is he not coming? Has she read it all wrong? What about his promise?

'I'll be there,' he'd said.

She reclines in the loveseat beneath the apple blossom, trying to hide her upset behind a rigid smile, listening to the others talk and feeling disinclined to join in, the scent of ripe fruit and raw disappointment, bitter bleeding blue.

Then, 'Margaret?'

That voice, like flowing nectar, honeyed amber.

She drinks him in, once again blown away by his beauty. Words failing her, the breath catching in her throat. Her heart at once beating too fast and not beating at all.

Suraj leads her to the seat beneath the rose arbour and she follows. It is as if she has no recourse; she is mesmerised by him. The others give knowing smiles and she notices them even as she breathes him in, his every feature. His eyes. That smile.

They talk late into the night about everything and nothing, the evening air sweet with possibility and promise.

When they retire to their rooms, she cannot sleep, the night passing even more slowly than the week preceding it. When finally the gloom of night is alleviated by grey fingers of pre-dawn light, she dresses, swiftly, silently, in the darkness, her fingers fumbling with the buttons of her dress, and slips out of the front door.

She is waiting for his footfall, hankering for his presence, his spiced clove smell, and then it is there. He falls into step beside her, easily, as if he was meant to be by her side. They walk along the ridge of the downs to her secret spot, where she likes to sketch among the reeds, land spread out below, a wide expanse of fertile green, sloping down to the sea, a cerulean, undulating, whispering vista, seemingly endless.

He slips a shawl around her shoulders, his touch making her shiver. She wants to lean into him. And as if he has read her mind, he leaves his arm on her shoulder and like this, they await the sunrise.

The sun peeps over the horizon, its perfect golden reflection on the glass of the water, the sky a kaleidoscope of pinks and reds, setting the clouds on fire, more beautiful than anything an artist could conjure, his arm on her shoulder, her body against his. They are quiet but it is as if they have spoken volumes. The silence between them charged with unspoken assurances, a conversation conducted without words.

*

The weekends continue, electric. Radiant.

'Who is this Suraj you mention in every sentence? Tell me more about him,' Winnie writes.

And Margaret needs no prompting.

'So, have you slept with him yet?' the Bloomsbury Group ask. And when she colours, 'Now that's what you should capture in your paintings, that smile.'

'What are you waiting for?' they tease. 'What if the world ended tomorrow? It almost did with the war. Life is short, Margaret, you need to grab it with both hands. Any fool can see there's something special between the two of you, so why dally? Live a little, girl!'

'Oh, but I *am* living,' she wants to say. 'I've never felt like this before, all my senses awakened, singing. I am savouring, cherishing, treasuring every moment.'

But she cannot explain it articulately, even to herself, cannot put into words how Suraj makes her feel. How, when she is with him, there's no one else, just the two of them in a world of their own. How they seem to read each other's minds, knowing what the other is going to say before they say it. That special, instant connection. That pull. Intangible but irresistible.

Her heart more charged and alive than ever before.

How to tell them that what she feels for him, what she has with him cannot be rushed, every moment seized, stretched, adored, prized, shared.

She can talk with him about anything, and sometimes they don't talk at all, just sit together in comfortable silence, entire conversations conducted through gazes.

'Teach me to paint,' he says and they set up easels side by side among the reeds.

'Painting is conversing with your soul,' she tells him. 'You're putting your feelings down through brushstrokes.'

He laughs at his efforts. She doesn't.

He attempts a self-portrait. Red spots on his cheeks. A clown nose.

He makes her laugh.

One day they walk into town, and they are jeered, booed.

A man spits at Margaret. 'Going with a coolie.'

Both of them flinch, but the sight of Suraj, small and wounded and ashamed, a cowering shadow of his usual dynamic self, shocks Margaret more than the abuse.

'Let's go back,' he says.

'No.'

Instead, she links her arm with Suraj's, and marches on, head held high. Suraj tries to pull away, but she holds on to him, refusing to acknowledge the taunts and the sniggers, the knowing smirks, the hostile glares and hurled obscenities, though shaken to the core.

Suraj is quiet for the rest of the afternoon, lapsing into a brooding silence.

That evening, he says, tight-lipped, 'I think we should stop being friends.'

'Why?' she asks, shocked, hurt more than she can say, panicked at the thought of never seeing him again, this man who is her reason for finally daring to be happy.

His eyes, fathomless pools of pain. 'You are precious, Margaret. I don't want you sullied by your association with me, subject to abuse such as we endured…'

Oh.

'You don't know me, Suraj. I'm made of harder stuff than—'

'But this is how it is, always, with me in the real world.' His voice, upset and frustration.

She wants to cup his face, gently rub away the furrows between his eyes.

'Here, nobody minds, we're in a blissful cocoon but it's misleading, you see...' Sorrow layering his voice the burnt ochre of a blustery sunset.

She recalls their very first meeting, when he had said: 'I can never gauge what reaction my presence is going to evoke here in England. Most often it is shock and distaste; people don't want me near them...'

She wishes she could soothe his pain away. 'I don't care for people who discriminate based on colour.'

'You may not care now,' his voice is a keening, hollow violet, 'but you will. It chips away at you, eating at your confidence, your sense of worth. I don't belong here in England, Margaret, and I don't want to drag you down with me.'

'Suraj,' she says softly, 'I don't belong either.'

It is his turn to be shocked. 'I don't believe it.'

She tells him then about her past, the air raid that destroyed their family, her anger at her mother for not leaving earlier, and at her father for not considering his daughters worth living for, her anger at herself for being, even now, angry at her parents, and most of all her guilt at not being able to rescue her sister, her upset at being the one who got to live.

For the first time she lays bare her soul to a person other than Winnie.

He looks at her and she is seen, known. All her layers peeled back, revealing the phantom selves of her sister and parents, of what might have been.

'Your sister dying wasn't your fault,' he says and his voice is tender as the whisper of wind on water, soft as a caress.

And although she doesn't entirely believe him, she is comforted.

She tells him of the lonely girl who talked to pigs while cleaning out the sty; the scholarship girl at university eavesdropping in corners, unable to join in, feeling other. 'I have learned to *pretend* to belong, but even here, although I was invited warmly into this group and I'm so glad for it, I'm unable to give of myself completely.'

'I don't fit either,' he says softly. 'In England I am judged for my colour. At home, I feel under pressure, as the only son, to do what my parents want for me.'

He tells her about growing up in India. How he has always known, from when he was a child, that he is to follow in his father's footsteps into the law. That he has never thought about doing anything else, dared try anything else, for his course in life was charted for him.

He takes her hand. His brown palm and her pale one entwined.

And again, that jolt of connection, that feeling of being right where she should be, of coming home.

She has been untethered, flailing since she lost her childhood home, Evie and Mother to the air raid.

In Suraj, she finds anchor.

Belonging.

'You've improved tremendously,' Mrs Danbourne says. 'Love has sharpened and honed your talent.'

'Love?' Margaret stares at her.

'Don't you know what's happening to you, child?' Mrs Danbourne laughs gently. 'You've never painted better, looked better. You are happy, bubbly, glowing. Transformed.'

It is love. Of course it is.

Margaret is desperate to see Suraj, be with him. She misses him during the week. She counts down the days, the hours, the minutes until they meet again. Her sketchbooks are filled with his likeness. She relives every single one of their conversations, over and over. He visits her dreams.

With him, she can be finally, uniquely, herself.

He is her life.

Margaret has never dared label what she feels for Suraj as love. For she is afraid. Afraid of and for her happiness.

Life can change in an instant, she knows. It can turn you upside down, inside out.

And a part of her wonders: Does she deserve this when Evie will never experience it?

Chapter Twenty-Five

1922

Archana

Favourite

Archana makes the journey to visit her sister, her last before her marriage. She doesn't know if, after her marriage, she'll get a chance to visit at all.

Her sister, eyes haunted, hair untidy. Her son clinging to her legs, daughter in her arms while she attempts to light a fire at the hearth. Looking flustered. Tired.

'Here, let me.'

After lighting the fire Archana distributes the gifts she has brought with her. A jar of pickle made from lime rind, pilfered from her mother's hoard – her sister's favourite. ('A good way to use the rind, instead of letting it go to waste,' her mother always says as she sets the lime rinds out to dry in the sunshine, shooing away the dog, who bounds up, sniffing curiously.) Some guavas and mangoes that Archana stole from Bhim's orchard, trying and failing not to recall that night raid in happier times. Those hell-raising boys, their neighbours. Radha could have married one of them; she would certainly be happier…

Radha's children start eating the mangoes immediately, their hungry eyes, so like her sister's, alight as they suck the juice.

Oh, Radha, she laments as she sees her sister handle the pickle gently. The desire and longing in her voice when she says, 'Ma made this?'

Archana nods.

'I miss Ma's food.'

'Nobody cooks quite like her.'

'She can conjure something out of nothing and make it taste so great too.'

'I'm getting married,' Archana says.

Her sister almost drops the baby in shock.

'Careful,' Archana says.

Radha is unable to hide the dismay that crosses her face. The sigh that escapes. 'I thought you wanted to study.'

The first time Archana visited her sister, Radha had clasped her to her chest and sobbed. 'I'm so sorry for ruining your chances, your future.'

Archana, distressed by her sister's appearance and her tears, had said, quickly, 'Radha, I don't want to get married. Ever. I want to study. You've done me a favour.'

Now she says, 'I've changed my mind…'

Her sister sighs again, and the infant, picking up on her mother's distress, begins to cry.

'Marriage is not all it's cracked up to be, Archana.'

'I know. But…'

'Who is he?'

She tells her.

'I know him. He's *old*! I attended his first wedding. You were just a toddler! Archana, you cannot.' Her sister's face wild with anguish.

A flash of anger, making Archana's tone sharp. 'I have to.'

'You don't.'

Archana knows her next words will hurt her sister, but something in her *wants* to. 'I haven't exactly had a glut of proposals, you know. This is the first I've received. The only one I will.'

Her sister grabbing her hand, her words urgent. 'He's thrice your age. What if he dies and you have to do sati?'

Trust her sister to tap into her deepest fear. Archana has lain awake at night beside her worn-out, sleeping mother, worrying about it: her husband dying and she burning on the funeral pyre with him, her life cut short – that is, if *she* doesn't die first, in childbirth, cursed by the same fate as his other two wives...

'Archana, say no.' Her sister pleading.

She thinks of her mother's face, lined before her time, her shoulders hunched, her tired body, devastation and disappointment written into every pore, her hands bruised and scabbed from sewing needles missing their mark as her eyesight worsens, her head dangerously near the candle in order to see the stitches.

Her face all lit up when the proposal came.

'It's not like I have a choice.'

'You do. You always do.'

'So you say,' Archana retorts and her sister's face falls.

Radha hears Archana's unspoken words: *You dared to take matters into your own hands, follow your heart. You believed you had the choice and look where it's got you.*

She says softly, 'I cannot break Ma's heart again. She'll never recover.'

Radha's face crumples. She turns away. The baby has stopped wailing and is vigorously sucking the mango, her face yellow with smeared juice.

Her sister does not ask if she is invited to the wedding. They both know the answer to that.

'Radha,' Archana says, gently, feeling immensely weary, so very tired of being the strong one. The one having to console everyone. 'It will be alright.'

She doesn't know if she is comforting her sister or herself. Perhaps both.

Her sister nods, her shoulders heaving.

'I'm going now. It'll be a while before I see you again.'

Her sister turns, breathing her in hungrily. They both know that it will be difficult to see each other once Archana is married, her first duty being to her husband. She won't be able to fool her husband and in-laws as easily as she has been doing their mother.

'I'll visit when I can.'

Her sister holds her as if she will never let go, her smell of defeat and hard work and poverty and sweat and ache, the baby, squashed between them, wailing again.

And Archana walks away, her head turned back, taking in her sister and her hungry-looking children standing in front of their little hut in the untouchable section of the village, watching them until they are specks in the distance, a haze of dust and blurry tears, telling herself, and hoping the thought will transmit to Radha, *I will come back*, the taste of desperation and sadness and missing and yearning in her mouth. For a different life. For what might have been.

Chapter Twenty-Six

1923

Margaret

Fever Dream

Months pass in a fever dream of sketches and meetings and happiness. Of delicious tantalising waiting until Margaret sees Suraj again each weekend.

They are watching the sun rise over the sea from their secret place, among the reeds on the ridge of the downs at Charleston, when he says, 'I graduate in a few months. Then I will return to India.'

India. Halfway across the world. A country of myth and mystics.

Suraj's birthplace. His home.

Although they talk endlessly, this is the first time either of them has brought up the future. When Margaret envisions the future, it always features Suraj.

Her heart drops, and she cannot hold his gaze.

'Suraj means sun,' he had said when she asked him about his name. 'My mother suffered many miscarriages; the doctor asked my parents to give up all hope of having children. Then I came along. When the priests decreed that the alignment of stars on my horoscope pointed to a name beginning with the sound *Sss* it was inevitable, my mother says, that they call me Suraj.'

'Your name suits you perfectly,' Margaret had said, thinking, *You are my sun, you light up my life.*

He had sighed. 'It's a burden, Margaret, being the only son, carrying the weight of their expectations. I just…'

He'd looked so sad that she wanted to hold him, console him. Instead, she'd sat on her hands in case they acted, involuntarily, upon the urge to touch him, soothe his pain, and made a flip comment that caused him to smile, the heaviness easing from his eyes.

And now that burden of expectation from his parents is drawing him back…

The same thing that drew her to him, their otherness that spawned that instant, electric connection, the way they felt separate, not part of a group even while in it, is now going to come between them.

He is going to India, to his parents, to his duties as only son, to take over his father's business.

Margaret's eyes sparkle. They sting.

They have never discussed their feelings for one another, but Margaret has always, naively, she realises now, assumed that he feels the same way she does. How else to explain the way he understands her, *all* of her, how he intuits her thoughts before she articulates them, how their silences are meaningful and loaded, conveying so much more than words…

Or so she thought.

Foolish, lovestruck Margaret.

She has been nothing but a plaything. He has been toying with her, passing the time until he has to go back home.

She swallows. Devastating loss, thick with brine.

'Come with me?'

Has she has heard right?

Those beautiful toffee eyes, wide with question, hopeful and hesitant. Vulnerable as if poised for hurt.

Her heart soaring, singing as she understands the implications of what he is asking.

She was not wrong. He cares. He reciprocates her feelings. He wants her to accompany him.

And, her mind racing ahead: India. So far from everything and everyone she knows. Her sister. Her life.

Her life.

She cannot imagine life without Suraj.

India. Tantalisingly exotic. A whole different world.

Far away from an England battered by war, felled by loss. From scorching memories of fire, the branding of guilt at not having been able to save her sister.

There is nothing really keeping her here, she realises, except Winnie. But Winnie is busy and content being a mother and wife; she doesn't need Margaret as she once did and Margaret wouldn't want it any other way – she is happy her sister's happy. And like Winnie says, often enough, 'It's time you moved on, Meggie, looked forward, not back.'

India with Suraj would be moving forward.

India would be, in the words of the Bloomsbury Group, 'Living a little'.

She will miss them, the Bloomsbury Group, who have accepted her and allowed her to come out of herself, for which she is so grateful. But she has always known that their friendship is transient – people leave all the time, new faces, fresh talent taking their place.

She will miss Mrs Danbourne. Her art course, which she enjoys. Her sister, her nephew. England.

But there is nothing pressing tying her here, holding her in place.

She is free to do as she pleases. What she wants.

And she *wants* this man beside her and what he is offering. A chance to begin again, begin anew, wipe out the past, sadness and sorrow, hurt and loss.

The sun rises, its soft morning glow gilding his face. His arm round her. His smell as familiar as her own.

'I cannot live without you. But I know it is asking a lot of you.' His voice soft, tender, choked with emotion. His face very near. 'I love you, Margaret.'

He loves me.

'I love you too.'

He kisses her then. The taste of a thousand feelings, a thousand lives concentrated into that one magical, wondrous moment.

The taste of her future.

'Marry me. Come with me to India.'

His lips on hers, her mind, her heart, suffused with him and the enchanting spell of his words. *Come with me to India.*

That evening, as they sit by the fire, toasting marshmallows and dipping them in hot cocoa, Suraj says, 'I know what I'm asking of you and I don't do it lightly. It won't be easy leaving all this behind, uprooting your life here.'

She opens her mouth, sickly sweet and sticky with marshmallow, to tell him that *he* is her life, that she is looking forward to her future with him: excitement and adrenaline, adventure and love; but he is continuing to speak, wanting to get his point across.

'It's just...' He sighs. 'Look around you, Margaret. Do you see anyone else like me?'

She knows what he is saying but tries for levity. 'You're unique, one of a kind.'

He does not smile. His lips are thin. 'Here, in this group, I'm accepted. But elsewhere…' He sighs deeply again, rubbing a hand over his eyes, the gesture weary. 'I… It's a struggle.'

'Yes.' She knows.

'If we lived here, you would be party to it too and I… I couldn't put you through it.' Such angst in his voice.

'I wouldn't care,' she says fiercely.

'But *I* do.' A pause then. 'I can't work here, Margaret. Nobody will employ me. And they need people like me in India – lawyers, men educated in England. Jawaharlal Nehru, who was also educated at Trinity, my alma mater, and Mohandas Gandhi are calling for men like myself to take part in their movement. Although I'll be working with my father, I'd still do my bit for my country.'

He has discussed with her his impassioned beliefs about India. 'I'm with Gandhi and Nehru. I want India to be governed by Indians.'

She agrees with him. She has read up on it.

Now, he asks, 'Are you sure you want to do this, marry me?'

The embers of the fire casting an amber glow on his beloved face.

Despite being excited and looking forward to it, Margaret knows it won't be easy, choosing love over the life she has established. But she cannot countenance living without Suraj.

Missing him during the week when he is at Cambridge and she is at her college is bad enough, made bearable only by the thought of seeing him at the weekend. She cannot imagine never seeing him again, being separated from him by an ocean.

Over the lonely years since the air raid she has longed for love, secretly wished to create a home of her own like Winnie has done, a happy, secure family like she remembers from her childhood before George was stillborn.

When she held her nephew Toby in her arms, when she looked at Winnie's face alight with love and pride, she had thought that perhaps holding her own child, holding the future in her hands, would finally exorcise the ghosts and sorrows of her past.

When she looks into Suraj's eyes and sees reflected there her own insecurities, her own emptiness – when they are together and they fill each other's hollow places with conversation, companionship, love, he anchoring the rootless part of her – she knows that he is the one with whom she can move on, fashion a family, a home, a future.

'I'm sure,' she says and he smiles, the worry in his eyes easing.

'Margaret.' Tender. 'I'll look after you, make sure you're never unhappy. And if it gets too bad or too much, we'll return to England. I promise.'

She looks into his eyes, intense, passionate, reflecting the dying flames from the fire, and she believes him.

She visits her sister.

'I love him.'

'I know you do,' Winnie says. 'I could read it in your letters, in the words that you were withholding, the excitement and happiness when you wrote of him. It was in practically every sentence, his name appearing everywhere.' Then, sighing as she strokes her stomach, just slightly showing with her second child, Toby sleeping peacefully in the crib beside them, 'It won't be easy for you, Meg.'

'But, Winnie…' Margaret smiles wryly. 'Nothing has ever been easy for me, and I don't think it ever will be.'

'Yes.' Winnie's eyes shining. 'You take things too much to heart, feel everything so deeply. It's what we love about you.'

'I'll miss you, and Toby.' Stroking her godchild's angelic cheek, velvet innocence. 'I won't be here to watch him and this little one grow up.' Placing her hand on her sister's stomach.

'Not only that,' her sister is gentle, 'not everyone will understand.'

Margaret nods. Winnie's own husband doesn't approve of Margaret's choice of husband, which is why, she knows, he is not present today. He must have made sure to be away when Winnie informed him of her visit.

Baron Andrew Cohen, stickler for propriety and reputation, had written to Margaret on hearing of her plans through Winnie, voicing his disapproval in no uncertain terms. 'You are a disgrace to your sister,' his letter said. 'If your parents were alive, they would be appalled. I am glad you are going to India. Stay there, if you insist upon this foolishness.'

Margaret has kept the letter from her sister. She was always unsure of the Baron, not able to completely trust him, although he loves her sister and is good to her, and this letter proved her instincts right. But it had hurt. Especially the mention of her parents.

Surely her parents would be happy for her? But too many years have passed since she lost them, and much as it depresses her, her recollections of them are now hazy at best, and there is no way of guessing what their reactions to her news would be.

'You cannot choose who you fall in love with.' Winnie sighs. 'I know it better than anyone. But, Meg, did you have to make it so difficult for yourself?'

Through her tears, Margaret smiles.

Her sister strokes Margaret's cheek. 'You're the strongest person I know. Although if it gets too much, I'm here. You can always…'

'Thank you, Winnie.' Her slender, beautiful sister, even lovelier in pregnancy, fragile but indomitable, with a steely core. 'I'm upset that I won't be close to you and your children, watch them grow up. But Suraj… He's the only one for me.'

*

Margaret visits the farm, informs her aunt and uncle, 'I've found someone to marry.'

'About time. We've heard of your shenanigans, gallivanting with all sorts, unchaperoned.' Her uncle snorts.

'He's a lawyer,' she continues, undeterred by this tirade.

Her aunt waits, eyes bright. Her uncle takes a big slurp of his ale.

Her cousins, who are both present, eye her eagerly.

Her cousins have heard of Suraj, Margaret understands, seeing their knowing smirks, the glances they exchange. This is why they contrived to be present when she was visiting, not wanting to miss their parents' response to Margaret's news about her choice of husband.

'He is from India.'

'A coolie?' Her aunt and uncle scandalised as comprehension dawns.

'Not a coolie, no. A lawyer. His name is Suraj.'

Her uncle florid, setting his ale down so hard that it spills onto the carpet, brown stain spreading darkly on beige. Her aunt's mouth working but no words coming out.

'The wedding is in...'

'You must be crazy,' her uncle roars.

'I love him.'

'This is how you repay us for taking you in? By dragging us down with you?' Her uncle getting louder the angrier he becomes, saliva foaming from the corners of his mouth.

She stands her ground, refusing to raise her voice to match his, saying coolly, 'You are invited to the wedding, all of you.'

Her cousins agog, shocked mirth, grudging admiration.

Her uncle is moved to stand up from his armchair, face suffused, eyes bloodshot, finger pointing at her in accusation. 'Get out of this house and don't ever come back!'

Margaret steps back to avoid her uncle's sour spittle, the venom in his screaming.

'Your mother must be turning in her grave.' Her aunt has finally found her voice; it is weak with shock, harsh with upset.

Margaret does not reply but walks out of the farmhouse, shutting the door silently behind her.

Before she leaves she visits the animals. She pets the pigs, the horses, the sheep, the cows, the goats and Bowie, old and tired now but happy to see her all the same, tail wagging, licking her face in joyful welcome.

She leans against the stile overlooking the meadow where she would come to escape and sketch, dandelions dancing, the scent of bluebells and wild roses, garlic and honeysuckle. The smoky green, fecund flavour of an English summer, Bowie sniffing the cow parsley at her feet.

Soft air tasting of lily of the valley and ripening apples brushes her face. She does a quick sketch, putting it all down on paper, committing it to memory. She buries her face in Bowie's flank, whispering goodbye into his fur.

And then she leaves the farm where she spent the second part of her interrupted childhood, for good.

Chapter Twenty-Seven

1922

Archana

Celebration

On the day of her wedding, Archana wakes on the mat beside her mother. The front door open for air, the smell of jasmine and dog.

Her mother bathes her gently, before dressing her in her wedding sari. Her hands are tender as they massage her limbs with coconut oil, like she did when Archana was a baby, hoping her mismatched feet, through these ministrations, would cooperate, magically becoming the same size.

By the time Archana's mother oils and combs her hair into a bun, adorning it with the jasmine garlands she has weaved from the flowers in the garden, they are both crying, the air thick and heavy with unsaid words, with everything and everyone missing.

If this was the wedding her mother had hoped and imagined for her daughter, all the womenfolk of the village would be here, getting Archana dressed, giving advice, urging her to provide her husband with a son and heir in nine months. They would be gossiping, cooking, boiling water, washing dishes, teasing each other and Archana, fighting over who would do the bride's hair, comparing weddings and husbands, arguing, making up, singing songs, shooing the men away until the bride was ready, the house festive, rent with noise and celebration.

*

The wedding is small. Archana's mother, her in-laws-to-be, her husband-to-be and a chosen few of his relatives.

The priest chants mantras, throws rice into the holy fire. Archana's sari is tied to her husband-to-be's dhoti. They walk round the fire seven times and just like that, she is a married woman.

Afterward, she touches her mother's feet, asks for her blessing, overcome by the expression on her mother's face: pride and happiness that shines through; naked hope in her eyes that Archana's married life will be better than the one she's led until now; and stark sadness, intense upset that she is trying but failing to hide at losing another daughter.

Aching for her mother who will be returning to an empty home, nervous and apprehensive, her heart beating fast and loud with trepidation, Archana accompanies her husband and in-laws to their mud abode, small but bigger than the hut she shared with her mother, nestling in the shadow of the mansion where she is to work.

Chapter Twenty-Eight

1923

Margaret

Prayer

'I heard from my parents,' Suraj says.

'Yes?'

He had written to them, informing them of his plans to marry Margaret. 'They'll accept it, I know it.' His voice fiercely hopeful, a chant, a prayer, when he told Margaret of the telegram making its way across the ocean.

For a long time there had been only silence.

Perhaps, she thinks, noting the slump of his shoulders, the hollowness in his eyes, that was better…

'They… they don't approve.'

She squeezes his hand. It hurts her to see him hurting.

And, a sudden, swift stab of fear. Is this it? Will he give her up at the first hurdle, choose his parents over her?

Please don't. I'm so ready to move to India with you. I want this like I've never wanted anything. A new beginning, a completely different experience, a fresh start with you.

But she knows how much his parents' approval means to him.

'All I've done, all my life has been to please them, to live up to their expectations of me,' he had said, his eyes haunted, as he worried about their silence.

'I'll not fit in with their plans for you, surely?' Voicing her fear, sitting on her shaking hands as she waited to hear his reply.

The darkness in his eyes, pain and melancholy, navy yellow, chased away by fierce resolve. 'Surely this one time when I want something for myself, they'll comply instead of dictating *their* plans for *my* life. And Margaret,' his eyes softening, squeezing her hand, '*you* are my life. My destiny. I believe we were meant to meet, that everything in my life before you was rehearsal, preparation for my time with you. I was not going to accept Strachey's invitation the day I met you – I had assignments to complete – but something compelled me to come anyway. And when I saw you standing under the apple blossom, smiling shyly, I knew then… A part of me that had been searching, lost, homeless, found shelter, succour.'

Margaret had stared at him, awed and overwhelmed by how he put into words exactly what she felt for him. Overcome that he felt the same.

'Our union,' Suraj was saying, 'is ordained, written in the stars. Why else the instant, intense connection? And it deepens every time I'm with you. You complete me, make me more than I can ever hope to be on my own.'

'They've disowned me,' Suraj says now, his voice a lament, stark navy with upset.

Suraj is their only son. They must have been incredibly hurt and shocked by his announcement to exercise such radical measures.

She'd known their union was not going to be easy, that people are not going to understand, that they will judge. Margaret was immensely hurt by the Baron's words and she doesn't even like him. It is even harder when loved ones disapprove, when they refuse to accept the person you love.

'I'm so sorry, Suraj,' she says out loud, although what she really wants to ask is, *Do you still feel the same way about me now? Or will you choose them over me?*

He looks up at her, eyes fiery, and her doubts dissipate like fog in the glare of the sun.

'I don't care,' he says. 'I love *you*. You are my anchor, all that matters, all I have.'

She feels her heart rise, fill, relief and joy taking her over as once again he puts into words exactly what she feels for him.

She had been flailing, rootless, even while at university, even as part of the Bloomsbury Group, until he came along and filled all the empty parts of her with love, and she discovered her capacity for the joy that she thought had been forever lost.

Ever since she lost her childhood home, despite her years at the farm, she has felt homeless.

Not any longer.

For Margaret, Suraj is home.

And she now knows for a fact that he feels the same way. Even at the cost of being disowned by his parents, he wants to be with her. Yet worry nudges her, insidious, palpable. She feels guilty for voicing it when Suraj is so upset. 'Does this mean we'll stay here?'

She has set her heart on going to India. For there, in a country she cannot begin to imagine, she will wipe out her past, start afresh with the love of her life, in time creating a family, recreating the happiness she remembers from her childhood.

His eyes darken. 'I can't work here, Margaret. I've tried. I applied for a few jobs and they all rejected me. But they take people far less qualified just because their skin colour is acceptable while mine is not.' His voice like pith, an unpalatable bitter yellow. 'And I want to do something positive, bring about change for India. I want to make a difference. I've written to my oldest friend. We'll live in Bombay with him. You won't regret it. If you're unhappy we'll come back.'

His gaze bright amber and liquid with passionate promise.

Bombay. She rolls the exotic name around on her tongue. Her heart full, she says, 'I'll go anywhere with you, Suraj. Being with you is what makes me happy.'

He smiles, the sadness in his eyes, the hollowness in his face easing.

She goes into his open arms, where she feels safe, loved.

Chapter Twenty-Nine

1922

Archana

Different Sides

Archana's mother-in-law wakes her up on her first morning as a married woman, by pushing aside the sari that acts as a curtain dividing the single room of the hut, separating the mat she shares with her husband from the mats where her in-laws sleep, apart from each other, on different sides of the bisected room.

It is barely dawn, the air sweet and perfumed with jasmine, and Archana sleepily rubs the drowsiness from her eyes as she adjusts to her new surroundings. She is sore between her legs and waddles a little as she walks, following her mother-in-law to the courtyard to pick flowers for puja, worship, and collect dew-moistened twigs to light the hearth. The sky is deep navy tinted pink-gold. Archana looks at its wide expanse, musing, with a tug of ache, on whether her mother is doing the same, sitting in the doorway, the dog at her feet, morning dawning gently, softly over the fields. She wonders if her mother slept last night or missed her daughter beside her on the threadbare mat, their dreams mingling in sleep.

All that long day, Archana's mother-in-law instructs her on the chores – seemingly endless – required of her. When she completes them to the old lady's satisfaction, she acknowledges it with a grunt.

But if she isn't happy with Archana's work – which seems to be almost all the time – she's not averse to expressing her dissatisfaction loudly enough for all the neighbouring wives to hear as well: 'This is what I have to put up with, a daughter-in-law not only slow, what with the limp, and dark as tea dregs, but green behind the ears as well! Do I have to explain everything? Did your mother not teach you anything, girl? What have you been doing all your life?'

Archana bites her tongue to check the retort that threatens to spill out of her mouth at the woman's insult to her mother. She scrunches her eyes to stop the tears of homesickness and tiredness that threaten to spill, even as she holds her thighs together to try to ease the throbbing, a reminder of her wifely duty to her husband the previous night and what is to come again tonight.

Finally, the sun begins its descent, slipping down behind the magnificent mansion in the shadow of which their village rests and where she will start work as a servant the next morning.

'You need to make breakfast, wash the dishes, cook lunch, pack some for your husband before you leave for work,' her mother-in-law instructs.

The sky is a kaleidoscope of colours, the yawning crimson of a scream, the mauve and bloodied orange of a bruise, like how her heart feels, stripped raw and hurting, wounded by yearning, missing her life as it was.

'Come,' her mother-in-law says, handing Archana a basket of tobacco and beedie leaves – the sight of them once again inciting in Archana an ache for her mother, who will be sitting in the courtyard under the tamarind tree, deftly fashioning beedies, missing her daughter, only the dog for company. Her eyes sting but she sniffs her tears away.

This is my duty. Ma wouldn't want it any other way.

'We don't own our daughters,' her mother would say when
Archana and Radha were children. Her mother plaiting Archana's
hair, her voice wistful, the cinnamon-scented breeze ruffling the
coconut tree fronds and spraying droplets of rain on their heads
like blessings. 'You belong to your husband's family – we only
look after you for them.'

Archana had laughed, uncomprehending. 'But, Ma, we are
yours and Da's—'

Radha had cut in, dancing around Archana and their mother,
the dog barking, a crown of marigold flowers in her hair, looking
like a queen, Archana thought. 'I belong to nobody but you and
Da and Archana.' Her voice firm, brooking no argument.

'Come on, stop dawdling,' her mother-in-law snaps, jerking
Archana sharply away from her daydreams.

Archana follows her mother-in-law with the basket, bending
to go through the small entrance to their hut. Her mother-in-law
is naturally hunched and doesn't need to.

Her father-in-law is dozing in the corner of the hut, which
is all he has done, all day. He had to be woken for meals and
afterward, he would sit for a bit under the banana trees outside
and would, once again, fall asleep, snore where he was sitting,
until his wife prodded him and told him to take himself indoors
to his mat by the window.

Beside and around them, from all the other huts, women spill
out, carrying similar baskets. They assess Archana curiously and
unashamedly, addressing her mother-in-law, 'She's a bit dark, isn't
she? And is that a limp?' Sounding unimpressed.

'She'll do,' her mother-in-law grunts, 'as long as she gives us
a grandchild and soon. My wish is to hold my grandchild in my
arms before I die.'

*

The women gather at a clearing – the grass flattened, the mud smooth, devoid of stones – their children running wild in the fields beyond, making the most of the waning light before the sun sets completely and dusk descends.

The women range in age from a bit older than Archana to grandmothers, but their eyes are all the same. Tired. Worn down by life.

They chew paan and chatter, teasing and joking – their laughter slightly manic, as if it has been reined in for too long – as they squat on the mud and start rolling beedies.

Archana sits beside her mother-in-law, gingerly, for she is still sore between her thighs, trying to suppress her sigh of relief as she realises it is the first time she has sat down all day. Even her lunch, a few mouthfuls of rice, left over after her in-laws had finished eating – her husband was at work in the fields – had been consumed standing up, her mother-in-law telling her to hurry up and wash the dishes.

'Mind if I sit here next to you?' asks a girl about her age, pretty but almost as dark as Archana.

Not waiting for a reply, she lowers herself to the space beside Archana.

Archana's mother-in-law is busy in conversation with a cluster of women as ancient as her.

Archana turns to the girl and, emboldened by her mother-in-law's distraction, says, archly, 'Why ask, if you're going to do it anyway?'

The girl laughs, pealing bells, birdsong.

Infectious.

And for the first time since getting married, Archana laughs too.

'I like you. We're going to be friends,' the girl declares, confidently. 'The moment I saw you, I knew it.'

The air smells of evening and delight. The sky, which a minute ago had appeared like a wound, a portent, now looks festive, a rainbow of celebration.

'I'm Pramila by the way and I know your name is Archana. I heard that witch' – the girl points surreptitiously at Archana's mother-in-law, who is deep in discussion with a toothless, hairless woman, and Archana swallows down a gasp at the girl's audacity – 'over there, yelling at you loud enough for the whole village to overhear. I saw you do your chores as she asked but there was something in your eyes... I hope you cursed her to hell, and if you did, the next time please will you include my mother-in-law as well?'

She nudges a shocked, grinning Archana with her elbow, at ease with physical contact.

'I've been waiting for ever for someone my age to come to the village. And here you are! We're going to have such fun together.'

Pramila's face glows and, despite being dark-complexioned, she reminds Archana of her sister, the girl Radha had once been: opinionated, bubbly and mischievous, twinkles dancing in her bright, soulful eyes. This girl is different from the other women here in that the weariness that characterises their every move-ment – even their laughter tinged with it, the disillusionment, the realisation that this is all there is to life – is missing. She is vibrant, lively.

'It hurts a couple of times, and then you get used to it,' she says, her face soft with empathy as Archana moves position and winces.

Archana cannot help the flush that takes over her face.

'Look at you, so demure.' Pramila smiles. And, winking cheekily, 'I close my eyes and imagine the boy I had a crush on growing up instead of my husband. It really helps.'

Archana blushes some more, Pramila laughing merrily.

And sitting there, stuffing beedies, part of this group of women, laughter and chatter around and beside her, sounds of children playing in the fields, her friend – her *friend* – next to her, for once not solitary and shunned and ignored because of what Radha has done, Archana muses that, apart from her tyrant of a mother-in-law and the soreness between her thighs, which her friend assures her will soon ease, being married is not so bad after all.

Chapter Thirty

1924

Margaret

Treasured

They are wed in the garden at Charleston, weak spring sun, wet grass underfoot sparkling with dew and the proximity of summer, yellow daffodils bright as promises, a profusion of crocuses and hyacinths, the fragile scent of budding life, the lingering taste of adrenaline, anticipation and excitement, of friendships, precious and treasured, and tentative hope for an unforeseeable future.

'I wanted my parents' blessing upon our union but since they're not inclined to give it, shall we get married in England?' Suraj had suggested.

'We were going to host a party for you: congratulations and goodbye, here at Charleston,' Vanessa had said, holding Margaret's palms in both of hers, eyes shining. 'So why not get married here? It's fitting. After all, this is where you met.'

A curious blend of joy (at being wedded to her love in the setting where Margaret has found acceptance), sorrow (at the impending parting) and thrill (at the new, bright future in an exotic country awaiting her). Marrying among friends, this group who have welcomed and included her in their coterie, thus making her not only a more confident version of herself and offering her a different, broad-minded, view of the world but also bringing about her meeting Suraj.

'Who would have thought,' they'd exclaimed, joyous and admiring, when she informed them of her plans, 'that you, of all people, would be brave enough to go through with this? We all take lovers but to marry someone of different race and background, move countries to be with him, defy convention in this way! Good on you, Margaret. You've proved the most daring of us all.'

The Bloomsbury Group have shared their lives with her and opened their homes to her. They have been warm and non-judgemental and accepting of both her and Suraj and their love. A gift that, the more prejudice and anger Margaret encounters for daring not only to love but *marry* an Indian man, the more she appreciates.

When applying for the marriage licence, the looks from people, ranging from shock to disgust, frowns and sneers: 'You're marrying *whom*?'

Even in the halls, her housemates giving her snide looks of contempt, puzzled bemusement. 'You're giving up your course and moving to India with a… a…?'

'He's a lawyer.'

Their gaze slinking away from hers. That's not what they were hinting at.

People she barely knows wondering if she is right in the head, asking if she knows what she is doing.

Advice from all quarters. Well meant. Unwelcome.

Winnie has travelled up for the wedding, heavily pregnant and yet stunning, garnering plenty of appreciative looks. She has not brought Toby along. 'He's with Nurse. He would only get in the way.'

'I'd like to have seen my godson, Winnie.' Margaret gently chiding.

Winnie's eyes filling.

Margaret knows it is the Baron's doing. He must have forbidden Toby from attending and she is sure he did not want Winnie to come either. But Winnie has.

Her sister. Defiant. Beautiful. Sad that Margaret will be moving so far away.

Winnie looks on proudly, eyes shining, as Margaret's friends read poems they have written for Margaret and Suraj, present paintings and sculptures they have fashioned for them.

'You have great talent. Make use of it, Margaret. Keep on painting. It is a shame that you have to give up your course, and I will miss you, immensely. I wish you all the very best in your new life.' Mrs Danbourne's eyes glowing wet, mirroring Margaret's.

'In a short time you've become a cherished friend, Margaret. It's been a pleasure watching you come out of your shell. Suraj, you've achieved quite the transformation; you've converted our quiet, shy Margaret into a daring adventurer, galvanised by love. It is a brave thing to do, leaving all one knows and is familiar with behind to embark on a new life in a different country across the world. We admire you for it, Margaret, and wish you and Suraj all the very best. We will miss you. Do write, keep in touch and keep painting.' Vanessa raises her glass and there are cheers of 'hear, hear' and much sniffing and eye-rubbing.

The party goes on well into the night, although Winnie leaves in the afternoon.

'I have to get back for Toby.' Her sparkling eyes reflecting all they have been through. 'Mother, Father and Evie would have been proud of you, Meggie. You have wonderful friends and

Suraj is lovely. You've chosen well. I know you will be happy.'
She swallows, holds Margaret tight, her bump between them,
planting a kiss on Margaret's forehead, her scent of crushed
lavender and love.

Sometime during the evening, as the fire dies down and friends
sit around sharing anecdotes, their faces flushed from drink and
the weak light from dying embers, burnt peach, the soft scent
of waning day mingling with pungent overtones of wine and
amusement, the peppery flavour of grilled meat, the sweet pink
taste of marshmallows, sticky and rich with melted chocolate,
Suraj, her *husband*, takes her hand and they slip away.

He leads her along the ridge of the downs, to their spot among
the tall grass from where they can catch a glimpse of the sea in
the distance, dark and gleaming, its roar gentle and subdued by
night. He kisses her and gently lays her down among the reeds.
And in the gathering, whispering darkness, the sky above them,
vast and wide, the land below them stretching to the sea, the
wind humming a lullaby to newly emerging leaves, rousing a
haunting chorus from the reeds, the call of birds flying home to
roost, the scent of green fecundity and an overflowing heart, he
makes love to her.

PART 4

HOME

Chapter Thirty-One

1923

Archana

Missing

When Archana goes on her monthly visit to her mother, she finds her missing.

She visits her mother on the last Sunday of every month, her day off at the mansion, when her husband takes a break from working the fields so he is around to keep his parents company. Her mother-in-law begrudges her even this, trying to pile her with chores before she leaves to hold her back, but in this her husband stands firm.

'Her mother is all alone. Archana needs to visit, check she's doing okay.'

For this kindness from her taciturn husband, who usually only grunts, allowing his mother free rein in the running of the household (which, Archana is beginning to realise, is a survival tactic as much as anything, for if not they'd never hear the end of it), Archana is infinitely grateful.

She longs for the one day each month when she gets to see her mother. If her mother looks well, Archana makes up some excuse and leaves early (although it wrenches her heart, seeing her mother's face fall), and walks the three miles to her sister.

The first time she had visited after her wedding, her sister had clasped her to her chest and cried, her children toddling around them.

Afterward, Radha held her at arm's length. 'You look well. Being married suits you.'

'You do too,' Archana lied; in truth she was shocked at how thin her sister was getting, how run-down.

'Tell me,' her sister said, clasping her hand, 'all about it.'

The children climbed all over them and Archana planted kisses on their dirty cheeks and said, 'It's alright. The in-laws are a pain.'

She didn't want her sister knowing that all things considered, it wasn't as bad as she had been expecting, certainly many times better than her sister's life.

'Tell me your routine. Everything.' Radha eager. A flash of the imperious sister of her childhood appearing briefly.

'It is hard, tiring, managing the household and working as a servant at the mansion,' she said, making it sound worse than it was.

Radha's son pestered her for stories. She tickled him and he giggled with the uninhibited abandon of childhood. When both children were tired, they climbed trustingly into Archana's lap, chewed on a lock of her hair and fell asleep, curled up against her chest, their long lashes sweeping over dirty cheeks, their warm weight anchoring her. And she wondered how it would be to have her own, a living breathing bundle that depended so entirely upon her, vulnerable and perfect.

On this Sunday she visits her mother, thinking as always, 'If Ma appears well, I'll go on to visit Radha.' But as she nears the house, she is filled with foreboding. The dog is running around the tamarind tree in circles; the air is charged with the calm stillness that heralds disaster, thick and cloying with the aroma of fermented fruit.

'Ma,' she calls, her voice barely above a whisper.

Normally, her mother would be sitting under the tamarind tree, the vantage point from where she could see all the way to the next hill, from which direction Archana would arrive. She would be fashioning jasmine flowers into garlands for Archana to take back with her as a gift to appease her mother-in-law, along with jars of her famous lime rind pickle (Archana not having the heart to tell her mother that nothing she or her mother did would appease her mother-in-law, except perhaps giving her a grandson). As soon as the dog started barking she would look up and when her anxious eyes found Archana she would stand and wave, one hand clutching her sari skirt, which held the jasmine flowers and wreaths, her face, her whole body lifting in a glorious smile.

Archana would run down the hill as fast as her limp allowed and across the stream and up the next hill, these last few paces seeming longer than her entire journey here, and throw her arms round her mother, the dog barking excited circles at their feet, her mother's scent of jasmine and fried onions and tiredness and joy.

But now, her mother is not to be seen and Archana is distressed.

She limps up to the hut as quickly as she can, breathless, her heart wild and stabbing, the dog whining and running up to the open front door, where her mother lies, a crumpled little waif in a worn sari.

Please, please, Archana prays as she approaches her mother, trepidation and panic. Her whole body trembling as she turns her over.

She is breathing in hot, ragged puffs and Archana is at once relieved and terrified. Gathering her mother in her arms, she trudges to the local wise woman's house, two fields away, as fast as she can, cursing her shorter leg, which is slowing her down, praying and sobbing and wishing her sister was here so she wouldn't have to deal with this alone; Radha, with her two strong, perfect legs, could have got their mother the help she needed faster.

Her mother is boiling, burning Archana's arms through the sari. Unresponsive.

Please, gods, Archana prays.

The wise woman takes one look at Archana's tear-studded face and allows her in. It is the first time since Radha eloped that Archana or her mother have been welcome in that house, or any other in the village for that matter.

Her mother had hoped Archana's marriage would change things, but evidently being associated with an untouchable trumps everything else. Archana tastes her mother's loneliness, all alone in the hut, shunned by villagers, every evening as she herself sits in the circle of women in her husband's village, as she laughs with her friend, Pramila, as she goes about her chores, her mother-in-law grumbling at her. She hurts for her mother, starved of human company, stuffing beedies under the tamarind tree, sewing by the light of the candle while talking to the dog, counting down the days until Archana visits.

The wise woman concocts pastes of strange-smelling herbs in her dark kitchen, making poultices that she applies to Archana's mother's prone and unresponsive, burning body.

As night falls, the wise woman's hut now pitch-black, scented with aromatic brews, the starry canopy of sky overhead vast and fathomless, pinpricks of fireflies piercing the dark, her mother's fever finally breaks.

Archana sobs with relief. The fields are a dark swathe, waving and whispering assurances in the perfumed gloom, the breeze tasting of fruit and spices caressing her face.

'She'll be alright.' The wise woman's voice is gravelly, sombre with the gravity of a thousand answered prayers. 'You should go. Your husband will be worried.'

It is only then that Archana remembers him, her duties as a married woman. 'I can't leave her.'

'She'll be fine, I promise. She needs to rest.'

'I—'

She is interrupted by voices outside, shattering the quiet gloaming. Candles flickering in the fields, competing with the fireflies.

'Archana?' A familiar voice. Her husband. Here!

She stares at the wise woman, wondering if she is capable of sorcery, if she has conjured Archana's husband up just by mentioning him.

'She's here,' the wise woman calls when Archana does not respond.

A moment later, her husband appears at the cloth door of the wise woman's hut, looking put out. 'We were anxious when you didn't come home. I had to leave my parents to come looking for you.'

He seems worried and it surprises her. He cares for her, in his own way, she realises then, her gruff husband who hardly talks to her and only touches her when he goes about the business of creating a child and heir.

'My mother…' She is unable to keep her tears in check. 'She…'

He pats her awkwardly on the shoulder, embarrassed by her tears.

'She's turned a corner, she'll be alright,' the wise woman assures.

'I'm worried about her here all alone. If I hadn't found her in time, she…' Archana shudders, unable to complete the thought.

'I tell you what, when she has recovered we'll ask her to move to our village. She makes her livelihood selling beedies and taking in sewing, isn't it? Well, she can do it at our village. Manthu died recently and since his wife was gone before him and his children have moved to the city, his hut's empty...'

Archana gapes at her husband in awe as his words sink in, a slow joy spreading through her. She has never heard him speak so many words at once. And what welcome words they are!

'You mean it?'

He smiles, nodding.

Much as Archana wants to believe him, take him at his word, it sounds too good to be true. 'Shouldn't you... check with your mother first?'

His smile disappears, a frown taking its place. 'I give in to her in most cases because it's easiest. But *I* am the breadwinner of the household. I'll decide what's best for my wife and her mother.'

She smiles tremulously through her tears.

'Come home.' His voice is gentle. 'Once your mother is better, she can move to our village. I'll make the arrangements.'

'Thank you.'

He smiles again.

The next morning, when her husband informs his mother of his plans for Archana's mother, as Archana had expected, there is mayhem.

'Bad enough your wife stayed out so late yesterday. You had to leave us to go look for her, fetch her back. We were worried out of our minds.' Sour spittle gushing from her mother-in-law's furious mouth. 'I kept quiet, didn't say a word because you asked me not to. But it's just not done. Archana's duty as a married woman is to her *husband's* family – when she married you, she chose to cast in her lot with us and *not* her mother. We are generous, allowing her to visit her mother every month, and now even that is not enough? You want to bring that woman here, into our village?' Her mother-in-law screeching. Women from neighbouring huts craning their necks to watch. Men on their way to the fields stopping to stare.

Pramila, from where she is sweeping the small compound in front of her hut with fresh cow dung, shaking her head.

'She's all alone. She might fall ill again. If she dies, it will be on us.' Archana's husband's voice calm, steady, in direct contrast to his mother's.

'How? Your wife's mother is *not* our responsibility.'

'Ma, she's old and frail.'

'She's bad luck, a widow, one daughter with a limp and another who is—'

'She's moving here.' Her husband's voice soft but firm, with steel in it. 'Archana will visit her today, and bring her back with her if she's up to the journey.'

'What?! And miss a day of work?' Her mother-in-law's voice as high-pitched as Archana has ever heard it, shock, fury and upset.

'Leela will inform them up at the mansion.'

Her mother-in-law's mouth open so wide that a crow could climb in. 'Your wife has turned your head.' Sniffing loudly and turning away. 'If she loses that job, I don't know how we'll manage. Such a cushy job we've got for her and she…'

Archana does not wait to hear any more. Her husband is nodding at her, mouthing, 'You go.'

He is kind, she thinks as she walks to the village where she grew up, past her mother's abandoned hut and through the fields to the wise woman's house, where the dog keeps vigil, bounding up in a frenzy of joyful barks upon seeing Archana.

A good man. Her heart warmed by her husband – not given to touching or displays of affection but, in his own way, caring for her.

And so it is decided.

Her mother moves into Manthu's old hut, a few paces from Archana's own.

Her mother-in-law takes to watching Archana through squinted eyes, grumbling about her bewitching her son. Archana ignores her, her heart snug, worry eased, knowing her mother is nearby.

She looks in on her mother every day on her way to and from work, as her hut is on the way, her mother-in-law's gripes falling on deaf ears. And the nights when her husband reaches for her, Archana, who, until now has only endured his fumblings, wanting them over quickly so she can sleep – knowing she has to be up before dawn the next morning to do all the chores her mother-in-law decrees urgent and inescapable, more every day – submits willingly. The thought of having a child who is like this man, quietly kind, honourable – provided Archana isn't afflicted by the curse his previous wives have succumbed to – is welcome.

'*Aiyyo…*' Archana's mother cries.

'Ma, are you okay?' Archana calls from where she is sitting next to Pramila in the clearing outside their huts, while her mother-in-law, sitting on her other side, grumpily mutters under her breath.

'Yes. I just pricked myself with the needle, that's all.' Her mother is blinking.

'Here,' one of the ladies says, deftly tearing a strip off her sari and bandaging Archana's mother's hand. 'You're getting too old to sew,' the woman chides gently, affectionately.

The other women stretch their tired bodies. 'Tell us about it.'

Everyone nodding agreement, even the younger women, old before their time. They are all sewing and stuffing beedies in the failing light. They keep an eye on their children playing in the fields, high-pitched voices calling out to each other, laughter, cows lowing, dogs barking, wind fragranced with waning day sighing in the trees above them; and on their hearths where rice, riddled with stones, is bubbling. They will have that with pickle or, if they are lucky, vegetables. The scent of dust and gruel. The evening rich with colour: the saffron of dust, the cerise-tinted, maroon-splashed grey of the setting sun.

The men are gathered in one of the huts, drinking liquor brewed from the sap of palm trees, the roar of their laughter reaching their womenfolk every so often.

When the sun has set and the mosquitoes are reigning, they will stumble to their huts and eat the weak, stone-riddled congee with pickle their wives place in front of them, cursing when their few remaining teeth connect with an especially hard pebble.

Beside her, Archana's friend Pramila, another young wife married to a much older man, like herself, muses, 'My husband didn't finish his breakfast today, he looked hot and bothered. I worried all morning that he was ill and going to die, and I'd have to do sati.'

Archana shivers. 'Oh dear, I hope he's…'

Pramila nudges her. 'He returned at lunchtime looking much better, and had double portions of my potato curry! Turns out he'd had constipation from my mother-in-law's cooking yesterday – I had been to the temple so *she* cooked for a change.'

Pramila giggles, a burst of infectious mirth, and Archana can't help but join in. Her mother-in-law shoots her an admonishing glare: 'Get on with the beedies now.'

'Witch!' Pramila snorts and Archana swallows down the laughter bubbling inside her.

It's been a year since Archana's wedding and she feels, if not happy, then settled in her role as wife and daughter-in-law, and servant at the big house. Her desire to learn, to go to college, is buried in the depths of her mind. She now has a friend and is part of a community, accepted into it, her limp ignored, her status as wife wiping out the cloud Radha's marriage cast on herself and her mother.

If she provides her husband with a child, her place within the family and in the community will be cemented even more, and she hopes she'll be able to do so soon. She prays that she'll survive childbirth, that whatever curse befell her husband's previous two wives will not strike her too – not that she believes there *is* a curse as such, but one can never be too sure…

She is even more content since her mother moved into the village, although it makes it harder to come up with excuses to visit her sister.

Archana misses her sister intensely, the Radha she knew growing up, feisty and full of life, especially when she is with Pramila commiserating over bossy mothers-in-law, the woes of being married, their husbands, their demands. Sharing with Pramila makes it possible to laugh even though there isn't much to laugh about.

If only Radha was close by, like her mother is now, Archana would be happiest, she thinks as she goes about her chores when she is back from the mansion: massaging her father-in-law's scrawny legs with oil, combing her mother-in-law's sparse grey, wiry hair, cooking supper and watching her husband and in-laws eat while her stomach contracts with hunger, making do with the meagre leftovers.

Yet still, I'm luckier than Radha. I have Ma nearby. I have found respect and have been accepted into this community. I'm blessed.

Chapter Thirty-Two

India 1924

Margaret

Tangible

When the ship anchors at Bombay Port, Margaret's husband squeezes her hand.

'We're home.' His voice singing.

Home.

All morning they've stood on deck, hand in hand, angling to get their first glimpse of land, India, the fizzy scarlet thrill of excitement and anticipation, barely contained, in Margaret's mouth.

And now here it is spread out before her, in all its exotic busyness.

Her new home.

The port bustling with people attired in eye-catching clothes that glint in the sun, strange smells, everything coated in dust, a peach sheen, the air thick with it, boats painted in bright colours dotting the surging yellow water.

She lifts her head up to the bleached-white, foreign sky, the sun hot and blinding, making silver spots dance before her eyes, moisture slide down her face, and she smiles, tasting heat and adventure, dazzling gold.

*

Suraj's friend Amit is there to receive them.

Suraj's familiar beloved features lift in joyous pleasure at the sight of his friend and they chatter away to each other, a rapid back-and-forth volley, catching up on their years apart, leaving Margaret free to take in the sights of the port, vendors hawking mounds of spices, cloth toys and multi-hued reams of gleaming cloth, the native men barely dressed, the women overly so, colourful saris covering them, veils shrouding their faces, their hands jangling with bracelets, multicoloured glass twinkling and musical, the slimy water, the air pungent with humidity, redolent with the piquant, tart aroma of exotic spices.

Amit's gaze rests briefly on Margaret before turning away shiftily, a look she has had plenty of occasion to get used to, having been on the receiving end of it often enough during their voyage here when people saw her and Suraj together and it dawned on them that they were *married*. It was a conversation-stopper. People did not know what to say or do. Most blushed, embarrassed, and changed the topic, avoiding looking at them again or talking to them.

Several matrons took it upon themselves to come up to Margaret, solicitous, scandalised: 'We heard a rumour that you and that… that native are married.' Disdain and disgust dripping from their voices. 'There must be some mistake, child.'

Margaret, her words biting: 'There's no mistake. He's my husband. I love him.'

Their faces uncomprehending that she would *choose* this.

They ignored her after, giving her a wide berth.

It was wonderful to be left alone with her new husband and they delighted in getting to know everything about each other, the music of the waves the backdrop to their love.

*

But now, Suraj's friend's furtive look stabs in a way all the others didn't and for a brief moment, Margaret's excitement, her joy at finally being here, in India – this place where she will begin again, creating a wonderful life for herself and Suraj and the family that will follow, replete with the happiness and contentment she recalls from her early childhood – is in danger of being doused. For Amit is judging her, just like everyone else.

His brief gaze accusing.

'I've known him from childhood. He's my oldest friend. His parents have a house in Bombay, where they were living until recently. But they've returned to their native village. Amit lives there now and he's kindly offered to put us up until I can convince my parents to see sense,' Suraj had said.

Margaret does not want to feel beholden to Amit. He is nothing at all like Vanessa, who had welcomed her into her home and life with open arms. But perhaps she is being sensitive, taking it all too much to heart. Making too much of his look. In any case, she will *not* allow him to cast a pall on her first day, her initial impressions of this incredible country that spawned her husband.

She looks at Suraj animatedly discussing the troubles in India with Amit. He is different here, she notices – he seems more confident. Standing straighter.

A woman sits beside a pile of bright yellow fruit that Margaret has never seen before, attracting a host of flies. She is draped in shiny maroon cloth, studded with sequins that catch the light, covering her completely, even her face, only her eyes showing, bright, inquisitive black. She flicks at a fly that has dared come too close, a slender brown hand emerging from the folds of cloth. It is choked by bracelets, red and gold and green, dancing and chiming a tinkly rhythm.

The horses clip-clop, the groom talking to them in a sing-song tongue. Vendors call out their wares, thrusting out flower garlands and toys, sweetmeats smelling of oil and spices. 'Mem-sahib, for you.'

A man beats a tambourine, and a bear – a real, live, shaggy black-furred bear! – dances beside him, a crowd gathered around, watching avidly, comprising of men and raggedy-clothed children. Even a cow and a couple of emaciated dogs weave companionably through the mob.

Margaret snakes her hand through her husband's. He smiles at her, squeezing her palm, while continuing to talk to his friend.

She takes a deep breath of zesty air, sticky with heat, heavy, almost tangible and so very different from the cool, honeysuckle-scented English breeze, and she smiles.

Chapter Thirty-Three

2000

Emma

Facade

'Please don't go public with this, Emma,' David implores. 'I honestly did not realise how big the paper would become and once it did, I couldn't…' Wiping his face with his hands, sweating, even though the heating isn't on and the house is cold.

'You shouldn't have published it at all. What were you thinking?' she cries. 'Do you realise what a tricky situation this puts me in?'

'If you don't *do* anything, there will be no situation.' His voice rising with urgency.

She barely registers him, thinking aloud. 'It will destroy our family. Chloe—'

'Forget family. What about *my* reputation?'

Now she hears him. Stops pacing.

He has stopped too, his gaze mortified as he realises what he's just said.

'I didn't mean it.'

But he *did*. They both know it.

'I'm sorry.' His eyes, the desperation in them. His hand, pockmarked with liver spots, stretched out towards her. And for the second time in the space of a few hours, she sees the real David instead of the elevated heroic version she has persisted, all these years, in believing him to be. A fragile, faulty, pathetic, *selfish* man. He doesn't care about her – or even Chloe – as much as he does himself.

She has fallen in love with a lie. A facade. Has been in love with a man who isn't real all these years, wasted her best years on him.

Even after he showed her a glimpse of his real self when he turned his back on Emma, pregnant and afraid, she still nursed her love for him – fool that she was. She then compounded the mistake by forgiving him and, years later when he came grovelling, welcomed him back into her life and that of her daughter, letting her daughter love him.

And it has led to this…

She should have known he would always put himself first.

Even now, he is panicking, she understands, only because his reputation is in her hands. He is not thinking of either her or Chloe. He is thinking of no one but himself.

She walks away from him, his pleading, his wretchedness.

She sits in her daughter's room, Chloe's beautiful, angelic face grounding her, calming her. She knows David won't come in here – Chloe is a light sleeper, waking at the slightest sound.

She sits out the night in Chloe's room, watching her daughter sleep, while in the living room the man she loves, who isn't the man she's wished him to be, paces.

She looks at her daughter and wonders if she can inflict the media circus, all the ugliness that will follow if she goes public with David's hoax, upon Chloe. What price Emma's principles if Chloe is dragged into the limelight of a very public, very dirty scandal, involving her mother and her father on opposite sides?

For a long time it had been just herself and Chloe. And it had been fine. Better than that even; close to perfect, at times. Worse at times too, of course.

Then David came, professed his love, declared, 'I've never really got over you.'

Gullible fool that she was, Emma, delighted that he felt the same way she did, took him back.

And Chloe, just like her mother unable to resist his charm, had accepted him, loved him, completely, unconditionally, wholeheartedly.

He never wanted you, she whispers to her daughter in her head. *But now that you're here in all your adorable perfection, he loves you. He'll always be part of your life. Can I bring this ignominy upon him, upon all of us? Will you hate me if I do so? Will you blame me for breaking up our family? Will you take his side, the side of the father who did not want you?*

Her daughter stirs in her sleep and Emma leans close, breathing in her peppermint and vanilla scent.

What should I do, Chloe? You look up to me for answers. Well, this is one question I don't know how to answer. Why did I choose that particular project? Why didn't I pay heed to David's objections? Why did I stupidly, stubbornly insist on following that line of research, digging out that discrepancy? Why, why, why?

If I break up our family, destroy your father's reputation, expose his work as fraudulent, you'll forgive me in time. Won't you?

As dawn washes away the sins of night, Emma decides what she will do, at least in the short term.

After dropping Chloe off at school, she will visit her grandmother. Margaret is calm and clear-headed and Emma has always turned to her, bypassing her hippy mother, when she's needed help and advice. Margaret has never once failed her and although she's ill and ailing, Emma knows she will not let her down now.

*

'Ah, Emma! Margaret's having a good day. She's not in as much pain and has been able to sit outside, in the bower. She asked after you just this morning. She was convinced you were coming to visit and here you are – she must be psychic.' Margaret's nurse, Anne, says, without taking a breath, sentences tumbling out at breakneck speed, as is her way.

Emma is not surprised that her grandmother sensed she needed her – Margaret has had a knack, over the years, of telephoning Emma just when she was at her lowest.

Despite the fact that her grandmother was always travelling with work, and was hardly ever in England, she was always there for Emma, at the end of a phone line, and giving the impression that if necessary she would drop everything and come to her aid.

Her grandmother has always instinctively understood Emma in a way her mother didn't. It was her grandmother to whom Emma turned in her crises, who patiently advised her. Her mother didn't mind. A free spirit – Emma had been conceived in a commune in Argentina – all she could tell her about her father was that he could be one of many men from all over the world. Often, in her dealings with her mother, Emma would feel as if she was the parent and her mother the child. And perhaps because of this, Emma muses, she has allowed David to be the 'parent' in their relationship; and now that he has proved to be feckless, a liar, a sham, she is free-falling...

During holidays from boarding school, with both her mother and grandmother away, Emma had stayed with her uncle (who, unlike his sister and mother, eschewed travel, content to settle in one place) – and she loved it. The comfort of knowing who your neighbours were, the milk delivered every morning, walking down the street and greeting everyone, the sameness, the rituals of a life.

It was what she desired most. What her mother sniffed at.

Roots, or rather her lack of them, were precisely why Emma had wanted to read history ever since she saw the programme featuring David. She wanted to research the past and in this way feel connected to it, to *something*.

When she told her mother of her offer from Cambridge, her mother had said, 'Are you sure you want to go to university? Come travelling with me. It's a better education than stuffy book-learning!'

But her grandmother, who was in Soweto at the time, was thrilled. 'Well done,' she had written. 'I'm proud of you.'

Emma went to Cambridge. She had an affair with David. Right around the time she found out she was pregnant with Chloe, and discovered David's true nature, her mother died in an earthquake in Bangladesh.

At the memorial service for her mother – they never unearthed her body – her grandmother took one look at Emma and said, 'What's the matter? It isn't just your mother, I know.'

Emma had sobbed in Margaret's arms, for her mother, for her lover who she realised, for the first time, was not the man she thought he was.

'It's at times like this you want your mother,' her grandmother had said softly, patting her back.

'She died doing what she loved.' Her grandmother's voice wavering. 'She wanted to see the world, experience everything it had to offer, and she did.'

'Yes.' Emma sniffed.

'You do what you think best,' her grandmother advised. 'It's what I told your mother. She chose to travel although I'd have liked for her to go to university. She was happy. That is the main thing. She wouldn't have been happy at uni. Your uncle on the other hand – staying put, settling in one place is what suited him best.'

'Yes,' she mumbled into her grandmother's comforting arms.

'Life is short. You need to do what makes you happy. You want to keep this child.'

Emma nodded, overcome by her grandmother's insight.

'Then move away. Start again. I have contacts at King's, my alma mater. They'll be glad to have someone as accomplished as you.'

The pride in her grandmother's voice. Although she was not around as much as Emma would have liked, she had always believed in her.

And so Emma had moved to London, teaching at King's while working on her Masters degree. She had had Chloe, saved up and bought her flat – her grandmother helped with the deposit. She had set down roots, just as she wanted.

And then she committed the incredibly foolish mistake of allowing David back into her life despite knowing that as much as he made her happy, he also made her unhappy, that he was fickle, not to be trusted…

A year ago, she had had a call from Margaret.

'Emma.' Her grandmother, indefatigable champion of disadvantaged children, now retired but, despite being in her nineties, still working with charities around the world on a voluntary basis, smart, sharp, no-nonsense. 'I'm dying. I have stage four ovarian cancer. I cannot travel any more, I'm returning to England for good.'

Emma was shocked, upset, more than a little scared, but she'd gleaned strength from her grandmother's bravery.

'I've booked myself into a hospice specialising in palliative care. It's in Kent, not too far from you, so you can come to visit,' her grandmother said.

Emma found her voice. 'Gran, if you'd told me before, I'd have looked around and found you the best—'

'I've decided that it is where I want to die,' her grandmother declared, silencing Emma, who shuddered, unable to bear the thought.

When they arrived at the hospice – Emma had insisted on accompanying her gran – and Margaret saw the bower thriving with busy lizzies and hydrangea, encasing an angel statue in the centre, she was transfixed.

'This is where I want to be,' she said, sounding overwhelmed.

'Let's look inside before you decide, Gran,' Emma said gently, although she could see that her grandmother's mind was made up.

Margaret picked the room overlooking the bower with the statue of the angel.

'It's occupied, Gran, what about…'

But Margaret would not budge.

The resident of the room Margaret coveted had agreed – after Margaret paid a substantial amount – to transfer to another room, and she had moved in that very week.

Emma worried that her grandmother, who had travelled all her life, would find it difficult to adjust to life in England, that she might be bored.

A few weeks into Margaret's stay, when Emma went to visit, she found her, as always, in the bower, keeping watch over the angel that reigned serenely over a starburst constellation of flowers, the glorious scent of blooms and promise, the tart green apple-blossom taste of an English summer.

When she saw Emma, her grandmother smiled and patted the seat next to her.

They had sat companionably for a while, watching butterflies flit among the flowers, a daring bushy-tailed brown squirrel dash across the lawn, bees buzz and striped yellow wasps drone. Her grandmother had turned to Emma, eyes shining even though the rest of her looked weak, insubstantial. 'Finally, I have come home,' she whispered, turning to gaze, once more, upon the angel.

Chapter Thirty-Four

1924

Margaret

A Ghost

The carriage turns into a tree-lined street. Still busy but not like the hubbub of the port, the main roads. Small tiled cottages here. Rubbish piled high in ditches, a vendor selling droopy vegetables in a basket slung across his body, a man sitting beside a pyramid of what Suraj tells Margaret are coconuts: green cones with shaved woody necks.

Boys play on the road, running away as their carriage approaches. Their laughter festoons the dust-soaked air.

The carriage comes to a stop at a gate, and Margaret can just see the house, square, squat, topped by red brick, set back from the road in a compound full of exotic trees.

Suraj helps her down, flashing that tender smile he reserves just for her, flush with promise and love.

'Are you alright?' he asks, softly.

'Yes.' She smiles.

A persistent tugging at her free hand. She looks down. A beggar, bare-chested, rags covering the lower part of his body, desperate eyes huge in his emaciated face, greasy, straggly hair, sitting cross-legged on the earth beside the carriage.

'Memsahib…'

Before she can say anything Suraj's friend, Amit, is beside her. 'Shoo!' he says. Then a string of words in the native language.

The beggar still locking eyes with her, his beseeching.

Amit's words increasing in tone and tempo. The beggar finally letting go of her hand, his expression defeated, dragging himself along on the dirt. He cannot walk. He sits cross-legged on the pebble-crusted earth and pulls himself along using his hands.

Margaret is shocked. A gust of gritty wind, smelling of earth and faeces, sighing through the trees and smacking her face. Her eyes stinging, whether from the dust or the state of the beggar, she cannot say.

'Come.' Suraj leads her gently to the gate, where a man in beige uniform has materialised and is opening it. He bows politely to her as she passes but she is too shaken to smile, nodding at him instead.

The courtyard is cool, made shady by the abundance of trees, ripe fruit she cannot identify, flies buzzing, mosquitoes hovering, indolent in the spiced heat, the air a fruity, piquant feast seasoned with dust.

The house is separated from its neighbours by mossy brick walls and as they approach it, Margaret is aware of eyes spearing her from the wall to her left. She turns. A woman in a sari, head covered, only her eyes visible, holding a scrawny cat in her arms. Two pairs of eyes, the green of the cat's and the deep caramel of the woman's, curious and scandalised, flitting between Margaret's face and her gloved hand intertwined with Suraj's.

It is Margaret who looks away.

To her right, from the other compound drift the voices of two women chatting in the native tongue, the tone and cadence rising and falling, intense and charged and expressive, the words coming fast and melodic, like stones rattling inside a glass, hardly a gap between them, each woman filling in while the other falters, a staccato duet. They might have been arguing if their chatter wasn't interspersed by sudden, sharp peals of laughter.

The heat, the hostile gaze of the woman with the cat, the beggar's despairing eyes: it is all overwhelming and Margaret shivers, suddenly wanting to be away, lying among the wet reeds in Charleston, looking at the sea. Rooks cawing, the susurration of the wind, the wide grey sky above. Peace.

She quietens the sudden, surprising ache, willing herself into the here and now, the life she has chosen with her husband, that she was – *is*, she reminds herself – so excited about and looking forward to, Suraj's hand in hers, warm, loved.

A loud, long screech, a high-pitched whistle, rhythmic hissing and chugging sounds choking the laughter of the neighbours, the chatter of the kids on the street, who had resumed playing when their carriage passed. Margaret startles and Suraj squeezes her hand. The woman at the compound wall continues to stare, unfazed; the cat, which has fallen asleep in her arms, undisturbed by the sound.

'Railway tracks nearby,' Amit says, pointing to his left.

The train goes past and then there is silence again, punctuated by the gossiping of the neighbours, the voices of the boys in the street calling to each other.

They approach a semicircle of flat ground, cleared of vegetation, in front of the house. A servant is sweeping it, her sari tucked into her waist, dust rising behind her in a cloud that ignites a sneeze in Margaret. The maid looks up as they approach, blushing as Margaret smiles at her, pulling the veil of her sari closer around her face. Her dark eyes are flustered.

Amit knocks on the door, ornate, carved wood, and it is flung open by a woman in a turquoise and gold sari that makes her ebony complexion glow. Her face is not covered by a veil like all the women Margaret has seen here up until now. Her dark brown hair is gathered into a thick plait, tied with pink ribbon, and is draped across her neck and down her left shoulder like a scarf. Ringlets of hair, having escaped the plait, frame her delicate face. Her eyes are gold-flecked, wide, almond-shaped. Her lips, bee-stung red, shaped like a bow. She is beautiful.

She smiles, her starburst eyes twinkling merrily, dimples dancing in her cheeks, and Margaret becomes aware of Suraj coming to an abrupt stop, his grip on her hand tightening. She turns to him, sees that he is pale, his face blanched of colour.

'Suraj?' she begins, but the girl speaks, her voice a cascade of water, tinkling and melodious.

'You look like you've seen a ghost, Suraj. Didn't Amit tell you I'd be here?'

And then, gaily, turning to Margaret, holding out her hand. 'I'm Latha, Amit's sister. You must be Margaret.'

'Yes, I—' Margaret begins but she is rudely cut off.

'You are the woman Suraj broke off his betrothal to me to marry.'

Chapter Thirty-Five

1923

Archana

Famous

'One day,' Archana's friend Pramila says, as she deftly fills the beedie, 'I'm going to be famous.'

Archana turns to Pramila, smiling. 'You are?'

Beside her, her mother-in-law pauses in her chinwag with her cronies to nudge Archana. 'Keep working. There's no reason why your mouth and hands cannot work simultaneously.'

Alright for you, Archana thinks, sourly. Her mother-in-law has stopped rolling beedies since her son's marriage to Archana – 'I've a daughter-in-law to do those things for me. After all, the only luxury of old age is being waited upon.'

'I'm sure those previous wives of your husband preferred death to her,' Pramila hisses and Archana laughs, while agreeing with her. 'I don't know how you put up with her. My mother-in-law is bad but not so…'

'It's like having a sore tooth. It's there, it's painful, and you've no choice but to endure it,' Archana says.

In truth, it is more irritating than a sore tooth. Her mother-in-law has become even more annoying and possessive since Archana's mother moved into the village.

If Archana is a little late coming home from work, she never hears the end of it.

'You've been to visit your mother, haven't you? We wait for you all day, we're old and ailing, your duty is to *us* first. When you married into our family, you became *our* daughter.'

Which doesn't mean I stopped being hers, Archana thinks, hiding her eyes so her mother-in-law can't read the rebellion in them.

Pramila makes a face at Archana's mother-in-law from behind her *pallu* and Archana suppresses a giggle.

Pramila always makes her feel better, no matter how hard her day has been, no matter how difficult it has been to dust the books in the master's study up at the mansion and not touch them, open them. She had succumbed to temptation her first day working there and Leela – also from the village, who had taken it upon herself to induct Archana into the workings of the house, act as her superior, although as far as Archana understands, they are both maids, underlings – had yelled at her, 'Are you mad? Your job is to work here, not read the master's books! I'll be in trouble for getting you the job. I might even be sacked alongside you.'

Leela is insufferable, always expecting gratitude: 'I got you the job as a favour to your mother-in-law.' Always putting Archana down, taking the easier jobs and leaving Archana the dregs, making the threat that her work is not up to scratch and she might lose her place.

She can be petty and sometimes a bit cruel, sending Archana up and down the stairs many times just to aggravate her limp.

If a job is well done, and praise bestowed, Leela takes all the credit.

Although Archana tries not to mind, she *does*.

*

'What's the matter?' Pramila had asked the previous week when, in reply to her question about how she was finding work, Archana couldn't hide her glumness.

'Just…'

'It's Leela, isn't it?'

Archana looked at Pramila, amazed by her perspicacity. 'How did you…?'

Pramila grinned, tapping her nose with her hand. 'I have my ways.' Then, making a face, 'She's bossy, her way's always right. I can't stand her. Look at her now, sitting with the older women, laughing at their jokes even if she doesn't understand them. Don't allow her to upset you. She's not worth it, she's jealous.'

'Of *me*? Why?'

'Why?' Pramila's eyes wide. '*Why?* Because you're lovely and she's as ugly as dried, peeling tree bark!'

Archana gasped, choking on her laughter. 'You're joking!'

'Don't tell me you don't know how pretty you are?' And softly, 'Archana, you're dark, yes, but your features are so even and arresting…'

'But…'

Her sister, Radha, is the beautiful one, Archana the runt, happy to bask in Radha's glamorous shadow.

'You're one of the most beautiful women in the village. Well… Apart from me, of course.' Batting her eyelashes, so Archana laughed out loud, earning an admonishing stare from her mother-in-law and a reprimand: 'What's so funny then?'

A child called from somewhere among the fields and the crows cackling merrily in the trees above them dispersed as one into the gold and orange sky. The air smelled of fruit and surprised delight.

Once Archana's mother-in-law had gone back to gossiping with her cronies, Pramila said, 'Why do you think they chose you? It's because you're beautiful.'

'I…'

'It's why they ignored talk about your sister.'

Archana's mouth dried up. This was the first time someone in this village had brought up her sister – she had thought no one here, apart from her in-laws and husband, knew.

'You must miss her so.' Pramila's hand on hers.

'I do.'

It was an evening of revelations.

Afterward, as Archana drew water from the well, to boil and cool and pour into tumblers for her in-laws' night-time use, she peered over the rim at her reflection. It was dark but the moon and stars were out. The silvery sheath showed a round face, almond eyes. But Archana could not see beyond the dark colouring, the same shade as the ebony sky, that she had been told all her life was ugly.

Pramila's talking nonsense, she thought, but her likeness in the undulating, star-spangled water was smiling.

The other revelation was that everyone in the village knew of her sister, and they *still* included her mother and Archana among them, accepted them. It was freeing. Wonderful.

After that day, no matter how badly Leela treated her, Archana told herself, *she is jealous. Bitter.* Looking at Leela's pinched face. Her mouth turned inward. Her pockmarked skin.

She did not quite believe she was beautiful and Leela was envious – who would be of a dark-skinned, limping girl? – but Pramila's words made her feel better anyway.

'So, how do you plan to be famous?' Archana asks Pramila now, humouring her.

'I'll be a movie star,' Pramila declares. 'You've seen my acting skills.' She simpers demurely. 'Especially when the in-laws are around.'

Archana giggles surreptitiously so as not to draw censure from her own shrew of a mother-in-law – Pramila always has this effect on her. She makes everything fun, all troubles bearable, reducing them to something that can be laughed about.

'But seriously,' Pramila says, her voice soft, wistful, 'I've always, from the time I was a young child, wanted to be famous. Looked up to. Admired. I *know* I'm destined for something more than this, Archana. I feel it here.' Dramatically clutching her heart.

Archana looks at her friend, her face glowing in the soft sunset, her eyes shining, this girl, younger even than her, who dreams big. *Who dares to hope.*

And even as she wishes with all her heart that Pramila's dream was possible, Archana can see Pramila's whole life unfolding. Children: one, another and perhaps more. Her eyes becoming tired and weighed down by their demands. Setting her dreams aside, bestowing them upon her daughters. And later, when they grow up, giving in, inevitably, to demands of family and in-laws, the pressures of duty and doing what is right, getting her daughters married, sighing wearily as she sees her dreams for them and their own dreams ground into the perpetual turmeric dust, chickens pecking on them.

'Hey!' Pramila nudges her and some of the stuffing in her beedie spills. 'No need to look so glum. I won't forget you when I'm famous, I promise.'

Pramila's laugh shaky, her voice tinny, ending in a plea, as if appealing to Archana to participate in her fantasy.

Archana tastes shame, bitter yellow on her lips.

Pramila has accepted her from the very beginning, easing her into life here, adding colour to her life. She boosts Archana, tells her she's lovely, takes her side, always, against her mother-in-law and Leela. She makes Archana laugh, however horrible her day has been. Pramila sees the best in her; she is the best of friends.

And now, Pramila has entrusted Archana with her secret, precious fantasies and Archana is trampling on them with cynicism evident in her lack of response.

She has no right. At least this girl has hope still. She is able to dream. She is not crushed, like Archana's sister.

Pramila's dreams may not come true but for now, she can bask in the luxury of imagining.

Archana smiles as bright as she can. 'You'd better not forget me when you're famous or I'll come after you with a scythe.'

'You don't really think I'll…?' Pramila's voice deceptively light but carrying an undercurrent of hope.

'Why ever not? I've heard of actresses being scouted from villages,' Archana says earnestly. 'And you're the most beautiful woman here, in your own words.'

This earns a giggle from Pramila.

'Your acting talents are second to none,' Archana continues. 'Why, my mother-in-law is completely fooled, which is why, I imagine, she doesn't object to my sitting next to you here every evening – in fact, she's glad for it! "That Pramila is so dutiful, so caring of her in-laws. You could do to learn from her," she grumbles when I do anything wrong in her eyes, which is all the time.'

The shadows crowding Pramila's eyes disappear completely as she laughs brightly, wholeheartedly, once more. 'Really?'

'Yes, but could you tone it down a bit, otherwise I think my mother-in-law might just swap me for you.'

Pramila chuckles, a merry waterfall of sound. 'What you said about actresses being picked from villages…' Raw hope pulsing in her friend's voice.

'I mean every word. It *will* happen, I know it,' Archana lies, wincing inwardly as Pramila squeezes her hand and beams happily.

'You're a good friend, Archana. The best.'

*

That night Archana tosses and turns, her sister's face, stripped of hope, tired and worn, looming before her eyes, superimposed with Pramila's starry eyes.

It has been months since she saw her sister, during which she has tried and failed to come up with an excuse to leave the village, thanks to her mother-in-law's hawk-eyed possessiveness. She knows that her sister waits for her visits, never knowing when she will come, only that she will.

In the morning, though bleary-eyed and groggy from lack of sleep, Archana comes to a decision.

On her way to work, she stops off at her mother's hut.

Her mother is in the courtyard, plucking jasmine. She beams upon seeing her daughter, and the dog bounds up and dances around her.

'Here,' her mother says, threading jasmine through her hair. The creamy smell of sweet anticipation.

Archana takes a breath. 'Ma, I've been lying to you.'

'Oh!' Her mother's hands, which were patting Archana's hair into place, stilling. Her eyes shocked.

'I've been visiting Radha.'

Her mother sits down, hand on her heart, not even bothering to push away the dog, who's taking the opportunity to lick her face. The pungent tang of cow dung mingled with jasmine. The look in her eyes, shock and fear and… something else.

Yearning.

Perhaps her mother has missed her prodigal daughter in recent months while living close to her other daughter.

Archana feels a thrill start at the base of her spine. Her heart glowing, she pushes her advantage. 'She's struggling, Ma.'

'She made her choice.' Her mother's lips sealed shut, turning inwards. Her whole body hunching as if to push away the longing that Archana has glimpsed.

'Please, Ma, can't you find it in yourself to forgive her?'

Her mother's eyes overflowing. 'I…'

'Don't you miss her?'

And her mother, so softly that Archana struggles to hear, 'Every day.'

'Then come with me, Ma, please. We'll tell my mother-in-law that we're visiting a temple.'

Her mother wavering.

'Come with me to see her and meet your grandchildren. Please.'

Almost imperceptibly, her mother nods.

Chapter Thirty-Six

1924

Margaret

Alone

'Why didn't you tell me?' As soon as they are alone, Margaret asks Suraj the question that has been on the tip of her tongue since she encountered Latha.

It had been a shock, meeting this girl who declared she had been Suraj's betrothed as Margaret arrived at the house that was the springboard from where her new life with her beloved would launch.

Suraj had squeezed her hand, mouthed 'later', and Margaret's racing heart had settled, comforted by her husband's gaze, those warm eyes the colour of autumn, radiating love for her, promising to explain. She knew Suraj would have good reason for keeping something this significant from her – she believed in their love – but nevertheless, she was a tad rattled. Her enthusiastic plans for a fresh start were ever so slightly dimmed by this girl and her unexpected announcement.

All evening, as she waited for when she and Suraj would be alone, thinking wistfully, longingly of their time together on the ship, Margaret watched her husband, mesmerised by his transformation. He seemed to have grown in stature, standing straighter, smiling wider, since their ship docked in India and she understood that the prejudice he had encountered in England because of his colour had chipped away at him, reducing him.

Here, Suraj was not an outsider: he belonged.

As if reading her mind, her husband smiled at her from across the table as they sat down to eat – a veritable feast, the maids shy as they flitted about serving and bringing in platters of rice and Indian bread and curries, a heady rush of flavours, spicy without being hot.

Suraj tucked in, eating with relish. 'This is what I was missing. Everything tastes so much better at home.'

Home.

And unbidden, she was struck by yearning for sun-warmed grass, the scent of lavender, honeysuckle and fermenting apples. The stile at the farmhouse with its worn, familiar grooves of wood, burnished velvet with moss. The soft button noses of the cows that would nuzzle up to her, the horses whom she fed with apples. The pigs with their placid eyes.

Blackberry juice sliding down chins, purple plums and wild garlic, pears and ripe strawberries and juicy red cherries. The sun, when it made an appearance, not harsh and blinding like here but mellow, the breeze, which smelled of ripening fruit, not gritty with dirt. Roses cascading down walls. Sitting with friends in the garden at Charleston and toasting marshmallows. The ridge along the downs from where you could see all the way to the sea.

'You can't change the past,' Suraj had said when he proposed, liquid almond eyes shining, like sun on grass browned by summer; he knew that she had lived almost all of her life with ghosts, carrying the weight of their hopes and desires within her, 'but you can shape the future. Live for yourself, Margaret. Take a chance, come with me. I will make you happy, I promise.'

Their room is suffocatingly warm, window closed to keep out mosquitoes, walls pushing in. The stale, lingering scent of spices: chilli and coriander, sharp, mouth-stinging heat.

Mosquito net covering their bed, the world pixelated, insidious with shadows, rendering ordinary objects sinister, planting darkness where there should be none.

The ceiling fan tiredly circulating musty air, humid and gritty. Sounds drifting in from outside, despite the secured window, the shut door. A vendor calling out wares in a sing-song voice – at this time of night? Somebody laughing. A dog barking. A child crying.

She thinks of the cold room in the attic of the farmhouse that she shared with Winnie, holding hands for warmth.

Winnie…

She had come to see Margaret onto the train that would take her and Suraj to the port. Her belly full with child. The child Margaret will only meet – when?

Toby had not come, of course. The Baron had not allowed it.

The busyness of the station, the toasted brown aroma of brewing coffee and departures. The tart yellow, burnt-indigo taste of distance and sorrow and endings and new beginnings a world away.

The station bringing to mind their goodbye to Father: that was the beginning of the end of their family as it was, their lives changed for ever, some lost. The memory reflected in her sister's gaze.

Mrs Danbourne at the station, come despite missing a day of lessons. Her teacher's eyes bright with emotion.

Brine in Margaret's throat, salt-green as she stood at the door of the train.

Mrs Danbourne holding her close. Her scent of lavender and turpentine.

'Paint, do. Don't give it up.' Her breath hot in Margaret's ear.

Vanessa had written to say goodbye and she too had reiterated: 'Keep on creating, Margaret.'

Winnie's face soft and vulnerable with tears, looking forlorn as the train pulled away, Margaret resisting the sudden urge to jump off, run to her sister, Suraj's arms anchoring her, holding her to him, her future...

Now, in this close room, she says with dawning understanding, 'This is why your parents disowned you, isn't it? They wanted you to marry Latha.'

'Yes.' And, his gaze hardening, 'I think they collaborated with Amit and Latha's parents to make sure Latha was here when we arrived. *They* sent her.'

'You really did not know?'

'Of course not!' He is shocked. 'I would not do that to you.' His gaze earnest, sombre. 'All my life, my future has been planned for me. I was sent to a boarding school of my father's choice, supposedly one of the best in India but which I absolutely loathed, then packed off to England to read law, follow in my father's footsteps. I was also meant to marry the girl they chose for me. But I... once I met you, Margaret, there couldn't be anybody else. Only you.'

'Do we... do we have to stay here?' She would, ideally, like her fresh start to be free of Latha's presence, a reminder of the life her husband was meant to live, the woman he would have married, had he not met Margaret.

Suraj pinches the bridge of his nose, the gesture weary.

'For now, yes. Until I find a job.'

She is quiet.

'Margaret, Latha... She's like my little sister. My parents and theirs – Latha's and Amit's – are close friends; Amit's father does the accounts for my father's law practice. We saw a lot of each other growing up. Amit and I were at boarding school together and our families contrived to spend the holidays together too. Lucky for us, Amit and I got on. And I treated his baby sister like my sibling too, since I did not have any of my own. I only found out before I left for England when my father insisted Latha and I formalise our engagement that our marriage...' His face contorts into a grimace '...had been arranged when Latha was born, agreed between our parents! I've never had feelings other than brotherly ones for Latha. I chose *you*. I've been disowned by my parents for it, but it doesn't matter. *You* matter. You're my anchor, my all. I love you.' His eyes burning fiery marigold. With passion. With love.

She believes him, for she feels this way about him too. And she thinks she understands why he kept something so momentous as his engagement to Latha from her – it didn't feel real to him, it wasn't what he wanted, so he pushed it to the back of his mind. In the time she has known Suraj, she's noticed this about him. He bats unpleasant things away, hoping that if he ignores them long enough they will magically disappear.

And yet, she wants him to explain in his own words. She doesn't want any secrets, any unpleasantness, anything unspoken between them just as they are starting their life together. 'Why didn't you tell me about her? Why did you keep your engagement from me?'

'Because I didn't want it – I had shut it out of my mind. Latha was not important, she wasn't worth our time.'

Just as she thought. She feels relief and love wash over her now that it is settled, put to bed.

Tenderly, Suraj kisses her. 'You came here, giving up all you know for me,' he whispers in her ear. 'I know how much it means and I don't take it lightly. I will make it worth your while,

I promise.' His scent, spiced clove and fresh mint. 'I love you, Margaret. You. Only.'

'I love you too.'

It is hot. Muggy. The walls are thin. But on top of sheets and under the mosquito net in Suraj's friend's house in a country thousands of miles away from Margaret's birthplace, the country that is now home, they make love.

Chapter Thirty-Seven

1923

Archana

Miracles

Now that her mother has agreed to come with her to see her sister, Archana, her entire being glowing as she imagines her sister's face when their mother visits, starts to work on her husband.

A few days later, in that mellow time after her husband has been with her, just before he is drifting off to sleep, she says, 'I'd like to visit the Vishnu temple in Kashi to pray for a child. I've heard miracles take place there.'

He turns to her, eyes shining. This is the first time she has mentioned a child in his presence and his face is bright with hope.

'My mother was telling me that at this temple, all one's prayers are answered. She said she'd take me, this Sunday. Will you talk to your mother, please?'

'I will. Don't you worry,' he promises, beaming at the thought of progeny.

Archana's mother-in-law, true to form, kicks up a fuss.

'It's too far away, it will take the whole day. Why can't you go to the temple in the next village?'

'Ma,' her husband intervenes in his gentle way, 'miracles are rumoured to happen there.'

'Well then, we'll all go.'

Archana's heart sinks. Her husband correctly interprets the desperate gaze she sends his way.

'It's quite a walk,' he says. 'It'll tire you out and Da cannot manage in this heat.'

His mother pouts, sulking. 'I don't see the point…'

'It's one Sunday, for a good cause – a grandchild for you.'

'Why does she have to go with *her mother*?'

'Ma…'

'I don't know what magic she has worked on you,' Archana's mother-in-law says with a sniff, 'but nowadays you seem more enamoured with your wife's mother than with us, your parents.' She bangs about the hearth so loudly that under the banana trees, Archana's father-in-law, who has been napping as is his wont, jerks awake. 'First, she comes to live here and now…'

'Ma!' Archana's husband soothes his mother's ruffled feathers. 'If Archana is to go to the temple, to pray for a grandchild for you, she needs someone to accompany her. Isn't it best if she went with her mother? If I took her, you and Da would struggle to manage.'

'You have a reply for everything,' his mother grumbles but Archana can see her shoulders relaxing. 'Just this once, mind.'

Archana nods demurely at her mother-in-law and from under her *pallu* smiles winsomely at her husband.

The battle is won!

On Sunday, Archana collects her mother from her hut.

She is nervous, apprehension and excitement, naked hope and anticipation pulsing in her face.

'What have you packed?' Archana asks, panting as she heaves the basket her mother has handed her onto her head.

'You said she misses my pickles.'

'That explains the smell that has been wafting from your hut on my way to and from work. Have you been cooking all week? Just because Radha likes it doesn't mean you need to concoct a year's supply!' Archana jokes and her mother laughs slightly anxiously along with her.

As they near Radha's village, her mother, who has been impatient with Archana's limp all this while, falls behind, fumbling with her sari.

'Ma, it's okay. This is your daughter and grandchildren we're going to see.'

'I...' Her mother's face raw. 'I'm worried.'

Archana stops, sets the basket down, indulging the brief flare of relief at the slackening of the load. 'Her marriage has not been easy. It has tired her, worn her out.' It is both request and warning. *Please don't show your shock* is what she really means to say. *Please don't cry at the state of your beautiful daughter.*

Her mother nods, understanding her unspoken plea. The anxiety in her face easing, replaced by a determined acceptance. 'I'm ready.' Then, as Archana bends down to pick up the basket, surprising her by cupping her face. 'You're a good girl.'

Her eyes fill up, mirroring her mother's.

As they walk to the section set apart from the main village, the home of the untouchables, with its shabby mud huts, its taste of desperation, its reeking, rubbish- and faeces-heaped gutters, its emaciated, unkempt children clothed in rags and dust, her mother's steps falter once more.

'Come, Ma.' Archana smiles determinedly as women collect in front of their huts and peruse them, unashamedly curious and suspicious, staring down the interlopers willingly entering their territory when most shun them, questioning their motives, their children with running noses, mud-stained, scrawny bodies, hungry eyes, gathered around them. A hundred unfriendly gazes boring into them.

Archana's smile sags at the corners as it always does when she comes here, no matter how many times she's been before. The feeling of being watched. The ache and upset at her sister for choosing this fate. Helplessness that makes her scrunch her hands into fists, open her mouth and bawl at the injustice of society labelling these people low-caste, unfit to mix with others, doomed to do the most menial jobs unwanted by everyone else.

Archana never gave a thought to untouchables until her sister married one, but now she is shocked and repelled by how they are treated. She knows how it feels to be marginalised, judged for no fault of hers; in fact, these people are doing it now – their eyes going to her face and then to the leg that she drags. Her limp that is now so accepted in her husband's village that she forgets about it, except when she comes somewhere else and realises that it is what people define her by. She is so much more than her mismatched feet, just like these people are so much more than their caste. They love, live, hurt and hate like everyone else, but are deemed untouchable because of the accident of their birth.

Yet her sister not only touched one, she married him...

'Oh, Radha,' Archana has wanted to yell, 'before you fell in love with that boy and risked everything by falling pregnant, you should have come to me. I would have told you how it feels to be judged, shunned, pushed to the fringes for something you can't control. I would have asked you to limp for a day or two and see how you liked being in the spotlight for all the wrong reasons. Perhaps then, none of this would have happened…'

There is a queue at the well.

Women with buckets, their children dancing in the water dripping from pails, fashioning mud cakes from the squelching dirt trampled to a wet, gooey swamp beside the well.

One of the women, slender, familiar, turns, hoisting a pail onto her head, carrying another, two children clinging to her like vines. Her vapid gaze drifts over them and away, indifferent, zoned-out. Then it comes back, sharp, alert, hopeful, brimming. Her face, tired and wan a minute ago, now aglow.

She takes a step forward, then stops as if afraid of her reception. One word escaping her mouth as she lifts the hand not clutching the pail to her heart: 'Ma!'

Then the pail drops from her head, water spilling everywhere. Her eyes rolling back in her head as she faints. Her children crying.

Instantly, her mother is running towards Radha, faster on her old legs than Archana has ever seen her, catching her daughter before she falls to the ground.

'Radha!' her mother says, gently nursing her daughter, prayer and love. 'Radha!'

Archana gathers Radha's wailing children in her arms. They plant kisses upon her face, her hair, wiping the salty wet from her face with their little fingers.

In that moment, despite a crowd collecting to witness this spectacle, point and nudge and comment upon it, Archana wishes what she had said to her husband was true, that she was really going to pray for a child. Holding her sister's children to her, she wants, more than anything, offspring of her own to love and care for. Trusting arms round her neck, warmth and adoration, precious innocence. She has longed for this without knowing that this is what she was missing, yearning for, she realises, as she carries her sister's children to their hut.

'Ma, you came.' Radha is luminescent, there's no other word for it. 'You forgave me.'

'I missed you.' Their mother looks younger than she has in ages.

Archana watches as her mother holds Radha's children, committing their every feature to memory, to tide her through the long days until she can see them again.

Archana notices her mother try not to show how upset she is by Radha's appearance, thin and exhausted; the hunger of her children, who stare disbelieving at the fruits they've brought before devouring them with the gusto of those unused to food, worried it'll disappear if left too long; the way Radha lives now: the smallness of her house, her meagre possessions; Radha's husband's conspicuous absence, her eyes sliding away when their mother asks after him, Archana surmising from this that he is, as ever, drinking away his earnings in the arrack shop.

On their way home, her mother breaks the brooding silence.

'I'll visit every Sunday, take some food for them.'

'Ma, you can't go alone. It's too far.'

'I can.' Her mother determined. 'I'll manage.'

Archana thinks of the basket she had carried here, so heavy and unwieldy.

'Promise me you won't take much.'

'Only as much as I can carry.'

Even so, Archana worries. She wonders if there is some way she can circumvent her mother-in-law, accompany her mother every alternate Sunday at least. She'll speak to her husband, tell him the priest asked her to come every fortnight to do a puja, get him to intercede with his mother on her behalf…

Chapter Thirty-Eight

1924

Margaret

Cusp

Suraj falls asleep easily that first night in India.

But Margaret cannot. She is excited, fired with ideas, restless to begin realising the dreams she has spun for her future here with her husband.

She stares at the ceiling, the plaster bubbled and yellow, cracking in places. Lizards with bulbous saffron eyes hunt for flies, forked tongues darting. She looks at her husband and is overcome with love for him, overwhelmed by what he did because of love of her: upsetting his parents by refusing to marry the girl they had chosen for him, thus leading them to disown him.

She and Suraj are a team, on the cusp of a new life, theirs to fashion any way they like. It is all ahead of them and together, they will make a success of it – Margaret is assured of this. Her mind buzzing with plans, sleep evades her, sweat turning her nightclothes soggy. She gets out of bed, quietly so as not to disturb Suraj. She fumbles with the matches, lights a candle and finds her notebook.

And through the muggy night, sounds filtering in regardless of the closed window, her husband snoring softly beside her, his face freckled with perspiration; in flickering candlelight, the scent of congealing wax, hot and sweet, the fiery amber taste of flames and dreams, she sketches, putting down on paper her hopes for a fresh start with her love in this exotic, exciting country.

Chapter Thirty-Nine

1924

Archana

Relentless

Archana admires the brilliant sapphire and gold butterfly perched on the red bellflower bush beside the road, smiling to herself, her heart as musical and alive as the birdsong serenading her, completely disregarding the dirt stinging her eyes as she walks home from work.

The monsoons are late this year and the heat is a dry, angry slap. Relentless. But again, Archana does not care.

She is happy.

Her period is late, which means that she might right now be growing a baby in her still-flat stomach. Her mother is looking happier than Archana has seen her in a long while, the worry lines ambushing her face having relaxed somewhat since she got in touch with her older daughter.

Archana shakes her head at all the time wasted in hurt and upset, the subterfuge she would employ in order to visit her sister while keeping it from her mother. Her sister and mother were longing to meet each other, but her mother needed urging, time to forgive and forget.

'After I moved here, close to you, after I left the village and all the associations there: your father's death, everyone shunning us, after being part of this community, where I was accepted, well, by most, by your mother-in-law grudgingly, I... I was able to let go of my anger towards your sister.' And, her mother's eyes haunted, 'She has suffered. I didn't want that for her. Neither did your father. That is why…'

Archana had squeezed her mother's hand. 'She's happier now she is reunited with you.'

'But she is not *happy*, Archana.' Her mother's voice a lament.

'Your visits give her joy.'

Her mother nodding while stirring the pickle that she would take when she went to visit Radha, the hot fumes from the crushed pepper, the mustard seeds, the ground chillies smarting their eyes in the cosy, boiling kitchen.

Archana plucks a cashew, red and juicy, from the tree growing wild by the road. It is pungently tart, almost but not quite fermented.

As she nears the scattering of huts that makes up their village, a skip in her step, touching her stomach and imagining how her mother will react to news of her pregnancy, she hears sobs. Loud, jarring.

The collective mourning of an entire village.

She shades her eyes with her palm, for the sun, though not as potent as at noon, is lower down in the sky and directly in her eyes.

A crowd collected by a hut.

Her mother's?

Then she is running, as fast as her limp will allow, the cashew dropping from her hand and staining the mud, splat, a host of flies alighting on it.

Her bare feet pounding the dirt, faster, faster, please, wishing she was able-bodied, wishing away the resistance, the throbbing in her shorter leg. Her heart loud with foreboding.

She is breathless, panting, by the time she reaches the edges of the crowd.

'What's happened?' she manages when she can speak, in between gasps. Her heart threatening to spill out of her mouth along with the question, waiting for the answer and afraid of it, too cowardly to push through the crowds, confront the truth. Have what she's dreading made real.

Please, gods.

'Collapsed,' someone says. 'Sudden as anything. One minute there, next minute gone.'

She closes her eyes, sways on her aching feet, as she gathers courage to ask who it is. Her whole body trembling, one word ricocheting in her head: *Please.*

A murmur spreads through the crowd, rocking her, making her open her eyes.

Her friend, Pramila, being led out of her hut.

It takes a moment to understand what she's seeing, for it to dawn on her that the villagers are gathered at Pramila's house, next to her mother's. She cranes her neck, looking above the heads of the villagers. Her mother is standing near the front with other wailing women, looking shocked.

Her mother is fine, but Archana cannot find relief as the horrible truth dawns on her.

Pramila's eyes swollen and tear-stained. Her forehead smeared with the remnants of the vermilion bindi – the mark of a married woman – which has been wiped away.

Pramila dressed in white.

Widow's garb.

As Archana watches, breathless with budding comprehension, Pramila's gaze meets hers, holds. There is no sparkle in it like usual. Instead, a deadened, numb acceptance.

Pramila, always happy, bubbly and full of life.

Not any more.

For she knows, as surely as Archana does, what is to come.

Pramila's mother-in-law lifts Pramila's hands up in the air, her emerald and scarlet bangles obscene on the white-clothed wrists. She brings Pramila's hands down with a thud against the wall of the hut. Pramila's eyes flinch in accord with Archana's as her bangles shatter upon contact.

Thud. Crash. Tinkle.

Gold, green and red shards littering the courtyard that Pramila sweeps every other morning with cow dung, winking bright, vulgarly festive.

Pramila's hands bare, bleeding. The blood looking to stain her white widow's sari the crimson of a weeping heart, the carmine of a married woman's bindi, but before it can, her mother-in-law, wailing herself, rubs it away.

Pramila. 'One day I will be famous,' she had said, her eyes shining.

That evening they sit vigil in Pramila's house, as her husband's body is anointed and the priest intones, the womenfolk gathered in the inner sanctum: the small, dark kitchen of the two-room hut hot and close, rank with grief, stunned with loss, smelling of burnt rice, spices and mourning.

Pramila sits in the middle of the circle of women, white-garbed and pale, welts on her hands where the bangles were broken. Her face and neck bereft without jewellery. She looks naked without her bindi and yet she has never looked more beautiful, Archana thinks.

She would give anything for this to be an ordinary evening, Pramila weaving her incredible, wonderful dreams along with the beedies, the smell of tobacco and evening, while children play in the fields and the sky is kaleidoscopic with sunset, Pramila's fantasies as brilliant as the stars that appear, piercing the canopy of dusk. The taste of impossible hopes and friendship, warm and comforting, sweet in Archana's mouth.

In the next room, chanting can be heard from the priest as the body of Pramila's husband is prepared for cremation.

Into the grieving upset, Pramila's mother-in-law announces, 'Pramila will do sati.'

Archana stares at her friend as the words settle inside her, hard and indigestible as stones.

Pramila does not even blink as a murmur goes through the assembled women, briefly puncturing their sobs. They've all known this was coming and yet...

And yet.

In the hubbub that follows the announcement, Archana corners her friend.

'Pramila?' she asks, urgently, 'Are you okay with this?'

Pramila's gaze heavy, tired. 'What choice do I have?'

In widow's whites, her enthusiasm, her zest for life crushed, along with her bangles. The girl she was wiped away with her vermilion bindi.

'But...' How can Archana put into words what she wants to ask? How to say, *do you know what they will do to you? You have to ascend the pyre alongside your husband's body, while they set fire to it. You will burn alive.*

'Oh, Pramila,' she says instead, squeezing her friend's hand.

'If I was pregnant, I'd be exempt, but I'm not.'

Pregnant...

It is then that Archana is aware of the tug in her stomach. The familiar stabbing pain that tells her that her period has arrived, crushing with it her hopes of having a child, now completely small and insignificant in the face of her friend's situation.

Pramila's eyes flutter and this time when she looks at Archana, they are no longer numb but alive with panic. 'I'm scared,' she whispers.

'Don't do it.' Archana's voice is trembling, with sympathy and fear and indignation on her friend's behalf.

'I have to.'

'You don't. I'll speak to them,' she says fiercely.

Pramila's hand, until now limp in Archana's grip, squeezes Archana's palm back. She nods in the direction of a woman sitting next to her mother-in-law, surrounded by three girls, all of whose features are a copy of Pramila's. 'It is my duty. My mother is expecting me to and so are my sisters. If I don't do it, I'll bring disrepute upon not only myself, but my entire family.'

Archana understands, having experienced first-hand the perils of not doing one's duty after Radha's actions, how they affected her family, the scandal and shame they wrought. Helplessness seeps into her very bones at her friend's dilemma.

'On the other hand, when I do…' Pramila summons a small smile that makes Archana infinitely sad, '…I'll achieve the status of a goddess. All of you will venerate me, revere me, pray to me. I'll be famous. See, my dreams are coming true. What did I tell you?'

In the face of her friend's bravery, Archana cannot allow her tears to fall, the terror she feels on Pramila's behalf to show. 'Yes, you will.' Then, trying one more time, 'But surely living with disrepute is better than fame after…' She cannot bring herself to say *death*, imagine her vibrant friend dying, although Pramila herself seems resigned to the fact.

'Archana,' Pramila says gently, and her voice is that of an older, wiser woman – something that, if she does sati, she'll never be.

'If I refuse, I'll bring disgrace upon everyone I love. How can I live with that? And what life will it be anyway, where I, and my loved ones, are vilified, cursed and hated? I have to choose between the pain of an instant and that of a lifetime: I choose the former. Wouldn't you?'

Would she?

All her life Archana has believed in the sanctity of doing her duty, especially after what happened with Radha. She has given up her dreams of education so as not to shatter her mother. But this... this sentence of death in the name of duty. This robbing of a life, is it right?

'Don't be upset. This is my destiny,' Pramila whispers in her ear. 'I wish you a long and happy life.'

Archana chokes back the salty sobs that threaten at Pramila's magnanimity, her incredible bravery. She throws her arms round her friend, this girl so vivacious, and yet, due to the cruel whims of traitorous fate, not long for this world, who dared to dream big in a small village, her scent of incense and sadness, sweat and fragility, her delicate shoulder bones, her pumping, beating heart, fiercely loving, wildly alive.

The evening of Pramila's husband's cremation and Pramila's sati, Archana gathers with the other villagers, disbelieving of Pramila's fate, even now hoping it will not happen, praying that someone will intervene, she herself not being brave enough to go against the crowd, bear the anger and displeasure of the people of this village who have accepted her and her mother.

'I feel such a coward, standing meekly by as my best friend goes to her death. I'm taking the easy way out by reassuring myself that she wants this,' Archana says to her mother. Her mother-in-law is too busy giving advice and support to Pramila's mother-in-law to admonish Archana for contriving to be next to her mother.

Archana's mother turns to her, brows furrowed. 'Of *course* she wants this. Hers is a hallowed fate. Untold glory guaranteed her and blessings showered upon her loved ones. If she refuses to do sati, it is worse ignominy than what your sister wrought upon us.'

'Ma...' Archana cannot phrase the question she wants to ask: *If it was me in Pramila's position, would you still feel the same way?*

She knows the answer, of course. Her mother's words reverberate in her ears: *worse ignominy than what your sister wrought upon us.*

'When your father died, there was nobody to ask me to do sati – given the circumstances. And much as I was tempted to do so anyway, I couldn't abandon you to an uncertain fate.'

Her mother sighs deeply and again Archana feels that familiar mixture of guilt and gratitude – that her mother suffered disrepute brought on by Radha's actions for Archana's sake. If Archana had not needed her mother, she would have died – like she wanted to – on her husband's pyre.

'It is a woman's greatest privilege,' her mother is saying, 'her ultimate duty to sacrifice herself on the funeral pyre of her husband. Look at Pramila's mother, how proud she is of her daughter, how high she holds her head. Pramila's sisters will make the best marriages now. All the gods will be smiling benevolently upon her family. They will have the choicest good fortune.' Her mother sounds almost *envious*.

'Archana.' Her mother gentle, gaze tender. 'Your friend is losing her body, that's all. Her soul will be glorified, she will be revered, a goddess...'

Archana's mother echoing what Pramila has always desired and hoped for.

And yet...

Archana watches as her beautiful, vibrant friend sits in the cart alongside the dead body of her husband, her heart beating with fear and a small, guilty spark of relief that she has been spared, her husband hale, sombre as he makes to follow the funeral cart alongside the other village men. She is more shaken than she can admit by her mother's words, the awe in her voice as she spoke of the majesty awaiting Pramila in the afterlife.

But what of *this* life? The small comforts, the daily joys: the scent of jasmine at dawn, crimson hibiscus petals opening like gifts with the kiss of sun, dew-laden air, soft and fragrant, brushing one's face, the juicy yellow taste of a perfectly ripe mango, the joyous sound of children calling from the fields, the comfort of the mat at the end of a long day...

If it was me, I'd want to live, experience these small, perfect moments just one more time...

Are you thinking the same, Pramila?

As if she'd heard Archana's unspoken question, Pramila looks at her once and her eyes that were bright and burning, full of life, those eyes that used to sparkle and glint with laughter, are as dead as the body of her husband beside whom she will be burned. This girl Archana loves, whose beautiful, vivacious, spirited heart will stop beating soon.

Archana tries to convey her love through her gaze.

But her friend now has her eyes shut, looking at no one.

The air has been still all day. Thick and moist, humid, angry.

After the procession passes – Archana's mother-in-law has asked her to stay behind with her father-in-law and Archana agreed only too readily, knowing she wouldn't be able to watch her friend burn – she paces the courtyard, unable to settle, her father-in-law dozing, as always, in the banana arbour.

Archana strides up and down, ignoring the throbbing ache in her stunted leg, imagining the village elders stacking the wood, leading Pramila onto the pyre, her living, breathing flesh beside the cold, unresponsive corpse of her husband. Are her eyes closed?

Her hands joined in prayer, perhaps, pleading with the gods to save her. Knowing that unless a miracle occurs, her fate is sealed. The chanting of the priest and villagers as they gather around the pyre.

What is Pramila thinking? How can she endure it, knowing that in a few minutes…

Archana shivers. She opens her eyes, realising only then that they've been shut. She stares at the sky, roiling grey with low-slung charcoal clouds.

Her face is wet.

She opens her mouth. She wants to keen.

But instead she stands there, staring up at the heavens, raging, but quietly, so as not to wake her father-in-law, who is dozing, as always, oblivious, as if today is just another day. As if a few minutes from now, Pramila isn't going to die, be burned, just because it is decreed, it is duty, just because her husband, many years older than her, has died.

How is this right?

Archana has willingly given up her dreams of studying further, perhaps working in the city, to do her duty. But if *this* is her fate too, was it worth it?

She is realising that duty is *not* the answer: freedom and education are.

But it's too late. She is trapped.

The still air, dense and humid, suddenly swirls and dirt lashes Archana's cheeks, pulling her hair out of its habitual bun and whipping it across her face. She welcomes the grit in her eyes – it feels like punishment.

She wants to scream so loud that it is heard all the way over at the cremation ground and they stop, the men who are even now, she imagines, circling the pyre with lit wood. The pyre catching alight. The flames performing a mad dance, licking the edges of the wood, cavorting towards Pramila as she sits, hands folded, eyes closed, awaiting her fate.

Does she flinch as her sari ignites, as the smoke assaults her nose, as flames caress her hands, her arms, hot, blistering, as they char her skin, as it peels off her in gaping gashes? Does she open her eyes, which sting from the smoke, the Titian-blue curtain of fire? Does she scream, with all the breath left in her body, all the life in her, 'To hell with duty, save me, spare me!', a version of feisty Pramila finally making herself known, too late? Does she then try to escape, as her husband's body crackles and snaps beside her as flaming twigs rain upon her, as her hair catches fire, as smoke chokes the vivid, spirited breath out of her?

Gods, how can you allow this, decree it? How can you say taking the life of a girl like Pramila is right? No matter what splendour awaits her in the afterlife, shouldn't she be allowed to live this one to the full? Why should her life be cut short just because her husband's has been?

Pramila, you shared with me your dreams of becoming famous, adored, admired. At the time I privately assumed they were fantastic, that they wouldn't come to fruition because you would have children instead, become weighed down by life.

That fate I pictured for you, of being mired in drudgery, bearing children, living to a ripe old age, would have been preferable indeed to this.

What price fame at the cost of your life?

The sky, brooding as Archana's thoughts, wearing a sulky glower of clouds, breaks in two, burning bright with lightning, thundering with the rumour of rain.

A burst of hope in Archana's heart, echoing the thunder, *Please rain. Drench the pyre. Save her.*

But it doesn't rain, the sky darkening instead into a tempestuous scowl.

A sudden sandy breeze, carrying the scent of fire, balloons of flame-tipped smoke seeping into the sky in the distance, convening into an ominous cloud.

All over the village, dogs howl, a mournful cacophony of potent grief.

It is only when the smoke colouring the air the waxy navy of sorrow has been swept away by the velvet pinks, sunflower reds and lemony peaches of twilight – a striking celebration at the soul of her gregarious, dynamic friend entering the heavens, Archana imagines – that the wind picks up and the storm portended by the thunder and lightning arrives, the sky roaring and raging at the waste of a life, dispersing sheet upon sheet of ash-flavoured water, too late for her friend, but soaking the mourners walking back home from the cremation ground by the river.

Chapter Forty

1924

Margaret

Lucky

Dawn streaks cerise splattered with gold through inky curtains, heralding Margaret's first morning in India.

Margaret, having spent the night sketching her dreams and aspirations for her future life with Suraj, cannot contain her enthusiasm about being here, finally, in this country she has only dreamed of, the birthplace and home of her love.

The noises from outdoors have not eased; if anything, they have increased in tempo. Horses neighing, cows mooing, carriage wheels squeaking.

The small room feels claustrophobic. Margaret wants to explore and experience Bombay, this place where they will be living temporarily until they find their feet. She wills her husband to wake but he is in a very deep sleep, his face young and vulnerable in repose.

A cock crows, persistent. Dogs howl.

A vendor calls out in a sing-song voice and bells ring, strident gold.

The city is awake. It beckons with its many voices.

Margaret comes to a decision: she cannot wait any longer, she *must* see what is outside.

Something long dormant is stirring within her – the curiosity, the insatiable thirst for knowledge and new experiences that had characterised her once. It is as if by coming here, to this new place, the old Margaret is coming back, the child she was, impatient, dynamic, unable to wait to know something, always asking questions, wanting to find out *now*.

With a last glance at her peacefully slumbering husband, Margaret slips out the door.

The house is largely dark and cool, languorous, shrouded in sleep. And yet, from the kitchen, she assumes, smoke rises. Clanking of utensils. The tinkle of a laugh. The maids preparing breakfast, she surmises.

She pushes open the front door and air, soft and smelling of flowers, fruity without the heat of the day to come, whispering secrets redolent with night, strokes her face.

The sky is velvet violet daubed with rose.

She walks up to the gate, rattling it gently, and the gate-keeper, snoring softly in his chair, startles awake and bows, obsequiously.

'Memsahib?' A question in his eyes.

She nods to the shut gate. 'I want to go for a walk.'

'Sahib?'

'He's sleeping.'

'I come…'

'Thank you, but there's no need. I'll be fine.'

He scratches his nose, appearing unsure, but opens the gate for her all the same, apparently deciding it is safer to do as she asks than go up to the house and wake up Amit, Latha or Suraj.

Margaret restrains herself from laughing out loud in delight – she is a married woman after all, and she doesn't want to startle the gatekeeper – so she settles for a smile and a gracious 'thank you,' even that making the man flush deeply.

*

The roads are busy, even at this early hour.

Beggars stir from where they are sleeping on the road, beside ditches overflowing with rubbish. Their emaciated bodies loaded with dirt and flies. Open wounds oozing pus.

A woman prays at a roadside shrine, an arch of rocks hosting a statue, the deity's face obscured by sweet-smelling garlands, bells tied to the tree beside it chiming festively.

Margaret walks, oblivious to the stones digging into her good shoes, taking everything in.

People living in huts by the road collect outside to stare at her as she walks by.

Shopfronts open, shopkeepers yawning as they arrange their wares. Children clad in rags gather, staring alternately at her and at the sweets displayed in glass jars, hunger mingling with desire.

A screech and a scream, the tired chug of carriages as the first train of the day goes by. She follows the sound, arriving at the railtracks after a couple of wrong turns.

She is just in time to watch the next train go by. So many people, stuffed into the carriages like matchsticks in a box, one on top of the other almost. Some squatting on the roof, grinning and waving at her.

There's a whole community of people living beside the railway tracks, Margaret notices with a start when the train has passed. Across the tracks, men defecate. Others wash the sleep from their eyes with water from pails.

Families sleep inside hollow construction pipes, upon them, seemingly unaware of or accustomed to the noise, their abodes, such as they are, shaking and juddering with the vibration from the tracks as trains go past.

Women chat to each other as they throw mugs of water on squirming, naked children. Steam, scented with spices, wafts from earthenware pots bubbling on outdoor hearths.

A vendor has put up an awning, the cloth torn and ragged, and is brewing tea and coffee, cooking rice and concocting lurid orange snacks in a vat of bubbling oil. A crowd collects beside him, people milling about, sharing rice and snacks, beverages and anecdotes.

Laughter from children playing on the tracks – who skip aside when the tracks start to vibrate, heralding an approaching train – colours the air, which is stained navy with smoke and mirth, spices and gossip.

It is deeply humbling: all these people living their lives in such abject conditions and yet seemingly happy, content with their lot.

Margaret takes out her sketchbook and tries to capture on paper the thriving, bustling humanity she sees here.

'Memsahib.'

A small boy. Holding out a pencil. One of hers. She must have dropped it.

His eyes wide, beautiful. His stomach concave, ribs in danger of poking through papery, dust-sheathed skin.

'Keep it,' she says, smiling at him.

His face scrunches up in befuddlement. He doesn't understand what she is saying.

She takes the pencil from him and then puts it back in his hand, closing his fingers over it. They are dirty and muddy but so small and fragile and precious.

'Keep it,' she says again.

'Queept, Queept,' he repeats, grinning. Dancing away, followed by a small crowd of children who have materialised, bright-eyed and smiling, in a matter of seconds.

She packs up and they follow, chanting 'Queept, Queept', the boy in the lead holding the pencil up like a prize.

She finds Amit's house after a few wrong turns, feeling like the Pied Piper with her procession of children, which seems to keep growing every minute.

At the gate of the house she turns to the children, giving them a smile and a wave, and they disperse, with a last loud chant of 'Queept', as if by seeing her safely home they have done their job.

She swallows, suddenly emotional, as the boy with the pencil disappears round the corner, nimble as a sprite.

I'm so lucky, she thinks. *I've never been hungry, destitute. Winnie and I were fortunate in that we had Aunt Helen to take us in after the air raid. We were always provided for, we've never experienced poverty like so many. And we've both found love, men who care for us.*

The feeling of gratitude intensifies as she sees Suraj pacing by the gate.

'Where were you?' he asks, throwing his arms round her, his face crumpled with concern. 'You can't go wandering off like that, Margaret, it's dangerous.'

She can feel his heart pounding as he holds her to him, tight, as if she'll escape if he doesn't.

'When I woke and found you gone...' His hot breath is flavoured with remembered panic. 'I love you, Margaret. I cannot live without you.' His eyes soft with care and worry.

'Nobody bothered me,' she says, hugging the secret of the army of children close, feeling light-headed from lack of sleep, a part of her wondering, looking at the dusty street empty of kids, if perhaps she imagined them all.

That afternoon when she and Suraj are alone, Amit and Latha having retired to their rooms for what she understands is the obligatory afternoon nap after lunch here ('It's too hot to do anything else,' Suraj has explained), Margaret says, 'This country, Suraj… Such joy amidst much poverty.'

'Yes.'

'When you talked about the need for India's freedom from British rule, I agreed with you, but…' Above her on the ceiling a lizard flicks out its tongue, long and sticky, and traps a fly. Hot wind flavoured with tamarind and grit wafts through the curtains. The ceiling fan circulates stale air soggy with humidity. '…I didn't really understand. If I thought of the colonies at all, I assumed we'd done good there.'

Suraj sighs, staring unseeing at the ceiling, where the lizard is placidly munching on its lunch.

'But the poor here in India, they need someone who understands them, knows how they live. Someone like Gandhi, who has chosen to live like them, poverty and piety.'

'Yes!' Suraj turns to her, hope mingled with surprise.

'I'd like to help, Suraj.'

Suraj beams, his eyes creasing into that tender expression reserved just for her as he pulls her to him, claiming her lips with his.

Over the next few weeks Margaret accompanies Suraj and Amit to Swaraj India meetings. Latha is disinclined to join them. They design posters for the Indian Independence movement, for which Margaret does the sketches.

Gradually, Amit's manner towards Margaret loses its iciness, his smiles reaching his eyes. Latha announces that she is bored and returns home to her parents.

Margaret settles into life in India, a new life, like she had hoped for, exotic and different, filled with purpose and energy, thanks to her participation in the Independence movement. Her relationship with Suraj growing stronger, deeper, with Margaret herself changing, opening up, discovering once again the girl she had been before the air raid.

As Amit and Suraj and Margaret concoct slogans, as they march through the streets in support of self-rule for India, Margaret one of the few white people taking the side of the Indians, she is aware of hope blossoming in her chest, the assurance that moving to India for love has been the best decision, the conviction that the dreams she sketched her first night here *will* come to fruition, that soon, she and Suraj will fashion the family she has been yearning for since she lost her parents and sibling, recreating the happiness she recalls from her early childhood.

Chapter Forty-One

1925

Archana

Commotion

Archana sits in the clearing, weaving beedies with the village womenfolk, her mother-in-law beside her keeping eagle-eyed watch, ready to find fault even as she gossips, when the commotion occurs.

This evening ritual that Archana looks forward to all day is now tinged with sadness, sorrow and ache for her friend; and desperation for escape before her fate mirrors Pramila's.

It's been months since Pramila's sati and yet her absence is still a raw, throbbing presence.

Pramila, are you looking down from somewhere up there? Are you the lone star twinkling in the tamarind and marigold dusk sky?

Every night Archana dreams of fire. Of being burned alive, flames lapping at her, caressing her, claiming her living flesh, branding her, stamping charred marks upon her like a grasping lover…

She wakes up screaming and, from behind the sari curtain, her mother-in-law yells, 'Stop making a racket! You're worse even than the neighbourhood dogs and crickets. Do you think you're a banshee, haunting the night?'

Beside Archana, her much-older husband is still. Not snoring like usual. She leans close. He grunts and she releases her breath.

She is safe yet.

Her heartbeat steadies but her fear does not.

I cannot die like Pramila. But if my husband dies before me, that's my fate.

Since Pramila's sati, Archana has taken to obsessing about her husband's health. She makes potions for him to drink, to ease the wind and reflux that dog him. She is worried about his wheezing, his weight.

She is living in dread, constantly studying him, checking to make sure he is okay.

I married you out of duty, giving up my dreams of education. I like you, respect you. You are kind. But I'm so afraid, for my fate is linked inextricably with yours.

'I want to make my own destiny,' Radha had stubbornly declared when Archana caught her with her untouchable lover in their hut.

Now, finally, Archana understands.

Radha, spirited and feisty as she was then, had wanted freedom. She'd yearned to escape the shackles of duty, the bind of expectation. Marriage, children and, if her husband died, death for her too... What sort of life was that to aspire to? Although, in the end, Radha's fighting her fate had only served to get her into a worse bind – her marriage to an untouchable meaning she was ostracised, delegated to the lowest rungs of society. But still, she had tried...

Archana drifts back into sleep to the soundtrack of her husband's sputtering snores, dreaming of escape, of education, of living for no one but herself.

The following morning her mother-in-law will complain of aching bones, a sleepless night, thanks to her daughter-in-law.

'Give me a massage,' she will command. 'I couldn't go back to sleep after your performance last night; for whose benefit was that? Do you want the neighbours to talk even more than they're doing already, say you're possessed, and that's the reason you're not providing us with a grandchild?'

As the months have passed with no child, her mother-in-law has got progressively more harsh and bitter. But Archana's husband is gentle and kind, insisting she go for her temple visits (she feels guilt at deceiving him by in reality visiting her sister, but she cannot risk her mother-in-law finding out and putting a stop to it), even when her mother-in-law avers that prayer is not working.

As Archana fashions beedies, catching her mother's eye every so often – her mother-in-law makes sure she and Archana sit at the other end of the circle of women from her, separating mother and daughter, laying claim to Archana out of pure spite, it seems – she talks to Pramila in her head.

You've got what you wanted, Pramila.

'I'm destined for something more than this… One day I'm going to be famous,' you said.

Well, you were right.

You are revered by the villagers. They look up to you, pray to you.

'What's that?' her mother-in-law asks, curiosity spiking her voice, jolting Archana out of her reverie.

A cloud of orange dust weaving towards them, coming from the mansion that houses Archana's employers.

'Oh!'

The women stand up as one, shielding their eyes. Children come running from the fields, gathering around their mothers. Archana can smell their sweet scent of sweat and inquisitive innocence.

The cloud comes closer and it is Nandu, the head of servants up at the mansion.

The women whisper among themselves, gossip and conjecture blooming on paan-flavoured tongues.

Leela self-importantly pushes forward from the group of older women she allies with, saying, 'It's bad news, I know it.' Her voice excited, a thrill to it.

Then Nandu is upon them, Leela asking, her voice officious while also unable to hide that sliver of glee at the hint of misfortune, 'What's happened?'

'The master and mistress have been in an accident.'

Murmur swelling into disquiet among the women.

'*Aiyyo!*' Leela theatrically clutches her chest. And to the women, 'They had gone out in the new motor car. They were due back this evening.'

'It overturned some miles away. I just got word.' Nandu's gaze haunted. 'They... They didn't survive.' His voice stumbling.

He takes a breath, then, 'I've already arranged for word to be sent to their son in Bombay. He'll be arriving within the next couple of days, I should imagine, with his wife.'

The air electric with this new nugget of gossip, flavoured a thrilling, ice-tipped blue. The wife who drove a wedge between son and parents: a white woman the son brought back from England, the reason why he hasn't been back home since, his parents having disowned him.

'The house needs to be made ready.' Nandu's voice easing into its normal, brisk cadence as he talks of work, looking over Leela's head, including Archana in his gaze. 'We'll need you both to come earlier, stay later, the next couple of days.'

Archana had seen the master and mistress that very morning and now they were no more. How fragile life was, how very precious. And again, the trepidation, the anxiety that has been her companion since Pramila's sati, biting.

I need to escape before something similar happens to my husband and I have to do sati.

She has always known that sati is a possibility, but it had seemed far away, a distant, vague concept like death itself. But now, it is the only thing she can think of. It haunts her every thought, a slumbering monster awakened, fostering apprehension, unease, dread.

My life so far has been decided for me by others: my sister's actions meant I couldn't bear to break my mother's heart and so I went along with her wishes for me. I sacrificed my dreams of education.

If my husband dies, I refuse to die along with him, just because it is my duty, what everyone says I must do.

I gave up my dreams for duty but I will not *give up my life.*

She is filled with resolve but there's a small part of her that wonders if she will be brave enough to shirk duty, turn her back on tradition.

'Archana,' Nandu is saying. 'Is that okay with you?'

She nods, thinking with a pang of the master and mistress, their lives snuffed out in an instant. The sadness shining out of the mistress's eyes, how she would touch the portrait of her son a few times each day, gently, wistfully.

When Archana first started working at the mansion, she had noticed that the young master's portraits were the only objects in the whole house that were not covered in a fine layer of dust (Leela having taken advantage of the mistress's absent-mindedness and not bothered dusting at all until Archana arrived and the job passed to her).

Once, Archana had overheard the mistress plead with her husband, 'Hasn't it gone on long enough? Can't he come home now?'

And the master, soft-spoken, had said just one word, 'No.' Final as a door closing. The wife leaving after a bit. The husband in the study getting steadily drunk.

Archana had found him in there, slumped over the table asleep, when she went in to dust in the morning. The room smelled sour, drink and sadness. She had taken quiet steps backward, softly closed the door and gone to dust the other rooms.

The wife had come down and sat in the living room, sipping tea with hollow eyes.

How will the new owners be? The son who caused all this upset, this distance between his parents because of marrying a foreigner. His wife, the cause of the rift between a son and his parents and, indirectly, among the parents.

She will be beautiful, Archana imagines. Aloof, perhaps. Snooty. Someone bewitching enough to make the young master forget where he came from, his roots, his duty: marriage to the girl his parents had chosen for him.

Will the new master and mistress stay at the mansion? If not, will they sell the house, she wonders as she gathers up the tobacco, the beedies and the betel leaves in the basket and follows her mother-in-law into their hut, to strain the rice, pound coriander and mint leaves along with chillies, ginger, garlic, onion and cumin seeds into a chutney, seasoned with mustard seeds and curry leaves sputtering in oil, for supper.

Chapter Forty-Two

1925

Margaret

Urgency

Margaret settles into her life in India with enthusiastic ease, and soon Suraj's friend's house and the city begin to feel as familiar as her own.

Within weeks of Suraj and Margaret's arrival, Latha had announced she was leaving, for it became apparent that there was no place for her.

Although Latha never warmed to Margaret, she herself felt sorry for the girl, for she could see in her eyes, read in her demeanour, her love for Margaret's husband. But Suraj did not love her back, not in the way Latha wanted him to; this too was obvious – he had eyes only for Margaret. And when Latha understood this, she had left.

Amit had accompanied Latha to their hometown, giving Suraj and Margaret a wonderful week together on their own. When he returned, they had begun taking part in India's struggle for self-rule in earnest, Margaret providing the slogans and being instrumental in creating the posters.

The first time Amit saw one of Margaret's posters, he was astounded. 'Wow, what talent! You're amazing, Margaret!'

'He doesn't give compliments easily. You've really impressed him.' Suraj glowing, happier at Amit's awe and appreciation of Margaret's skill than Margaret was herself.

Participating in the freedom struggle, making posters, taking part in rallies with Amit and Suraj, and each morning, meeting with the slum children, teaching them to sketch, Margaret felt she was giving something of herself, making a difference, a change for the greater good. In the process, the two parts of herself: the insatiably curious, affectionate and bright girl she had been before the air raid and was discovering again since she first stepped foot in India, and the introspective, creative, deeply feeling adult she had become were fusing, and Margaret discovered that she quite liked the woman, a composite of the two halves of herself, who was emerging.

Suraj noticed it too. 'India has transformed you,' he said often, his eyes soft with awe, pride, love. He was changing himself, becoming an ever more confident, assured version of himself, although always at the back of his eyes was the pain of his parents' disowning of him.

'I wish they would come round.'

'Write to them,' she had urged. 'Try again.'

'I will, but not quite yet. I'm still so angry and hurt, Margaret.'

She understood. It had taken her a long time to move past her anger at her parents: her mother for deciding to stay at home instead of going to Aunt Helen; her father for giving up on life after the death of his wife and eldest daughter, rendering Winnie and Margaret orphans. It was meeting Suraj and coming here to India, being with the slum children, seeing what they had to endure every day as a matter of course, that was allowing her to let go of past hurts, move on.

She pulled Suraj close, trying to show him through her loving that they would both carry scars, hurts, sorrow, but they had each other now. He kissed her back, telling her in this way that he understood. They had never needed words and in India their relationship was becoming stronger as they both came into their own.

Every morning, the children of the slum beside the railway tracks waited for Margaret by the gate, beaming at her, their dirty faces glowing. They'd follow her all the way to the tracks and back – her very own urchin army.

She drew them and when they saw the sketches she had made, they were delighted, holding the paper aloft and mimicking the expressions she had captured on paper, jumping in the air, churning dust, cinnamon-speckled, grit-flavoured happiness.

The beggar who had accosted her on her first day in India found her too, as did his friends, a veritable cabal of vagrants with limbs and body parts missing. With Amit's permission, she would take them left-over food, old clothes she found in the house belonging to his parents.

They had become her friends now, these people she saw on her daily morning walk.

'Memsahib!' they called, grinning and waving wildly, and when she distributed her gifts – they were happy with so little – they bowed low, even kissing her feet, which embarrassed her no end.

The women smiled at her from beneath their veils, their smiles tired, weighed down at the edges with years of weariness, their eyes haunted and hurting, as they went about their chores: cooking, washing, drawing water from the one well they all shared (which she'd been told by the gatekeeper dried up in the summer, many of the slum dwellers dying of dehydration), praying – there were countless shrines dotted around, small homages to gods, marigold garlands, a festive celebration of bells tied to tree branches above the deities, the heady perfume of incense.

Amit's house, which Margaret had had such mixed feelings about when she first arrived, was now home.

Suraj had found a job, working as barrister for a local firm.

Margaret had settled into a routine. When she returned from her walks, she had a wash. Then she read or sketched. She wrote to Mrs Danbourne, Vanessa and especially Winnie, enclosing some of her sketches.

They all wrote back, sending news from home, and despite Margaret revelling in her life in India, when she read those letters she felt the pull of homesickness, missing, briefly and yet intensely, the wide green vistas of England. Winnie wrote to say she had had her baby, a little girl – named Evelyn for Evie. When she saw the name, Margaret cried.

After lunch she had taken to the Indian habit of siesta. Then she would wash again and wait for Suraj to come home.

After supper, Margaret, Suraj and Amit would lounge in the courtyard on hammocks (fashioned from old saris tied to the trunks of palm trees), palm fronds fanning them with a breeze soft and seasoned with twilight, tasting of waning day. Spiced cinnamon tea and gulab jamuns (sweet balls of powdered milk, fashioned into a dough with clarified butter, deep-fried and swimming in syrup) to hand, they would plan their agenda for the weekend, when they would organise Swaraj protests. The life from the street – hawkers and beggars, laughter and gossip, arguments and barking from stray dogs, the mooing of cows, the clucking of hens and mewling of next door's cat – would filter in, until the evening became full of shadows, the light switching from bright gold to mellow pink to grey, and mosquitoes buzzed and flies circled despite the sweet-smelling herbs the maids lit to dissuade them.

Margaret, Suraj and Amit are preparing to go on a Swaraj rally, the posters and banners Margaret has fashioned waiting by the front door, when there is a furore at the gates. Someone is rattling them with great urgency.

Margaret, dressed and ready and pacing in the courtyard, watches alarmed as the gatekeeper comes running up to her, all of a fluster. In all the months she's been here, he's never done this, preferring to walk sedately, head held high, taking his time, unwilling to bother his sahib, making whoever is at the gates wait.

'Telegram!' The gatekeeper is panting.

Margaret goes indoors and sits down hard on the first chair she encounters, her heart beating very fast.

The gatekeeper, in his urgency, has left the gate wide open and an army of beggars is peeping in, curious. Margaret recognises most of them. But she is inside the house and although she can see them, they cannot see her and she is grateful. For she is disconcerted, petrified, her heart threatening to explode out of her ribcage.

Please let Winnie and her children be safe.

The gatekeeper hands the telegram to Amit, who has come out of his room, hurriedly buttoning his shirt, to see what the commotion is about, and rushes back to his post, decisively closing the gate and shutting out the beggars.

Amit reads the name on the envelope – so innocuous, a pale blue flap of paper, but bearing the potential to change lives.

And lives can change in a moment, Margaret knows.

Please.

'Telegram for you, Suraj,' he calls, his eyes meeting Margaret's.

Margaret breathes a sigh, relief mingled with fear on her husband's behalf.

Suraj emerges from their bedroom, rubbing his wet hair with a towel. When he holds out his hand for the envelope, it trembles. Margaret goes up to him, places a comforting hand on his arm.

He opens the envelope, unable to stop his hands from shaking.

His eyes scanning it.

Then, looking at Margaret, his face ashen, gaze haunted: 'My... my parents. They are...' His voice breaking. Margaret holding him as the envelope flutters to the floor.

She leads him to the chair she's just vacated.

He sits, looking shell-shocked. 'They... they were in an accident. Father, he'd just got a car. It overturned.' His eyes wet. 'I need to go home.'

PART 5

COMMUNITY

Chapter Forty-Three

1925

Margaret

Nostalgia

'This is the village where I grew up,' Suraj says, weariness and grief and nostalgia coating his voice.

His village is a smattering of huts surrounded by fields, tired and yellowing, dabbed a ubiquitous shade of red by dust.

Margaret squeezes his hand, offering comfort, even as she thinks of the village where *she* grew up, lush and green in the summer, coated in a blanket of snow in winter, the image forever overlapped with their house ablaze, memories and happy times razed by fire, the stench of smoke and sadness, devastation and loss…

The train they had taken to travel here was one she had watched pass every morning during her walks, her following of street kids clustered around her as Margaret taught them to sketch. They were so careful and diligent, tongues clasped between their teeth in concentration as they tried to copy her sketches.

These children, clothed in rags, concave stomachs, hungry eyes, living on the streets, skilled at picking pockets, wise beyond their years – and yet their pleasure at drawing was much like any other child's. When they held up pictures for her to admire, their gazes shy and hopeful, she spied the innocence, cruelly nipped by fate, shining through; the natural guilelessness of childhood that should by rights be a given.

Margaret had chosen the seat by the window, the pane a bleak yellow, rendered almost opaque by years of grime and dust.

'Can we open this?' she'd asked.

'Dust will enter the carriage, and smoke.' Suraj's eyes red-rimmed.

'Please.'

He had stretched across her to open it, his smell of peppermint and clove tinted blue with grief.

A rush of hot, sun-baked air when the window was finally open, smoky with coal dust, infused with cinnamon and crushed ginger, laughter and noise, sizzling onions and spiced coffee.

She had pressed her face to the iron bars, the tang of ammonia, rust-spattered bronze. Giggling and banter, drifting down to her from directly above.

Above? Surely not?

Just as the thought crossed her mind, bare feet, coated in dust, smelling of earth, dangled right in front of her on the other side of the window bars. The skin on the feet was cracked, studded with pebbles.

She scooted away from the window, shocked, to a ripple of chuckles from above.

On the platform, a veiled woman, overweight and laden with jewellery, lectured a harassed-looking train guard. She was giving the guard an earful, judging from the man's face and the way he was obsequiously nodding as her entourage of servants, wearing identical cotton saris and no jewels, waited patiently beside her. When her monologue finally ground to a halt, the guard was all but bowing.

A young boy dressed in rags, taking advantage of the train guard being otherwise occupied, latched onto the bars of the window Margaret was peering out of, grinning at her. He had only a couple of teeth, badly damaged and stained yellow, left in his mouth. Before she could react, he climbed up the train on the outside, agile as a monkey.

Margaret watched, aghast and admiring in equal measure, as his foot got stuck in the window bars. He bent down, eyes pleading with her, and she gave the dirty little foot a shove until it disentangled in a shower of dust. He flashed her another grin and disappeared from view up the train as if scaling a tree, a loud cheer emanating from directly above her.

Another boy started to climb up but this time Amit, who had come to wave them off but had been momentarily distracted when he encountered an old friend and struck up conversation, saw him at the same time as did Suraj, who had been making sure the case they had brought into the carriage with them was secure. They both yelled at the boy, who slid down in surprise, his companions booing from atop the carriage.

In the time it took for Margaret to blink, a crowd had formed, drawn to the hullabaloo, nudging each other and murmuring excitedly, the scent of anticipation, the taste of gossip.

The guard, looking relieved to be free of the veiled woman, ambled over, the mob that had assembled seemingly from nowhere parting for him.

He yelled something at the boys in the native language, which Margaret had come to understand was Marathi.

'What did he say?' Margaret asked.

'He asked them not to sit atop the first class carriage. He said they can do whatever they want in third class – sit on top, hang off the sides, he doesn't care,' Suraj translated.

A clatter above her as the daring gang started – she assumed from the thudding – walking atop the carriages to the third-class compartments, the couple of boys left on the platform running alongside on the ground. Margaret watched from the window, her head craning as they reached the third class carriages and climbed up nimbly.

The crowd dispersed. The guard sighed and made his reluctant way back to the woman, who despite her covered face was somehow managing to convey impatience and indignance at being kept waiting.

'Monkeys!' Suraj said, shaking his head.

'I know, they're good, aren't they?'

'I meant…' he began. Then he smiled weakly, perhaps for the first time since he heard about his parents. He laid his hand on her knee, squeezed. 'Yes, they are.'

Margaret left the window open as the train pulled away, juddering and groaning, Amit fading from sight. It gathered speed, rushing past the backs of houses and then that familiar section, the slums by the tracks. And there they were: her army of urchins, waving like crazy. Their eyes eagerly scanned the train, trying to peer into compartments. In addition to the children, there was the beggar she had met on her first day in India, with his friends. The whole community she passed during her morning walks was there, it seemed, come to say goodbye.

She pressed her face to the window bars, the tang of iron and emotion, and waved her handkerchief, a fluttering white flag.

'I'm leaving,' she had said to the children. Their faces had fallen as the gatekeeper translated her words – she had asked him to accompany her for just this reason.

She distributed the sweets she had brought with her, their eager eyes watching her lips as she formed words, repeating them even though they didn't understand.

When the gatekeeper translated, 'I'll be back', they smiled, and asked through him, 'Very soon?'

She nodded. Then, 'I'll be taking the train.'

'We'll wait,' they told her via the gatekeeper. 'We'll look out for you. We'll wave.'

And so, as she put on her hat, her gloves, she had also tucked a white handkerchief into her pocket.

They cheered when they saw her – they must have kept vigil all morning, looking into and waving at every train just in case, until they found her – and the boys atop the train cheered back, thinking the slum children were calling for them.

Her troop running with the train heedless of the thorny bushes, the rubbish beside the tracks, cutting into their legs. They ran a long way, skinny brown limbs, yellow teeth, calling, 'Memsahib, Memsahib,' shouting words in their language, which Suraj translated as: 'Come back soon.'

She waved the handkerchief long after they fell behind and were out of sight, her face pressed to the bars. Dust stung her eyes, making them water, and she sniffed, using the handkerchief to impatiently rub at her eyes before dancing it out the window again.

'Shall I shut the window now?' Suraj asked gently once the city had fallen behind.

'Yes,' she said and the fields rushing past became a reddish-green blur through the grime-encrusted pane.

She wiped her eyes and laid her head on his shoulder.

'When they disowned me,' he said softly, 'I didn't think for a moment that I'd not see them alive again.'

She held him tight. The train rocked and hissed, juddered and grumbled and it felt like they were the only two passengers, locked in the bubble of their grief.

'I understand.' She did.

'I thought I'd have years,' Suraj said with a sigh, 'to indulge the luxury of my anger. That in time I would introduce you to them and when they saw how happy you made me, they would…'

'Yes.'

'I never imagined this. That I'd be going to perform my duties as only son, to light the funeral pyre for their bodies.'

She kissed his tears, brine and pain.

And as the train bore them towards his childhood home, to his dead parents, as evening descended, weary and dirt-tinted, they made love. Salt and comfort.

And now they are in the carriage that arrived to pick them up from the train station, Suraj's hand on hers tightening. 'There it is. My home.'

A mansion, sprawling wide, bricks glowing pink and gold, resplendent in the setting sun. Rising up glorious from the pebble-encrusted apricot dust.

'My ancestors were landlords of this village. My father broke the mould by reading law. He started his practice in town; he didn't move away, because the farmers depend on him – we still own most of the land around here,' Suraj had told her.

It is like a fairy-tale manor in the middle of nowhere; so huge as to be obscene in the face of the small shacks of the villagers, their poverty.

A man is waiting at the open front door, older, grey-haired, besuited.

He comes forward, hands outstretched. His eyes are tired, sorrow grooved into them.

He claps Suraj on the back.

'Uncle.' Suraj manages a weary smile.

Over Suraj's shoulder, his gaze meets Margaret's. It is cold, calculating, even as it is familiar. Margaret recoils, a chill shuddering through her, making her shiver although it is hot.

'Margaret, this is Mr Varun Karanth, Amit's father. He was my father's best friend—' Suraj's voice breaks.

Oh. This man is Amit's father; Latha's too.

'Pleased to meet you,' she says, not offering a smile when faced with his hard gaze.

He blames her for Suraj breaking off his betrothal to Latha, Margaret understands.

'Son, it was so sudden. It's been hard on all of us,' Amit's father says to Suraj, ignoring Margaret.

She turns away from him – if he can be rude, so can she.

She looks instead at the land spread out around them, shimmering red and hazy in the distance, dotted here and there with huts and copses of trees.

What must it be like, she wonders, for the villagers to live in the shadow of the mansion, forever beholden to Suraj's family, working on farms they can never hope to own?

'Margaret,' Suraj says, shaking her from her reverie, 'a maid will lead you to our room and you can freshen up. I have details of the cremation to discuss with…' His voice wobbly again.

'Yes,' she says, following the men inside, Amit's father's shoulders rigid, unyielding.

Chapter Forty-Four

1925

Archana

Vantage Point

'The young sahib and memsahib are here,' Nandu calls, his usually serene voice slightly shaky, a rare display of nerves.

Even he *is apprehensive*, Archana thinks, her stomach somersaulting.

Nandu, although just a couple of years older than Archana, is head of the servants, promoted after his father, who previously fulfilled the role, passed on.

'Nandu practically grew up at the mansion – he was doing all the duties long before his father died; his father had some sort of prolonged disease and was often ill, so Nandu would fill in. And he picked up English too along the way,' Leela had informed Archana imperiously when Archana on her first day had remarked, surprised, when told they all reported to Nandu, 'But he's so *young*!'

Now, Nandu speaks directly to her: 'You're to attend to the memsahib, show her to her rooms, in Leela's absence.'

Leela had to go home, suffering a severe stomach ache.

'An anxiety attack, more like!' Archana hears Pramila's voice in her head.

She experiences a stab of panic mingled with excitement at attending to the memsahib: this woman who has turned the sahib's head so he went against his own parents, ignoring duty, upbringing, in order to marry her.

How must the sahib be feeling now, his parents dying without his having made peace with them? Perhaps he doesn't care. Archana sends a small prayer of thanks to the gods that her sister is reconciled with their mother.

She waits just inside the hall, ready to be called to attention when the memsahib needs her, from this vantage point seeing everything without drawing attention to herself.

The carriage that has been steadily edging closer comes to a stop and the new sahib, the prodigal son, emerges.

He is a younger, thinner version of the old sahib; clean-shaven, his face worn and tired, run down by grief. A lacklustre version with none of the panache or gravitas the moustache, the beard and age had provided the older sahib. Sorrow has paled him; his whole being seems defeated, hunched. It is hard to believe that this man would go against everything that had been decreed for him, turn his back on his roots.

Then the reason for his, Archana assumes, uncharacteristic rebellion steps out. She is wearing a green dress the colour of mint washed with the star-spangled dew of morning, and a matching hat. She is as tall as the sahib and she is beautiful. Truly eye-catching, but not in the vampish, aggressive way Archana had been expecting. Her every movement is graceful, her gaze bright and inquisitive, as she stands there, framed by the red-gold aura of evening, and takes in the house.

This woman has successfully followed her heart, marrying a man of different race and culture to her, and accompanied him halfway across the world. There must have been uproar and outrage from her family and friends as well as the sahib's family at their union, yet despite this, she has married for love.

Archana has heard from the other servants that the memsahib is educated, that she went to college, that she is an artist, famous in England.

The memsahib is everything Archana is not, but wishes she was. Smart, educated, thinking for herself, loving and living for herself. On equal terms with her husband. Unshackled by duty.

Free.

Chapter Forty-Five

1925

Margaret

A Beautiful Sound

The interior of the house is cool, dark. Grief pervading the walls, ghosts of previous owners haunting it.

The impression of wide, long rooms, high ceilings, tapestries, intricate furniture. The pungent aroma of loss and spices, the stunned hush cast by death.

Beams of mellow evening light, burnt pink, angle unevenly from the high, vast ceiling, creating small spotlights on the chequered floor tiles, throwing everything else into shadow.

'Memsahib.' A maid appears in the gloom in front of her, anklets chiming a festive melody at odds with the sombre mood permeating the house. A beautiful sound.

'Please come,' the maid says in English, bowing slightly, then turning round and walking away, expecting Margaret to follow.

Margaret takes a step, and stops in shock as the woman ahead of her walks through a lance of light, coming sharply into focus.

Evie.

She blinks once, then again. Are her eyes playing tricks on her?

The woman is small. Wearing a sari the colour of sugar-crisped custard, walking with a slight limp. But it is the way she handles herself, that gentle grace, so like Evie…

Margaret makes a noise: a scream, strangled as it gathers steam, so it escapes her mouth as a choked half-whisper.

'Memsahib?'

The maid turns. Her head is covered by the veil of her sari, only her forehead, nose and eyes visible. But those eyes! Tawny almond flecked with honey, glinting in the half-light.

Evie. All grown up.

Margaret blinks, her gaze blurry, mouth tart with shock and reminiscence and longing.

From somewhere to her left, men's voices, Suraj and Amit's father, low and rumbling.

The maid's head tilted to the side like Evie's used to when she was thinking.

Margaret shakes her head to clear it. It is the journey. The disconnect she feels at this sudden change, just when she was getting settled into life in Bombay.

But... The maid's intelligent, dark gaze. It really *is* so very like Evie's.

'Memsahib?'

Her voice like bells.

'What's your name?' she hazards, knowing that the maid may not understand.

But... She spoke in English before, did she not?

'Archana,' the maid says.

'You know English?'

'I went to a school run by missionary nuns until I married.'

'You are married?' Margaret cannot keep the surprise from her voice. The girl looks barely sixteen.

Margaret knows from the slum children she was teaching to sketch that they marry early here. Girls used to appear for a couple of lessons and then disappear. When she managed to ask – they had developed a system of communicating through sign language and the children, sharp and bright, had picked up some English – they would tell her they were married. She would see girls, barely older than children themselves, hoisting babies onto their hips. She had thought they were siblings until one of the children called a slip of a girl 'Ma', *mother*.

'I wanted to study,' the maid is saying, her voice the dream-tinted blue of wistfulness, 'but I had to do my duty and get married.' There's a heaviness there, sadness, the purple wash of what-might-have-been.

'Oh,' Margaret says, her mind galvanised into action.

Since the telegram arrived, followed by a frenzy of packing and goodbyes, she's felt a tad apprehensive about leaving Bombay, coming here. She knew of course that they couldn't stay with Amit for ever, but she had assumed that in time, once they were financially able, they would move into a place of their own, ideally near Amit's house. Suraj would continue at his workplace and Margaret her work with the slum children. At the weekends they would do their bit towards the Independence movement alongside Amit. Margaret had not really discussed this with Suraj, but she knew it was what he wanted – they had never needed words to read each other's minds.

But with his parents' sudden and unexpected demise, everything had changed.

Margaret knows that it will take a while for Suraj to sort out his parents' affairs, although she hopes that at the end of it, they will move back to Bombay.

She has grown to love the city. She's well on her way to achieving the dreams she'd spun when she left England for India; Bombay has more than delivered on the fresh start she'd hoped for.

Since arriving in Bombay, she has become reacquainted with her old self, the girl she was before the air raid. She feels complete, whole again. Working with the slum children has taught her to appreciate what she has, be thankful for her blessings, her life, rather than wallow in all she has lost.

She's loved having a sense of purpose, being useful. Painting is something she enjoys and is good at, but she's discovered what she loves most is sharing that joy with others, teaching the slum children to sketch.

This is why, when the telegram arrived, a small, selfish part of her was anxious. She felt for her husband, but she also worried about going to his hometown, where she had not been welcome when his parents were alive. She had decided Bombay was where they would live and love and realise their dreams and she was wary of change, coming here. Especially under these circumstances.

She fretted that she'd be at a loose end – she had enjoyed being busy, doing something worthwhile with her time.

And now this girl who reminded her so very strongly of her long-dead sister was providing her with the perfect opportunity!

'I'll teach you,' she says.

'Memsahib?' The girl looks puzzled. The way she scrunches up her nose, the crease between her eyebrows: pure Evie.

'I'll tutor you in English. And any other subjects you'd like to learn – at least as far as I'm able.'

'Really?' The maid's eyes aglow.

Why do you remind me of Evie so?

The yearning that pierces is physical, a rush of ache.

'We'll start tomorrow.'

The maid's – Archana's – gaze dimming. 'Oh, Memsahib. I… There's another maid, she's supposed to tend to you. She's ill today so I took her place.'

'Well, I can teach her too.'

'She doesn't speak any English and I don't think she'll approve.' Archana worries her sari so her veil slips, her downturned mouth visible.

'Well, if this other maid doesn't speak English then she's no use to me. *You* can be my personal maid. I'll speak to Suraj.'

Then, 'Once it's all sorted, we can start the lessons. And this other maid... if she doesn't approve, she needn't know.' Her voice lowers conspiratorially.

Archana laughs, tinkling bells. It warms Margaret, chasing away the tiredness of the journey. It is amazing how at ease she feels with this girl, as if their meeting was meant to be.

'Thank you, Memsahib.' Then, as if emboldened by her happiness, 'When I first started here, Leela, the other maid, caught me reading one of the books in Sahib's study. I never heard the end of it.'

Now it is Margaret's turn to laugh. 'You like to read?'

'I *love* reading.' Then, softly. 'But I haven't had a chance to since I got married. I might have forgotten how...'

'It doesn't work that way.' Margaret smiles kindly. 'It's splendid that you enjoy reading. We'll include a reading session in your lessons.'

Archana beams, a brief flash of brightness, like lightning illuminating the night sky. Her smile spearing Margaret's heart, for it *is* Evie, all grown up.

Bittersweet being with this girl. Her sister come back to her, and yet not.

Margaret climbs the stairs behind Archana, who is markedly jauntier, almost skipping despite her limp, happier now that she has a purpose here. She won't be waiting around while Suraj sorts out his parents' affairs.

She had not expected this instant connection with the maid, for things to fall into place quite this soon.

Despite the sad circumstances of her arriving here, as she follows Archana, this woman who reminds her so strongly of her sister, past endless, cavernous rooms, she is fired up with energy, renewed hope.

Chapter Forty-Six

2000

Emma

Peaceful

Her grandmother's nurse, Anne, leads Emma to the bower.

Margaret, bundled up in her winter clothes, sits watching the angel, the plants in the bower frost-tipped and waiting, patiently, for the reviving kiss of spring. Margaret likes to sit here, rain or shine, summer or winter, except when she is feeling *really* ill, which has been quite often lately.

But today, her grandmother looks happy. Peaceful.

'Look who's here, Margaret.'

She turns and when she sees Emma, her face lights up in a smile. She holds out a hand.

'Emma, darling…'

Her grandmother's eyes are clear, not clouded over with pain as they often are nowadays despite the ever-increasing mountain of pills she takes.

'I was thinking of you today. I had a feeling you might visit.'

Emma takes her grandmother's hand, feeling her devastated heart settling a tiny bit. The arbour is peaceful. The angel serene. Margaret's hand warm in hers.

'What's the matter, my love?' Margaret asks, softly.

Perhaps it is the gentleness in her grandmother's voice. Perhaps it is the tone, like the one Emma uses when her own daughter is upset. But it is enough to unleash all the emotions Emma has been holding in since the previous evening when her world overturned.

'I... I...'

Her grandmother waits. And sitting there, the icy breeze bleached with snow caressing their faces with frosty fingers, Emma tells her grandmother everything.

Afterward, Margaret pats Emma's hand, her touch soft as comfort.

'Sometimes,' Margaret says, 'the hardest thing in the world is doing what is right.' She sighs, her voice burnished yellow. 'Believe me, I know.'

Her grandmother understands. It is a gift.

'What you need,' Margaret says, 'is a break.'

'A break?' Emma looks at her grandmother. 'But I... Chloe...'

But even as she speaks, her mind is providing alternatives. The Christmas holidays are looming – family time – but with what she knows now about David, his choosing reputation over family, she is dreading just that.

With regards to her project, she had been at that stage where she could see the finish, and it fired her up. Well, now the fire the project has stoked has consumed her; it has leapt up and singed her.

She could do with a break.

'You need time to think over what to do. This is going to affect all of you,' her grandmother says.

'Yes.'

'You see, in my case I... I didn't take time to think, I acted impulsively. That was my mistake.'

'Gran?'

Margaret blinks, patting Emma's face with her papery palm. 'You need to go somewhere far away from all of this.'

'That would be nice.' Emma smiles wryly. 'But I can't afford—'

'Here.' Margaret digs around in the pocket of her dress. She holds something out to Emma. An envelope, perfumed with lavender.

'Open it, go on,' her grandmother prompts.

Inside, thick yellow paper, officious, legal.

'Gran?'

'I had a feeling, you see, that you might come today so I tucked this in my pocket…'

'Ah,' Emma says, but she doesn't understand.

'They are the deeds to my house in India,' her grandmother clarifies.

Chapter Forty-Seven

1925

Archana

Bargains with the Gods

When Archana slips onto the mat after washing the dishes under the coconut tree in the silvery half-moon's light, under a canopy of twinkling stars, the night scented with herbs and cooling earth, alive with sounds, she is aware of pulsing heat radiating from her husband.

The sense of relief she experiences at finally resting her aching body, tired out with the day's work, is replaced with intense panic.

She had been praying softly as she cleaned the dishes, unease nagging her, because her husband had struggled to finish his dinner and refused a second helping – something he usually needed no urging for. She had tried and failed not to read too much into his unusually flushed face.

My prayers are not working, she thinks desperately, her mouth sour violet with the taste of dread as she strokes her husband's forehead and finds it burning to the touch.

Please. No, she thinks even as she stands, her whole body protesting as muscles that were just beginning to relax are galvanised into action again.

Her mother-in-law stirs but doesn't wake as Archana pushes aside the sari curtain that separates the one room they all live and sleep in, and fetches water and a cloth. Her father-in-law continues to snore in his section of the small space.

Throughout the night as she sponges her husband's hot, fevered body, Archana prays, making bargains with the gods. *Please don't let him die. I'll be a dutiful wife, I'll not dream of escape, if only you spare him. I've only just started my lessons with the new memsahib, I enjoy them so much. Please can I have some more time? I'm not ready to sacrifice my life just yet. If you spare him, I'll be a good wife, the best.*

And even as she promises the gods to do her duty by her husband, another part of her is frantically devising escape routes: *The new memsahib has taken a shine to me, made me her personal maid. She's teaching me, and she is so friendly and approachable. I know she will help – she's even mentioned it a few times. Now is the time to run away, escape this marriage, before he dies and I'm well and truly trapped.*

Her husband cries out in his sleep and Archana is assaulted by guilt, vivid purple.

You're horrible. He's suffering and all you can think of is escape. You want to abandon him when he's been nothing but kind to you.

He thrashes about on the mattress, restless, hot to the touch, sweating all over.

Archana pulls the sheet off her husband. She holds him to her – something he normally doesn't like, claiming he can't sleep when someone is touching him. He isn't a tactile person, only touching her when he wants to be with her, but now he is too ill to notice or mind. His heart is beating very fast.

Please get better, she prays.

Archana startles awake when the cockerel crows loudly just outside the mud walls. She had fallen asleep holding her husband.

Dawn tinges the dark edges of night ashen grey.

Her husband, asleep within the cocoon of her arms, is no longer hot and his breathing is even, normal.

She sobs silently with sheer relief even as she gently frees her arms from around him and gets up to go about her chores.

When he sits down to breakfast, he looks washed out. Old. But he is not flushed and doesn't appear feverish.

'Are you feeling okay?' she asks.

Please, gods.

He blinks as if far away. 'Yes.'

'You were not very well last night. Perhaps stay at home today?' she suggests tentatively.

Over by the entrance to the hut, her mother-in-law stops in the act of oiling her hair and meets Archana's eye, a question in her gaze.

'I'm feeling alright,' her husband says, but although he finishes his tea he doesn't eat all of his breakfast. Normally, he polishes it off and has seconds, but even though she has made rotis, soft and plump, fresh off the fire, and served them with her mother's lime pickle, his favourite, he takes only a few bites before pushing the banana leaf which serves as plate away.

Once again, her mother-in-law looks at Archana, the worry in the old woman's eyes mirroring her own.

'You'd better go to the temple this evening after work to pray for your husband's continued good health.' The accustomed sharpness in her mother-in-law's voice is tempered by anxiety.

'I will.'

Archana returns her mother-in-law's apprehensive stare, and there's communion in their complicit gaze. They are both worried, afraid. It is the first time they have agreed on anything.

Archana's breakfast: her husband's half-eaten roti – he couldn't even finish one when usually, he eats at least four – tastes like mud in her mouth, unease uncoiling venomous in her stomach.

She sees her husband off to the fields along with her, for once silent, mother-in-law, who has been rendered mute with anxiety. Then she walks to work, her steps heavy, sombre, hoping her lessons with the memsahib – accomplished and inspiring, a woman who has fashioned her own destiny instead of meekly awaiting fate to direct her life – will take Archana's mind off her fear. She prays that some of the memsahib's courage in doing what she felt was right – marrying the sahib because she loved him even though he was of a different culture and race – regardless of what others, even loved ones, might think, will rub off on her.

Chapter Forty-Eight

1925

Margaret

Tradition and Superstition

Margaret sits on the balcony of her room, her husband's land spread out before her, listening to Archana read as she sits cross-legged on the floor beside her – 'I'm more comfortable here than on a chair, Memsahib,' she had protested when Margaret insisted they bring the armchair from the room onto the balcony for her to sit on.

Margaret hadn't expected this instant connection with Archana, transcending their differences. It is similar to what she felt with Suraj, but whereas that was the electrifying, all-consuming pull of love, in this case it is the soft, gentle and yet no less heartwarming bond of sisterhood. This slight, sweet girl halfway across the world reminds her of the sister who resides in her heart, the girl she loved so absolutely and failed so completely when she needed her the most.

'Do you believe in destiny?' Suraj had asked when they first met, and Margaret had hesitated.

Now she would unequivocally say, 'Yes, I do.'

For she believes that she was destined to meet Suraj, and Archana too. In a secret part of her heart, she believes Evie sent Archana to Margaret. Perhaps it is her way of saying, gently, 'Lay past ghosts to rest, Meggie. Move on. Create your dreams, realise the hopes you have invested in India.'

Soft light angles into the room, burnished gold, mirroring Margaret's whimsical mood, making the dust motes glow, suspended nuggets of treasure.

Archana reads slowly and deliberately, taking a moment to understand the words and if she doesn't, looking up at Margaret, wide-eyed.

'Break up the word, Archana. Take out the *in* and *able* from indisputable, and what have you left?'

Archana's face lighting up as comprehension dawns. 'Dispute. I know that word.'

Margaret looking at the starburst radiance of her smile, those eyes, sea-glazed pebbles rubbed smooth by centuries of waves, once again being reminded forcefully, poignantly of Evie.

Being with Archana, teaching her, has not only given Margaret purpose, but also restored Evie to her. The sister she was not able to save.

Somehow, in Archana, this woman who is as different as can be from Margaret in upbringing and race, Margaret sees the woman her sister would have become, had she had the chance to grow up.

You are giving in to whimsy.

Why not? For in this country, steeped in tradition and superstition, the notion of rebirth is commonplace.

In Bombay, when Margaret said she wanted to learn more about India and its people, Suraj had declared, 'You must begin with the stories that we grew up with,' and gifted her the *Mahabharata* and *Ramayana*.

Margaret had devoured the epics, mesmerised by the extravagant tales of war and love among gods and humans. Since then she has been reading up as much as she can about India, especially recently, having raided Suraj's father's substantial library of books, as much for her sake as Archana's.

The idea that Evie might have come back to Margaret through Archana makes very real sense in this setting.

'Archana, you can borrow some books to take home with you,' Margaret had said when they first started these lessons.

Archana had smiled wryly. There was such ache in that smile that it hurt Margaret to look. It spoke of being left out, other. Had Evie smiled like this and Margaret been too young to read the pain in it? It spoke to the lonely girl Margaret had been before she became part of the Bloomsbury Group, peering from the sidelines.

To the child Margaret's untrained eyes, Evie had always handled her disability gracefully; she accepted it and made the best of it. But there must have been times when Evie was frustrated by the constraints of her wheelchair, by all she couldn't do. Her disability was in the end what cost her her life, trapped in her room, relying on Margaret to get help.

'Memsahib, there is no time as it is to do all the chores my mother-in-law sets me. She would banish me from the house if I indulged in reading,' Archana was saying, making light of the drudgery she surely faced at home.

'Would that be such a bad thing?'

The possibility of freedom dancing briefly, fiery bright, in Archana's eyes. Then her shoulders slumping, defeated. 'It's not easy, Memsahib.'

'Why not?'

And Archana had told her, in her halting but precise English, scrabbling for the right words, her story. How her sister had been shunned for daring to love an untouchable. How Archana was the good daughter, expected to do her duty. How those bonds were almost impossible to break, cut free.

'But…' Margaret was upset on behalf of this intelligent girl constrained by duty, reined in by tradition, family expectation.

'My husband is a good man. He's gone out of his way to look out for my mother. He's kind, he doesn't hit me…'

Margaret flinched at the matter-of-fact way Archana said it, like hitting was the norm and anything else was kindness of the highest order. 'Archana—'

'Memsahib, I can't. Not yet.' Archana pleading.

Margaret had heeded her plea. The *not yet* sounded hopeful. The girl was conflicted, she could see. She understood how much duty meant to Archana, but she could also sense the ambition, the desire to learn and better herself, the yearning for something *more*, coming off her in palpable waves.

Margaret would wait. This would be her purpose while she was here: not only to teach Archana, but to get her away from her husband – whom she clearly liked and respected but equally clearly didn't love – and her in-laws. To give her access to the dreams she thought were out of her reach.

They have taken to having their lessons in this room.

Suraj is busy; he wakes with the dawn and works in the study, settling his parents' affairs, before going into his father's office in town after breakfast, returning late in the evening, hollows under his eyes, grooves wrought on his forehead that she tries her best to kiss away during the night.

Her first morning here, Margaret woke to an empty bed.

She had gone downstairs in search of him, past brooding, shadowy rooms, an aura of melancholy pervading the very bricks as if the house was mourning its previous occupants.

Her husband was surrounded by books in the study, where he had been sequestered with Amit's father the previous night.

A bottle of whisky on the desk, three-quarters empty. Suraj's head on the table, eyes closed, small snores escaping his open mouth. An ashtray with cigar butts. The air in the room dense with the acrid fug of smoke, alcohol and mourning.

She'd coughed and Suraj had startled awake.

'Margaret?' He blinked, rubbing his bloodshot eyes.

He looked so young, his hair dishevelled, the shadow of a burgeoning beard, his cheeks criss-crossed with lines from the table, grief etched into the grooves of his tired face.

She'd gone up to him and ran a hand through his tousled hair.

'What's the time?' And, noting the light angling into the room despite the curtains pulled shut, 'Oh… I fell asleep.' Colour rushing into his face. 'I meant to come up.'

Suraj's gaze. Something in it…

'What's the matter?'

'My father. When he disowned me, I thought he'd cut me off completely, but… He's left this house and his practice to me.'

His eyes shining, raw with pain.

'My father wanted me to follow in his footsteps, Margaret. I let my parents down and I feel… I feel so *guilty*. They loved me, I was their only son and they died thinking that I—' His voice breaking. He swallowed. 'You know about guilt, Margaret, more than anyone. I *have* to do this…'

Her band of slum children of whom she had become so fond, who she had been teaching to sketch and who in turn had been teaching her to forget everything that came before and everything that would follow and to live in the moment, who showed her every morning how to find joy in small things, be happy with so little. They had followed the train that conveyed her here as far as they possibly could. 'Please come back,' they had called.

One day, she and Suraj would return there. Perhaps not as soon as Margaret planned or hoped, but they *would*. Until then, she'd just have to recalibrate her plans, change the setting of her happy-ever-after from Bombay to here, Suraj's hometown.

'I know you wanted us to settle in Bombay. I wanted that too, but the people my father represented, they need me.' He wiped a hand over his eyes. 'My parents would have come round. I should have listened to you, tried again with them. I didn't realise it would be too late.' His tone bleak. 'That is why I have to do this…'

'Of course you must.'

'But not at your expense. You'll be happy here?'

Naked hope and pleading in his eyes.

'I'm happy where you are, Suraj. You are my anchor, my home.'

His spiced cinnamon eyes shone, relief and love mingling. 'I don't deserve you, Margaret.' Gathering her in his arms, burying his face in her hair. 'I'm so incredibly lucky in you.'

He kissed her, stale cigars, sour alcohol and loss.

She kissed him back, whispering, 'I'm the lucky one.'

Suraj had written to Amit telling him of his decision, and Margaret had added a letter of her own. 'Please could you ask the gatekeeper to pass on a message to the children by the railtracks that I'll be away for a while, but I will come and see them as soon as I can. Please tell them to sketch anything and everything, like I have taught them, until I am back.' She had enclosed some paper and pencils to be handed out to them.

*

Margaret and Archana have taken to working in the morning under the guise of Archana helping Margaret to dress and change.

'If the other servants knew you were teaching me, they'd be angry. I'm getting ideas above my station, they'd say. As it is, Leela is annoyed that you've chosen me to be your personal maid,' Archana says.

They talk about what Archana has just read out loud and afterward, Archana tells her stories of village life. But she always veers the topic round to Margaret; she loves hearing Margaret's stories.

'My life is boring, Memsahib. All I do is work. But you… you've *lived*.' Her eyes shining, admiration and envy.

'You're amazing, Memsahib. You and Sahib have defied duty for love and it has worked, unlike with my sister.' Her voice wistful and awed.

'Oh, I—'

'You've been to university. You're a successful painter in your own right. And the sahib is so proud of you.'

When seen through Archana's eyes, Margaret's life is magnified, glorious.

'Tell me stories of England,' Archana asks as she goes about her chores. 'Tell me about the Bloomsbury Group.'

She listens, bright-eyed, forgetting to stuff the pillowcase, or stopping mid-sweep, her mouth wide and gaping, a gust of wind from the open balcony scattering the dust she has just swept, undoing her work; but Archana does not notice, rapt as she is by Margaret's tales.

'Really?' Her mouth a wide 'o' of wonder. 'They do that?'

'They say, quite rightly, that life is short, that one might die tomorrow, so why not live a little?'

'Why not indeed?' Archana muses, as she tucks her sari in and resumes her sweeping, thoughtful.

'So, will you follow their advice?'

'Memsahib, for now, I think it is safest if I live a little in my head only.'

And Margaret laughs, although it is desperately sad. But she will chip away at the girl. Try to get her to see past her overarching regard for duty and put herself first.

Archana is trapped, conflicted. She wants to please others and she wants to please herself, but she can't do both for they are at such odds. Margaret's aim is to help her see that her duty to herself comes above and before that to others. If Archana's mother and in-laws expect otherwise *they* are the ones being selfish, and not Archana for wanting to look out for herself. For if she doesn't, then who will? Not, in any case, that husband of hers…

'Does indisposed mean to throw away? Oh, there's an *in* so it must be to not throw away – dispose means to throw, get rid of, no?' Archana asks, eyes questioning.

Margaret sips her tea, sweet and zesty with cardamom and ginger. She has grown to like it. 'Indisposed means ill.'

Archana's face falls.

'Sometimes English makes no sense,' Margaret soothes gently. In the time she's been teaching Archana, she's marvelled at the girl's determination to get everything right, her upset and disappointment in herself when she gets things wrong or when she encounters words that are exceptions to the rules they should, by rights, follow, and which thus confound her. She finds Archana's fierce resolve, the high standards she sets herself, endearing.

'It's not that.' Archana fiddles with the end of her sari as she does when she's anxious, Margaret has noticed. 'My husband has been ill on and off recently. I'm worried.'

'Oh, I'm sorry to hear that.'

'I grind potions for him from medicinal herbs. I pray for him, but he is weak and I worry…'

Margaret knows that Archana's husband is a lot older than her. She had assumed from their conversations that Archana cared for her husband but did not love him. But perhaps she drew the wrong conclusion. Archana's concern about his health implies so. Perhaps this is why she resists Margaret's suggestions for her to leave home.

'I worry he will die and I will have to do sati. My mother-in-law has been hinting at it. She's worried too, even more than me.'

'Sati?'

Archana, her voice throbbing with sorrow, loss, explains about her friend Pramila and what happened to her. Margaret is stunned, shocked, appalled.

'Archana, how could they? This is *barbaric*.'

'Memsahib…'

'Surely it's against the law?'

'They have their ways around it…'

'Archana, you're a third of the man's age. You have your whole life ahead of you.'

Archana's eyes dark as storm clouds. 'I won't allow him to die, Memsahib.'

'It's not in your power, Archana,' Margaret says, gently.

Archana's eyes wide with fear. Cloudy with defeat.

'If anything happens, you'll come here and stay with us. You understand? We'll protect you. I— Oh…'

'Memsahib, what's the matter?' Archana hovering, worried.

'I… I felt a bit light-headed just then.'

Archana leads Margaret to the bed, props her up with a nest of pillows and gets her a drink of water. 'I shouldn't have brought it up,' she says.

'It's not you. I've been feeling like this lately – I think I need to eat something.'

'I'll get the spiced semolina dish you like, and send for Sahib.'

*

Suraj, eyes haunted with anxiety and panic, sends for the doctor.

He is reluctant to leave her alone even for a minute, pacing just outside the door during the doctor's examination – Margaret can hear him.

He almost stumbles in the door when he's allowed back inside, wringing his hands and trying to gauge the doctor's expression.

'Suraj, calm down, you're making me nervous.' Margaret smiles, squeezing his hand.

'There's nothing to be nervous about. In fact, congratulations are in order,' the doctor says, smiling. 'You're going to be parents.'

Suraj glows as the news sinks in, his delighted gaze mirroring Margaret's.

'Margaret, I've been distraught at being orphaned. And now, you, my love, are carrying our future, our child. We're making a family of our own!'

And Margaret, overwhelmed, suffused with joy and gratitude, thinking, *Everything I had hoped for when marrying Suraj and moving to India is coming to fruition.*

PART 6

EMOTION

Chapter Forty-Nine

1925

Margaret

Question

'What separates a good painting from a great one, Archana, is emotion,' Margaret says, as they paint side by side in the garden, the wind carrying the promise of fresh rain, smelling of churned earth. The taste of wistfulness on her lips. 'It should speak to the viewer, make them feel, think, experience, ponder, question. Put your heart into it, don't hold back.'

As she repeats Mrs Danbourne's words, Margaret feels, as always, a pang of intense ache for her teacher, who recognised her talent, encouraged her, loved her even. Her eyes had shone bright as she waved goodbye to Margaret. Even now, her letters arrive with wonderful regularity alongside Winnie's, while Vanessa's and the rest of the Bloomsbury Group's have dwindled.

Ah well, she thinks, as she pushes homesickness away. *They are busy; they have their lives as I have mine.*

She touches her stomach where her baby – her baby! – nestles, still just a speck, but making itself known through Margaret's mood swings, sudden emotional highs and lows.

She and Archana are in the grounds of Suraj's ancestral home. Vast and sprawling, verdant green, the rains having arrived, bringing fecundity, the perfume of mulched earth, the sound of relentless rain tapping against the roof. Bugs and frogs.

It's freeing to be outdoors after days of almost non-stop rain, windows stippled with sheeted water, lashing and roaring, thunder and lightning and extravagant performance.

These monsoons were certainly showy, Margaret had thought, drinking sweet tea and eating brinjal pakoras dipped in spicy green mango chutney. She's been craving tart, tangy food, the spicier the better. Suraj teases her, when she takes another helping of lime pickle at supper, 'Our child is definitely more Indian than English, Margaret.'

Our child. The joy when he says it making her heart fill, eyes overflow as they've taken to doing without warning lately.

She is a host of emotions, homesickness assailing her at the oddest times, manifesting in vivid dreams of England, her childhood home, always ending in fire so she wakes up, crying out, heart thudding, the taste of singed hopes, promises going up in smoke in her mouth. Suraj soothing her, his arms, his smell: mint, cloves and comfort. 'It's alright, Margaret. I'm here.'

In the secret recesses of her heart where she conceals her fears, she worries something will go wrong now she is so happy, so incredibly content, all she hoped for in her new life on the verge of becoming reality. She knows luck can turn in an instant, lives can be lost. She tries not to think of her mother's last, ill-fated pregnancy, George's stillbirth; how after that everything changed. Both her parents never the same again...

And through it all the soundtrack of the rain, wild, lashing the windows, whipping the ground into a frenzy of mud, growls of thunder exploding like omens, warnings.

This morning when she woke, there was stillness, a hush, expectant.

She was entangled in the sheets, Suraj's side bereft of him. She was used to him leaving early, before she woke, and some nights coming home only after she had given up waiting for him, had a solitary supper and was in bed, already asleep or getting there when he slipped in beside her, smelling of industry and apology.

'I'm sorry,' he'd whisper. 'I lost track of time. There was just so much to do. I'm so sorry, my love.'

And as always, in his arms, looking at his face, earnest and shining with love for her, tired and burdened, she would forgive him and they would make love to the drumming of the rain on the roof tiles.

This morning, the sun angled through the curtains, not shining through a sheet of rain but from a white, cloudless expanse.

She had pushed off the sheets and when Archana brought in her tea, they had had their lesson on the balcony for the first time in days, Margaret looking out at a freshly washed, glowing world and feeling grateful to be here, thankful to have a friend in Archana, a husband who loved her, a child on the way. Her eyes pricking with gratitude, great joy and at the same time a sliver of trepidation at being this happy, irrational worry that it would all be taken away from her...

Archana paused, perusing a word with intense concentration, her mouth puckered in a frown.

'Are you alright, Archana?' Margaret asked, feeling as if she was looking at her sister: Evie used to sport the very same expression. Margaret's eyes filled, *again*.

'I'm fine, Memsahib.'

She refused to call Margaret anything else, although Margaret had tried. 'It doesn't feel right. You're Memsahib to me.'

'And your husband?' Margaret asked, as she had taken to doing every day.

Archana sighed. 'I'm praying for him. I went to that temple I had been lying to him about, when I used to visit my sister. I navigated the temple on my knees, praying to all the deities.'

'What? Didn't it hurt?'

Archana flashed that smile that radiated intense ache, making Margaret's eyes prick again. 'That's the point, Memsahib.'

'Shall I ask Suraj to send for the doctor?'

'No need, Memsahib,' Archana said quickly. 'In the village, they're suspicious of doctors.'

'But surely—'

'Anyway, he's improving, I'm sure.' Fierce determination in Archana's voice as if she could make her husband better through sheer force of will.

'Well, you know you can come to us if anything happens—'

'Memsahib, it's bad luck to think like this. He's weaker than he was, but better, I think.' Hope shining in her eyes.

This girl, a mass of endearing contradictions. So intelligent, amassing book knowledge and yet believing in superstition. Filled with ambition and yet held back by tradition. Regarding duty to others over duty to herself.

One day she would make the girl see that she was doing herself a disservice but right now, she wanted to chase the sadness from Archana's eyes.

'Come,' she said. 'Let's paint.'

'But, Memsahib…'

'I'll teach you. We'll set up by the stream.'

They are beside the stream that marks the end of Margaret and Suraj's property, the opposite bank of which the village women come to wash their clothes and gossip.

Once the clothes are washed they put them to dry on the rocks, a colourful explosion of saris, and sit on the grass, sharing paan, plaiting each other's hair, soothing their babies, their children dancing around them and splashing in the water.

'Ah!' Archana exclaims, eyes aglow, and Margaret startles into the present. 'Memsahib, you've created magic!'

She has been painting furiously while lost in reverie. Her painting is a glorious clash of colours. Emerald and gold, garnet and ochre, turquoise and lilac and black all fighting for space on the page, ringing a woman sitting serene in the midst of it all, owning the beautiful chaos.

'What do you see?' Margaret asks.

A kaleidoscope of emotions flit across Archana's eyes. The way she considers, head cocked to one side, tongue poking out of her teeth in concentration, makes Margaret's heart ache.

For her sister used to ponder exactly that way, gaze pensive, her head tilted to attention.

'I think...' Archana begins. She hesitates, fiddling with the end of her sari.

'Go on,' Margaret urges, keen to know what she has made of her painting.

'The girl in the painting... At first glance she looks happy. But her eyes, they are sad. She is young, but she has lived, suffered. And she is... what is that word I learned with you... Oh yes, she's conflicted, I think. Afraid to be happy, perhaps?'

Margaret is aware of colour draining from her face as she stands rooted to the spot. The stream swollen in the rains gushes and gurgles. A crow cackles, butterflies flutter. The air is alive with the scent of wet heat. The taste of stale spices and churning dirt.

She did not realise she had put so much of herself – her fear that something will go wrong now that she is so very happy, with a child on the way and all her dreams set to come true – into the painting.

'Art is self-expression. Essentially, through it we artists try to make sense of the world and of ourselves, to equate who we really are with the persona we project to the world, the scars we all carry, the

haunting ghosts of our bad choices,' Vanessa had said one evening at Charleston, the fire burning low, the honey-gold flavour of marshmallows, wine and friendship.

Margaret experiences a sudden, fierce longing for the downs of Charleston, the whisper of the reeds, the sea glassy silver, the horizon the deep blue of promise.

Archana's gaze mortified. 'Memsahib, I… I'm sorry. I…'

'Please,' Margaret says. 'Don't apologise.'

It is a novel feeling. Archana is only the second person to read her work so accurately, the first being Vanessa. None of the other Bloomsbury artists, writers or critics, not even Suraj, has ever interpreted her work so cannily.

And yet this slip of a girl has got to the heart of what she was trying to convey.

Clouds have gathered above them. Dark, threatening. Thunder rumbling.

'Memsahib, we should go in.'

Archana reverently collects the painting, shielding it with her sari. She gathers together the paints, urging, 'Come, Memsahib, let's go inside.'

Lightning illuminating her world in bright white light. Somewhere a dog yelping, mournful. A sudden slick flash in the rushing water of the stream: a water snake gliding past.

Margaret feels light-headed. Archana's voice comes as if from far away.

'Memsahib…'

Archana tries to reach for her, but her hands are occupied with the paints, her half-finished effort and Margaret's painting.

'Come indoors,' she says instead, her voice urgent.

Margaret is too hot suddenly, although the sun has disappeared behind an overcast, glowering sky the colour of swirling smoke, charred ash. She feels as if she is fading, heat smacking the joy out of her, melting away her optimism, enthusiasm seeping out of her in endless sweat droplets. She is tired. Intensely, immensely weary. She wants to lie down right here, sink into the ground.

Archana hobbles towards the house, the limp impeding her, turning every so often to call to Margaret: 'Please come, Memsahib. It's not good to get wet in the monsoons.'

And Margaret is reminded again, sharply, of Evie, her wide-eyed, big-hearted sister.

Evie, who couldn't outrun the fire.

Evie, whom Margaret promised to rescue…

The heavens open with a grimace and a crack that sounds like fireworks.

The air raid that night had sounded like fireworks, Margaret recalls, as rain falls, warm drops tasting of earth, heavy and huge. She turns her face upwards, catches them on her lips.

Margaret watches as Archana rushes inside and deposits the painting carefully on the table before she comes running back out as fast as her limp will allow.

She links her arm through Margaret's and says softly, 'Memsahib, come.'

The rain has flicked her veil away and her dark plait is soaked through. Her hair plastered to her face, her eyelashes wet with rain.

'Evie,' Margaret says, 'you came back.'

Gently, Archana leads Margaret inside.

Her hands soft as they wipe Margaret's hair, tuck her into bed.

'Night, Evie,' Margaret says.

Chapter Fifty

1925

Archana

Out Of Turn

'She's calling for you, again!' Leela huffs. 'I don't know what magic you've woven upon her. Even when she's comatose with fever, she wants you.' Leela is both suspicious and jealous at once.

'It's because you act tongue-tied around her that she prefers me,' Archana snaps.

Leela is in awe of the memsahib and is hesitant to employ even the little English she knows.

'Humph! It's your English airs and graces. Show-off,' Leela grumbles. 'And why does she keep calling you Yeevi? Is that her nickname for you?'

'She's been ill, delirious. I think perhaps I remind her of someone.'

Leela's harsh bark of a laugh. '*You?*' Then, 'Mind you don't get fever yourself or pass it on to your husband or in-laws,' she goes on. '*We* won't survive it, you know. We don't have the nourishing food, the luxury of lying in bed, waiting for it to pass.'

At Leela's words the worry that has been dogging Archana these past weeks is dragged sharply to the fore. Her husband is still distinctly off-colour, unable to shake off his lethargy, the fever that assaults him every night, so he is boiling hot one moment and sweating profusely the next. She lays cool cloths on his head, applies poultices of medicinal herbs, makes potions – as advised by the wise woman her mother-in-law has consulted – for him to drink. But he is clammy in sleep, calling out, plaintive, assaulted by nightmares.

'Shall we call the doctor? The memsahib—' she had begun the other day but her mother-in-law had not allowed her to finish, almost biting her head off with the vitriol she unleashed.

'You're getting ideas above your station, working up there. *We* don't want anything to do with fancy doctors. The herbs and medicines the wise woman dispenses are good enough. What my son, your husband, needs is a dutiful wife who'll pray to the gods to make him better.' Her mother-in-law sighed deeply. 'And if not, if it's the will of the gods to take him, then like a good wife, you'll share the pyre with him, although hopefully, it's not his time yet.' Her mother-in-law's voice quivering, so very unlike her, sparking a chill in Archana's heart.

When the memsahib kindly suggested the doctor, Archana had thought of secretly getting her husband to see him. But how? And what if, when her husband, and worse, her mother-in-law, found out how close she was to the memsahib, they stopped her working there? She values this friendship with the memsahib. It is her escape, her respite.

Is she being selfish, wanting to preserve her relationship with the memsahib, the lessons that give her such joy, that have opened up her life, at the cost of her husband? After all, if anything happens to him, it is she who will pay the price…

But the memsahib herself is having the best of care, the doctor visiting twice a day, and she is *still*, after weeks of illness, showing no signs of getting better.

'Are you going or not? The memsahib's calling for you. I don't know how you get any work done with your constant daydreaming,' Leela complains, her face twisted as a gnarled root.

*

Archana sits by the memsahib, laying cold cloths on her boiling head. The curtains are drawn, the room close and humid with the scent of illness, populated by the fragmented wisps of the memsahib's incoherent ramblings.

It is a far cry from their lessons in this very room, punctuated with laughter and stories, colourful accounts of the memsahib's life in England, her larger-than-life friends.

'Get better, Memsahib,' Archana whispers.

This woman, a world apart from her and yet, incredibly, as close to her as was Pramila. Her benefactor and teacher.

The memsahib does not talk down to her, and has insisted, several times, 'Call me Margaret, Archana, at least in private if you're afraid of what the other servants will say.'

She understands, instinctively, that Archana will not fit in if she is marked as favoured, different, and so she makes sure to treat her the same as the others when they are around. In this way, as in everything she does, the memsahib is kind, understanding.

In the deep, secret recesses of her heart, Archana goes so far as to think of her as her friend.

If one day Archana *does* escape her life, these lessons with the memsahib will stand her in good stead. In any case, she has loved learning with the memsahib; she fills the Pramila-sized emptiness in her life. She has liked having a secret she can harbour while enduring her mother-in-law's moods and scoldings, and to stave off the worry of her husband's illness.

She has hoped that via these lessons with the memsahib, hearing stories of her daring friends in England, some of their daring will rub off on her.

What this Bloomsbury Group say: 'You may not be alive tomorrow, so live for the moment. Live life to the full,' makes sense in an abstracted, storybook way. But how to equate it to her life, mired in duty? When the whole point of her life is to do as expected. How to escape these bonds of duty and obedience? When her mother looks to her as her good daughter, when her husband, though old and taciturn, is kind.

Anyway, it's pointless speculating about the lessons for the memsahib is ill. Archana worries for her and her child, the fact of whom the memsahib was so thrilled and happy about. Glowing with joy and contentment. Archana has overheard the doctor tell the sahib that the child is safe as long as the memsahib's fever breaks soon.

During the long hours while she tends to the prone, unconscious memsahib, Archana tries reading the books Memsahib had procured from the study for the purpose of her lessons. She doesn't understand some words but she can garner their meanings after reading the sentences once and again, and sometimes by breaking up the word like the memsahib taught her. She's become adept at putting the books aside quickly when she hears footsteps in the corridor.

Spending time with the memsahib has afforded her the tantalising possibility of freedom. The memsahib makes it look so *easy*, to live for oneself.

'Leave them. Come and stay here, with us,' Memsahib has said, as if it is Archana's choice. As it should be. If it wasn't also the hardest thing to do. The burden of upsetting so many people, carrying their hurt.

She wishes she could be like her sister, who blithely did what she wanted. It was Archana who had to carry the consequences, she was the one who experienced how her sister's actions affected herself and her mother, which is why she gave up her dreams of studying, unable to bear being responsible for her mother's heart breaking again.

Her mother had wanted to die with their father, but she had lived with ignominy, endured hardship for Archana's sake.

If Archana did leave her husband like she wants to, what if her actions proved too much for her mother's heart and she died, like their father had done when Radha's pregnancy was discovered? Archana would be responsible for her mother's death, as she holds Radha responsible for their father's.

It would be a travesty, for her mother is happy, accepted as part of a community, reunited with her estranged older daughter, revelling in her grandchildren.

It doesn't bear thinking about, but it is all Archana can ponder on, late at night, lying beside her sickly husband, worrying about him, wanting to escape before something happens to him, feeling trapped and chastising herself for her selfishness. Too afraid of the consequences to break free of her bonds, although she'd like that more than anything, especially when she considers how precarious her situation is: if this illness takes her husband, she's done for.

A knock on the door. The sahib, worry lines crowding his face, arrives to sit beside his wife as he has been doing every day since she fell ill.

Before the memsahib's illness, Archana loved watching her with her husband, how her face lit up when with him, her eyes sparkling with life and love. The sahib's demeanour softened when he looked at his wife, which was all the time, his gaze following her around the room. Despite their differences in upbringing and race, they are the perfect couple, so in love, as if they are one being, Archana secretly thinks, their love transcending barriers. And since the memsahib's pregnancy, they seem even closer, the sahib so gentle, little nuances not meant to be seen but not escaping Archana's scrutiny, a touch here, a caress there. They are formal with each other in front of the servants but their connection is palpable, their joy at creating a family together tangible almost, the sahib's grief at the loss of his parents receding slightly in the memsahib's presence.

Archana thinks of her husband, then, who she likes and is grateful to, for his kindness towards her. But that is all. And she wonders: if she had taken the nuns' advice, studied further, would she have had the courage to fall in love and marry someone even if the whole world was against them? Then she laughs softly at herself: 'Look at you, trapped but afraid to leave, thinking this way.'

The sahib works hard at his father's office in town.

'He's a good man,' she's heard from more than one villager. 'Despite the fact that he married the English memsahib against his parents' wishes.' A sniff here, a shrug to indicate they are laying that blame squarely on the English memsahib's shoulders. 'He helped Bhiju free of charge with his court case when his uncle was bent upon grabbing his land. And also, Duja with the stolen bullock cart, again free of charge. Perhaps it's his way of doing penance for the heartache and upset he caused his parents.'

Archana has seen him in the study since his wife has been ill, sitting before the photograph of his parents adorned with flower garlands. Touching them, gently, conversing with them, much as his mother used to do with his photo when they were estranged. It has made Archana warm to him, this man who has material things that she cannot even dream of, and yet not what he craves: the forgiveness of his parents, the peace that parting with them on a happy note would have brought him. It makes her even more grateful that Radha is now reunited with their mother and, at these times, sure that she should not leave her husband and marriage, for if anything happens to her mother, she will be just like this man, wanting absolution after the fact, living with regret.

Sahib sits beside his wife, holding her unresponsive hand, as Archana sponges her scalding forehead.

'I can't bear to see her like this. I'd much rather *I* was ill than her.' His voice softer than a murmur.

Archana startles. Is the sahib speaking to her?

These weeks of his wife's illness, he has sat beside the sickbed, talking to his wife sometimes, but mostly silent, and although Archana was shy to tend to the memsahib with him present at first, now she goes about her business not minding him.

In all this time he has never once talked to Archana.

'Punishment,' he says, 'for what I did to my parents.'

He is looking right at her, eyes pensive. Does he expect a response?

'Sahib,' she says, looking at the memsahib, pulling the veil closer around her face, 'this fever… it takes time to heal.'

'You think so?'

Out of the corner of her eye, she can see his gaze. Hopeful.

'It will break soon,' she says, with more conviction, her shyness easing.

'That's what the doctor says. And with the child…' His head in his hands. 'It's what she's wanted, what we've wanted. I…'

He sounds so plaintive, forlorn, hopeless. She can't help but say, 'She'll be alright. And so will your babe.'

He nods, smiles, the smile not quite reaching his eyes. Haggard, with a day-old beard – he has always been clean-shaven but now, with his wife ill, he is not so fastidious with his grooming – he looks even more like his father.

'The doctor says the baby should be fine.' Hope and anxiety mingling. 'But she's not responding to medicine. And I can't bear it if... My parents... It's punishment,' he says again, his voice a dirge.

'Your parents...' She wonders if she dares.

'Yes?' His gaze focused fully on her now, wide and alert.

'They wouldn't want this, to hurt you, to cause pain.'

'Why do you say that?'

She is pinned by his gaze. Such desire in it, such longing, to hear about his parents. Exactly as Radha's used to be when Archana visited her before she made peace with their mother. It gives her the courage to continue. 'They missed you. They would have forgiven you, eventually.'

His eyes widen with surprise.

She didn't mean to say the latter part, or perhaps she *did*, for if she was in his position, she'd want to hear it.

Nevertheless, she says, 'I'm sorry, Sahib. I spoke out of turn.'

'No, go on.' There is naked hope in his eyes. 'Please.'

It is surprising, jarring, hearing the sahib plead.

'You were here, weren't you, when they...' he says.

She nods.

'You think they'd have come round?' His voice pulsing with the need for absolution.

'Your mother would touch your photograph, talk to it. Your father kept his own copy of your photograph in the study. I...'

'Go on, please.'

'I came upon it while dusting. Your father liked to keep the windows open, and you know the study, it's a real dust trap. But your photograph, it was... It didn't need dusting, Sahib. Ever. It was the only thing in that study that didn't...'

His eyes shine and he looks away, down at his hand, entwined in his wife's. 'Oh.'

'If the accident had not happened, I think they'd have got in touch with you,' she ventures. 'They'd have been over the moon at news of a grandchild.'

Now she is speculating, but he is still, his whole body angled as if to hear more. And so she says, 'They'll be intervening with the gods, Sahib, on your behalf and that of their grandchild. Memsahib's fever will break soon.'

He is silent for a while, looking at his wife, his jaw working furiously.

Archana busies herself with changing the water for the memsahib's cool compress.

After a bit, he looks up at her, his voice soft. 'Thank you so very much. You have no idea how much this means to me.'

And leaves the room.

As Archana places the umpteenth cool cloth on the memsahib's forehead, she realises that the memsahib is not as hot as she was even an hour ago when the sahib was here. Her sleep is peaceful, not delirious like before. Her breathing clear, not hot, but soft and even.

Just as Archana had predicted to the sahib, the memsahib's fever has broken.

Relief and joy overwhelm her, even as she hopes this means her husband too will turn the corner with his illness, get better, as Archana has been praying for him and the memsahib simultaneously…

She is debating whether to get the sahib when she hears noise outside, someone hurrying up the stairs in a terrible rush.

Has the sahib somehow intuited that his wife is better?

'The memsahib's fever has broken,' she opens her mouth to say, her chest tight with happiness as the door is pulled open with urgency.

It is not Sahib but Leela who bursts into the room, breathless, panting. 'Go home at once.'

Her expression…

'Why?' Archana whispers, happiness wiped away by leaden dread.

Leela's face, the unusual compassion there, the pity, so out of place, makes the dread explode into wild panic.

And yet, when she opens her mouth, she cannot find words.

'What is it?' she manages finally, her throat hoarse, voice scraped out, even as her eyes plead with Leela not to give voice to the awful news that has contorted her face into this unfamiliar expression of sympathy.

But she knows. Even before Leela opens her mouth she knows.

'They found him in the fields, he had collapsed.'

'No!' Her hand on her heart. Terror in her throat, coated yellow with bile. 'No!'

One thought coming to the forefront of her fear-frozen mind.

Run.

Run away.

But where? And how? She has no money. Nothing to call her own.

She looks at the memsahib's sleeping face, serene now, not harangued by fever. She will come to, and she will give Archana shelter. She will protect her, Archana knows.

And yet…

If Archana abandons her dead husband, these villagers who have accepted them will turn on her mother like the others did when Radha eloped. Then, her mother had endured their shunning, the ostracism, for Archana's sake…

Archana knows how much the acceptance of the villagers, inclusion in their fold, means to her mother.

Can she abandon her mother to their venom to save her own skin? Can she allow her mother to be shunned again? Will her mother bear it?

But if you go back to the village, you will die.

She shivers.

'Archana?' Leela's voice is uncharacteristically gentle.

It jolts Archana into action.

And then, like that other time when she saw the crowd gathering outside Pramila's hut and thought it was her mother they had come to mourn, she is running as fast as her limp will allow, *towards* the village, praying, *Please, gods, please*, her mind purposefully stripped of everything else, especially the knowledge thundering in her agonised heart.

I'll find a way to escape. Perhaps I'll convince Ma to accept the protection of the memsahib along with me. But I cannot abandon my mother now, visit upon her the shame of being the mother of the wife who abandoned her husband at his deathbed.

She runs all the way to the village, breathless. The crowd gathered around the hut she left so innocently this morning, when all was well in her world, parts mournfully for her.

Her mother-in-law's wails, echoed by that of her cohort, grating in Archana's ears as she arrives, panting, in front of her husband's body: lifeless, still. His chest, not moving. Not at all. Not even when she places her head on it, listens carefully, her gasping, heaving, obscene breaths serving only to underline her husband's absolute rigid silence. Not when she throws her arms round him, shakes him, begs, 'Wake up, please.'

Her mother, face swollen with grief, comes up to her, holding her as she collapses.

Then, very gently, Archana's mother rubs away the bindi, the mark of a married woman, from her face.

Chapter Fifty-One

2000

Emma

Warmth

'They are the deeds to my house in India,' her grandmother repeats.

'Your…' Emma is tongue-tied.

She knows her grandmother was briefly in India, married to an Indian man, Suraj, but Margaret doesn't like to talk about that time.

Her mother had told her this in hushed tones, when Emma, young and curious, had asked, eyes wide, 'Gran, I heard there are tigers in India. Have you seen them?'

Margaret had shut down, her eyes blank, no evidence of the twinkle that usually resided there when she looked at Emma.

'Don't talk about India. It's upsetting to her,' her mother had warned and Emma had nodded solemnly, despite not quite understanding *why*.

Now, despite her mother's long-ago warning echoing afresh in her ears, Emma hazards, 'Is it the house you shared with Suraj?' After all, this time it is *Margaret* who's initiated the topic.

Margaret nods, her eyes briefly clouding. 'He left it to me when he died.'

'Oh… I'm sorry to hear—'

Her grandmother cuts her off, obviously not wanting to dwell on Suraj's passing. She is still touchy about India and her past there, Emma observes.

'Emma, my love, going to India would do you a world of good right now. You need a break and I… I'd like a favour.'

Now Emma understands why her grandmother has brought up India even though she's clearly uncomfortable talking about it.

Margaret has always been self-sufficient. She's always looked out for Emma, never the other way round. Her grandmother asking a favour of *her* has never happened before.

A small warmth blooms in Emma's shattered heart.

'I… There's a woman in India. Archana. She and I… It's a long story.' Her grandmother sighs. 'I… I never felt able to…'

Upset at watching her articulate grandmother struggle to put her feelings into words, again something she's not seen her do before, Emma says, gently, 'Gran, would you like to go to India? Do you want me to take you?'

Margaret pats Emma's hand, eyes shining. 'Thank you, but I don't think, in my condition, my doctors would advise it…'

'Gran, if you really want to, we can work around it. Don't you want to meet this Archana in person?'

'No. I… I couldn't. It's taken me a while, but now I…' Margaret clears her throat. 'If you do decide to go to India, please find Archana for me.' She stands, grimacing only slightly, refusing Emma's offer of help. 'Come.'

In her room, Margaret tugs down the painting that is above her bed, one of two paintings she's never without. This one is of a girl, surrounded by a sea of colour, her eyes haunted by secret pain. The other is of paint dripping like blood, shocking red on white canvas. Her grandmother painted these, and others that hang in museums alongside the work of leading artists of her time.

Before her grandmother toured the world, helping disadvantaged children, she was a painter, one of the famed Bloomsbury Group. But her grandmother does not speak of that time, another of her taboo subjects.

And in all the years Emma has known her, she hasn't picked up a brush.

'I don't paint any more,' she says brusquely when anyone brings up her past as a reputed painter. 'That phase of my life is over.'

Now, she says, handing Emma the painting with the girl in it, 'Give this to Archana when you find her. Please. And tell her... tell her that I understand why she did what she did, that I forgave her for it a long time ago.' Margaret pauses, swallows. Then, 'And ask her, please, to forgive me.'

Even as she commits her grandmother's words to memory, Emma is surprised.

Margaret is not a hoarder – she's not sentimental, hardly accumulating any stuff in almost a century of living – but this painting and the other one of the crimson splotch have always travelled with her, her most precious and indispensable possessions. And now, she is gifting the painting to this Archana, accompanied by a message asking the woman for forgiveness!

Emma will ponder it all later, but now her grandmother's gaze on hers is urgent, keen.

'It's yours, the house. I've left it to you, in my will.'

'Oh.'

She doesn't know what to make of it. This is the first she's heard of this house in India and now to find out that her grandmother has left it to her...

'Thank you, Gran, but—'

'I know your nomadic childhood put you off travel. But I believe India will be good for you, especially now...'

Her grandmother blinks, looking exhausted. Her face fixed into that rigid pose, the tight, thin smile that suggests to Emma she is holding herself together with everything she has.

'I'm tired, I'll rest now,' Margaret says. 'Thank you, Emma. Your visit has done me a world of good. My girl, please don't feel under pressure to go to India just because of the house and the favour…'

Emma fingers the envelope containing the deeds. It is all too much, too big, too sudden to take in, and her grandmother knows it.

'Take your time, think it over,' Margaret says. 'And Emma, what you're going through… it feels devastating, insurmountable. I know.'

And looking into her grandmother's pain-clouded yet earnest eyes, Emma believes Margaret *does* know. Briefly, curiosity about her grandmother's past flares, but before she can ask, Margaret speaks. 'It's not about what David has done, it's how *you* feel. You need to take time out to process it all. A bit of distance, a change of scenery, will help. Trust me, the answers *will* come.' She smiles tenderly at Emma. Then, her eyes drooping, 'Send Anne with my pills on your way out, will you, please.'

Emma kisses her grandmother's parchment cheeks, lined with experience.

As she is leaving, her grandmother grabs her hand. 'It will be okay. You'll be alright, my love.'

Emma goes in search of Anne, holding the painting to her chest.

'Margaret palmed that off on you, did she?' Anne chuckles, nodding at the painting. 'She did say she'd ask you to give it to someone called… Archie?'

'Archana,' Emma says.

Whoever this woman is, she clearly means a lot to Margaret.

Why else would her grandmother, who is unsentimental, give one of only two paintings she owns to this woman?

And she sounded so sad when talking about Archana.

What happened between her and this woman? Why does Margaret want Emma to find her?

Her message: 'Tell her that I understand why she did what she did, that I forgave her for it a long time ago. Ask her, please, to forgive me.'

What was Archana's relationship with Margaret that requires mutual bestowing of forgiveness?

It sounds to Emma as if her grandmother, faced with imminent death, has taken stock of her life and realised she has unfinished business: she wants to make peace with this Archana before she passes on.

Given how little time Margaret has, Emma knows that she needs to go to India as soon as possible, to have a chance of finding Archana, giving her her grandmother's painting and her message and telling her gran what happens.

She *will* do it, she thinks, suddenly fired up despite her broken heart, her indecision regarding David. It will be her gift to her grandmother, who has always been there for her.

And perhaps, like her grandmother says, the distance from David will help put things in perspective.

Perhaps in India Emma will come to a decision as to what to do about her own, suddenly fractured, life.

Chapter Fifty-Two

1925

Archana

Colourless

They take her hands and hit them against the walls of the hut, cracks appearing in the mud, her bangles smashing in kaleidoscopic shards of red and bright green that catch the light and wink gold.

They take off the worn yellow sari she wears for work and dress her in white: white skirt, white blouse, white sari. All these women handling her, their smell of onions and spices and tiredness and empathy and sweat, their hands, chapped and rough from hard work, yet gentle when they touch her, when they wipe the tears from her face along with remnants of the vermilion bindi she had applied to the centre of her forehead that morning, by rote, not giving it a second thought, not knowing that it was the last time she would apply red colour to her forehead and between the parting in her hair.

They work on her efficiently, sorrowfully, transforming her from married woman to widow, all to the accompaniment of piercing sobs from her mother-in-law.

Her father-in-law sits shell-shocked, for once not dozing in the banana arbour, tears rolling down his stunned cheeks. He is wide awake for the first time Archana has seen, grieving the son he barely acknowledged while alive.

The village women, when they've finished transforming her into a widow, sit her down, squatting around her in a circle and setting up a funeral dirge, hitting their foreheads and lamenting the loss of a good man.

The men shuffle and mutter and cough their upset, shifty eyes hiding the relief that they've been spared.

The neighbourhood dogs howl to keep time with the sobbing, nipping at feet and being shooed in between cries.

Archana watches it all, unbearably weary, incredibly afraid.

Her mother wipes Archana's wet face with her *pallu*, gently, even as she wipes her own.

Archana looks at her mother in her widow's garb and thinks, *Now, we are alike. Incomplete, undefined without our husbands.*

Colourless.

But I will not be allowed to stay this way. Instead, I will have to combust in a blaze of duty alongside my husband.

Her husband, whose body had lain close to hers the previous night, his heart beating, his chest rising and falling, now motionless. Face waxen.

'He died without issue, the child he longed for,' her mother-in-law keens and that lament pierces the fug of fear that has descended over Archana.

A child. Her husband yearned for one, she knows. And yet he never pressed her.

'It'll happen,' he had said, hope and desire. 'You keep going to the temple.'

The temple. She had lied about going there, using it as an excuse to meet her sister.

She had lied to her husband, and he had fought with his mother on her behalf.

'Ma, she needs to go to the temple,' he had insisted. 'Let her go.'

His voice gentle, never rising no matter how much his mother harangued and yelled and grumbled.

He had cared for Archana in his own, taciturn way and all she wanted was to run away, feeling trapped when with him, worrying about her fate inextricably linked with his.

Even now, there's a frantic thought ricocheting in her mind: *I have to convince Ma to come with me to the memsahib. I need to escape. I cannot be the dutiful wife who sacrifices herself for her husband.*

I'm so sorry, she tells her husband in her head. *I should never have married you. I should have stood up to Ma then.*

They sit. Mosquitoes bite. Flies hover and drone. Dusk colours the silky rose sky the bunched navy of foreboding. Archana tries and fails to find a suitable time, the right moment to speak to her mother, surrounded as they are at all times by mourning village women.

The priest comes.

More wailing.

And then, a sudden silence followed by an ominous ripple. Everyone looking at her. Her mother's hand in hers, holding tight.

Here it comes.

'Archana will do sati,' her mother-in-law announces.

Sati. The word sparks a frisson of pure panic, scalding her, branding her with fiery tentacles. It reverberates through the gathered people, a shudder that echoes through the women, the men momentarily rendered still.

No, I won't. I don't want to.

Her mind screaming like a terrified toddler in the throes of a tantrum.

Archana's mother is crying afresh, and yet her head is higher, standing straighter on the stalk of her neck. There is serenity on her face, along with sadness. Acceptance. Resolve. Pride as she looks at Archana.

Everyone staring at her, whispering. Men and women alike nodding. Sighing. Rubbing their faces. Only the children guileless. Bored. Slapping at mosquitoes. Whining.

Her mother leaning into her, patting her hand. 'When your father died, on the heels of your sister eloping with that boy, I was ostracised. Nobody gathered around me, nobody helped me with the grieving, the cremation. And nobody suggested I do sati.'

Terror, roiling blue-black, enveloping Archana.

This is the nightmare she's had every night since Pramila's sati – except now she understands it wasn't a nightmare at all but a premonition.

She cannot countenance dying, not experiencing any longer the small beautiful joys this life affords. Watching the sun set, a tangerine dream setting the charcoal sky on fire; tasting the first rain of the season, warm drops seasoned with peppery air and churned mud, the feel of wet earth under her mismatched feet; clouds parting to reveal the sun like a smile after days of storms, sunshine on her head like a blessing; the bright yellow grins of marigold, the creamy scent of jasmine, the festive rainbow cascade of bougainvillea; the syrupy nectar of coconut water, the tart brown zest of just-ripe tamarind, the eye-watering kick of raw chillies; her mother's arms, her sister's smile, her nephew and niece's hugs, their small arms wound tight and trusting round her neck, their smell of innocence and love; the slick glinting scales of tiny fish in the shimmering water of the well; the full moon on a blustery night; the susurrating wind in the branches; the gurgling of the stream, velvety coolness on a hot day.

She wants to grow a child, be a mother. She wants to experience another sunrise and then another. She wants to watch her sister's children grow.

She wants to see the smile on her mother's face, the feel of the dog bounding up to her, wet snout, joy and warm welcome.

She wants to share confidences, to chatter and giggle, to grumble and moan, sing and feel.

She wants.

She wants her life, however imperfect.

She *must* speak to Ma, convince her to accept the memsahib's protection.

'Ma…'

Her mother reads the terror in her eyes. Her own widen and before Archana can speak, she says, 'It's okay to be afraid. But remember, you have a whole community behind you. You'll be revered, you'll be a goddess.' Her mother's eyes shining like they did when she was speaking of the glories awaiting Pramila.

'But, Ma, I… I can't—'

Now her mother sharp, biting. 'You *have* to. If you don't…' She shudders. 'It will be a thousand times worse than what Radha did.' And, softening, 'It's natural to be scared, but it is just a body, Archana.' Tender. 'A covering, that's all, and imperfect. Especially yours. Your soul, on the other hand, will be hallowed by sati. You'll be a martyr, the ultimate *devi*. The last of the dishonour sticking to us due to Radha's actions will be washed away by your sacrifice. Your sister dragged us through the mud. You will saint us. Raise us to great heights.'

Her mother's voice passionate. Her wet face shining as she looks at Archana, love and hope and pride.

But even so, Archana tries, 'The memsahib said I can go to—'

Her mother cuts her off, fierce, her grip on her hand insistent, urgent. 'When you were born, I looked at you, your dark complexion, your stunted leg, and I worried that you were destined to remain unmarried, on the fringes of society, scrounging off people's charity, pitied and tolerated. Instead, my love' – her mother's voice thick with awe – 'you're destined for greatness. To rain good fortune upon us by becoming a *devi*. Your sister's sins will be forgiven.' She releases her clenching of Archana's hand. 'You will lose your body, but gain spiritual reward.' Her mother looks at her as if devouring her, breathing her in. 'You're a good girl, the best.'

That again.

'I'm so proud of you.'

Archana opens her mouth, then closes it again, her rebellion crushed. Defeated by her mother's pride in her. By the weight of expectation, familial and that of a community.

Just like once before when she set aside her desire to study, go to college, in order to get married, do what was expected of her, once again she is felled by duty. That time she gave up her dreams, now she is giving up her life.

For a brief, wistful moment she pictures that alternate life where she did not get married, going instead to college like the nuns at her school had recommended...

Where would she be now?

Her mother is still looking at her, warm eyes, love and pride.

What is the point of thinking of what might have been? What can she do except what is decided for her? She who has always been dutiful, always toed the line.

If you don't, it will be a thousand times worse than what Radha did... Her mother's words echoing in her head.

A searing flash of anger.

Why do I have to be the good girl? Why am I always making up for what Radha did? Why do I have to give up my life? Why didn't I run away when I could? Why didn't I take up the memsahib's offer?

What if she stands up now and says, 'I don't want to do sati. I don't want to die with my husband.'

But... her mother's sweaty palm in hers, as binding as the tightest of cords. Her gaze, fearful and expectant, naked hope and proud love. Her mother who has suffered so much, more than her fair share. Who wanted to die with her husband rather than bear the ignominy wrought by Radha but endured it for Archana's sake. Who has withstood the ostracism of one set of villagers and will surely break if she has to endure another. And this time it will be Archana's fault.

She has seen first-hand what Radha's actions did to their family. She cannot do the same or worse... How will she live with it?

She'd rather die.

And so, she swallows down her wants, her wishes, her desires.

I want to live.

I choose to die.

She will be burned alongside her husband and once the flames have claimed her, her imperfect body, her limp, her dark skin, her failure to provide grandchildren will matter no longer.

She will be burned. And once she is, she will be revered.

She will be burned and in the process the ignominy surrounding her mother and sister will be wiped away.

She will be burned in this life but achieve glory as a goddess.

She will be burned.

PART 7

SCARS

Chapter Fifty-Three

1925

Margaret

Custom

Margaret wakes to sunshine trapped within her closed lids, dancing a persistent, percussive rhythm.

The first thing she sees when she opens her eyes is a painting. One of her own. That of a girl surrounded by a turmoil of colour, haunting sadness in her eyes.

And then she sees the figure by the bed.

'Evie?' Her throat feels scratchy, dry. Unused.

It's not Evie but Suraj, sporting an unkempt beard that is at least a day old, looking worn out. His eyes are closed but at her voice, more of a croak, really, he stirs, startles awake.

'Margaret.' Her name on his lips, prayer and love song.

'Evie,' she says, knowing how foolish she must sound, yet unable to keep the hope from her voice. 'She was here?'

Suraj kisses her. 'You've been ill. Hallucinating.'

But… Those gentle hands administering cool cloths to her head. A soft voice reading to her. She hadn't dreamed it all? It had felt so real.

Then, as Suraj's words sink in, her hand going to her stomach. 'The baby.'

'…is fine.' Suraj tender, his eyes shining with love. 'Growing nicely, the doctor says.'

She releases the panic-infused breath she has been holding, her heart gradually settling. She leans back on her pillow, worn out already. 'For how long have I been ill?'

'Three weeks.'

'*Three* weeks?'

'Typhoid. It's particularly vicious and draining.'

'Winnie will be worried that I haven't written. And Mrs Danbourne. And—'

'I've written letting them know, don't you worry.'

'You're not at work?'

'I… I couldn't leave you. How could I work when you're…' His eyes softening, brimming over. 'It was touch and go for a while, you gave me quite the scare. At one point…' A tear travels down his cheek. 'I thought I'd lost you both.'

Again, a wash of pure fear taking her hostage. 'Are you sure the baby…?'

He takes her hand. 'I promise, Margaret, the baby is fine and doing well. The doctor has been checking on you regularly. In fact,' Suraj glances at his watch, 'he should be here soon. He'll tell you himself, but you're advised complete bed rest for the rest of your confinement, given the typhoid and how close you came…' His voice trembling like a sapling in a storm. He rubs a hand across his face. 'And now, what with Archana…'

'It was her. Putting cold compresses on my head. Ministering to me.'

'Yes. She's been constantly by your side.'

Archana. Friend. Soul Sister.

Margaret recalls hearing her gentle voice reading, a comforting soundtrack to her delirium-addled sleep…

Reading.

Archana had continued with their lessons despite Margaret being ill. Margaret smiles. It had soothed her no end, that soft voice that in her illness-riddled mind she'd equated with her long-dead sister. It warms her and makes her tearful at the same time – the sudden, sharp realisation of how much the lessons mean to Archana.

'It's such a shame, her husband dying just as you—'

'*Dying?*' Oh no!

'Heart attack, most likely. He was at least three times her age and grossly overweight. I saw him once in the village. Anyway, sadly, this means Archana won't be coming back. Poor thing. So young and another victim of sati – such a waste of a life.'

'Sati.' Margaret's heart sinking. Archana's in-laws have not wasted any time. But they've not reckoned with Margaret. She will *not* allow her friend, bright, eager to learn, *young*, with so much to offer, to go the way of Pramila.

'It's a custom they have where the wife is sacrificed on the funeral pyre with her husband's body,' Suraj is saying, his voice bitter. 'It's banned, illegal, but they all do it. My father tried to outlaw it, used force, but…' He shrugs, sadly. 'It's had no effect. They do it in secret. And the women purport to want it.'

A wave of irrepressible fury briefly pushing aside her exhaustion.

Burned. Archana. The girl who reminds Margaret of Evie. The girl she believes is Evie come back to her. Her friend. Who's tended to her through her illness. Who had led her, she recalls with sudden clarity, in from the rain, that day when they painted by the stream. Archana had dried her hair and put her gently to bed, while Margaret believed it was Evie ministering to her.

Archana had made sure the painting was safe, first. She has hung it up here in Margaret's room, in Margaret's line of sight.

For Archana to be burned alive…

No. Never.

'Don't you worry about it,' Suraj says.

She looks at the painting – an amalgam of fiery red, angry coral, stormy violet and startling black, the girl sitting serene in the midst of the maelstrom of clashing colour.

'You did that the day you fell ill. It's powerful, but it hurts to look at it,' Suraj says, following her gaze.

'Oh.' An epiphany.

'What is it, Margaret?' Suraj concerned.

She cannot answer, her mind working frantically.

The Hindus believe in destiny, that you are on this earth, in this life, for a purpose, she has read. Now she knows hers. She understands why she felt this strange connection to Archana. Why she reminds her so strongly of Evie.

Now Margaret understands with perfect clarity why she is *here*, in her husband's ancestral home.

I could not save Evie from burning alive, but I can save Archana.

'She is so young,' Margaret says, urgently, speaking her thoughts out loud, 'we can't let her *die*.'

'We cannot go against them – the whole village is in on it. Believe me, my father had been trying for as long as I remember to end this custom. He used force, he even tried imprisoning the village leaders – none of it worked.' Suraj sighs. 'Their argument is that the woman is willing. And the women when brought before the magistrate swear that they want to do it. It is tradition, Margaret. You know as well as I do how much in thrall to tradition we Indians are. This is why my parents disowned me…'

'It is murder,' Margaret spits.

A knock on the door. A maid comes in, the one who can't speak English, who was supposed to be Margaret's personal maid until she chose Archana instead.

The maid says something to Suraj in the native language, head down, gaze averted, veil pulled over her face.

'Margaret,' Suraj says, 'the doctor…'

'Suraj,' she holds onto his hand, 'we can't let her die.'

'Margaret, you are with child. You shouldn't be worrying—'

'About a maid?' she snaps.

'No.' He is gentle. 'About anything at all. Your illness has weakened you, endangered our child. Please. You are my everything. I cannot lose you, either of you…' Tears in his eyes.

'But, Archana… she's just a young girl. She reminds me of my sister. Of Evie.'

'Margaret, it doesn't do to—'

A decisive knock on the door.

'Ah, Doctor!' Suraj says, with palpable relief, as the doctor comes into the room, smiling benevolently at Margaret, and she allows her husband to change the topic to her health.

For now.

Chapter Fifty-Four

1925

Archana

Vigil

The villagers keep vigil by Archana's husband's body all through the night, the priest chanting prayers, her mother-in-law's wails a dirge in themselves, the cool air perfumed with jasmine and settling dust, nocturnal animals scared away by the villagers' keening.

Darkness, intense black easing as a new day stains the sky pink and cream. The sun, a mellow turmeric ball, appearing in a soft golden haze.

This is my last dawn in this life, Archana thinks.

And what a dawn it is, beautiful enough to rouse desire for just one more dawn like this one!

No.

Through the long night she has – grudgingly – accepted her fate, alternating between anger and resignation. As if knowing she might waver, her mother had held her hand throughout, a gentle reminder of her duty.

Several times during the night Archana opened her mouth to persuade her mother to change her mind, come with her to the memsahib, but the sight of her, eyes bright, lined face looking younger and more hopeful than Archana could recall ever seeing it, stopped her.

She thought of how defeated her mother had been after Radha's eloping and her husband's untimely death. She thought of Radha and her children – how happy they are to have Archana's mother in their lives.

'Thanks to you, little sister, I've been reunited with Ma,' Radha had gushed. 'I can bear anything, anything at all now that Ma has forgiven me, and has accepted and loves my children, her grandchildren.'

If Archana refused sati, it would devastate her mother. She might slump into despair, give up on her daughters, even Radha. Archana could not do that to her mother, her sister and her children.

I want to die a good daughter, she told herself, biting back a burst of hot, pulsing rage at the sheer injustice of once again having to put duty first, this time at the cost of her life, the frustration at being trapped by tradition, angry at herself for not having run away when she could, escaped earlier, dumbing down the desire to live just one more day, to sit on the balcony of the memsahib's room and read, to listen to her stories…

I want to die hailed and hallowed by these villagers who have accepted myself and my mother as one of them, she told herself.

Pramila, like you, I too choose fame, reverence, glory after death instead of disgrace in life.

For if I don't go through with it, it will be worse than when Radha—

Her sister… It is too late to send word.

'Tell Radha and the children,' she says to her mother, 'that I love them.'

Her mother nods, eyes brimming, overflowing, love and pride.

Chapter Fifty-Five

1925

Margaret

Conviction

'Archana, sati, when?' Margaret asks the maid, Leela, while Suraj is talking to the doctor in the corridor outside her room, aware that Leela doesn't speak English, but hoping she understands her query.

The maid holds up a finger.

'In one day? Tomorrow?' Margaret is incredulous, but the practical part of her realises that it makes sense. They have no means of preserving the body and they probably want to get the sati over and done with before the authorities intervene.

Oh, Archana, why didn't you listen to me and leave your husband before? But don't you worry, I will not let you die.

Margaret closes her eyes and all she can see is the fire, burning, consuming Archana, the intelligence that shines out of vivid eyes, those eyes that so remind Margaret of her sister. Her vibrant vitality, all that promise, charred, wasted, burned.

The image morphing into Evie, the nightmare that haunts Margaret. Evie trapped in her room, waiting for her sister to come with help, rescue her, convinced Margaret would arrive in time, even as flames claimed her.

She cannot get the picture out of her mind.

*

'Suraj,' Margaret says, urgently, when her husband comes in after speaking with the doctor, 'we cannot let Archana die. I can't leave my bed, so you'll have to…'

He sighs. 'Margaret, you're compromising your health, our child, if you carry on like this, worrying, upsetting yourself. The doctor has advised complete bed rest and this means not agitating—'

'Suraj, a woman is sentenced to death for no reason other than because her husband has died. A woman we *know*, who has worked for us and your parents before us. Where is your humanity? Where is your passion? You, who're so passionate about Indian Independence…'

'Margaret, you don't understand. The villagers' customs—'

'She must be terrified…' Her voice breaking.

'Margaret, listen.' He holds her palms in both of his. '*You* are important. And this baby. Our child. It has already been compromised by your illness…'

She pulls her hands away from his grasp, frustrated. Incredibly angry. 'Suraj, this is not about us. Please, for God's sake, *do* something. Where are your principles? What's happened to your conviction, your zeal to do what is right? If I could, I'd go myself, reason with the villagers who are deciding Archana's fate…'

Her husband's mouth closing, lips thin, a grim line. A muscle twitching in his jaw. He is angry with her. She doesn't care; she's angry with him too. He has shown himself to be less of a man than she's always believed him to be.

He nods at her, as if she's a passing acquaintance. 'I'll try.'

'Thank you.' She smiles before collapsing back on the pillows, smelling of illness and delirium, exhausted.

Suraj does not smile back, does not acknowledge her thanks. He leaves the room without looking back.

Chapter Fifty-Six

1925

Archana

Omen

With morning, a dust cloud, rising and approaching like an omen.

The villagers murmuring, wondering.

When it reveals the sahib, a ripple rushing through the crowd.

Sahib alights from the carriage, paying his respects to Archana's prone, unresponsive husband.

This man here, so out of place. Although not tall, he seems too big, somehow, for this hut. Too different.

Sahib folds his hands and addresses her in-laws. 'I hear Archana is doing sati.'

Her mother-in-law does not reply, continuing with her relentless, unstopping wails. Her father-in-law is catatonic, dumb with grief.

It is one of the village elders who answers. 'It is her duty.'

'It's against the law.'

The village men crowd around the sahib, anger coming off them in hostile waves. 'It's our tradition, going back centuries. This law brought by foreigners' – *like your wife* is the implied subtext – 'is nothing whatsoever to do with us.'

'You could be arrested.' Sahib stands his ground.

'Archana will do sati regardless. You think we care for your laws? Sati has been practised for countless generations. We'd rather break the law than break with tradition. You think we're afraid just because some foreigners with no knowledge of, nor inclination to understand, our religion, our customs, deem it unlawful? Why should we respect these laws they impose upon us when they don't respect our culture? In any case, Archana's sati will ensure our community is blessed by the gods. In return, if we have to suffer punishment for breaking your law, then so be it.'

The sahib's eyes grazing the huddle of women, settling on Archana. 'Is this what you want, Archana?'

Her name on Sahib's lips, foreign. Sharp.

This is the first time the sahib has spoken directly to her except for that stilted conversation in Memsahib's sickroom when she had the expectation of a longer life, and even then, he had not said her name. She had no idea he even knew it.

Everything feels so sharp and, at the same time, dulled around the edges. It is as if she is watching from a distance, as if her body is gone already and only her soul hovers.

I hope I feel this numb when the fire takes me.

Her mother nudges Archana.

The sahib is waiting for a reply. And so are the villagers. Even her mother-in-law has lowered the tone and pitch of her keening.

She looks up at the sahib, only her eyes visible through the veil of her widow's sari. For a minute, recalling their conversation – was it just the previous day? – when he had looked at her with such naked hope in his gaze when she spoke of his parents, Archana feels something pierce the numbness that has arrived with acceptance of her fate. A small rebellious flare. What if she says, 'No, it is not what I want'?

But even as she thinks it, she is aware of her mother's hand on hers, the caution in the gentle pressure her mother applies.

She opens her mouth, wills her throat, which feels inflamed, hoarse, to work.

'Yes, it is my duty,' she manages and is surprised her voice is clear.

'Are you sure?' His gaze piercing.

And again that brief, sudden, damning impulse to say, 'No, I'm not. Save me.'

Her mother's gaze on hers, warning and love.

'Yes.'

The sahib nods once.

Her mother-in-law's wails increase in tempo once again, but they now have a sing-song, approving quality. Or perhaps she is just imagining it…

Archana watches the sahib leave and experiences longing, brief and intense, for lessons with the memsahib, companionship, laughter and the daring thrill of possibility proffered via Memsahib's stories; sitting beside the burbling stream, the song of the honey-flavoured breeze ruffling the trees, watching the memsahib's eyes shine with passion as she talks about painting.

The sahib's carriage leaves in a haze of dust.

Her fate sealed. Accepted.

No looking back.

Or forward.

No future. Not in this life. Only flames.

Chapter Fifty-Seven

1925

Margaret

Disbelieving

Margaret jerks awake when Suraj returns from Archana's village.

'I spoke to Archana. She wants to go ahead with the sati, she insists it is her duty.'

The heat of the anger is like a slap. She wants to break something, hit her husband. She has never felt this impotent. 'And you accepted that?' Her voice disbelieving, sharp, cutting, incensed.

'Margaret, despite the law against it, despite the villagers being imprisoned for it countless times, this custom has continued in the village for years, generations. And besides, we can't...' Suraj frustrated. 'She's determined. Nothing we say or do will stop her.'

'Because it is ingrained in her to do her duty. Because—' A sudden stabbing pain in her stomach. She lies back down among the nest of pillows, reeking of her anger, her upset.

'What's the matter?' Suraj coming to her, losing his earlier stiffness, his face concerned.

'N... Nothing.'

But it is *not* nothing.

Another stabbing pain.

And then she feels it, a gush between her thighs. Unmistakable.

'Call the doctor,' she whispers, and she closes her eyes and prays even as her stomach hurts and she feels wetness seep into the bedclothes around her thighs.

*

'Just some spotting, nothing to worry about,' the doctor says and Margaret's sigh of relief is echoed by Suraj, who is holding her hands, tears in his eyes.

'You're still not fully recovered from your fever. Your body is weak. Please, no worrying about anything. You need rest, both for your body and mind.' The doctor is gentle.

She is too fatigued to do anything but nod.

After the doctor leaves, Suraj, eyes holding the sheen of tears: 'Please, Margaret. I cannot bear if anything were to happen to you or our child.'

She nods.

'I know you care deeply for Archana and it is commendable, it really is. But she *wants* to do this – it is her wish. *You* have to concentrate on *us*. Our child. Our family.'

She closes her eyes, tries to rest.

But in front of her closed lids, Evie, being destroyed by flames, morphing into Archana.

She wakes gasping. Her face wet, sobs building in her chest.

She has met Archana for a reason, she is convinced of this.

I have to do something.

Later that morning, she has her opportunity.

'I have a court appointment that I cannot miss. I'll only be away for a couple of hours, there and back before you know it.' Suraj looking drawn, worried.

'I'll be fine. Go.' She smiles.

It is an effort to stand, a greater one to move, but she does both, ignoring the pull on her lower abdomen, the siren call of her body to fall back into bed, offering a small prayer instead, just one word: *Please.*

The safe where Suraj stores their money is locked. She cannot find the key. She takes all of her housekeeping money and the change Suraj keeps in a jar beside his toiletries. It isn't much, but it will have to do.

Then she summons Nandu, the head servant, who, like Archana, can speak English.

'Bring Archana here.'

Nandu cannot keep the alarm from his face at seeing her up and dressed. 'Memsahib, the sahib and Doctor Sahib…'

'Please.' Even talking requires effort. She has never known this level of fatigue. It would be so easy to give up, give in. Lie in bed, close her eyes, forget…

I can't. For Evie's sake. Archana's. *I can't.*

Nandu looks completely undone by her pleading; uncharacteristic behaviour from a memsahib. A flash of pity on his face, sharing space with concern, before he wipes both out, makes his expression impassive. 'Memsahib,' his voice gentle, 'the villagers, they'll not allow Archana—'

'Try your best. Use threats if you have to. I'll wait for you to return.'

Chapter Fifty-Eight

1925

Archana

Dissent

Some time later – an hour, three? – as the priest prepares Archana's husband's body, makes arrangements for the procession to the crematorium, another dust cloud approaches from the direction of the mansion.

This time Nandu, speaking directly to Archana: 'The memsahib wants you up at the house.'

Memsahib. Her friend. She must have recovered from her fever, found out about Archana's fate. She must be upset, incensed on Archana's behalf, wanting to help, to save her.

Too late now, Memsahib. I've made up my mind. I cannot go back on this.

A gasp through the crowd, morphing into a growl of dissent: 'Do they think they own us? What's this interference?'

Archana's mother-in-law's grieving falters, coming to a stop. Her voice gravelly when she says, 'What they're asking is unacceptable. She's a new widow, she's doing sati in a few hours.'

Nandu looks directly at Archana but speaks to her mother-in-law: 'The memsahib just came to from her illness and found out. She has a fondness for your daughter-in-law, who has worked for her and looked after her. She wants to say goodbye. It'll only take a few minutes.'

'It's unusual. Goes against…'

This time Nandu includes the village elders in his gaze, his voice conspiratorial. 'The sahib's a lawyer, as you know, and sati is illegal in the eyes of the law. He can bring the magistrate down on you…'

The mourning stops completely to be replaced by uproar. 'Let him try! His father has before to no avail! They think they own us, up at the mansion, ordering us about and disrespecting our customs with their threats and newfangled laws, stuffing them down our throats, interfering with our age-old—'

Nandu put his hands up in surrender. 'Look, I'm just the messenger. The sahib is a good man. He's defended some of you and not charged for it.' His gaze cannily seeking out the men in the crowd whom the sahib has represented, the baying anger easing ever so slightly as the men pay heed to what Nandu has to say. 'He has not interfered in village customs up until now, knowing it is tradition, although some of them go against the law…'

The cries of dissent start up again, threatening to balloon into roars.

Nandu speaks above the crowd, his voice high and urgent. 'The memsahib has not been well. She is with child and delicate during her convalescence, easily upset, advised complete bed rest. The sahib is worried for her and his child.'

The crowd quietens somewhat, the women exchanging looks, whispers blooming in eager mouths even in this grief-stricken setting: *The memsahib pregnant! Who will the child take after?*

Archana watches all this unfold as if from afar, taking it all in even as it pours off her numb, cauterised soul.

'The memsahib has taken a liking to Archana as she has tended to her so diligently through her illness. All she wants is a chance to say goodbye.'

'Why should we oblige? Why do we always have to do what *they* want? Why do our lives have to run on their say-so?' someone shouts and others echo the sentiment.

'If Archana is allowed to go and see her, you can continue with sati. The sahib will turn a blind eye, there will be no further interference, from either the sahib or the law...' Nandu leaves the threat hanging.

More frustrated, angry bellows from the men.

From the women, disdain and disgust. 'Why does she want to see a widow and invite bad luck into her life, upon her child? Don't suppose she knows any different.'

But then, a village elder, 'Let's ask the priest.'

The priest grave, stroking his chin as he considers. 'Hmmm, although it's highly unusual there's no reason why she cannot go. But she needs to be back before three – it is the auspicious hour.'

A beat of silence at this unprecedented sanction.

Her mother-in-law nodding before shattering the silence by striking her chest with her palms, keening afresh her sorrow at her son's passing.

And thus, another decision made on Archana's behalf, during the course of her last morning in this life.

Chapter Fifty-Nine

1925

Margaret

Effort

Margaret dozes on a chair, not trusting herself to rest in bed while awaiting Nandu, knowing that she may not be able to gather the strength to get up again, her body a painful, roiling mass.

When Nandu returns, again that look on his face: concern warring with more professional impassiveness, the latter winning. 'She's here, Memsahib.'

Through the open doors of the balcony Margaret sees Archana making her way to the back entrance used by the servants, that limping, distinctive, graceful gait, looking hunched and colourless, reduced somehow, in her widow's whites – or perhaps this is just Margaret's fancy, knowing the fate that has been decided for her.

Although it is hot, Margaret shivers.

She wants to reassure her friend that she will be fine, that she is fixing things for her, that she needn't worry, but there is no time. Also, she doesn't have the strength to meet her friend *and* do what she must. She'll speak to Archana later – there will be plenty of time then.

She turns from the balcony and nods at Nandu, even that small action taking considerable effort, sending spasms down her neck, her back, her stomach. 'Thank you.'

Then, as he turns away, 'Take me to the village.'

Nandu, uncomprehending. 'But Memsahib, Archana is here.'

'I know.' She has to concentrate not to sway on her feet, fall in a heap on the floor. Every word is an effort. 'Please take me.'

He nods, although she knows he still doesn't understand.

They leave through the front door as Archana lets herself into the house through the back entrance, only just missing her.

Margaret rests her head against the cushions of the seat but feels every jolt of the carriage, every rut in the mud road, every pebble ground under the carriage wheels as a physical stab of pain. She strokes her stomach, the bump solid, substantial, having grown even during her weeks of illness. Her child, whom she loves so very much, who is the glorious embodiment of her dreams and hopes for her future, her love for her husband.

At the village she knows at once which is Archana's house from the crowd collected in front of it, wailing and moaning.

A small mushroom-shaped dwelling, cracking mud walls, hay roof. The scent of dung and flowers, incense and hunger. The taste of dirt and despair. A scrawny goat tethered to a guava tree. Emaciated dogs weaving between humans.

Archana's husband is laid out in the courtyard, draped in white cloth, ash on his forehead, flower garlands round his neck, flies hovering, feasting, a priest chanting mantras; the sweet, sharp tang of death.

The whole village turns from their vigil to focus on her as she gets out of the carriage, swaying a little, her head swimming from the sudden movement. Nandu holding her hand, respectfully, discreetly offering support.

The villagers' cries grind to a halt; the priest stumbles on his chants.

For a moment, the villagers just stare at Margaret, their gazes switching between her face and her stomach, which is beginning to show. She is uncomfortable, pinned by their unfriendly gaze, curious and dark looks levelled at her bump.

Then they all start talking at once among themselves and hurling questions at Nandu.

The dogs, agitated by this disturbance, begin to howl, babies to cry, stirring in their mothers' arms.

Margaret's stomach stabs and she fights the ache to sit down right there on the pebble-littered earth.

The goat thrashes at its post, ramming its horns into the guava tree trunk.

'Memsahib, these are Archana's in-laws,' Nandu pointing to an old, wrinkled couple, 'and this is her mother.'

Archana has inherited her mother's eyes. Bright. Inquisitive. But Archana's mother's eyes are not so feisty as Archana's nor as lively. They are battened down by life. Wearing its many scars.

The mother-in-law is small and wizened, with shrewd, sharp eyes dulled by grief. The father-in-law looks distinctly grey and unwell.

'They want to know why you're here, especially when you asked for Archana to come to you and they honoured your request despite the fact that she's a new widow and about to...' Nandu falters.

'Is it necessary for Archana to do sati? Is there some way she can be spared?' Margaret asks.

When Nandu translates, for a brief moment the crowd is silent, then they all erupt. Shouts. Fingers pointed in her direction. Shaking heads. The women's veiled glances just as scandalised as the men's hostile faces, contorted with outrage.

Archana's mother closes her eyes, rocks on her feet.

Archana's mother-in-law spits on the ground, vehemently spewing a rattle of words. Invectives, no doubt, that Nandu, who has moved slightly so he is in front of Margaret, protecting her from the crowd, will keep from her.

When Archana's mother-in-law finally stops talking, Nandu translates, 'She says this has already been discussed with the sahib. She says it is none of your business.' Nandu flushing deep orange as he relays this message.

'She's a young woman, her whole life ahead of her.'

The mother-in-law's face puckers into an angry frown when Nandu translates, the look she gives Margaret one of pure disgust.

Margaret cannot care. The heat is making her dizzy, the tugging on her lower abdomen getting worse.

'They say a widow's life, without her husband's protection, is worse than death.'

At the mother-in-law's words, which Nandu translates for Margaret, Archana's mother, in widow's whites herself, seems to shrink, pulling her veil closer around herself. Margaret briefly wonders why she was spared sati, but the discomfort she is feeling puts paid to her musings. She wants this to finish so she can go back, sink into her bed, give her growing child the rest it is demanding.

Just a little longer, my babe.

She takes out most of the money she has brought with her. Holds it out to Archana's mother-in-law, upset afresh at how little there is, hoping that Archana's life will not be lost because Margaret could not procure enough money to buy her freedom. 'Perhaps this will make you change your mind.'

A gasp flusters through the crowd, their gaze flitting between the money and Margaret's face.

'Money for a new start, in exchange for Archana's life.' She speaks to the mother-in-law.

The entire village mesmerised, as Nandu translates.

The mother-in-law's gaze meets Margaret's, flashing bright yellow with hatred. Margaret flinches, this woman's animosity at last piercing the fug caused by the agony that has taken her body captive.

I'm doing this for Archana.

Standing here, pinned by a collective angry gaze, the sun beating down on her head, her stomach sore and cramping, she feels light-headed with pain and weariness.

When this is over, I'll go to bed and rest until you're born, my babe.

The woman looks over at her husband, then at her son's corpse, worrying her lower lip with her teeth. Finally, her gaze returns to Margaret, pulsing with loathing. The money is clearly tempting. To Margaret it had appeared so very little, but to her it obviously isn't.

She hates me for putting her in this position, giving her this impossible choice. Money versus age-old tradition, custom.

Margaret, although shaken, will not be deterred by the woman's obvious hatred.

I have not come here, disobeying my doctor's orders, for nothing.

As if to chastise her for spurning her doctor's advice, her stomach spasms, a thousand knives attacking all at once. Margaret bites her tongue in an effort to endure the pain, tasting fear, sharp, sour yellow as she wonders for the first time if she really *is* risking her child's life by overriding the doctor's caution.

Please, no.

Foolish of her to only just consider it now. Too late to turn back. She has to do what she has come here for. The sooner she saves Archana's life, the sooner she can get herself and her babe safely back in bed. She rides out the pain, swallows down her dread and turns to Archana's mother-in-law.

'Without your son to work and bring home money, you will be destitute. This will help.' She drives home her point.

'We don't need your charity.' Archana's mother-in-law holds Margaret's gaze as Nandu translates. 'If my daughter-in-law does sati, the villagers will look after us.'

Another sharp pull on Margaret's lower abdomen. Prolonged and excruciating. Margaret sways on her feet, holding herself together with all she has, until it passes.

'Archana doesn't want to do it. She told me so when she came up to the house. She begged me to save her.' It is a lie, but not far from the truth. If she had had a chance to speak to Archana, Margaret is sure this is what she *would* have said. 'If you still insist on going through with this, my husband and I have no option but to go to the police.'

Nandu looks at her askance, his lips thinning, as he translates.

The villagers explode into angry tirades, a few of them shaking their fists at her, their bodies tense and charged, eyes bright with loathing.

Margaret is more shaken than she is willing to admit at the strength of the villagers' agitation, but she means to leave with a positive outcome. She has come here ignoring her body's complaints, the well-being of her child, the ire of her husband. She has lied and will continue doing so if it saves Archana's life. She takes a deep breath that reverberates through her ailing body. 'Up until now, you've got away with sati, escaped the repercussions of the law because the women showed willing. But Archana is not. She will back us up, say she doesn't want to do it and you are forcing her.'

More loud yelling. Two of the men advancing towards Margaret, hands raised.

Margaret tries not to recoil, but she can't help flinching, taking a couple of steps backward, her whole body complaining, her stomach jarring and hurting even more than it has been doing.

This is bigger than she naively assumed.

She's not just risking her life and her child's – please, no – but the peace of the village, their relationship with the villagers; something she hadn't thought to consider, her care for Archana overtaking everything else. She has acted with her heart, assuming it her destiny to save Archana because she couldn't save Evie, when she should have taken a few moments to think things through with her mind. She has been rash, impulsive.

Foolish.

'Don't worry, Memsahib,' Nandu says to her in English, which the mob cannot understand. 'This is all bluster. They would not be foolish enough to dare do anything to you.'

But his voice dips ever so slightly as the men crowd him, close enough for Margaret to feel the heat from their bodies, their sour breath, their quivering rage.

Archana's mother's eyes, the only part of her face visible through her widow's veil, are a study in upset and anger and shame. She seems to have made herself even smaller, as if she intends to disappear, burn in place of her daughter.

Archana's mother-in-law, on the other hand, is a small but determined ball of incredulous, incensed fury. Archana's father-in-law is wilting, grief and pain.

Why are you here? What are you doing? You're out of your depth, her conscience cries.

Nandu, trying to ward off the men, is thinking the same thing, she can tell.

I'm doing this for Archana, Margaret reminds herself, once more.

At what cost? Look at these men, primed for violence. You're risking your life, your child's. You're causing trouble for Suraj and yourself, enmity with these villagers beside whom you'll have to live.

She cannot bear to dwell on the repercussions of what she is doing. Right now, all she wants is to finish this, go home. She wants, more than anything, the safety of her bed. Her hand protectively snaking to her stomach, Margaret speaks directly to Archana's mother-in-law, via Nandu: 'It is in your best interests to accept this money and let go of this notion of sati for Archana.'

The woman looks at the furious villagers, their anger wanting outlet, and then once more at her husband, who is quite ashen and looks set to faint, a bit like how Margaret herself is feeling, holding herself together with her remaining strength – which is not much – and every ounce of her willpower, of which she has a formidable amount.

And just like that, as Nandu finishes translating, the fire goes out of the woman's eyes. Her shoulders slump and with that defeated gesture, Margaret knows she has won.

The mother-in-law nods, once, very slowly.

There is quiet.

Then her hand whips out of her sari and she grabs the money. It shocks Margaret, how little it takes to buy a life.

A whisper surges through the crowd, trumpeting into a rumble.

'Here, for you.' Margaret hands the remaining notes to Archana's mother.

'What will happen to Archana?' she asks, via Nandu, her eyes, the eyes she has bequeathed to her daughter, wide and luminous, sparkling with tears. 'She'll not be welcome in the village.'

An understatement. The villagers are baying for blood.

But Margaret does not have the energy to worry about that. The smarting pain in her stomach is now a dull, persistent throbbing, dragging her body down. 'Archana can stay with us up at the house.'

The crowd hostile, restless, seething, pacing, yelling and ready to riot.

Nandu says, 'We'll leave now, Memsahib.'

She does not need to be told twice. She has accomplished what she came for: she has saved Archana's life. But as the carriage pulls away, the crowd's shouts volleying against it, harsh and loud, staccato as bullets, she feels no joy, or guilt at her barefaced lie, only exhaustion. A bone-weary tiredness. Ache in her very soul. The longing for sleep. Rest.

Chapter Sixty

India 2000

Emma

Spooky

'Wow, Mum, this is *so* spooky!' Chloe delights.

'Yes.' Emma hugs her daughter close, revelling in her joy, feeling excited and rejuvenated despite having hardly slept either during the journey here or in the days leading up to it. 'It is so very different to home, isn't it?'

India has been a revelation. The city where they landed hot, crowded, sticky with spices and scents and people. In contrast, the village where the house nestles is quiet. Surrounded by open land, brown-tinged fields, dust-sheened grass waving lazily in the unrelenting sun. A few small cottages dotted around and the mansion rising above it all – for that is what it is; her grandmother had forgotten to mention its size. Emma had been expecting a dinky little cottage, and had peered into each one they passed.

Margaret's house is huge but dilapidated, weary yet radiating history from its every brick. Bearing witness to a chequered past, carrying the weight, the secret longings and vivid hopes of generations within its moss-encrusted, crumbling walls.

As the taxi drove up the rutted road, fields on both sides, the house looming ahead, Chloe scooting closer to her, eyes agog, her breath coming in awed gasps, Emma realised suddenly why her mother and grandmother had travelled so much, why her mother had sought out new experiences. She was excited, enthralled, her emotions replicated in her daughter, who was a budding historian herself. And she would be, with parents…

Don't think of David, not now.

But thoughts of David came anyway, insistent.

'Chloe and I are going to India during the Christmas holidays,' Emma had said two days after her visit to her grandmother, having looked up air fares and made calculations and decided that the trip was possible if she raided her emergency fund. And once she'd decided that, she'd realised just how much she wanted to go, to be away from David and the choice she faced regarding him.

He had looked at her blankly.

'I need a break to think about what to do,' she'd said.

'Why India?'

'My grandmother has a house there.'

'Ah.' And then, the audacity. 'Can I come?' That charming smile she could never resist, now only repelling her.

'No. The reason I'm going is to have a break.' *From you* is what she didn't say.

'But, I… Chloe. I'd like to spend Christmas with her.'

'You can spend it with your other children.'

'But…' She heard what *he* was not saying. *They don't want to spend it with me.* 'I've missed so many of Chloe's Christmases already.'

And whose fault is that? she thought. *If it had been up to you, Chloe wouldn't be here at all.*

'You don't want added complications – the Masters is hard enough,' he had said, when she told him she was pregnant.

He had called Chloe a *complication*. That was when he broke her heart for the first time.

The more David spoke, the more she was realising that what had charmed her once, made her fall in love with him, stay in love with him, take him back despite everything, was now the very thing she loathed. His oily charisma. His confident insistence about getting his way.

She had rubbed a hand over her eyes. 'I need these two weeks, David. Away from you.'

The hurt, wounded-animal look in his eyes…

'I'll come back,' she said, 'when Chloe's Christmas break is over. By then I'll have decided what to do.'

Now, she looks up at the house, awe and giddy enthusiasm pushing aside her gloom about David, and thinks, *Why didn't it occur to me to visit India, find out about my own history, my grandmother's too?*

This woman, Archana, and the story that is hinted at between her and Margaret intrigues Emma.

Chloe sidles up to her as she knocks on the great wooden door, carved with figurines of Indian gods. The air that smacks their faces is gritty, spiced. Is that cinnamon she can detect, or cardamom? The plaster of the mansion is crumbling in parts, showing the red bricks within, but it stands regal, though decrepit, creepers climbing up its walls.

The house, from what she can see of the exterior, needs love and attention and she imagines it must be the same inside.

Chloe tugs at her hand, pointing upwards, her eyes wide with delight.

Emma follows her gaze and takes a startled step backward.

She is staring at a buzzing black, droning, living mound.

'Is that a… a beehive?' she whispers, just as two fat bees rumble past her, brushing her ears, to join the growing, U-shaped whispering hive nestling in the rafters, dripping honey.

Chloe laughs. A cascading whorl of pure joy.

Emma can't help joining in and all the tiredness from the journey, the stress from the last few days, eases. She tilts her face to the sun and allows the hot rays to warm her. Her heart feels lighter, less burdened, and she can feel the beginnings of hope unfurling, the assurance, as she delights in her daughter's glee, as she participates in it, that things will work out after all, just like her grandmother promised.

Emma waits in front of the huge wooden door with her daughter, smelling of strawberries and candy floss, pressed against her. Bees rumble above them and there is a scattering of cottages in the hazy, dust-tinted distance. She feels slightly light-headed in the pungent, moist, orange heat.

The minutes pass and she presses her ear to the door, but all she can hear is the low rumbling of bees, the gritty air tasting of spiced earth.

She has been in constant communication with the solicitors, whose name and address was in the letter that her grandmother gave her along with the deeds. They had assured her they would call ahead, let the caretaker know about Emma and Chloe's visit.

What if they didn't? Why hadn't she checked? But there had been so many things to do that it had slipped her mind.

On the journey here, Chloe had slept in between bouts of extreme excitement, but Emma couldn't. What she had discovered, David, her grandmother, the woman called Archana who she had undertaken to find, this sudden travel she was doing, the expense of the tickets, going round and round in her head. What was she doing, taking her child with her to a country, a house she didn't know, even if Chloe was thrilled about the adventure?

When she saw the house, her excitement had chased away her doubts but now they circle again, as insistently droning as the bees. She doesn't have much spending money left over. Her plan was to stay in the house, familiarise herself with it, find Archana, convey her grandmother's message and hand over the painting and discover, if she can, what exactly Archana's connection is to Margaret, why she is Margaret's unfinished business, the woman she wants to contact and make peace with at death's door.

Footsteps on the other side of the door.

Emma lets out the breath she's been holding, allowing the feverish excitement that had briefly deserted her access once more.

Chapter Sixty-One

1925

Margaret

Duty

Archana is at the house, waiting. She looks incredibly young and wan in her widow's whites.

'You called me, Memsahib.'

Margaret blinks, trying to ignore the sharp and persistent, mind-numbing pain that is making her feel more than a little faint and focus on this slight girl who, in such a short time, has come to mean so much to her, whose life she thinks she was destined to save for she missed the chance with her sister.

Archana's eyes are dull, lifeless and waxy as the body of her husband, so different from the bright-eyed girl Margaret is accustomed to.

'You loved him?' she asks, unable to help it. In the time she has known Archana, she has speculated about her relationship with her husband, but has never asked her directly about it. But looking at her now, beaten, the spark drained from her, Margaret wants to know.

Archana looks down at her feet, embroidered with dust, lurid orange in contrast to the starkness of the rest of her; no jewellery, not even the bangles all the women here wear, multicoloured glass that catches the light, chiming a melody when they move. 'He was my husband.'

Not an answer.

And now, too late, Margaret asks, already knowing what the reply will be but wanting Archana to say it, give truth to Margaret's lie after the fact. 'You're willing to die with him?'

Would she die with Suraj?

Of course not, no matter how much she loves him.

And anyway, much as she loves her husband, right now she is upset with him, angry at his reluctance to do anything about Archana, well, except under extreme duress…

'It is my duty,' Archana says.

'Oh, Archana, you can't go on about duty. Not now with your life in the balance!' Margaret is exasperated. If she wasn't so intensely, immensely weary and in pain, she'd shake some sense into the girl. 'No woman should die for her husband or for *anyone*. Your life is precious, it is yours alone. There are enough people dying senselessly as it is – victims of events out of their control – war, for example.'

Archana is still gazing at her feet. 'It is my duty,' she repeats in a monotone.

'They've brainwashed you, I see,' Margaret says, thinking to herself that it was a good job she intervened on Archana's behalf. If it was up to this girl she would sacrifice herself on the pyre even though she has such ambition, an intense desire to learn, better herself, so much to live for. If Margaret hadn't met her, didn't know this…

She shudders as she pictures this girl, her friend, consumed by flames, like her beloved Evie…

'You no longer have to do sati.'

Now Archana looks up, eyes liquid ebony and fathomless. 'Memsahib?'

'I've just returned from talking to your in-laws and mother. They've agreed that you're to be spared.' A shudder of remembered fear briefly transcends the agony consuming her, as Margaret recalls the reaction of the villagers, their barely controlled anger.

Incomprehension, bemusement written into Archana's gaze. 'I... I don't understand. It's my duty as a wife to do sati.'

Duty again.

Archana has put her life and desires on hold for duty and in the end this duty she values so highly, placing it above personal freedom, ambition, self, so much so she's willing to give up her life for it, was worth just a few paltry rupees!

Margaret sways on her feet, her stomach throbbing. 'Not any longer. You'll be staying here, with us. You needn't worry about your in-laws or mother – they're compensated.'

'But, Memsahib...' The bit of Archana's face visible outside of her veil is blanched white, as pale as her sari.

'The room off the kitchen where you rest in between jobs is yours now to stay in.'

'Memsahib, but how... Why?'

Archana sounds puzzled, her voice a wail, a keen.

Why is she crying, a funeral dirge, when her life is saved? Margaret wonders, but the momentary thought is replaced by a ringing in her ears. Archana's voice is coming as if from afar. 'Memsahib?'

The pressing down on her stomach now a flame, a bright-orange burn of pain, devouring her whole self, it seems, pulsing hot and liquid between her legs. Not small spurts like before but a scorching, endless gush.

No. Please, no.

The tiredness that has swamped her, the cramping ache she has been keeping at bay with the last of her strength and all of her willpower, overcomes, overwhelms, takes her over.

And then blackness.

Chapter Sixty-Two

1925

Archana

Bad Luck

As the memsahib falls, Leela yells, 'Don't touch her!'

Leela holds the memsahib instead, trying to revive her, all the time shouting at Archana, 'Now look what you've done, brought your widow's bad luck here with you! Go, you shouldn't have come at all!'

Archana, with a backward glance at the memsahib, who is bleeding and unconscious and unable to answer the questions that are swarming in her brain, runs, the memsahib's words, *You no longer have to do sati. You'll be staying here, with us*, echoing in her head.

She runs, once again, all the way to the village. Her shorter leg hurts. But what does it matter when she is dying anyway?

But the memsahib said…

She drags her faulty leg and sprints, coming to a shocked halt as she enters the village, a hollow feeling in her stomach, as if she cannot get enough air.

No crowd at their hut. Her husband's body lying abandoned outside. The flower garlands placed upon his person wilting in the harsh sunlight, bees buzzing around it, flies hovering undisturbed, no one to shoo them away.

People standing at the doorways of their own huts, not gathered at her hut to lament her husband's loss together, as a community.

Their gazes accusing. Angry. Violent.

It is as if she has gone backward in time.

For she has experienced this feeling of being speared by a community's hostile stares when her sister left to marry her untouchable. And then too, her father's body forlorn, surrounded, not by a village grieving his loss, but by two mourners only, herself and her mother. The incredible desolation of it: no wailing womenfolk, no grim-faced men friends to share the burden of loss, carry the weight of memories, happy and sad, of a life lived among them, with them. Archana had experienced the soul-destroying loneliness of it once and that was enough – she had vowed it wouldn't happen again.

The villagers hiss at her as she walks past their huts. They curse and yell insults. Dollops of spit land at her feet, spatter her widow's whites with pungent, foamy loathing.

This was *not* meant to happen.

She was meant to be glorified, not vilified.

Distress piercing the fug of numbness that has enveloped her since she decided to do sati.

Memsahib, what have you done?

A sudden, roiling breeze flings grit at her as if in cahoots with the villagers. The taste of dust and upset in her mouth.

The womenfolk turn away, these same women who used to laugh and joke with her as they wove beedies in the gathering dusk, sharing gossip and problems as they washed clothes together by the stream, who had dressed her gently in her widow's whites, now sullied by saliva.

Her own mother is nowhere to be seen.

Her mother, who was relying on Archana to wipe away the last of the ignominy Radha's actions had wrought. She will not be able to bear this…

Oh.

Her in-laws sit beside their son's body, looking bereft, alone, abandoned.

Through her panic, her disorientation, Archana feels a pang for them even as her mother-in-law pauses in her sobbing, then stumbles to a stop at the sight of her.

She stands, eyes flashing venom, thrusting an accusing finger in Archana's face.

Even as Archana takes a startled step backward, she can sense the neighbours gathered in their doorways edging closer to see what will happen next.

'How dare you show your face here,' her mother-in-law screams, 'after what you've done!'

'I… I've come for the cremation…'

A dog howls in the fields. Otherwise the street is still; even the breeze has stopped, the air thick and heavy with dust and suspense, the villagers avidly watching the drama unfold from their huts.

Her mother-in-law's screech whips the silence into turmoil. 'You won't do your wifely duty but you want to attend the cremation? To gloat that your husband is dead, sent to an early grave by his disrespectful little slattern of a wife?'

Her mother-in-law spits at her feet. Archana flinches but does not move away, staring at the froth on her dust-spattered feet, white to match her widow's garb.

'She said you're to live with her. So why are you here now? Go to your memsahib.' Her mother-in-law mocking.

Archana's stomach hollow, her head dizzy with upset.

Where is her mother? She wants her mother.

'We chose you for our son knowing your sister had brought disgrace, despite your limp, and now, instead of doing your duty by your husband, you send the woman!'

'It wasn't my… I didn't…'

'A white woman coming here on the day of my son's cremation, threatening to send us to jail…' Her mother-in-law's voice floundering.

What has the memsahib done? Anger, bright white. It wasn't her place, her right to interfere. How dare she?

A baby wails. Its mother impatiently shushes it.

Archana's mother-in-law, having recovered her voice, yelling, 'What possessed us to think you were a worthy wife for our son when your sister had already proved your fickle, flighty blood…?' Beating her forehead, crying, 'Our son deserved better.'

Archana breathing in the villagers' acrimonious anger as the truth of her situation settles in her befuddled brain. Frantically going over Memsahib's every word, recalling: *they are compensated.*

'You took money from the memsahib.'

Her mother-in-law looks at her. Disgust, disdain and is that a quiver of shame in her eyes? 'How else are we supposed to provide for ourselves? If you had done sati, the villagers would have looked after us, as relatives of the sainted woman. But now… Look at your husband, lying abandoned, alone. Nobody mourning him but us.' Her voice shaking. '*You've* done this. You've dragged us down to the pit you and your mother were in when we rescued you by accepting you as daughter-in-law. Do you think we'll have respect here? We'll have to move away, start again. Leaving everyone we know, the life we are familiar with, behind. We're too old for this, did you think of that? Leave! Take your shameful self away from here.' Her voice rising to a scream.

'Can't I stay for the cremation?'

'And make a further mockery of it by watching your husband burn while you don't accompany him?'

'I can still accompany him, I'd like to…'

'Then why,' her mother-in-law screeches, 'did you tell her you didn't want to? Why go crying to your memsahib? Saying one thing to them and another to us. You two-faced witch! We were well and truly taken in by you, my poor son included. We gave you a chance, trusted you, welcomed you into our home, our lives and in return you've made a fool of us. By your claiming that *we* wanted you to do sati, that *you* didn't wish it, we would have ended up in prison! How dare you! Leave! I cannot bear to look at you.'

Another blob of spit from her mother-in-law's mouth, this time landing near her face, brushing her ear, sour and fiery.

But Archana is too stunned to care. The memsahib *lied*.

The memsahib, who believes in personal choice, freedom of self. Who would lecture Archana on how she should stand up for herself, do what *she* wanted, instead of going along with decisions made for her…

This very memsahib taking matters into her own hands. Making this decision for Archana without asking her if it was what she wanted. Not only that, *lying* on Archana's behalf…

'I didn't…'

A sneer curls her mother-in-law's lip into a grotesque parody of a smile. 'She bought you off us like chattel. You are her possession now.'

Dirt assaults Archana's eyes, inciting tears. 'I never… I did not ask her to… I…'

She cannot finish her sentences, cannot frame any, her mother-in-law's words reverberating in her head: *She bought you off us like chattel.*

'Please,' she begs instead, asking for the one thing she's always yearned for since she was tiny, tagging after her sister, dragging her awkward leg along, and had, for a brief while, found here: belonging.

Her mother-in-law sighs, sounding infinitely weary, looking like a very old woman. When she gazes at Archana, her eyes are dead. 'It's over, it's done. My son is gone. You belong to the memsahib. We're leaving here since you've made us unwelcome in our own village. Happy now?'

'I…'

'No use making a scene. Go to your memsahib.' And when Archana opens her mouth to plead her case again, sharply, 'Leave.'

Archana goes to touch her husband's feet like she used to when he was alive, asking for his blessing, the sweet-stale odour of rotting flowers and flesh.

'Don't you dare.'

She flinches, her outstretched hand inches from her husband's feet. She stares mutely at her husband's waxy features, still and expressionless in death. Then she does as her mother-in-law asks, her mouth salty, face wet, taste of shame and sorrow. She leaves the village where she briefly found happiness, of a sort, and belonging, accompanied by the venomous glares, from their huts, of the villagers, of whom she had foolishly assumed she was a part, even though she'd known from experience that allegiances could change in an instant.

PART 8

SHAME

Chapter Sixty-Three

2000

Emma

Magical

The door is pulled open with grunts and several tries on the other side.

An ancient man stands hunched in the doorway. He beams at Emma and Chloe, his crinkled face lighting up so his face unfolds, the creases swept back like the pages of a book.

'Hello.' Emma smiles. 'I'm Emma and this is Chloe.'

'My name Nandu.'

Chloe momentarily shy, peeking from behind Emma's thigh.

Emma holds out her hand. 'I hope you were expecting us. The solicitors did say they'd let you know. If not, I'm really sorry.'

He beams even more if possible, his whole being glowing. 'No trouble, no trouble.' He nods vigorously. 'Come.'

The house is huge but falling apart, just as Emma had expected. An impression of ornate staircases, high ceilings, multiple floors stuffed with antiques. The scent of mildew and dust and decay. The doorposts eaten by woodlice and hosting anthills. Chloe's eyes huge, reflecting the wonder and delight Emma herself feels.

Their footsteps echoing. Sunshine angling on the worn chequerboard tiles of the floor.

A sudden flutter and, in the eaves, cooing. A flash of ebony wings.

Nandu shakes his head, muttering to himself.

Chloe laughs. A burst of sunshine.

Nandu stops muttering and smiles.

'Mum, I love it here. It's magical. There are birds *inside* the house and an actual gigantic beehive just outside!'

Emma grins, taking in this house, each disintegrating, anthilled, woodlouse-infested, crumbling wall breathing dust and stories of decades past, witness to her grandmother's time here. She feels awed, standing where her grandmother once stood, coming here as bride to Suraj, an Indian man – a marriage that must have shocked society, both English and Indian, greatly.

How must her grandmother have felt, what emotions was she experiencing when she had her first glimpse of this house? Was she filled with the enthusiasm, the thrill, the sheer wonder of being here that Emma and Chloe are experiencing?

Walking in the footsteps of her grandmother from so long ago makes Emma feel closer to her. The grandmother she's always turned to for advice seems more familiar, known.

When Emma had introduced David to Margaret, she had said, 'In my opinion he is—'

'Too good for me. I know,' Emma had cut in, smug, headily, gloriously in love.

'No,' her gran chastised softly. 'I was going to say *you* are too good for *him*.'

'Oh, Gran.' Emma had given her a hug of gratitude and her grandmother whispered into her hair, 'I'm not joking.'

Her grandmother had seen through David, like almost everyone else.

Why hadn't Emma?

*

Emma looks up at the impossibly high ceiling criss-crossed with wooden beams letting in chinks of sunlight that show up the dust in the room, the aging grandeur, the faded tiles reflected in the patches of sunlight, the birds nesting in the eaves, and she knows with absolute conviction that, notwithstanding all her bad decisions involving David, she has made the right decision coming here.

Standing in the hall of the house her grandmother had called home long ago, now decrepit but seeping memories of past grandeur, every brick whispering stories of a colourful past, she feels her shattered heart settling, her mind emerging from the fog of worry, upset, indecision and self-flagellation it has indulged in since she discovered David's hoax and realised that she was to blame for taking him back, for Chloe loving him – for Emma has always known David's faults, she had just been wilfully blind to them. She saw David as a saviour and parental figure, she understands, but no longer. From now on she will take responsibility, be the adult. Which is why she is here, as much for herself as for her grandmother.

A shaft of sunlight snakes down and warms her head like a blessing, as if sanctioning her decision to move on, look ahead instead of dwelling on past mistakes, and she is aware of excitement nudging aside the ache in her heart as she considers all the secrets from her grandmother's past this house has been keeping, waiting for someone to share them with.

Chapter Sixty-Four

1925

Archana

Scandal

Archana's mother is cowering in her hut, sobbing as she stuffs her belongings into a sari whose ends she will tie in a knot around her shoulders, the dog – not normally allowed inside, but these are exceptional circumstances and she must feel in need of his company – licking her tears.

The strong, all-pervading sense of déjà vu, the scent of jasmine and sorrow.

'Ma…'

Her mother rounds on her, eyes flashing, upset and rage.

Archana recoils. She has seen her mother like this, anger and grief intermingling, once before, but that time the ire was directed at her sister. Her mother has *never* been this angry with Archana. She has always been the good daughter and she was willing to die to keep it that way…

'Ma.' Hurt and panic intermingling, so her voice is a timid, wispy thread. She swallows, tries again, 'I didn't have anything to do with…'

Please believe me.

'Get away. Out of my sight.'

'Ma…' Trying not to flinch at the venom in her mother's voice. Her own refusing to do her bidding – the whine of a terrified infant.

'You're dead to me. Go to your memsahib.'

Nausea rising, bitter green, in Archana's throat at the thought of the woman who by her lies has condemned her to this ostracism, turned her own mother against her.

'Live out the life you so desperately wanted at the cost of...' Her mother's voice, rage, ache, breaks. Dissolves.

'Ma...' Archana takes a step forward, unable to bear the sight of her mother's slumped shoulders, the defeat etched into the lines that are once again crowding her face, that seem to have multiplied, the happiness that had given her face a sheen when she was part of a community no longer in evidence.

'Do *not* sully this hut – which I have no choice but to leave now – with your luckless presence.'

The dog whimpers, looking from Archana to her mother.

Archana does not heed the tears running freely down her face.

'Where will you go?' Hurt coating her throat, roiling charcoal.

'Did you think of that when you went running to your memsahib, saying you didn't want to do sati, eh?'

'I did not—'

'I'll go to your sister. Cast in my lot with the untouchables. Anything is better than this dishonour, this shame you have wrought...' Bitterness and agitation colouring her mother's voice the dark purple of a rotting brinjal.

The thought of her mother preferring being with the untouchables to being associated with her is a stab of pure pain that drives Archana dizzy with hurt and upset.

'Isn't there anywhere else?' By allying herself with the untouchables, her mother will never be part of a community again. She will always be shunned.

'No.' Her mother's tone short, sharp. 'I'll not be welcome anywhere else. And perhaps even the untouchables might not want to be associated with us, relatives of a woman who will not do her duty by her husband, who threatens to bring the police upon her community.'

Anger directed at the memsahib, seething blue, seeps into every part of Archana's body. 'I didn't…' She is shaking with rage, violent poisonous indigo.

'Hope your life, such as it is, is worth it.' Her mother finally looks at Archana, her eyes soft and sad. Weary. There is love there and grief, anger and sadness.

Her mother is saying goodbye, not in a blaze of veneration as they had both pictured, but hiding in her hut from the villagers, in shame and trailing scandal.

Bile and vomit in Archana's throat, threatening exit.

'You'll be in Radha's village?' Archana asks, wanting to confirm her mother's whereabouts, knowing this is probably the last conversation she will have with her, unable to keep the longing from her voice.

Her mother turns away, not bothering to reply, her whole demeanour subdued. The dog runs a wet tongue over her face and then bounds up to Archana and does the same, smearing slobber and her mother's tears all over Archana's cheeks.

Archana realises then that this is the closest she can now hope to get to her mother, their tears intermingled with the dog's saliva. She stands there on the threshold of her mother's hut, in the village where they were both accepted but will now never be welcome again, looking at her mother's thin body, memorising it.

She thinks of the previous night, her mother's hand linked in hers, the warmth and solidity of it.

She imagines the feel of her mother in her arms: fragile, a body of bones.

'Ma, I'll leave now…'

Her mother does not turn.

'Can I touch your feet, have your blessing?' Her voice hopeful and tremulous, that of a child again.

Her mother seems to shrink even further. Her shoulders move up and down and Archana realises she is crying, like Archana. But she does not acknowledge Archana's words, does not give her permission to come inside. She is silent, hunched, only the movement of her bony shoulders giving her away.

Her own mother will not face her, allow her inside her home – not that it will be her home for much longer.

Archana kneels down and touches the mud of the doorway, imagining she is touching her mother's feet, that she is smiling at her. She imagines her mother's hand on her head, giving her blessing.

The dog moans, reflecting Archana's pain.

'Goodbye, Ma,' Archana says, breathing her mother in, her bent back, her face turned away, her vanquished shoulders.

In a few hours, she should have been dead.

No flames claiming her body now. Her body unscathed. Alive.

Yet she feels defeated, tears falling unchecked as she leaves the village that gave her mother and herself succour and identity, where, for a time, they belonged.

Chapter Sixty-Five

1925

Margaret

Disappearing

When Margaret comes to, her husband is sitting by her bed, tight-lipped, hollows in his eyes. Flinching when her gaze meets his, his lips disappearing.

'What's the matter?' she manages, her throat rasping and dry.

'You lost our baby.'

She recalls the hot gushing between the legs, her hand instinctively going to her stomach.

No. Please, God. No.

The pain is a river. Undulating. Accusing. Taking her over.

No.

'Was it worth it?' Suraj throws the words at her, biting them out from between pressed-thin lips, and there is a world of hurt in his throbbing voice, tight with anger.

She closes her eyes, unable to look at him, see his hurt when her own is threatening to swallow her whole.

My babe. I loved you for the short time you were with me. I love you still. I always will.

'Why, Margaret? You were advised to rest and you… Did you think you were infallible?'

His voice a lament. She can't bear it, his ache on top of hers, she can't.

But she has to – it's what she deserves.

'And the villagers... they're so angry. My office was vandalised. Windows smashed. Door battered down. Important papers destroyed. We've lived harmoniously beside them for generations and now... Now they are baying for blood!'

She swallows past the lump in her throat, finds her voice. 'I'm sorry, I...'

'You made light of their age-old custom, bought off tradition with money, cheapening it. It doesn't do to bulldoze your way into what they've been doing for centuries just because you think it is right...'

Her husband's words. So very harsh. More hurt piling on top of the raw, pulsing agony of loss. 'Archana—' she begins.

'She did not want to be saved, Margaret. She will not thank you for it.' His voice sharp in a way it has never been with her. Biting.

'I do not want her thanks.'

I do not want anything except my child back.

'It does not do to interfere with tradition, to go against duty. I know – I married you against my parents' wishes and I have to live with the guilt of their anger, of not having made up with them, for the rest of my life. But I could bear it, bear anything, for I had you with me. We were making a family, forging a future. Together. But you... You wilfully disregarded the doctor's instructions at the cost of our child. You...'

She closes her eyes, trying to shut out his raw pain. She cannot deal with it right now. She wants to mourn quietly, in private, for her child.

When did it come to this, that she cannot grieve for their child with the man she loves with everything she has, her soulmate, her destiny, her future? When did it become so that his sorrow for the loss of *their* child is an intrusion upon hers?

As if he has read her mind, he says, 'I'm going now. You need to rest.' His voice ironic when he says the word 'rest'.

At the door, he turns to her, his dark eyes flashing, bottomless pools of misery. 'Margaret, who is she that you regard her as more important than your family, the life we made together, for whom you sacrifice our child? Who is she to you?'

He slumps at the doorway, broken, and then he pulls the door closed behind him.

And now she is free to cry, sob, rail. Scream her hurt into the pillow.

But she finds she cannot. She is dry-eyed, stunned, agitated.

Her child.

Lost.

Was it worth it?

Did she do it for Archana's sake or for Evie's? Because she couldn't save Evie and felt she was being given another chance? Does it matter? Hasn't she done good? But at what cost?

All that night she tosses and turns, holding her empty stomach, scoured of her child.

Was it worth it?

In that darkest time just before dawn, navy shadows blanking the moon, stifling the stars, she is finally able to be honest with herself.

I didn't think of my husband or my unborn child; not even Archana, not really.

I did it for myself. To redeem for the failures of my past, for failing Evie when she needed me most.

Was it worth it?

Archana's face when she found out she was to be spared sati. Paler than the widow's garb she was clad in.

Those eyes. Archana's eyes, Evie's eyes.

Was it worth it?

Margaret cradles her stomach, barren, empty of her child, her starry-eyed hopes, her rainbow-hued dreams for the future. She thinks of her husband's anger, his raw, blistering agony.

By not letting go of my past, being haunted by it, I have lost my present, maimed my future.

Chapter Sixty-Six

1925

Archana

Portent

Archana enters through the back door, reserved for servants, a door she thought she would never grace again.

The staff are gathered at the little table in the storeroom, sharing samosas and gossip, egg pakoras and carrot halva left over from the sahib's tea, it being that time after tea and before dinner when there is a bit of a lull.

The friendly chatter halts abruptly when Archana enters, smiles freezing on faces. Leela harrumphs when she sees her, her gaze moving to the sari pouch containing Archana's worldly possessions and then away. The others do not meet her gaze, not even Nandu, who looks fixedly at a point above her.

Archana stands there, unsure, faced with their collective indifference, still reeling from her mother's rejection, the mem-sahib's lies. For a brief moment, as the servants resume eating and drinking their tea, she wonders if she has died, if she is not present at all, watching all this from the afterlife.

She shakes her head, clearing away the whimsy, slipping past the servants and into the house via the kitchen, the chatter starting up, loud and busy, as soon as the door closes behind her. Then, ashamed of herself but unable to resist, knowing no good can come of it, she stands with one ear pressed to the storeroom door, listening to them talking about her.

'How dare she, the cheek of her!'

'Her place is with her husband, on that pyre, not here! Wonder what black magic she has woven on poor Memsahib, desperately ill again, losing her baby for her.'

Oh.

The wood of the door pressing against Archana's forehead, the smell of sawdust and the flavour of gossip, tears of upset and anger once again stinging her eyes. Because of the memsahib's impulsive, thoughtless action, her lies, her refusal to allow Archana to make her own choice with regards to *her* life, an innocent life lost – the memsahib's child's life traded for Archana's own.

She climbs up the stairs, her shorter leg cramping with each step, reminding her with each pulse of pain that she is alive, she is here, that this is the first day of the rest of her life, a life she was not meant to have.

To the memsahib's room, the thick fug of illness and grief shifting in a sighing whisper when she opens the door, then settling over her.

The memsahib still and unmoving. She could be dead except that her chest rises, ever so slightly, barely disturbing the close air of the room.

The sahib is slumped by her bed, his head in his arms. It is like those long weeks when the memsahib was ill, delirious with fever, but whereas then she was hot and flushed, thrashing around on the bed, now she lies motionless. Pale.

The sahib looks up as Archana enters. And as he registers her, rage, throbbing and toxic, directed at her.

She should be used to this by now, this fury and loathing aimed at her from all sides, and yet she recoils at the strength of the sahib's hatred, trying not to flinch, wanting to run away from the room, all the way to the funeral pyre, throw herself on the flames' mercy. The same sahib who had looked at her so hopefully, intently, in this same room, when she talked to him about his parents…

Now she feels consumed by his anger, his contempt.

'You!' he spits. Then he stalks out of the room, pulling the door so hard behind him that it almost comes off its hinges.

The memsahib sleeps through it all, a porcelain doll.

Archana stands there, shaking, setting down the sari containing her meagre belongings.

Later, she will take it to the room beside the storeroom, where she would rest on those days when asked to stay later than usual. It will be her home for the foreseeable future, a future she thought she would not have. But what future this, she thinks, feeling cheated as she looks at her unresponsive mistress, the fury that had fired her to come here straight after being dismissed by her mother denied outlet.

Archana had left the village with a heavy heart and unconstrained rage at the memsahib, wanting to ask her why.

Why did you interfere? Why lie, say I was against sati? Why didn't you do me the courtesy of asking me whether I wanted it or not?

Just because you're my memsahib, did you think you had the right to decide on my behalf?

It was my *life,* my *choice.*

You of all people should have respected that. All those lectures you gave me about personal choice being more important than duty…

All my life nobody *has let me decide my own fate. My mother, my in-laws do not know any different, constrained as they are by culture. But you… You professed to be different. You expounded on freedom, personal choice.*

And yet you went ahead and made this choice on my behalf, lied on my behalf.

Why didn't you ask me first?
It was my *decision to make.*
Why, why, why?

It was what she has been screaming internally since she arrived at the village to find the villagers turned against her, her mother shunning her.

Everyone choosing to believe the memsahib over her.

But the memsahib is comatose. Having lost her child. Looking like a pale copy, a wax effigy of herself.

Archana cannot have it out with her, and that makes her even more furious.

Her hands are shaking with hurt and upset, sorrow and rage with no outlet. She sits on them, wanting to yell, to scream, to cry, to rant. Wanting her mother, her sister. Wanting to go back to the time when her da was alive and they were happy.

What have you done, Memsahib? Why did you have to do it? In the process, both of us have lost so much.

The balcony doors are open and the breeze that ruffles in is haunted by the memory of blinding sunshine, cool with the portent of night, harangued by the sharp turmeric grit of lingering dust. The sun is setting and in the distance she fancies she can just see the silvery flash of winding river, the crematorium resting on its banks, a curl of smoke staining the vermilion sky the bruised grey of anguish.

She should be there, burning alongside her dead husband, her rising ashes, entwined with his, arching towards the horizon.

She shouldn't exist but she does.

Chapter Sixty-Seven

2000

Emma

Adventure

Nandu, takes them to a room on the ground floor, two beds neatly made, a door that locks and a wardrobe that is blessedly woodlouse- and dust-free.

There's hot water in buckets for them to have a wash, scented with woodsmoke and kindling.

Chloe giggles as she scoops water from the pail onto herself: '*Everything's* an adventure here, Mum!' Her eyes shining as she scrubs away the grime of the journey.

Afterward, feeling clean and fresh, fatigue suddenly overcomes Emma, every inch of her body aching.

'Let's have a rest,' she says, lowering herself onto the bed, her eyelids pulling closed.

'I'm too excited to sleep, Mum,' Chloe declares, but she yawns widely, setting Emma off. 'I'll just lie here to give you company,' her daughter says and Emma smiles, for in two minutes Chloe is fast asleep, the weariness of travel catching up with her.

When they wake, there's noise in the house, chatter. The piquant zestiness of spices, the aroma of a feast drifting into their room making Emma's stomach rumble.

A wide-eyed, pretty girl, not much older than Chloe, introduces herself and the very old woman beside her. 'I'm Anju and this is my great-grandma, Leela, the best cook in our village.' She nods at the older woman. 'We're here to help.'

'Are you sure your great-grandma is up to…' Emma begins, taking in the older woman's hunched posture, grappling for words to express her concern without causing offence.

But Anju understands, giggling as she waves Emma's concern away. 'She's been working here since she was younger than me – nobody dares take her place, she wouldn't allow it. She doesn't look it but she's fierce. Everyone in the village is terrified of her.'

As if she has understood her great-granddaughter's every word, the older woman shoots her a vile look.

Anju laughs, bringing to mind a tumbling cascade of kaleidoscopic flowers. 'She understands very little English but seems to know just when someone is speaking ill of her.' She lowers her voice conspiratorially. 'Some people in the village think she might be a witch.'

Chloe gasps, delighted beyond measure, taking in the old woman, her face hidden by the veil of her sari, only her beady black eyes showing, hard and uncompromising. She stares mesmerised at Anju's bright pink sari, the glass bangles, green and gold, winking on her wrists, the anklets on her legs that chime a melody when she takes a step.

'Come and eat,' Anju says.

Anju's great-grandmother has concocted a banquet. Rice, plump grains marbled red, fish curry, tart and spicy, green beans with coconut, mango, ripe, but made into a sauce with chillies, again sweet and tart and oh so hot, yogurt – they call it curds, this also with chillies. It is the best meal Emma has eaten. Chloe enjoys it too, both of them ending up red-faced, noses running but absolutely sated.

Afterward, 'Let's explore the house, Mum.' Chloe tugs at her hand.

'Just what I was thinking.' Emma grins down at her daughter.

There are many rooms, mouldy and timeworn, swollen with damp, paint peeling, doors and wardrobes nibbled at by woodlice.

This house, teeming with secrets and history, going to ruin; a travesty.

Upstairs, Anju pushes open a door at the end of a corridor. She crosses the room and draws thick curtains, releasing a small avalanche of dust, making both Emma and Chloe sneeze.

When she has stopped sneezing, Emma gasps. The curtains were hiding a door that leads onto a balcony from where you can see for miles around: the road leading up to the mansion, the scattering of cottages that make up the village.

The room is large, even by the standards of the other rooms in this vast house. Dust motes dance in sunlight like trapped thoughts in a busy brain. The air is thick with ghosts, spectral wisps of past occupants' memories. A big four-poster bed in the centre of the room, a mosquito net, yellow and torn, draping it, both translucent with dust. A wardrobe and a dressing table, both in a state of decay.

The room smells of neglect and old sweat trapped in the walls, also a faint tinge of perfume. Emma, not usually given to whimsy, is nevertheless struck by the notion that this room gives off melancholy vibes.

'This was the memsahib's room,' Anju says.

Emma startles, a hand creeping up to her heart, emotion choking her as she understands what Anju is saying. *This was her grandmother's room once.*

She pushes open the wardrobe. The scent of mothballs and confined memories. A few old-fashioned dresses, powdery to the touch, gone to ruin.

Tears sting her eyes as she touches these relics from her grandmother's past, releasing golden dust and silverfish. Her grandmother wore these once, but when she left this place, for whatever reason, she left them behind. And here they wait, satin and silk, whispering and swishing, for a woman who is dying in a hospice across the world.

These dresses carrying the imprint of the girl her grandmother once was, younger even than Emma, a faint hint of flowery perfume among the staleness.

Oh, Gran, she thinks, *what happened to make you leave these behind? I've never asked or given it a second thought. Why did you leave when you came to this country flushed with love, braving censure, starting a new life with Suraj?*

Chapter Sixty-Eight

1925

Archana

Fault

When Archana opens the door to the study to dust it, the sahib is in there, slumped upon his desk, pipe smouldering, whisky bottle three-quarters empty.

The sahib has been holed up here a lot recently, drinking and smoking, the study permanently coated in tobacco ash and the sour fug of stale spirits. But Archana had thought she'd heard him stumble upstairs late last night and, thinking the study empty, has taken the liberty of entering very early this morning in order to do a quick clean, the house quiet and slumbering, blessedly free of servants, dawn not as yet washing the horizon with pale fingers of light.

The sahib must have returned sometime during the night, or not gone up at all, Archana having misheard and misinterpreted the sounds from her room.

The sahib has been understandably low since the miscarriage of his child and his wife's illness, which has come back with a vengeance. He's spending all his time in the study; his office in town has been vandalised and broken into by the villagers angry at his wife's interference in their customs, her stopping Archana's sati.

The mistress has been bedridden, rendered unconscious by the double setback of the relapse of her fever – from which she hadn't completely recovered when she intervened in the matter of Archana's sati – and miscarriage – where she lost more blood than she should have, and to make matters worse contracted an infection.

'She's had the worst of it, but what is holding her back most is motivation. She seems unwilling to recover,' Archana has overheard the doctor tell the sahib, the doctor's voice sounding grave and containing barely masked admonishment directed at Archana when he noticed her lingering nearby.

The doctor, along with everyone else, blames Archana for the memsahib's ill health.

The servants hold her squarely responsible: the gloom pervading the house, their sahib and memsahib's unhappiness and illness is Archana's fault. As punishment, they leave both the dusting of the sahib's study and the care of the memsahib to her, while at the same time ignoring her, acting as if she doesn't exist. Despite this, they are very good at getting their opinion across through pointed slights and loud conversations among themselves in Archana's presence.

It is the biggest irony, Archana having to care for the memsahib when she is raging at her, when she wants to shake the reason for her lie out of her, when she wants to yell, *What did you think you were doing? Couldn't you have thought to ask me what I wanted first? Were you so used to giving orders, being the boss, that you assumed you were God?*

But the memsahib is wan, unconscious, unresponsive. She looks so pale, reduced, a slip of a thing. Archana is livid and yet she cannot vent her anger at this version of the memsahib. It feels unjust, like stabbing someone when their back is turned. And so she tends to the memsahib, wanting her to get better, if only so she can have some answers.

*

Now, Archana backs away from the study softly, and is almost at the door when the sahib lifts his head from the cave of his hands and looks up, right at her.

He blinks once, twice, recognition dawning on his unshaven face, inebriated eyes wild, flashing fire.

'You!' Again, that word seeping poison, like that day by the memsahib's bedside, after which Archana has made sure to try to keep out of the sahib's way. '*You* were meant to die, not my child.' Every word blazing, doused with pain, seeping fiery hurt.

'Yes, Sahib.' She agrees with him.

'Why you?' He peers at her, befuddlement warring with loathing and anger in his gaze. 'Why do you mean so much to my wife? If not for her strange fascination with you, *everything* would be alright…'

He stands abruptly, the chair toppling backward, falling into a wardrobe of books with a crash and a thud. 'I gave up so much for her. My parents disowned me when I broke my betrothal to the girl they chose, and I couldn't get to make my peace with them before they…' His voice a low keen of sorrow.

He continues and it is as if he is talking to himself. 'She is my all. For her sake, I gave up my duty, went against my culture. When she got pregnant, I knew that it was all worth it. We could put the past behind, concentrate on creating a family, a future. She was everything to me, she *is* everything to me, and our child would have been the proof of that love. But then, you… You…'

The way he says it, like he detests her.

'She disregarded everything, our love, our child… For you!' he spits.

Archana winces, rooted to the spot, shock and fear as the sahib lurches up to her. 'What is it about you, huh? What do you have that she finds irresistible? Why has she taken such a fancy to you?'

He is so near she can smell his sour breath, his unwashed skin, smoky and stale.

She wants to take a step back but she is afraid of what he might do. In his current state, hatred and rage coming off him in pungent waves, the sahib is not the remote, kind figure all the servants have come to expect, but someone wild, provoked, unpredictable.

As if to prove her point, he suddenly lunges forward and grabs her shoulder, his hand digging into her flesh through her thin sari. Stunned into rigidity – the sahib has never touched her before, never come within a foot of her in fact; did he lose his footing or mean to grab her? – Archana is afraid to breathe.

The pain of the sahib's pincer-grip is sharp, intense, but strangely, she welcomes it. She wants to feel something after the days of numbness. She wants human touch even if it hurts, although she knows *this* is not allowed. No man, apart from her father when she was a child, and her husband, has touched her.

But she should have died with her husband. Yet here she is, living a half-life where she is a ghost, drifting on the periphery of others' lives. Denied entry into the village that was her married home; spurned by her own mother. Haunting the empty rooms of this huge mansion after the servants have gone home to their families, conversing with spectres. Cleaning up after the sahib who despises her, blames her, cannot stand the sight of her. Tending to the prone, unconscious memsahib, doing her duty by the woman who has, through her interfering, granted her this punishment of an unasked-for, bonus lifespan – thinking, no doubt, that she was doing good, expecting, most likely, Archana to be grateful – with a strange mixture of rage, resentment and pity: for she feels sorry for the memsahib too, her pale, wraithlike self washed out by illness and the loss of her child.

The servants invoke the gods to ward off the bad luck associated with her when Archana chances upon one of them, looking through her as if she doesn't exist, recoiling from anything she has touched.

Over the last few days she has wondered more than once if she is real, or a ghoul in someone's nightmare.

So, despite knowing it's wrong, she welcomes the sahib's abrasive touch. She welcomes his hatred, his angry words. At least he is looking at her, acknowledging her.

'You should have died,' he repeats, frothy spittle blooming on his lips.

After all these days of feeling invisible, being seen, spoken to, shouted at, evokes a reciprocal flare of anger that has been brewing ever since she was rescued from her fate into one worse than death. Relegated to a phantom existence while still alive.

Without her meaning to, a reply scorches from her mouth, 'I did not ask to be rescued. I would have preferred to die than to be here, living this half-life.'

The words sizzle in the air and she is both shocked and relieved. They are out there now, these words like boulders that have been weighing down her fiercely alive, relentlessly beating heart.

But to say them to the sahib, of all people, to be so openly ungrateful and insubordinate!

But with his scathing grip on her arm, his vinegary breath on her face, his unkempt body so close to hers, all boundaries crossed, redefined…

And after all, what does she care?

All these years she has been dutiful, done what was expected of her, and where has that got her? Displaced, not belonging anywhere, ostracised from the village, renounced by her mother, treated worse than an untouchable, not part of the servants' clique, living at the mansion but not belonging there either…

Who is she?

The sahib blinks at her words, then he is laughing, harsh, mirthless, loud and manic in the close, rank room populated by alcohol fumes and grief, the rancid taste of musty tobacco and regret. 'The irony! You did not even want to be rescued.' Tears running from his rheumy eyes, and Archana can't tell if they are from sorrow or laughter, 'Did you tell this to my wife?'

'She didn't ask.'

The laughter switches off abruptly. He sighs, deep and long. 'No.' Then, squinting at the white of her sari flopping over his hand where he is still clasping her, 'Why are you dressed like this?'

An inferno, torrid orange, igniting at the base of her stomach, blistering the air when it leaves her mouth in a broiling blaze. 'Widow's garb. But should I, a widow who did not do her duty by her husband, be wearing this? I don't have the right. I have no identity any more. I am no one.'

The sahib recoils as if shocked by her words, her wrath.

Then, he chuckles softly, and it is almost worse than his maniacal laughter of before. It is rueful, sympathetic, understanding. It *hurts*. 'She thought she was saving you. Instead, she has consigned you to hell. And me with it.'

'Why *you*?' she spits, anger, viscous scarlet, directed at the sahib for likening his fate to hers, wiping away the last of her inhibitions, her worry at being insolent to her employer. What does *he* know of what she is going through?

With the hand not holding her, the sahib cups her face.

She gasps.

Is he going to hit her?

But he says, mournfully, 'What is this life, eh? My parents dead while estranged from me because of my actions. My father's practice going down the drain, office broken into, documents destroyed. My child dead. My wife ill...'

Her anger explodes into wrath that overtakes her whole body, making it shake violently. 'Your parents loved you, they had forgiven you. The practice will thrive again – there's always need for lawyers. Your wife will get better. I'm sorry you lost your child, but you will have more children.'

'You're saying *your* desperation is worse than mine? You're *here*, living with us, not in a hut with a man thrice your age and his parents. My wife's pet, saved at the cost of our child…' He spits out the last sentence, still cupping her face, and pulls her closer, his saliva spraying her face through her veil, rank and pungent.

In trying to pull away from his grasp, her veil falls.

She feels bare without it, exposed.

His eyes dark and bright at the same time. Hungry.

She has wanted someone to look at her, not through her, but not like this.

This she doesn't want.

'No, Sahib.' She attempts, once more, to pull away from his clasp.

A mistake, as she only succeeds in lurching closer so she is pressed against him.

'Sa—'

Her mouth captured by his.

Every inch of her is screaming *This is wrong*. She shouldn't be here, in the study with the sahib while the memsahib is ill, comatose upstairs.

Did she think of me when she lied on my behalf, when she bartered for my life without checking if it was what I wanted?

And it is the all-consuming fury, the rage that has been hounding her since the day the memsahib informed her she didn't have to do sati, *informed* her instead of asking her, that makes her succumb to the sahib's insistent lips upon hers, his body pressing against her.

Once she has made her decision, she shuts her eyes tight, pushes all thought away, wipes her head clean, a blank space to be filled, for a brief while, only with sensation.

For, truth be told, it feels good to be held even like this, violently, angrily, after days of loneliness, ache, angst, nights when she has had to pinch the soft skin on the underside of her arm to remind herself she exists, that she is alive and not a ghost whom no one sees.

Afterward, the sahib turns away, falling into a drunken, spent sleep.

She opens her eyes to light. Outside the window, dawn leaks through the edges of night, a new day scraping darkness away with creamy rose brushstrokes.

The door to the study is not fully closed, she realises, cautiously peering outside, heart thudding wild in her chest.

A flash of red and green disappearing to the kitchen. Leela? She has a sari that colour.

Archana shakes her head, rubs her eyes. It's too early for Leela or any of the other servants.

It's fear that is twisting her stomach, making her imagine things.

But I did not imagine what happened.

Shame and disgust crawling through her body, mingling with horror, a panic-flavoured cocktail.

What on earth have I done?

PART 9

IMPLICATIONS

Chapter Sixty-Nine

2000

Emma

Heartache

The only two rooms in the house that are presentable and seem to have been lived in until fairly recently – all the others exude the damp, musty scent of disuse despite having been cleaned in honour of their arrival – are on the ground floor: the bedroom given over to Emma and Chloe, and the room adjoining it, which is lined with bookcases. Books spill out of them onto chairs, with more piles on the floor; the scent of ink and knowledge, musty blue. Like all the rooms in this house, this one too is huge, but the myriad books on every surface lend it a cosy feel. Nevertheless, it too exudes misery, flavoured with tobacco, sorrow and loss, Emma decides, giving rein to the fanciful thoughts this house seems to induce in her.

'This was the sahib's study,' Anju says. 'The room next door, where you are sleeping, was the sahib's bedroom. He had it converted from a drawing room. He lived in these two rooms, towards the end.'

That explains why the rest of the house reeks of loneliness, exudes neglect. Ghosts flit through it, whispering tales of intrigue and mystery, scandal and heartache.

'My great-grandmother and Great-Uncle Nandu knew your grandmother,' Anju says.

'They were here when she arrived?' Emma feels excitement prickle her spine.

The girl nods vigorously and Nandu grins, showing reddened stumps of teeth. The lines around Leela's eyes – the only uncovered part of her face, the rest covered by her sari, one end of it wrapped round her head like a veil – crinkle to show that she is smiling assent.

'You look like your grandmother. Very beautiful,' Nandu says.

Emma grins, warm happiness blooming in her stomach, both at the compliment and at the unexpected but very welcome knowledge that these people knew Margaret back then, a younger, raw version, the girl before the woman she became.

When Margaret was bequeathed this house by Suraj in his will, and she subsequently updated her own will to leave the house to Emma, when she suggested her granddaughter come here, did she know that she was also giving Emma access to people who knew her before she became a mother, a grandmother?

Of *course* she did.

When she was bequeathed the house, Margaret would have found out everything about it. Margaret is nothing if not thorough.

Emma is overwhelmed by love for her gran as she understands the extent of the gift she has given her. Margaret knew full well that when Emma came here, she would meet Nandu and Leela, who were part of the past that her grandmother doesn't talk about, witnesses to her youth. She is giving Emma permission to dwell on her past, dig it up, bring it into the open. She's left this house to Emma and not to her son or his children because she knows that Emma is the one who will be most interested in her grandmother's past.

By presenting her with the deeds to this house, her grandmother has given Emma access to herself as a young girl.

Chapter Seventy

1925

Archana

Complicated

When Archana slips into the memsahib's room, she does a double take, for the memsahib is pale, weak but awake, her eyes not clouded and delirious but alert, for the first time in Archana's presence since her miscarriage after releasing Archana from sati.

This is what Archana has wanted: for the memsahib to come to her senses so she can ask her why she did what she did, why she didn't take a moment to check with Archana first. She's been waiting to rage at the memsahib, rail at her; but not now. Not like this.

For now, all she feels is immense guilt. Inordinate shame.

Does she know what I've done?

'Archana.' The memsahib tries on a smile, but it is drooping at the edges, her gaze hunted.

Can she sense my betrayal?

'Memsahib,' Archana says softly, all the anger and resentment she has harboured for this woman wiped away by the bitter guilt in her mouth, flavoured tart yellow with the sahib's kisses. 'How are you feeling?'

She can't meet her employer's gaze. This woman who saved her – whether Archana wanted it or not – and lost her child.

And in return, Archana has slept with her husband.

What have I done?

'I've been better.' Again, that weak, not-quite smile.

She doesn't know.

Relief. Shame.

'And you?'

Archana knows what the memsahib is asking, what she must say. This woman for whom she feels such a complicated mix of emotions.

Memsahib, she's railed over and over to her employer's pallid, unresponsive form when caring for her, *you should have stayed out of it. Or if not, you should have at least talked to me first, considered the implications, before barging in and rescuing me from my fate at such great cost to everyone involved.*

Why did you do it? she's wanted to cry. *Why did you lie on my behalf?*

But right now, shame and guilt, vivid purple, choke those questions, spawning others.

Why did I do it? What on earth possessed me?

It was loneliness, the ache for connection, the yearning to feel something, anything. The need to wipe out all the hurt, the pain, the missing – rise above it for a brief while.

It was revenge. I wanted to hurt you, as if you aren't hurting enough already.

I am sorry. So sorry.

She's left it too long to reply. The memsahib's eyes flutter closed, her face looking flushed again, the fever rising, coming back to claim her.

Fresh guilt, festering and contagious, edges out the small, bright flare of relief at having been spared the need to answer, to thank the memsahib for saving her life.

A heavy tread on the stairs. *The sahib.*

Is he going to come in, sit with his wife?

Archana looks out the balcony at the buttercream sky, a ghost of a prayer on her lips.

What god will listen to her now, a fallen woman who has betrayed her husband twice over, and also this woman before her, suffering with fever and heartbreak, innocent of the perfidy the woman she rescued has wrought upon her?

The sahib's steps faltering at his wife's door, then going past.

Archana releases the breath she was holding.

The memsahib sighs in her sleep, her hands cradling her stomach, empty of child, eyelashes fanning cheeks rosy with fever, a starburst jewel of a tear adorning one lash.

Chapter Seventy-One

2000

Emma

History

Dear Margaret,

Hope you are well and enjoying India and married life! My dear, I can picture you having the most fabulous of adventures. England must positively pale in comparison! We miss you and Suraj, but we do hope your travels inspire you to paint more…

Emma sets down the postcard sent to her grandmother by Vanessa Bell, celebrated artist, sister of Virginia Woolf, whose writing Emma admires. She experiences thrilling excitement at this discovery, awe for her amazing grandmother consuming her.

Emma is in what used to be Suraj's study, rooting through his things, searching for traces of her grandmother, taking advantage of the fact that Chloe is exploring the garden with Anju, Nandu and Leela keeping watch.

Much as Emma has loved spending time with Chloe, being just the two of them again, she had jumped at the chance to be on her own for a bit. Since she saw the study, she had been wanting to explore it, peruse Suraj's paperwork for some traces of her grandmother.

And it has been most rewarding.

She's discovered Swaraj posters bearing her grandmother's signature etchings – proving that Margaret was involved in India's fight for freedom from British rule. Emma is at once excited and upset about not having found these things out about her grandmother sooner.

And in the past hour she has been so absorbed that she has not given a thought to David and the dilemma she faces. All these years, since she saw David on television in fact, she has been in his thrall, her life revolving around him. Even when he left her when she was pregnant with Chloe, she had still hoped, waited, her every decision geared towards his return. She'd even gone so far as to take up where his paper left off – in a misguided attempt, she realises, to feel closer to him, although it served to do the opposite. But now finally she is no longer under his spell and it feels good. Freeing. She misses him, she hurts, but she also sees David for who he is, rather than the perfect persona she fashioned for him.

And now she has this house and its treasures to occupy her…

She, a historian, is discovering so much of her own history, juxtaposed with the history of colonial India and Britain in between the wars as well, and she is so grateful to her grandmother for giving her this opportunity to do so.

Chapter Seventy-Two

1926

Margaret

Cost

'I know it must be difficult for you,' Margaret ventures, gently, as she and Archana sit by the stream and paint. 'Living here, missing your family.'

She catches the flash in Archana's eyes – a spirited look, but one Margaret cannot decipher – before she focuses again on her painting, demure.

It is a bright, hot day. The first that Margaret has felt well enough to come out of her room, spend in the gardens. She has been ill for a very long time, and she hasn't seen Suraj since she found out from him about her miscarriage.

'Your body was weakened intensely due to fever combined with the loss of blood during your miscarriage, and the infection you contracted in its wake made it worse. For a while you had me quite worried,' her doctor said, smiling with relief, when she started on the long, slow road to recovery.

Margaret knows that her state of mind didn't help either. After she found out she had lost her child, she lost her sense of purpose; she saw no point in getting better – Suraj was staying away from her, she had done her duty by Archana at great cost to herself and she was far away from Winnie and others she cared for. She preferred to spend her days and nights delusional – she had more company then: Winnie and Mrs Danbourne, Vanessa and the Bloomsbury Group, her husband before he became her husband, Evie and her parents, her dead brother and her dead child – a little girl the image of Evie.

In her dreams she was at Charleston, Suraj feeding her sugary marshmallows dipped in chocolate. The taste of love. Afterward, hand in hand, they walked along the ridge of the downs to their favourite spot among the reeds, the tall grass, dew speckled bright, whispering secrets. Birds sang, squirrels dug in the soft mulch in the base of trees and velvet emerald meadows marched to the sea, a sheet of glowing silver. Suraj looked at her with such love in his honey-tipped caramel eyes.

When her fever finally broke, she woke tasting salt and ache, her heart hollow with loss, her stomach bruised with it, a great big emptiness in place of their child.

Her husband conspicuous by his absence. Suraj, her soulmate.

Was their love so weak that it could not withstand this small assault? Was it so flimsy that it stumbled at the first obstacle?

We will have more children, she wanted to tell him, if he would visit her sickbed, even as they grieved, together, for the child they had lost.

The previous night, Margaret had dreamed of her mother.

Her mother waited at the window looking out onto the grounds and in the distance, instead of the postwoman, her father came, wearing his uniform. Her mother ran downstairs, into his arms. Then she turned and spoke to Margaret, who was a grown woman.

'Go to him. He is your love.'

*

The dream was the reason Margaret felt much better that morning, finally ready to shrug off the garment of mourning and face the world again, determined to make peace with her husband. When she felt able to get out of bed – it took a couple of tries, as she was light-headed and weak – she went in search of Suraj.

He wasn't in the house, although the study smelled of him: cloves, mint and ginger, the pungent tang of alcohol, tobacco and despair. His ghostly presence but no husband.

She sat on the balcony of her room watching the path leading up to the house from the village, dust and patience, waiting for him.

He didn't come.

If he would not come home then she would go to his office – that was where he probably was. She would apologise if that was what it took, although she didn't think it was to Suraj she should apologise but to her child, who did not get a chance to grow because of her…

Archana came into the room with a cold compress, stopping short on seeing Margaret sitting on the balcony instead of prone in bed. Colour surging into her face, at odds with her widow's whites. 'Memsahib, you're awake. I… I'll get…'

She turned to go but Margaret, looking at her friend properly for the first time since that fateful day when she saved her and lost her child, said, 'You don't have to wear widow's garb any more. The past is the past. You're free now to make your own future. We'll resume lessons soon. I'm better now.'

Archana nodded, not saying a word. No enthusiasm, like Margaret had expected; no reaction at all.

But her eyes, those eyes so like Evie's, full of unspoken words, fiercely emotive with an added layer of darkness, sadness. Sharp with messages that would not leave her mouth and that Margaret was too tired and spent to interpret.

Her hand went of its own accord to her stomach, to stroke the child as she had taken to doing before…

Before…

Before melancholy could drag her down, she said, 'Let's paint by the water. It's too glorious a day to spend inside.'

'Memsahib, I… I've work to do.'

'Come, Archana, give me company, please.' Her voice stumbling.

Archana nodded, but she looked trapped.

They've set up easels by the stream, water lilies floating serenely on the water, white hearts with sunny centres roosting majestic on a seat of green. The scent of earth and heat and dust. The sky a wide, cloudless white. The fragrant air stroking Margaret's face tastes of nostalgia, bruised yellow.

'I've been ill more than twenty weeks! These Indian fevers do completely floor one, don't they?' she muses to Archana, who is quiet, pensive – quite different from the girl she used to be. Perhaps it is to be expected after what she's been through, what very nearly happened to her.

Margaret would like to draw her out, get her to talk, but she's not up to it right now, weak and worn out as she is by illness and grief.

'Has the sahib been staying over at the office all this time?' Margaret asks.

Archana goes very still, a flutter of something darting across those expressive eyes too quickly for Margaret to make sense of it.

'Most days, yes,' she replies, her voice a monotone.

'Well, this is quite the state of affairs – me ill for weeks on end and the sahib working himself to the bone!' Margaret says, wryly. 'I'll visit his office this afternoon and ask him if he knows the way home or if he's conveniently forgotten the fact that he has a wife waiting here for him.'

Archana is quiet, giving no indication of having heard. The girl is really behaving distinctly oddly. Perhaps she *should* try to make an effort with her.

'Are you alright, Archana?' she asks.

The stream gushes and warbles, and crows gossip in the branches of the trees above them.

'Yes.' And again that expression flitting across Archana's eyes. One Margaret recognises.

Guilt.

But why?

And then it comes to her. Archana feels responsible for Margaret and Suraj losing their child. She blames herself. Did Suraj say something to her, shout at her perhaps? Is that why she went rigid just now at the mention of him?

Margaret decides that she will not bring it up now, embarrass her friend. She will give some thought as to how best to talk to her about it.

'What are you painting?' she asks instead, her voice gentle. Then: 'Oh.'

Archana's painting is a swirl of bold, out-of-control orange.

'You're drawing fire.'

Suraj's words come to her, vivid as the painting: 'She did not want to be saved, Margaret. She will not thank you for it.'

Before she can stop herself the words are out: 'Do you wish you had died with your husband, Archana?'

Once again, the girl's hand stills in the act of painting.

Then, after a pause that goes on too long, she says, 'I owe you my life, Memsahib.' Her voice expressionless as she deftly sidesteps Margaret's question.

Before Margaret can push further, the other maid comes with snacks. Samosas with chutney. Egg pakoras. Khichdi: spiced rice with lentils and smoked fish.

'I'm ravenous. It's a sure sign that I'm better,' Margaret says, tucking into the khichdi.

A gagging sound at her side.

Archana's face is as pale as her widow's garb even as she covers her mouth with her hand and turns away.

'Archana, what's the matter?'

But Archana has dropped the paintbrush onto the grass, orange spatters on emerald, and is running away.

She is back in a few minutes.

Margaret has started painting again, having set aside her khichdi, the joy she was gleaning from it quite destroyed by Archana's odd reaction.

A frog croaks brashly before tumbling into the stream from its perch on a water-lily leaf with a resounding splash.

'I'm sorry, Memsahib. I've been feeling a little ill.' She looks ashen, pale. A wraith in her widow's whites.

'I hope you aren't coming down with my fever.'

'No, Memsahib, I think it's just something I ate.' She turns away, bending to pick up her paintbrush.

And that is when Margaret notices. The slight but unmistakable rounding of Archana's belly, so at odds with the rest of her, which is fading away.

'You... you're not *pregnant*?'

'No, I...' Archana's eyes wide with shock, upset and... is that guilt?

'Didn't you know?' Margaret is gentle, even as her heart is breaking. The taste of grief, salt and ache in her mouth for her own lost child.

And then as the implications of Archana's pregnancy dawn. *I was right doing what I did, even if I lost my child. Even if Suraj is angry with me. I saved* two *lives. Not only Archana's but also her child's.*

Archana is standing there stunned, so Margaret says softly, 'We'll get the doctor to confirm it, but I think you're definitely pregnant. That will be why the smell of smoked fish made you sick.'

Archana looks pale as the fog that used to wreath the downs at Charleston. She's whispering something to herself in her language over and over.

Margaret feels the sorrow she has been keeping at bay assault her afresh, along with a brief flare of outrage – *Why does* she *get to have a child while mine is lost?* – promptly quashed.

You're being petty, childish.

'Archana,' Margaret says, trying for gentleness. 'This is a *good* thing.' Her voice trembling only slightly.

Archana looks at her, her eyes wide, unfocused with panic. 'No, Memsahib. You don't understand. I'm so sorry, Memsahib.'

'Why're you apologising, Archana?'

'I did something horrible, Memsahib. I was so angry.' Archana is crying now. Tears running down her cheeks, unchecked. 'It turned me mad. Made me lose my mind. But I know it's not an excuse…'

This girl is making no sense. 'I don't understand, Archana. Why were you angry?'

But Archana is crying too hard to speak, snot trailing down from her nose, mingling with her tears.

A crow startles nearby, cackling, its companions setting up an encore.

'Don't worry, it will be alright,' Margaret says, although she doesn't know what it is she is consoling Archana about. And truth be told, *she* is a little angry now. Here she is, just recovering from a long illness exacerbated by the loss of her child, and this girl she's considered her friend is weeping because she is pregnant! Shouldn't she have some consideration for Margaret's feelings?

But Archana continues to sob, her arms round her burgeoning stomach, rocking and repeating, over and over, 'I'm so sorry, Memsahib.'

What on earth is she apologising for?

The stream spills and burbles, carefree. A wide-winged bird Margaret doesn't recognise dips into the water, sweeping ripples in its wake.

'I didn't mean to. It just...' Archana's voice, upset and guilty. Guilty.

A nauseous feeling in the pit of Margaret's stomach, the air coloured blue with unease.

'It was... I was so *angry*,' Archana says again.

What does she have to be angry about?

Was she angry at *her*? Margaret? Is that what she is trying to say?

'You were angry at me?' she hazards.

Archana nods.

'But *why*?' Her voice stunned.

'You lied, Memsahib. You told them I didn't want to do sati. You did not ask me first.'

'I—'

'All my life, nobody has asked me what I want. I've been told what to do, how to do it. You, who believed in self-choice, preached about it, I thought would be different. But you were the worst. You acted on my behalf, *lied* on my behalf without a second thought.'

'It saved your life...'

She will not thank you for it, Suraj had said. *It does not do to interfere with tradition.*

'A life I did not want! A life where my mother has disowned me, the villagers have shunned me. In thinking you were giving me a choice, you imposed *your* decision upon me, regardless of what *I* wanted.'

Margaret's stomach roiling, the unease now a great uncoiling serpent, Archana's words, 'I did something horrible,' ringing in her ears.

'What did you do, Archana?' Her voice a mere whisper, barely audible above the merry gurgle of the stream.

The other maid, approaching with the tea tray, drops it on seeing Archana holding her stomach and bawling. A loud, noisy clanging. Tea spilling, staining the grass brown, oozing into the dust, colouring it the red of spilled blood.

The maid says something rapidly in the native language, her voice rising in tempo, her expression hard, eyes flashing venom as she points to Archana.

Margaret can make out some of the words but not all. She hears the native word for 'child', knowing it from the servants' effusive anticipation when she herself was pregnant. *Was.* A brutal wash of pain. Then she hears 'Sahib'.

Margaret's hand jerks, the paintbrush, which she's been clutching in her hand like a talisman, shaking. Paint from it dripping bright red, like the blood she lost along with her baby, onto the canvas, a splodge of messy crimson. *The scent of turpentine and betrayal.*

'Nothing excuses what I did, Memsahib,' Archana pleads. 'But I didn't mean for this to happen.' Holding her stomach. The baby growing there.

The air smells of tamarind, tart brown, and tea, spiced cardamom, gritty with shock, pungent with spilled secrets.

It is the other maid who holds Margaret as she falls, in whose arms, smelling of onions and sweat and righteousness, she is held as she reads the guilty truth in Archana's eyes, written upon her face.

It cannot be.

'*Suraj's* baby…?' Her voice a whisper tasting of treachery and incomprehension.

'You're the only one for me,' he had declared.

She does not want to entertain this wretched thought even for a minute, but it persists. In a warped way, it makes sense. Archana's strange behaviour. Suraj staying away, at the office. She had thought it was because he blamed her for the loss of their child, unable to bear being with her. But all this while, has it been guilt keeping him away?

'She will not thank you for it,' her husband had said of Archana. But Margaret never expected that she would do *this*.

'Who is she to you?' the love of Margaret's life had asked.

Who is she to you, *Suraj?*

PART 10

FIRE

Chapter Seventy-Three

1926

Margaret

Bruised

Margaret blinks awake, disorientated, groggy.

She is in her room, the sheets smelling of illness and loss.

A brief moment of confusion before the events of the morning torpedo into her, devastating her all over again, making her nauseous. Her mouth acrid, foul with knowledge she would give anything to disgorge.

Her husband and the girl she considered her friend...

The thought is a hot lance of betrayal, potent fiery red, inescapable.

She stands, fighting waves of dizziness, and rushes to the basin, where she is sick, over and over, trying to scour away the image of the two of them entwined in the way she and Suraj have not been for a very long time, these two souls she is closest to: the man she loves with her everything and the woman who reminds her so very much of her dead sister.

The thought of Archana touching her, carrying her to bed after she'd fainted by the stream, this woman who knows *her* husband intimately, who bears his child, inciting another wave of nausea...

Archana has betrayed her in the worst possible way, creating a child with her husband when Margaret had lost *her* child saving her...

But through the anger, the hurt, her conscience prodding.

What Archana said: 'I was so angry, Memsahib. You acted on my behalf, lied on my behalf without a second thought.'

Although it shatters Margaret to admit, she knows Archana has a point. She had lectured Archana about freedom of self, that doing her duty meant she was denied personal choice, that decisions were always made for her. And then, Margaret had gone on to do the same. She had bartered for Archana's life, but without asking if it was what she wanted. She had behaved exactly like Archana's mother, her in-laws, all those people she had railed against and asked Archana to leave because they didn't respect her, allow her the freedom to do what she wanted with her life.

For the first time, Margaret considers the possibility that perhaps Archana didn't *want* to be saved. At the very least Margaret should have asked her, given her the chance to confirm that this was what she wanted before she lied to the villagers that Archana did not want to do sati. She recalls the villagers' anger and shudders. She did not stop to think of the effect of their collective rage on Archana, what it must have cost her to be shunned when she had finally found acceptance after her sister's actions had caused her mother and herself to be ostracised. Archana's longing for acceptance was why she wouldn't leave her husband, despite his being ill and the possibility of his death and her sati. Margaret had known this and yet she blithely disregarded it, convinced of the righteousness of her actions, her lies on Archana's behalf, not considering the aftermath, the repercussions…

Margaret had justified the lie to the villagers by telling herself she was doing it for Archana, but she had really done it for *herself*. She wanted to save Archana because she hadn't managed to save Evie.

Her projection of her past onto the present has cost her her future – she has already lost her child and now she's discovering she has lost Suraj too…

*

She is sick until her throat is sore and bruised, but no matter how sick she is, she cannot gouge out the understanding sitting heavy and jaundiced in her heart – that of Archana and Suraj together, her lost baby, Archana's baby, her own culpability, how she used Archana's sati as a chance to absolve herself of past mistakes, all the while telling herself she was doing it for Archana.

Afterward, she wipes her face with a flannel, dresses, managing very well without a maid, berating herself for having one in the first place. If she hadn't, then perhaps…

She pushes the thought away and stares in the mirror. Once the initial shock at seeing her pale, gaunt likeness wears off, she works at schooling her face into an impassive expression until she is satisfied with the result.

Then, she summons Nandu.

'Can I trust you, Nandu, or is there something you too are keeping from me?' Her throat, abused by her scouring, hurts when she speaks.

'You can trust me, Memsahib.' His voice shaking with upset, worry for her clouding his kind eyes. 'I'm sorry about Ar—'

'Please,' she says, holding up her hand. 'It's not your place to apologise for anyone.' She is surprised and grateful that her voice does not betray the turmoil inside of her. 'Take me to my husband.'

Husband.

Traitor.

Suraj's office is a long room in a small tiled building, one among the hotchpotch collection of cottages that make up the nearest town.

The windows are boarded up with cardboard and the door is hanging off its hinges. She recalls, with a twist of guilt, Suraj telling her of the villagers vandalising the office, angry at Margaret's interfering with tradition.

The muggy breeze tiredly displacing the mud coating the roadside bushes is hot and bright and gritty on Margaret's face, stoking tears.

At the sight of Suraj, bent over his books at his desk, tired, dishevelled, with an untidy beard, a stab of love blindsides her, making her forget momentarily why she is here. She wants to go to him, put her arms round him, soothe the worry lines on his face. He is anxious, she knows, about the villagers' dissent caused when she bargained for Archana's life.

Archana. A slap of pure pain. The heat of betrayal making her illness-battered body feel faint again.

'Suraj.'

He startles at the sound of her voice, looks up and, at the sight of her, he smiles, surprise and pure joy. That special smile reserved just for her. Tender and full of love. As if nothing has happened, no woman has come between them, as if he has not spent all the weeks of her convalescence avoiding her…

Despite everything, seeing that expression on his face, her heart spins with hope.

There must be some explanation.

But as she watches, all that has come between them clouds his face, wiping away his initial spontaneous reaction, the involuntary joyous smile upon seeing her.

'Margaret.' His voice formal. 'Why are you here?'

Hot white rage biting, wiping away the flash of love, the burst of hope, her mind invaded, once again, by suspicion. What right does he have to use that voice with her when *he* is the one in the wrong?

'Archana is pregnant,' she says. And even as the words soil her mouth, igniting agony, again fledgling hope rears, at odds with her voice: cold, expressionless. 'I don't think the child is her dead husband's.'

Please. Be shocked. Be outraged. Convince me.

I cannot stand for you to have done this, cheated on me with the girl I traded our child's life for.

She watches, heart shattering like a stone splintering a frozen lake, as his face colours.

His eyes flustered. His gaze sliding away from hers.

Her knees buckle and she is grateful that she is leaning against the door jamb.

Her hand cradling the stomach bereft of her child. *Their* child.

This man she loved with her everything. Betraying her with the woman she rescued at the cost of her child.

No, her mind screams. *No, no, no!*

She realises that she had come here hoping, wishing to be proved wrong.

But on his face, stark, bruised purple with guilt, her answer.

'Margaret, I... It was just the once...'

She cannot bear it.

She *has* to.

With all her strength she turns away from the man who has betrayed her in the worst possible way.

'Margaret, wait!' His voice desperate. 'I was hurting, angry with you for not heeding the doctor. I blamed you for the miscarriage... We were a team, you and I, and together we had created a child, our future. Yet you acted as if it didn't mean a thing. You risked our child's life, lost it... I was furious...'

So you created another baby with the woman who, in a roundabout way, was the reason for my losing our child?

Some revenge.

She cannot speak. The words are in her chest, her throat heavy with them, but they won't settle on her tongue.

She concentrates on putting one step in front of the other, walking slowly, tiredly away.

'Margaret, it's you I love.'

The pain in his voice. Even now, after all this, her first instinct is to go to him, hold him, kiss his pain away.

Crash!

She shudders but does not turn back. He has pushed the table away, is coming up to her, taking her hand. His smell of musk and ginger, sweat and remorse.

She flinches from his touch.

'Margaret, it was just the once.' He is crying.

She believes him. She even understands, at a push, why he did it – he was hurting, lonely, raging, lost. He missed her. He was angry with her.

But…

She cannot forgive him. The pain raw, naked, flaying. Her ears ringing with the final, irrevocable shattering of her hopes, the dreams she'd sketched for them, heady with love.

How naive they were, how hopelessly ingenuous, to think that their love would be enough.

They were living in a fantasy, escaping the sadness of the loss of their families with this unreal life.

She understands now, too late, that love cannot exist in a vacuum. They needed people around them but they foolishly believed that their love was enough.

And into this came Archana. Both of them using her for their own ends – Margaret to atone for her past, for letting Evie down; Suraj because he was hurting and lonely.

Archana. Bequeathed a new lease of life regardless of whether she wanted it or not, by Margaret, and a new life by Margaret's husband. What future for her? A pregnant, disgraced widow…

An endless scream, the crimson-spattered violet of a weeping wound, in Margaret's heart. A chasm opening up inside her, eating her whole as she gets into the carriage, ignoring Suraj's beseeching. A crowd spilling out of the neighbouring buildings, gathering on the road to watch agog the spectacle of the sahib sobbing, turned mad by his white wife.

All Margaret and Suraj had wanted was love, children, a happy family like Margaret's own when she was a child. Instead, they've ended up destroying each other, their love toxic, tainted, imploding under the weight of their mistakes.

Chapter Seventy-Four

2000

Emma

Great Expectations

In a rose-scented bureau in Suraj's study, Emma comes upon a file titled 'Margaret'.

The file – fading orange – is a treasure trove. There are photographs of her grandmother's paintings – some of which Emma didn't know existed until now – all catalogued and dated in Suraj's neat handwriting, and snapshots of a youthful Margaret and Suraj.

Her grandmother, dazzling, radiant in her husband's arms. Emma has never seen her smile so joyously and openly.

'Did Suraj remarry after my grandmother…?' Emma had asked the previous evening.

Nandu did not let her finish: 'No. He loved Memsahib only.' His rheumy eyes far away, clouded with sorrow.

Emma is finding proof of that. All paperwork pertaining to Margaret carefully preserved, well-thumbed, as if Suraj went over it again and again.

In a locked section of the bureau – the key in a hollowed-out copy of *Great Expectations* sitting on top of it, found by chance when Emma dropped the book and it fell open – she finds several letters from Suraj, sealed but unposted, all of them addressed to

Margaret wherever she was travelling with work at the time they were written. So, Emma muses, Suraj had kept tabs on Margaret, knowing exactly where she was over the years. His handwriting on the address labels, firm in the beginning, tremulous as he got older and his eyesight dimmed. His hands shook, but the yearning she senses exuding from the letters – the intuition that seems to have been aroused when Emma stepped into this house once again announcing itself – was as strong as ever, coming across despite the envelopes now brittle with age, fragile to the touch, the ink faded lavender. Yet he lacked the courage to post them and they have lain here, patiently waiting to be found.

Seeing those letters, the love Suraj harboured for Margaret long after they separated, she thinks of David, the love of her life. Why has it taken her so many years to see that *she* was never the love of *his* life? When Emma took David back, it was with the hope that he had realised, finally, that he loved her best and only, her hopeful, optimistic heart trumping her mind that cautioned she was being a fool. It has taken her this, the evidence of Suraj's enduring love for her grandmother, to see David's love for the sham it has always been.

Now she understands that throughout their relationship she refused to see the real David, preferring the glorified version of him in her head, even when he hurt her; *especially* then. This edified David was the suave, smooth-talking professor she had seen on television as a teenager. So when the paper through which he entered her life via the screen was revealed to be a lie, her own fictional David fell apart.

She is as much to blame as David, she realises now. She fostered this version of him, did not see the real man. The flawed man.

'You have this exaggerated sense of who I am,' David would accuse during their arguments, frustrated and upset. 'I will never measure up.'

She is as much to blame.

*

When Suraj died eighteen months ago, he left the house and its contents to Margaret, in this way hoping she would see, through all the mementoes of her he so carefully preserved, her things treasured, her photographs much-thumbed, the letters he wrote to her over the years, what he was not able to tell her: that he never stopped loving her. Margaret too never remarried. Given this, Emma surmises that Margaret and Suraj were the loves of each other's life. If so, then why did her grandmother return to England?

What secrets are you keeping, Gran? What did you and Suraj do to each other that meant you went away, leaving your things behind and never came back?

Why did you never reconcile with the love of your life? And what has Archana got to do with it all?

Chapter Seventy-Five

1926

Archana

Stupid

Archana cowers in her room – this small space that has been given to her, along with her life, her future, by the memsahib.

And in return she has stolen the memsahib's future.

The memsahib lost her child to save her and she…

She cradles her stomach. How could she not have known?

She has, she realises now, stubbornly refused to see the signs. Her sari skirt pinching, her stomach tightening, swelling, while the rest of her remained the same.

How could she have been so foolish, so utterly, utterly stupid?

She has been on edge since that fateful day when, instead of always doing what was expected of her, she spoke her mind, to the sahib of all people. And then, she did something that she has regretted, over and over, since.

Since that day, she has tended to the memsahib and kept away from the other servants – to their relief (she's heard them eavesdropping: 'The atmosphere's so much better now she's taken the hint and stayed well away from us.') – taking her meals in her room, what is left for her after the servants have had their share of leftovers from the sahib and memsahib's meals.

Not that the sahib has been at home; he has been staying at the office since that fateful morning. Archana knows it is guilt – he cannot bear to face the memsahib, and Archana is relieved for she doesn't have to face him, the knowledge of what they did sitting between them.

Tending to the memsahib has been hard enough. The remorse assaulting her. Stabbing her with recriminations.

The look on the memsahib's face when she found out…

How could I have been so ungrateful?

What shall I do now?

I cannot stay here, I won't be allowed to.

Footsteps outside her room. One of the servants, she imagines, on their way to the storeroom next door. They stop outside her room.

Splat! Droplets of foamy froth spill into the tiny gap between the door and the floor. They've spat at her door.

She deserves it.

Chapter Seventy-Six

2000

Emma

Photograph Album

'Anju, will you please ask your great-grandmother if she knew of someone called Archana? Nandu, have you heard of her?' Emma asks.

She has not been able to find a mention of Archana in any of the documents in Suraj's carefully ordered study – Suraj had named and filed everything; he was a meticulous man.

The only thing she did find that was out of place and did not have a context or explanation was a photograph album, a recent one, at odds with all his other photographs, which were taken in the 1920s when Suraj was with Margaret. It was as if his life had stopped with Margaret leaving; there wasn't anything personal after she left – except for this photograph album.

What was most odd about the album was that there were no pictures of Suraj – they were mostly of a woman in her sixties, and what appeared to be her children and grandchildren. Suraj's mistress? Somehow Emma didn't think so. Suraj had steadily written to her grandmother over the years – although he'd lacked the courage to post the letters. The only personal mementoes, other than the album, that he had kept seemed like a shrine to Margaret. It was obvious he had been in love with her until his death.

That did not mean he couldn't have had a mistress, of course. This house seemed to radiate loneliness, and his solitary existence must have made him yearn for company, the comfort of a companion. But Nandu seemed to think he'd had no one else – and he would have known. Perhaps the woman in the photographs lived in town, near his office, most likely.

In any case, the album was a mystery.

But there was no mention of Archana. Had Margaret met her somewhere else? Was she not connected to this house at all? That couldn't be right; her grandmother had given Emma the deeds to this house and asked her to find Archana. So, Archana *must* be linked to this house in some way…

Now, at the mention of Archana's name, Emma sees Leela, who was fetching tea, stop in her tracks, the stainless-steel tumblers in which she serves the tea shaking.

Nandu is also still, his face frozen. He and Leela exchange a glance, taut with silent communication.

They knew Archana, Emma understands, and from the sudden tension in the room it appears that whatever happened, whatever it was that caused her grandmother to leave, *did* have something to do with this woman.

Anju, cheerful, young, completely oblivious, turns to her great-grandmother, who, Emma's been told, cannot speak or understand much English (but evidently recognised Archana's name), and translates Emma's question.

It is Nandu who answers, looking directly at Emma, his rheumy old man's gaze suddenly sharp. 'She was a servant here.'

'Oh.'

Somehow Emma wasn't expecting this.

You think you are modern, above preconceptions. You pride yourself on an open mind. And yet, when you find out that this woman, who is so important to your gran that she wants to give her one of her paintings and convey to her a message asking for forgiveness, was a servant, you are shocked.

Leela speaks, her voice low and gravelly. Her words slow, as if she is thinking deeply about each one. She is talking to her great-granddaughter but her sombre gaze doesn't waver from Emma's.

Anju translates. 'It seems Archana was close to your grandmother as she was the only one, apart from Nandu, who could speak English.'

And suddenly, Emma understands. Her grandmother here in this big house, just a girl really, younger than Emma, far away from all she knew. Her husband at work, busy. Margaret reaching out to the maid, who could converse in English…

'Where is she now, do you know?' Emma asks, looking at Nandu and Leela in turn.

A weighted pause.

A thought striking Emma as she calculates the years that have passed since her grandmother was last here: *I hope, for Gran's sake, Archana is still alive.*

Then, Nandu, wringing his hands: 'In the city.'

Emma tasting relief on her lips.

'Is it far? I have a message for her from my grandmother.'

Again, that thinning of their lips, the sudden tautness in their movements, the closing of their open faces.

'Not that far. The round trip can be done in a day.'

'Is there a bus that can take us there? Or a taxi service I can call?'

And at this, finally, Nandu grins, dispelling the agitation, chasing away the pall caused by Archana's name. 'Come with me.'

'Chloe,' she calls, and her beautiful daughter comes bounding down the stairs, her dress dust-stained, knees grimy, hair dishevelled but face radiant. 'Mum, I found four anthills – three of them were growing into doors – two centipedes, one millipede that curled into a ball when I touched it, seven moths, two butterflies, one completely yellow and one blue with white spots, several mosquitoes, bees and flies, and two huge spiders. One of them was pregnant! Also, a dead rat and three live cockroaches.'

Emma shivers. 'O… okay.'

'Where are we going?'

'It's a surprise.'

Nandu leads the way out of the house and round it along an overgrown path, Emma shivering every time a blade of grass brushes her legs, imagining snakes or some other animal lying in wait that she has yet to find out about.

Leela follows him, both of them sure-footed despite their great age.

Chloe, swinging from Emma and Anju's hands, brings up the rear.

Tucked into an alcove at the back of the house is an annexe, which seems to have been haphazardly added on – it doesn't match the original house in style; it is not tiled, but terraced. A square cement block, not much to look at, but functional, and a good size.

Nandu digs out a key and with some effort, unlocks the rusted padlock.

It takes them a minute to adjust to the gloomy interior after the short walk in the brilliant yellow sunshine.

And then: 'Wow!' Chloe exclaims, taking the word right out of Emma's mouth.

For in front of them, gleaming in the darkness, cobwebs littering the walls, little animals Emma doesn't want to think about scurrying away, the scent of chrome and rust and dead things, mould and metal, is a vintage Rolls-Royce, the sleek green of envy. Polished and elegant.

Beautiful.

Emma claps a hand to her mouth.

David would love this.

And her next thought, *I don't care if he would love this or not. I like it. And it's about time I enjoyed something without wishing he was there to share it with me.*

'This was Sahib's car, his pride and joy,' Nandu says. 'Runs beautifully. We will send word and tomorrow morning, the driver will come to take you to the city.'

Emma stands there, awed, Chloe's excited words echoing in her head, she agreeing with every one: 'This is the best holiday ever!'

Chapter Seventy-Seven

1926

Archana

Detrimental

Archana paces the room all night.

What to do? What shall I do?

She wonders if the memsahib is okay. She had finally recovered from her illness. Archana had tended to her impeccably, her guilt providing impetus. Even the doctor has started nodding at Archana, his brusque manner with her – he held her responsible for the memsahib's miscarriage and subsequent ill health – gradually easing as he tells her what pills to give the memsahib. Archana has been her sole carer, the sahib having not come home since that fateful morning.

She hopes this setback is not detrimental to the memsahib's health.

How dare you! You have no right to hope anything, to even think *of the memsahib.*

Dawn cleanses the darkness from the room, but nothing can chase the darkness within her.

Her stomach rumbling. The baby making itself known, asking for sustenance.

I wish I was dead. I wish I had died on my husband's pyre.

Chapter Seventy-Eight

2000

Emma

Spectacle

The city is teeming with crowds, scents and noise, vendors and hawkers, shops and beggars spilling onto the road. But they all stop what they are doing to gawp at the car, the eyes of the children, dressed in rags, hungry and sunken, lighting up at this spectacle.

Emma is glad she is not driving. She was tempted to, but Nandu and Leela looked worried, Anju voicing their thoughts: 'It's not easy, driving in the city. Please take a driver this time.'

'Mum, look!' Chloe says, her voice high-pitched, and they watch a man emerge from a pothole in the middle of the road, his whole body stained orange, dripping mud and water, traffic weaving around him.

'Wait, how—' Emma begins, but the question she was going to ask is interrupted, forgotten at the sight of an elephant – *an elephant!* – painted and garlanded, bejewelled cloth draped over its body, gold plate covering its forehead, approaching them, the ground beneath it shaking with each heavy tread.

'Wow!' Chloe whispers as it passes them, jewellery clinking, their car half in the ditch to make space for the beast, its eyes placid, trunk swaying gently.

*

The driver turns into a narrow road crowded with small shops selling all manner of knick-knacks: boiled sweets in glass jars, yellow tubes in plastic bags. Bangles. Saris.

A tailor working busily on his sewing machine.

An ironing cart, a mountain of colourful saris, checked shirts, waiting to be ironed. The pressed clothes pile is small and neat. The woman sets down her steaming iron and wipes her face, her tired eyes briefly meeting Emma's.

'How does the driver know where Archana lives?' she had asked when Nandu said he would summon him to take them to see Archana.

Nandu had coloured then, exchanging a loaded glance with Leela.

'Sahib used to visit Archana twice a year,' Nandu said, finally. Leela's dark eyes flashed with upset.

Emma was puzzled. 'Did Suraj make a point of visiting all the servants who had been in his employ?'

It was a genuine question. Perhaps this was the way it was here, she had thought, the sahibs looking after the well-being of their servants long after they had left.

But again, a look passed between Nandu and Leela: Nandu shrugging, Leela turning away.

It was obviously not done.

So why was Suraj visiting Archana?

Why did her grandmother want her to contact Archana, pass on the painting with a message asking for forgiveness?

What had happened here?

She meant to find out.

*

The car pulls up in front of a gate.

Archana's home is a modest bungalow, wedged between two similar houses in this narrow street. It is a quaint, charming dwelling. Painted the bright blue of a cloudless summer sky, topped with orange tiles.

The gate creaks as they open it.

'Who are we visiting, Mum?' Chloe, for all her curiosity, has not really wanted to know this until now, happy to travel in the car, out on an adventure.

'A friend of your nana's.'

Chloe, when very little, had heard Emma call Margaret 'Gran' and in an effort to imitate her had ended up with 'Nana', and it stuck.

'Are you going to give her Nana's painting?' Chloe nods at the painting Emma is carrying, wrapped in newspaper.

'Yes.'

Curious faces peer out of the windows and courtyards of the other bungalows lining the street, everyone staring first at the car and then at them. The woman ironing shirts wheels her cart close and starts a conversation with their driver.

Another woman comes up to the gate and joins in. A couple of men who were at a nearby kiosk drinking coffee from thimble-sized tumblers sidle up to the car. A bullock cart comes to a stop, the animals impatient as their minder cranes his neck out and admires the car. Soon, their driver has quite the audience and he chats away, gesturing to Emma and her daughter, Emma feeling suddenly quite shy, pinned by these myriad gazes.

A veritable feast of flowers and fruit trees greets them from the little courtyard of Archana's house, a potpourri of scents, a profusion of dazzling colour.

Purple and red bougainvillea cascade down the front door, interspersed with the bright green, palm-like leaves of the money plant.

Emma knocks, her heart drumming against her ribcage. She is about to meet Archana, solve the mystery of her grandmother's connection to her.

The scent of sandalwood and roses, the rust and metal taste of adrenaline.

I should have checked if Archana was home, Emma thinks as they wait, Chloe's hand warm and sweaty in hers. But how? She does not have a number for her. Oh well… It's too late now to turn back.

And why is she apprehensive? Why does she feel anxiety trickling down her spine like when she found out about David…?

David. She hasn't thought about him much, if at all, today.

It is as if being here, soaking up experiences, trying to piece together the puzzle of her grandmother's past, has made her life, her dramas, seem not as urgent, put them in perspective. There is a whole world out there, so many lives being changed by factors beyond their control. When did she falter, lose sight of the bigger picture, become mired in her own troubles? When and why did she allow one man so much power over her, to change and direct the course of her life?

She has always thought herself strong, a modern woman. But she understands now, standing here on a strange doorstep, waiting for a woman from her grandmother's past to answer the door and her questions about her grandmother, that she has been neither strong nor particularly tough, having allowed David to navigate and dictate so much of her life.

Not any more.

She doesn't yet know what she is going to do about her discovery regarding David's paper, but she knows this much.

*

She knocks again, clutching the painting with one hand and Chloe's hand with the other.

A crowd has collected at the gate, peering in curiously through the bars at her and Chloe, and more people are gathered around the car, chatting with the driver; everyone talking at once, some questioning, others lecturing. A beat of silence and into it, someone laughs. Almost at once, everyone erupts, a cacophony of happy mirth.

A baby cries, the mother shushing it impatiently while also querying something in a high-pitched voice. A dog howls and Emma notices that the neighbourhood dogs are now circling and sniffing the car. A cow has joined in too, giving the bullocks a wide berth, lifting its tail and defecating beside the ditch, a wet splatter of green dung, attracting as if by magic and out of thin air, an army of flies. The road, previously relatively quiet, now seemingly in the throes of a chaotic party, thanks to them.

Perhaps it's the noise outside, both Emma and Chloe distracted by the laughter, because Emma has not heard footsteps or the door being opened when they hear a soft voice say, in English, 'May I help you?'

Emma turns around, startled.

A small woman is at the door. She is wearing a white sari with its end draped like a veil over her head, and no jewellery. She is bent over with age and her face is very lined, like crêpe paper, but her eyes are a beautiful brown, sharp and intelligent, and right now, as she gasps, her hand clutching her heart, shining with tears.

'Sorry to come like this without…' Emma begins, feeling apologetic and more than a little puzzled at the emotion their arrival has aroused in this woman.

'M… Memsahib?' the woman says, softly.

Now Emma understands. 'I'm her granddaughter,' she says gently, knowing at once that this must be Archana for her likeness to her grandmother to have provoked this reaction.

'Of course.' The woman wipes her eyes with the trailing end of her white sari. 'For a minute there I thought… Is she…?'

'She has cancer, she couldn't travel.'

Archana closes her eyes, saying softly, 'I see.'

'She asked after you.'

Tears shine again in Archana's eyes, her hand snaking up to her chest once more. 'Oh. I…'

Chloe pipes up, curious, 'Why're you not wearing any jewellery?'

Her daughter, unashamedly inquisitive.

Archana smiles at Chloe through her tears.

'I'm sorry,' Emma begins.

But Archana is squatting down to Chloe's level, in a move that would have made Emma, despite being so much younger than her, wince. Archana in contrast appears completely comfortable sitting on her haunches. 'It's because I'm a widow.'

'So, a widow can't wear jewellery?'

'Not in Hindu custom. And they must wear white.'

Chloe nods solemnly.

'But you see, I wouldn't be here, now, if not for your great-grandmother…'

'Oh?'

'I owe my life, all this, to her.' She waves her hand around to indicate her house, the press of people at the gate having multiplied manyfold in the few minutes they have been talking.

Archana stands up, bones cracking audibly but showing no discomfort whatsoever, and smiles graciously at both Emma and Chloe. And in that smile that lights up her face, Emma sees how beautiful this woman must have been once, even as she mulls over what Archana just said.

What exactly does she mean?

'But, please,' Archana is saying, 'come in and we will talk.'

Chapter Seventy-Nine

1926

Archana

Shadows

Much later, as pink-tinted shadows claim the room, heralding dusk, Leela comes, standing outside, whispering harshly, 'I saw you that day, in the sahib's study, too early in the morning to be decent. I had come in early, I can't recall why now.'

Oh. That flash of sari. It *had* been Leela.

'I didn't want to believe what I saw. I kept quiet, watched you. Hoping you hadn't done something silly.' Leela's voice, not gloating and spiteful, or outraged, as Archana expected, but as tired as Archana feels. 'And it was only when I came to the same realisation as the memsahib – that you were with child – that I put two and two together. I kept expecting you to disagree, to shout at me, to be shocked at the unfounded accusation. But the look on your face...' Leela's voice choking. 'How *could* you, Archana? I never expected it of you, of all people.'

Archana stands with her head pressed to the door, listening to the first words Leela has spoken to her since she came here, having foregone sati. Her voice full of disappointment, upset. The way she said her name – with the harassed affection of an older sister.

In her own way Leela does care for her. It is a realisation that comes too late. Tears sting.

Why are you crying?

'I was lonely and lost, living a half-life that I hadn't asked for. I was furious with the memsahib,' she whispers almost to herself.

'So, you slept with the sahib? Got pregnant by him?' The scorn and disdain in Leela's voice spark anger in Archana.

'You haven't been in my position. You've no right to judge me.'

'Too right I haven't and thank the gods for that!'

At Leela's sobering words, her anger dissipating, renewed desperation at her situation taking its place.

'What would your mother say?' Leela asks from behind the door.

And at that the tears Archana has been holding back overflow.

'I hope she never finds out,' Leela is saying.

'Me too,' Archana whispers.

Her mother, living now with the untouchables. This disgrace, a pregnant widow carrying a child not her husband's, is a thousand times worse than foregoing sati. Even the untouchables would shun Archana.

'You can't stay here.' Leela is quiet, her voice soft. 'You are to leave immediately. There's food outside your door. Eat and then leave. The memsahib has paid your salary for the last few weeks – she needn't have done so, but she has. The envelope is beside your plate.'

What do I do? Where do I go? Panic agitating in her stomach. *Why didn't I think of the consequences when I did what I did?*

'I know of a convent in the city run by missionary nuns – they take on destitute women. It's right next to the train station.' Leela's voice gentler than Archana has ever heard it.

Why now, too late, is she discovering that Leela has a heart after all?

'Goodbye.'

A pause and then Leela's footsteps receding, the musical chime of anklets.

Archana opens the door. An envelope, sitting on paint supplies, her painting of fire and a sketchbook. Salt in her mouth. Once again bowled over by guilt and remorse at the memsahib's kindness, her thoughtfulness that Archana doesn't deserve.

She eats the food left for her by Leela, more kindness that she is not worthy of, but grateful for, and opens the envelope. More money in it than her salary, much more: enough to start over.

Tears run unchecked down her cheeks.

She is humbled and shamed by the memsahib's generosity despite what she has done to her. Gifting her her own life – whether she wanted it or not – and now enough money to provide for the child she has made with the memsahib's husband when the memsahib lost her own while saving her.

She gathers her belongings and the memsahib's gifts into a sari, fashioning a pouch, and waits until the shadows in her room lengthen and multiply, until the mansion lapses into silence as one by one, the servants leave for the night.

Then, under cover of darkness, she opens her door. At the base of the stairs she hesitates, looking up towards the memsahib's room.

Should she?

She won't want to see you.

But I want to see her, need *to see her.*

She was kind to me, my mistress, teacher, storyteller, friend and saviour. The least I can do is thank her, apologise and say goodbye.

She climbs up the stairs one last time.

She pauses outside the memsahib's door, almost losing her nerve.

Almost.

But then she thinks of their lessons, laughter and learning, the memsahib's stories of the Bloomsbury Group…

I've been granted this new lease of life, a life I did not ask for. In this life, from now on, I will try to be brave. Live for myself, if I can. And right now, that means going in there and thanking this woman who has given me so much.

And so she takes a deep breath, gathers her flailing courage around her and pushes open the door to Memsahib's room.

The room is mostly in darkness, the bedside lamp serving only to cast long, brooding shadows outside its immediate circle of light.

The memsahib sits up in bed, blinking. 'Who is it?' Her voice hoarse.

She has been crying.

Her face, illuminated by the lamp, is wan, washed out. Her eyes swollen, the lids bruised red. They widen as they register Archana. *The hurt in them. The pain.*

It will haunt Archana all her life, she knows.

Archana wants to shut her eyes. She wants to back out of the room. Run down the stairs and away. Instead, she swallows, forces herself to say, 'Memsahib, I'm so sorry, I—'

The memsahib lifts her hand, holds it out palm-up. 'I should have asked you,' she says, her voice gravelly. 'It was not my choice to make. I… I couldn't save my sister and I thought…' She swallows, tripping up over her words.

'Memsahib…'

'I convinced myself I had to save you. I did it for me, not you, that was my mistake. And my husband…' Her voice tormented, drowning. 'He…'

She cannot bear to see the memsahib like this.

Broken.

What have I done?

'He loves you, Memsahib. He was angry and upset. Hurting. And I… I was there, I suppose.'

The memsahib's hand falling back on the sheets, limp, defeated.

'He loves *you*, Memsahib. This, me... It was all a mistake...'

The memsahib closes her eyes. She looks so tiny, insubstantial, the bed dwarfing her.

'I had hoped for so much.' Her voice is so soft that Archana edges forward slightly to hear. 'A family of our own like mine...'

And that is when it comes to Archana what she must do, how she can set things right.

'Memsahib, you can still have the family you wanted...'

The memsahib shudders, opening her eyes and looking, bemused, at Archana, almost as if she had forgotten she was there. Her puzzled look from those distraught eyes asks, *what are you still doing here?*

Archana pushes on, regardless. Resolute now she's found the solution to their dilemma. Wanting to say what she has to before she loses courage.

'Memsahib,' she says, gently, very tenderly stroking her stomach. 'You lost your child saving me so it is only fair that you have mine.'

The memsahib blinks, once then again.

'The sahib loves you, Memsahib. You can be a family again.' Archana's voice slightly desperate as what she's offering begins to sink in. And it is at that moment, as she pledges her child to the memsahib, that she realises how much she loves it, how much she *wants* it.

And it is also when she realises, for the first time since she was saved from sati, that, despite everything, she is glad, she is grateful, to be alive.

The memsahib sighs deeply, her eyes wet with tears. 'We thought our love could weather anything, Suraj and I. But we've made a mess of things.'

'No, Memsahib, you still can… You can have my baby.'
Although I want it. Oh, how I want to keep this child!

The strength of her love for her unborn child makes her understand, with an agonised pang, how the memsahib must have felt when she lost her own child. How undone she must be, how desolate. No wonder she took to her bed, losing the will to recover.

'Archana, you and your child will always remind me of my husband's betrayal. Please leave. I… I know life for a pregnant widow will not be easy, so I've made sure you have enough money to start anew.'

Archana feels relief ambush her at the realisation that she doesn't have to part with her child. And gratitude to this woman, who has given her so much. From whom she has taken so much.

'Memsahib—'

'Please,' the memsahib says, and her voice is a keening lament, 'just go.'

She buries her face in her pillow, as if in this way she can smother her pain.

'Thank you, Memsahib. For my lessons, for your kindness. For my life. I'm… I'm so very sorry for what I did.'

And having said this, mostly steadily, Archana resolutely turns away, cradling her stomach where her child grows, slipping out the servants' entrance into the terrifying unknown, the cool night air stinging her wet cheeks, leaving the father of her child and the woman who gave her her life back, and the mansion that has been home in recent months, for the last time.

Chapter Eighty

2000

Emma

A Temple Bell

Emma and Chloe follow Archana into the small, but beautifully furnished house, perfumed with sandalwood and spices, a homely warm aroma.

'Why do you limp?' Chloe asks.

'Chloe!' Emma says, mortified, and to Archana, 'I'm sorry she…'

'No, it's okay.' Archana smiles.

She means it, Emma can see. She breathes out in relief, rehearsing in her head the conversation she will have with Chloe later.

'I was born with one leg slightly shorter than the other. That's why I limp,' Archana says, matter-of-factly. Then, 'I love your name, Chloe. It sounds like a temple bell ringing.'

Chloe beams, shooting Emma a look as if to say, 'See, Mum, it's fine.'

The living room is cosy, wooden benches lined with cushions, several sculptures and paintings of various gods, house plants, a glass almirah full to bursting with knick-knacks and photographs.

The photographs are familiar.

Looking at them, the mystery of the album in Suraj's study is solved. But why does Suraj have photos of Archana's daughter, grandchildren and great-grandchildren?

A delicate matter, but Emma resolves to find out, albeit in a more tactful manner than Chloe's when asking about Archana's limp…

Emma's gaze is arrested by a painting, obviously done by an amateur – one of Archana's children or grandchildren, perhaps. It depicts a fierce, out-of-control tornado of raging tangerine flames. The painting is not skilled, but it radiates a certain wild energy, Emma thinks, carefully setting down the painting she herself is holding.

Once they are seated, Archana says, 'Now, you will have some tea and snacks.'

'No, we…'

'I insist.'

After she's plied them with hot, sweet tea, spicy peanuts and sweet and salty biscuits, Archana says, 'You look just like your grandmother.'

'Genetics, eh? Although I'm Winnie's granddaughter, I took after her sister…'

Archana looks bemused. 'Sorry?'

'My grandmother, Margaret's sister Winnie, fell ill with the consumption in 1926. Margaret travelled back to England to look after her. By the time she arrived, my grandfather – Winnie's husband – had also contracted the disease. Margaret nursed them both but they never recovered. On her deathbed, Winnie asked Margaret to look after her children: my mother and her brother. And so, Margaret adopted her sister's children, when her sister and her husband died, very soon after she returned to England from India.'

'Ah.' Archana winces as if in pain. 'She never remarried?'

'No.'

Archana closes her eyes, tears squeezing out from her shut lids. 'I… I thought when I saw you…'

'Margaret maintains that Uncle Toby and my mother, Evelyn, were twin blessings at a very difficult time. She was recovering from the breakdown of her marriage and the loss of Winnie. She said Uncle Toby and my mother saved her.'

Archana nods.

Emma clears her throat. 'Suraj used to visit you. He has an album with the same photographs you have here…?'

'Yes, I…' Archana sniffs, wiping her eyes with her sari. 'It's a long story.'

'I'd like to hear it, but first, I have a message from my grandmother.'

Again, Archana closes her eyes, her hand on her chest, tears trembling on her cheeks.

Chloe is watching Archana's tears, open-mouthed and fascinated.

I shouldn't have brought her along, I should have left her with Anju.

Before Chloe can give vent to the questions Emma knows are forming in her mind, she says, slightly desperately, having spied a small patch of garden at the back of the house, 'Um… Can Chloe play outside? She loves looking for worms, centipedes and bugs.'

Please let her not come upon a snake or a scorpion.

Archana once again wipes her face with her sari, only serving to spread her tears all over her face, giving it a salty sheen.

'Yes, of course, sorry. Come, Chloe.' She opens the door and Chloe beams, happily distracted from Archana's tears.

'Chloe, be careful. If there's a snake or…'

'I *know*, Mum. I'll come for you at once.' Chloe grins at Emma.

Once Archana and Emma are seated again, Emma keeping an eye on her daughter out of the window, tells Archana, 'My grandmother asked me to come here. She asked to give you this.'

She hands the parcel to Archana, who reverently opens it.

When she looks at the painting, she gasps, fresh tears running unchecked down her cheeks.

'She said to tell you she understands why you did what you did, that she forgave you for it a long time ago. She's asked if you can forgive her.'

More tears arrive, collecting in the grooves of Archana's lined face.

Emma, alarmed and more than a little uncomfortable, feeling like she's intruding on private grief, tries desperately to lighten the mood. '*I* don't understand what she means at all, of course, I'm only conveying her message and I hope I've got it right – she never liked to talk about the past or her time in India.' Her voice a tad hysterical in the face of this stranger's sorrow.

She reaches across and pats Archana's hand, wondering if it would be too forward to put her arms round her.

'She painted this by the stream.' Archana's voice heavy with nostalgia. 'She taught me to paint – I painted that under her direction.' She nods at the painting of fire that Emma had assumed had been painted by one of her grandchildren. 'Painting has been my comfort all my life. When I am upset, sad or worried, it soothes me.'

'My grandmother never painted again after her return to England.'

'No?' Shock and incomprehension stilling Archana's tears. 'But she was so talented…'

'She said it was something confined to her past, a stage in her life that had passed. Finished.'

More tears, huge, choking sobs.

It is distressing, watching this old woman cry with the messy abandon of a child.

Emma is grateful that Chloe is not witnessing this.

'I should have been grateful for what she did,' Archana whispers, finally, sniffing and wiping her nose with the end of her sari. 'Instead, I... I...' She breaks down again. After a while she swallows, gathering herself together visibly. 'It's not for me to *forgive* her but to thank her, profusely, with my everything. Your grandmother,' she says, looking at Emma with swollen eyes, 'is an amazing woman. She gave me the greatest gift a person can give another – the gift of life, all these years to experience my child, grandchildren and great-grandchildren – at huge cost to herself.'

'She gave you the gift of life?' The words sounding grandiose as Emma repeats them. 'What do you mean?'

Archana wipes her eyes. 'She saved me. She gave me a new lease of life and in return, I took everything from her. And now, once again she overwhelms me with her generosity, her big-heartedness...'

'Tell me what happened,' Emma prompts gently.

And Archana does.

When she finishes, there are tears in Emma's eyes too.

'You must hate me,' Archana says softly, fiddling with the trailing end of her sari.

Emma tries to speak, to put into words what she feels. When Archana spoke of her betrayal, she was angry on Margaret's behalf, but because of what she herself is going through with David, she understands how complicated, complex and unfair life and emotions can be. Nothing is black and white, there are so many swathes of grey in the mix...

Her grandmother had said, when Emma confided her dilemma about David, 'Sometimes the hardest thing in the world is doing what is right.'

Oh, Gran, you comprehend perfectly what I'm going through for you have been through far worse yourself…

She understands now her grandmother's need to reinvent herself, put distance between herself and her past, even if it meant giving up her passion, the thing that had defined her: her art.

Why did her grandmother never remarry? Did she love Suraj all her life but couldn't reconcile with what he did?

She pictures Suraj's letters to her grandmother, so many, over the years, unposted, reeking of sorrow and yearning.

Two lovers separated by one rash action, pining for each other but too proud to admit it, one living with his mistake, the other unable to forgive it.

And all linked to this shrunken woman before her…

'I can see now why Suraj visited you…'

'He fell ill in his eighties, you see; had a massive heart attack and was faced with his mortality. So, he searched for me. It must have been his lawyer's instincts – he found me and asked if he could visit his child and grandchildren. He found some joy in them, especially as his health deteriorated.'

Emma looks out the window at her daughter, on her knees in the mud, peering intently at something, her whole being absorbed, rapt.

'He left us some money in his will,' Archana says softly.

Emma turns her attention back to the woman. 'I don't…'

'I just… I wanted you to know.'

'And you,' Emma says after a bit, for she wants to understand, to be able to tell her grandmother, should she ask when Emma gets back, 'what happened after you left them? You were pregnant, alone…'

'Leela had told me about this convent in the city. I took refuge there.'

'Leela?'

'I've heard she's still going strong up at the mansion, daring anyone to oust her from her position. She always wanted to be top dog.' Archana smiles through her tears.

'She's brilliant, an amazing cook,' Emma says.

Archana nods. 'The nuns were kind and accepted the story I prepared – that my husband had died tragically just when I found out about my pregnancy, that I was a destitute widow. When they realised I could converse in English as well as the local language, they enlisted my help in teaching at the school they ran for orphan children. I discovered I was very good at it. And when my own daughter was born, she fitted right in – she was reading almost before she could walk! Time brought me legitimacy and I became a respected teacher; I gathered up the courage to visit my mother and sister. Radha's husband had died of alcohol poisoning and she was living with our mother; she had never fit in among the untouchables, tolerated only because of her husband, so upon his death she wasn't asked to do sati – a blessing. They were barely making ends meet. I coaxed them into coming to live with me in the city. Radha too eventually started teaching at the school – the nuns didn't care about her untouchability, there were several untouchable children at the school.'

Archana pauses, once again choked by tears. 'Every day, I thank your grandmother for her generosity, her strength of conviction, for saving me from burning alive on the funeral pyre, giving me another chance, another life.' A breath. Then, 'I volunteer at a women's refuge. I've done so for many years. My daughter and granddaughters work there too. I've battled my guilt by giving back to society, although nothing will excuse what I did…' Archana's gaze bright, earnest. 'One of my granddaughters was in an abusive marriage. She refused our help, refused to see what was happening to her. And that was when I understood exactly what your grandmother had done for me. I was willing to go along with sati, do my duty, give my life, because that was what had been decreed. But your grandmother, brave woman that she was, saw what was best for *me* even when I couldn't. My mother wanted me to do sati, but because I didn't, I was able to save her and my sister, provide for them both.'

Archana sighs deeply. Then, 'For a long time, my mother was angry with me. Although she had no choice but to come and live with me – she and my sister and her children would have been destitute otherwise – she was stubborn, and refused to speak with me, except when she was dying.' She takes a hitching breath. 'On her deathbed, my mother said, "I'm glad you're here. I'm so glad." We were foolish to think sati would solve anything.' Archana pauses.

'Your granddaughter,' Emma ventures, 'Is she…?'

'Yes. I intervened and dragged her and my great-grandchildren away, against her wishes. She hated me for a while. It took her two years to see the light. When she thanked me for rescuing her and her children, I told her about what your grandmother had done for me…' She swallows. 'She is an amazing woman.'

Emma nods. 'That she is.'

I thought I was strong, Emma muses as she collects Chloe, as they make their way back, the street, packed with people, cheering as the driver gingerly navigates the car through the crush, Chloe waving like royalty, her face alight; Archana standing on her doorstep, her body hunched but face looking lighter than before.

But true mettle is doing what is right despite the circumstances, like my grandmother did, saving Archana. It is being true to oneself, one's principles. And mine... well, it would never sit right with me, hiding what David has done, being complicit in his deceit.

Gran, you loved Suraj but you were unable to forgive his betrayal. In contrast, I... I've forgiven David over and over, even when he has been undeserving.

I finally see David for who he is – he'll never love me like I once loved him. He'll never love me selflessly. I'm not willing to settle for that any more. I deserve better.

You and Suraj loved each other all of your lives, although, tragically, you lost each other along the way and couldn't find your way back.

Have you forgiven him? If so, why didn't you come back?

That evening, as they prepare for bed, Emma brushing her daughter's glorious hair, scented with sunshine and citrus, asks, 'Sweetheart, are you missing Dad?'

'Yes,' Chloe says. 'But there's so much to do here, Mum. And we'll see him soon.'

'You know you said Darcy's mum and dad have separated and she goes to her dad at the weekends?'

'Yes?' Chloe turns to her, wide-eyed.

'I think... Your dad and I... We might do the same.'

'Oh.' Chloe's face falls.

Emma gathers her in her arms, her warm, soft little body against hers.

After a bit, Chloe says, 'Mum, can we stay here?'

'Here?'

For a brief moment, Emma entertains the possibility. They could hide here while the story broke about David but then she would be running away, not facing up to what she is doing to him. She has to take responsibility for her actions.

'I like India. I want to see more of it,' Chloe says.

'Tell you what, we'll come back in the summer holidays and see what we think, eh?'

'Yes! And Mum?'

'Yes?'

'I miss Dad but I also like it when it's just the two of us.'

Emma holds her daughter close, burying her tears in Chloe's hair.

She knows the way forward will not be easy, that Chloe will pine for David, that there will be wobbles, that it will take time for her to accept their new reality.

Emma understands that, if not now, then sometime in the future Chloe will be angry with her for breaking up their family so publicly. She pictures Chloe yelling at her for destroying her father's credibility, shattering their family unit. It terrifies her, this image of her daughter turning against her.

But then she thinks of Margaret, how she did the right thing – for the wrong reasons perhaps, believing she was being given a second chance at saving her sister, but the right thing nonetheless – at great cost to herself.

Emma too will do what is right and she will face the consequences. It won't be easy, not at all, but her conscience will be clear and she hopes that one day her daughter will understand, that some day her daughter will be proud of her as Emma herself is of Margaret.

Chapter Eighty-One

1926

Margaret

Knowledge

'Memsahib, paint?' the children ask.

Margaret picks up the paintbrush.

But... the smell of turpentine is forever now linked to betrayal, bringing to mind the splodge of dripping crimson on canvas: her pain, the guilt in Archana's eyes.

She sets down the brush.

'We will write,' she tells the children. 'It is like drawing but this way, you get to read, to learn. Here, look, I'll teach you.'

And in helping the children, teaching them to read, she finds brief respite from pain, ache, loneliness. She finds momentary peace.

Margaret is in Bombay.

'Please don't go,' Suraj had begged. 'Forgive me,' he pleaded.

Once upon a time, not too long ago, they had communicated without words, reading each other's minds. But now, she couldn't find the words to tell him that she could not begin to forgive herself for her many mistakes, so how could she forgive him; who was she to forgive him? She couldn't tell him that when she was with him, there would always be the spectre of Archana. And Margaret would be reminded that she had done the very thing she had preached against. She had not given Archana a choice concerning her own life and it had come back to bite her.

She and Suraj loved each other, but their love was not enough. It was tainted now, smeared with betrayal, battered by their mistakes.

'I can't,' she said, Suraj's tears doing nothing for her, her heart stark, empty, numb, as if her insides had been scooped out, spattered onto the canvas, created accidentally, when she found out about Suraj's betrayal.

'Painting is expression. It is our voice. We show what we feel, *everything* we feel through it,' Vanessa had said one indolent afternoon in the garden at Charleston, the air piquant with Earl Grey tea, sticky sweet with crusty bread and thick orange marmalade.

Margaret's hand had reacted to the knowledge of her husband's perfidy by creating that splodge on canvas, the bright scarlet of spilled blood from a bleeding heart, when she found out.

The train had approached the outskirts of Bombay at dusk and Margaret startled awake, pressing her face to the window, the smell of grime, the taste of iron and dirt. It was pitch-black outside, the darkness alleviated every so often with a bright yellow glow here and there.

She remembered waving her white handkerchief to the slum children when the train was taking her away from Bombay, Suraj beside her, star-spangled dreams for a sunny future with her beloved bright in her heart.

Now, she was alone. She had left behind most of her possessions, packing only a few dresses and the two paintings: the one of the girl she had created while painting side by side with Archana beside the stream when she was pregnant and hopeful, her dreams intact, and the painting with the scarlet splotch, created once again while painting next to Archana, when Margaret found out Archana was pregnant with her husband's child.

The slum was shrouded in darkness, reeking of rubbish and desperation, hunger and humanity, whole families asleep within the concrete construction pipes by the tracks.

I have no right to feel sorry for myself. I have a roof over my head, food when I need it.

She could just about make out cloth huts, shadows dancing within, silhouettes against the flimsy material that flapped in the secretive breeze.

A stirring inside her, a flash of something close to wanting, yearning, piercing the cloak of numbness that had enveloped her, taken her over since Suraj acknowledged his perfidy.

She would see them soon.

Her children.

Amit had rented a house near his for Margaret, with her own household of servants.

'When you're ready,' he said, hesitantly, 'I'd like your help with the self-rule campaign.'

He had made sure the gatekeeper at her place was *his* gatekeeper, Raju, the one she knew, who understood English and spoke some, who had accompanied her to the slums to translate her goodbyes to the children when she was leaving Bombay. 'So you can take him along on your walks, which you're sure to begin again.'

That garnered a small smile from her. Just a tilting upwards of her lips, but she felt a lifting of her heart. Very slight.

She was not completely numb after all. She was looking forward to her walks, seeing the children again.

*

She settles into a routine.

She takes Raju along on her morning walks; he's good company and eager to improve his English, and she in turn attempts to learn the local language from him. He asks one of the boys who does odd jobs for her household and Amit's to guard the gate and accompanies her, happy and keen. He tells her stories of his life in Poona, the youngest of six children, the only son after five girls, the apple of his parents' eyes.

'I sending money, for dowry, my sisters,' he says. 'They proud I in big city.'

The children bring her gifts, treasures they have collected and saved – a perfectly oval pebble, polished to a shine, warm and sweaty from their grasp; a forked twig fashioned into a catapult; a snake's skin, shiny and slippery, reflecting sunlight; a small rat with beady eyes and a chewed-off tail, which she politely declines.

The adults collect outside the huts and the pipes that are their home and listen to the lessons – Margaret teaching their children to read and write English and the children teaching her all the bad words in their language, their tired faces lifting in wide smiles when she swears in the local tongue.

When she is with the children – their faces, wide open, trusting, sandalwood-coloured, their shock of dark brown hair, their rangy, nimble limbs – she is able to look ahead, to a future without Suraj, and although it appears bleak, she can see occasional glimmers of hope.

Margaret had sought, in her relationship with Suraj, redemption, freedom from her past, and that was her mistake. For too late she is realising that she alone is the architect of her happiness and that redemption is to be had here, working with disadvantaged children, seeing their faces glow when they read a sentence unaided.

*

And in this way her days pass.

But then a letter arrives in her beloved sister's handwriting: 'Margaret, I am ill. Please can you come.'

Fear. Turbid, potent black.

Please, God, let nothing happen to Winnie. I cannot bear it.

She appoints a woman whom she met while campaigning with Amit to teach the children.

She bids tearful goodbyes to the friends she has made in Bombay: the slum dwellers, both children and adults; Raju the gatekeeper.

The children cling to her. They cry.

'Don't go,' they say, these children she loves. Who have taken her empty being, scoured by betrayal and hurt and upset, and made her feel, care again, the sheer joy they glean from her company a balm to her devastated soul. Who have shown her the way forward.

For she knows now what she will do once Winnie is better: she will work with disadvantaged children. And in doing so, she will find the redemption she has been looking for all her life.

'I'll try to come back,' she promises.

She thanks Amit. 'Please tell Suraj,' she says, finally bringing his friend, her estranged husband, into their conversation, which, all these months, has carefully edged around him.

'You won't?' he asks.

She shakes her head.

He nods once. 'We will miss you.'

As the ship leaves Indian shores, she watches the churning water, muddy yellow. The people waving goodbye, Amit among them.

The shore slips further away, separated by dancing waves, sunshine-streaked, tawny green, boundless.

She concentrates on the strip of red, freckled with colourful dots of people.

What hopes she'd had.

One day, perhaps she'll come back.

But now, her sister needs her.

Chapter Eighty-Two

England 2000

Emma

Love

Margaret is not having a good day. She had a setback while Emma and Chloe were in India and she has been in hospital all this while, in intensive care, drifting in and out of heavy, drugged sleep.

She only returned to the hospice the previous day and is weak, fragile, but smiles widely when Emma arrives, patting the seat beside her bed. 'It's good to see you, Emma.'

Emma takes her hand, delicate and papery. 'Gran, thank you for the house in India. How did you know we'd love it, that it would be perfect for us?'

'India.' A light coming into her eyes. 'Archana…'

'I met her.' Emma describes Archana's cottage, the people collecting at the gate and around the car.

A smile from her grandmother, a small shake of her head. 'I'd forgotten about that, how everyone would be interested in everyone else's business.'

'I gave Archana your message, and the painting,' Emma says. 'Here, this is a letter from her. Shall I read it to you?'

Her grandmother nods, her eyes leaking tears as she hears Archana's words – the letter, then everything she told Emma in person about what happened to her after she left Margaret's employ.

'She had her chance to live life her way this time round.' Her grandmother smiles. And, when she hears about Archana's work with destitute children, 'It was what I was doing, in Bombay, before I came to England to nurse Winnie during her illness. I always meant to return, continue my work with the slum children; somehow I never could... Instead, I assuaged my conscience by helping children in need in different parts of the world. Meanwhile, serendipitously, Archana also found her salvation working with disadvantaged children...' She pauses. Then, 'Everything occurs for a reason. Although you don't realise that until after. When I left Suraj, I put to bed the dreams I had so naively spun, my fantasies of a fresh start, a new life in India with my love. But bringing up your mother and uncle, working with disadvantaged children all over the world, has fulfilled me. It's delivered a different kind of happiness.'

Emma squeezes her grandmother's hand. 'I'm sorry, Gran. For your baby... For everything.'

Her grandmother is quiet, but tears escape from beneath her closed lids. She swallows, then, 'I've had a good life, though not necessarily the one I pictured for myself.'

'You never remarried...' Emma says tentatively.

'There never was anyone else. Suraj was the one for me.'

'I... I found letters from him,' Emma says softly. 'He wrote them, regularly, until his death, but he never posted them.'

Her grandmother handles the letters very carefully, bringing them to her nose as if to catch a whiff of her ex-husband's scent, gently running her hand over her name in his handwriting. 'I loved him so very much. But I... I invested too much in our love. I believed that I would find redemption and peace through love rather than from my sense of self. It was only later, through taking on Winnie's children and helping and caring for others in the community and abroad, that I was able to find true contentment.'

'Suraj's house, Gran... Your room, a shrine, just as you had left it. He lived like a recluse. He converted the room next to the study into a bedroom. Nandu said he would stand at the window, looking towards the village and beyond, waiting, pining… There was no one else, he only ever loved you.'

Her grandmother's eyes full and overflowing.

'Have you forgiven him?' Emma asks gently.

Her grandmother sighs. 'I found it harder to forgive myself. We both made mistakes and neither of us could come back from them. When the letter arrived from the solicitor in India informing me of his death and the house being left to me… It confirmed what I had known all along, that he had loved me all his life, like I did him.' A tear sparkles on her cheek. 'It was too late with Suraj and too late for me to travel back to India – I had just received my diagnosis. But I decided then that before I left this world, I would make my peace with Archana. I couldn't leave it too late, carry more regret… And thanks to you, that's been possible.' She smiles softly at Emma.

'It's a tragedy. You and Suraj, true loves separated by one mistake. Then there's me, refusing to see David for who he is, forgiving mistake after mistake, loving this caricature, my idea of a man he never was…' She takes a breath. 'Gran, I've left David.'

David had met them at the airport when they returned from India and one glance at Emma told him all he needed to know.

'You're going ahead with it,' he said that evening.

'I wouldn't be able to live with myself otherwise.'

His face hard before crumbling.

In the morning, he said, 'I'm going to Canberra.'

'Canberra… In Australia?'

'I… have a friend there.'

And there it was. In that pause she understood. He had come to her when his marriage broke up because Australia was too far away – he was too lazy to uproot himself. But he'd always had backup. He must have been keeping in touch with this… friend of his. Another starry-eyed student whom he had seduced, no doubt.

'And does *she* know about the paper?'

'Yes.' Defiant. 'I emailed her last night.'

'Ah.' She was right, her suspicions confirmed. Her heart felt a pang, but that's all it was, a pang, and mostly on Chloe's behalf.

David didn't care, either for Emma or for his daughter. He was selfish through and through, interested only in saving his own skin.

'You'll have to come back to face charges.'

'If there are any,' he said.

Eternally hopeful, thinking his charm would get him out of this scrape too, like every other.

Or perhaps he meant to disappear.

Emma processed what she was feeling: upset on her daughter's behalf, and that was all. She would deal with Chloe's sadness and confusion, perhaps anger, guide her through it, be there for her daughter. But she understood now that her love affair with David, the grandest passion she had known, which had lasted all these years, was finally over.

Now she says, 'It didn't hurt as much as I thought it would. I was in love with the idea of him rather than the person he was. But, Chloe—' Her breath hitches.

'Emma, darling, by taking David back, you've given Chloe a chance to get to know and love her father. Despite everything that is happening now, she will always have that – fond memories of her father.'

Her grandmother's words make Emma feel warm inside and alleviate some of her hurt and anger at herself. She has been chastising herself for her short-sightedness, her foolishness, but put like this, she realises that she should forgive *herself*, not be too hard on herself.

Her grandmother has made Emma see that her choices have not been in vain. Despite being wrong, they've wrought some good.

Emma takes a breath. 'While you were in hospital, I… I made it public, David's deception…'

Her grandmother squeezes her hand.

'I'm waiting for the media circus that will erupt any minute. We're not in London – we're renting a place near here, close to you. I've taken a sabbatical from teaching and I'm putting my project on hold for the time being. I'm home-schooling Chloe, so hopefully we'll miss the brunt of it. I'm sure a few intrepid reporters will find us, but it may not be as bad as it would have been if we'd stayed put in London.'

'How's Chloe taken it?'

'It's all an adventure for her, a continuation of our holiday. I don't think she's quite understood that David is gone from our lives…' Her voice trembles.

'Chloe is resilient, and she has you.' Her grandmother looks at her with such love in her eyes. 'You'll both be okay, I know this.' Her eyes bright with assurance. 'I'm proud of you.'

'*I'm* proud of *you*, Gran. You're my inspiration,' Emma says.

She sits there, her grandmother's hand in hers, until the lump choking her throat has eased somewhat. Tears glisten bright on her grandmother's face as she smiles at her.

'I used to think I was a homebody, that travel was not for me, but I was wrong,' Emma says. 'Both Chloe and I, we loved India. My plan is to travel all over the country with Chloe, using the house in India as our base. I've decided to continue home-schooling her – it's not as daunting as I thought. I wish Mum was here so I could tell her she was right, all those times she told me that one learned more through travelling than in school.'

Her grandmother smiles, her eyes shining. 'Oh, how your mother would have loved that! I'm sure she's crowing with delight from up there.'

Emma takes a deep breath, working up the courage to put forward the idea that has been brewing in her head since she returned from India. 'Gran, I... I'd like to write a book. About our own history. About you.'

'Me?' Her grandmother's eyes twinkle, briefly pushing away the pain that has taken them hostage, dulled their glow. 'But, child, surely there are more interesting subjects?'

'None as interesting as you.'

'Arguable, but you have my blessing.'

Emma beams.

The phone call Emma has been dreading comes a week later.

Her grandmother is in bed, her eyes closed, face peaceful, a small smile playing on her lips, looking for all the world like she is just resting.

In her hands she clutches Suraj's letters, pages and pages of words, spanning decades and continents and transgressions, held tight next to her heart, the opened envelopes in a neat pile on her bedside table, her name facing outward, the scent of lavender, fading ink and love.

A Letter from Renita

I want to say a huge thank you for choosing to read *The Girl in the Painting*. If you did enjoy it, and want to keep up to date with all my latest releases, just sign up at the following link. Your email address will never be shared and you can unsubscribe at any time.

www.renitadsilva.com/e-mail-sign-up/?title=the-girl-in-the-painting

What I adore most about being a writer is hearing from readers. I'd love to know what you made of *The Girl in the Painting*, and I'd be very grateful if you could write a review. It makes such a difference and helps new readers to discover my books.

You can get in touch with me on my Facebook page, through Twitter, Goodreads or my website.

Thank you so much for your support – it means the world to me.

Until next time,
Renita

 RenitaDSilvaBooks

 RenitaDSilva

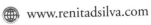 www.renitadsilva.com

Acknowledgements

I would like to thank all at Bookouture, especially Abi Fenton – the best editor one could wish for. Thanks for your brilliant advice, encouragement, patience and kindness. You are the very best.

A huge thank you to Jenny Hutton, editor extraordinaire. You are amazing and I cannot thank you enough. Thank you also to Jacqui Lewis and Jane Donovan for your wonderful, eagle-eyed scrutiny of the manuscript.

A million thanks to Lorella Belli of Lorella Belli Literary Agency for your untiring efforts in making my books go places and also for your friendship and support during a difficult year. It means more than I can say. Thank you also to Milly and Eleonora.

Thank you to my lovely fellow Bookouture authors, especially Angie Marsons, Sharon Maas, Debbie Rix, June Considine (aka Laura Elliot) and Rebecca Stonehill, whose friendship I am grateful and lucky to have.

Thank you to authors Chris Babu and Manuela Iordache for your wonderful friendship and support.

Thank you to all the fabulous book bloggers who give so freely of their time, reading and reviewing, sharing and shouting about our books. I am grateful to my Twitter/FB friends for their enthusiastic and overwhelming support. An especial thanks to Jules Mortimer, Joseph Calleja and Sandra Duck, who I am privileged to call my friends, and who are the best cheerleaders one could wish for.

I am immensely grateful to my long-suffering family for willingly sharing me with characters who live only in my head. Love always.

And last, but not least, thank you, reader, for choosing this book. Hope you enjoy.

Author's Note

This is a work of fiction set around and incorporating real events and people.

Mrs Danbourne is a fictional character I made up – she did not teach Vanessa Bell.

Charleston is not as near the sea as I have made out. It would have been quite a long walk. I have manipulated the distance for the purposes of the story.

Sati is also known as suttee but for ease of reading I have referred to it as sati throughout this book.

Sati was banned in India in 1829. However, it has continued to be practised, although not as widely, well into the twenty-first century.

In the early twentieth century, during which time the bulk of this story is set, sati did take place but the custom was not as prevalent as in the nineteenth century.

When practising sati, some widows took their place next to their husband on the pyre attired in their wedding sari. In this story they wear widow's whites.

I have taken liberties with regards to the Indian setting, picking characteristics – food, vegetation and customs such as the practice of sati – from different villages in different parts of India to fashion my fictional villages; the areas I have set them in may not necessarily have villages like the ones I have described.

I apologise for any oversights or mistakes and hope they do not detract from your enjoyment of this book.

Made in the USA
Columbia, SC
26 September 2019